Robert Barr (16 September 1849 – 21 October 1912) was a Scottish-Canadian short story writer and novelist. Robert Barr was born in Barony, Lanark, Scotland to Robert Barr and Jane Watson. In 1854, he emigrated with his parents to Upper Canada at the age of four years old. His family settled on a farm near the village of Muirkirk. Barr assisted his father with his job as a carpenter, and developed a sound work ethic. Robert Barr then worked as a steel smelter for a number of years before he was educated at Toronto Normal School in 1873 to train as a teacher. After graduating Toronto Normal School, Barr became a teacher, and eventually headmaster/principal of the Central School of Windsor, Ontario in 1874. While Barr worked as head master of the Central School of Windsor, Ontario, he began to contribute short stories—often based on personal experiences, and recorded his work. On August 1876, when he was 27, Robert Barr married Ontario-born Eva Bennett, who was 21. (Source: Wikipedia)

Literary works:
"The Face And The Mask" (1894)
In the Midst of Alarms (1894, 1900, 1912)
From Whose Bourne (1896)
One Day's Courtship (1896)
Revenge!
The Strong Arm
A Woman Intervenes (1896)
Tekla: A Romance of Love and War (1898)
Jennie Baxter, Journalist (1899)
The Unchanging East (1900)
The Victors (1901)
A Prince of Good Fellows (1902)
Over The Border: A Romance (1903)
The O'Ruddy, A Romance, with Stephen Crane (1903)

A PRINCE OF GOOD FELLOWS
&
LORD STRANLEIGH ABROAD

ROBERT BARR

PRINCE CLASSICS

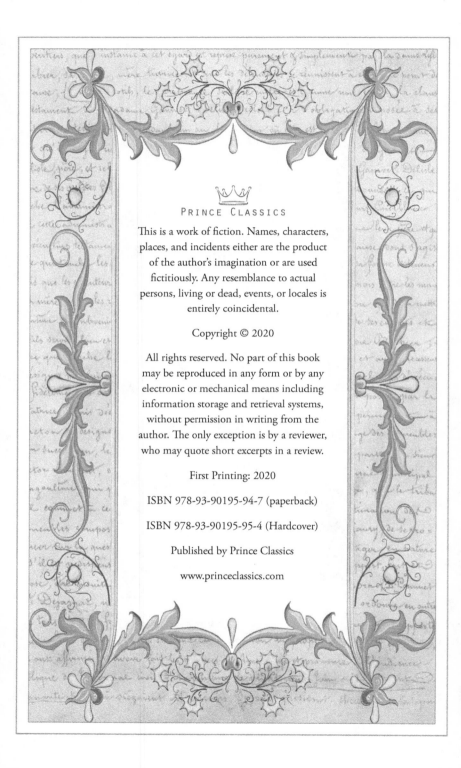

PRINCE CLASSICS

First Printing: 2020

ISBN 978-93-90195-94-7 (paperback)

ISBN 978-93-90195-95-4 (Hardcover)

Published by Prince Classics

www.princeclassics.com

Contents

A PRINCE OF GOOD FELLOWS   9

The King Intervenes   13

The King Dines   28

The King's Tryst   37

The King Investigates   53

The King's Gold   73

The King A-Begging   92

The King's Visit   112

The King Explores   126

The King Drinks   142

The King Sails   156

The King Weds   172

LORD STRANLEIGH ABROAD   197

I.—LORD STRANLEIGH ALL AT SEA.   199

II.—AN AUTOMOBILE RIDE.   221

III.—THE GOD IN THE CAR.   240

IV.—THE MAD MISS MATURIN.   260

V.—IN SEARCH OF GAME.   280

VI.—THE BUNK HOUSE PRISONER.   304

VII.—THE END OF THE CONTEST.   331

About Author   359

NOTABLE WORKS   362

A PRINCE OF GOOD FELLOWS
&
LORD STRANLEIGH ABROAD

A PRINCE OF GOOD FELLOWS

To

Thomas Spencer Jerome

in his Villa of the Castle on the Island of Capri,

this book is respectfully dedicated, with

the hope that some of the facts

herein set forth may aid him

during his historical

researches.

The King Intervenes

Late evening had fallen on the grey walls of Stirling Castle, and dark night on the town itself, where narrow streets and high gables gave early welcome to the mirk, while the westward-facing turrets of the castle still reflected the departing glory of the sky.

With some suggestion of stealth in his movements, a young man picked his way through the thickening gloom of the streets. There was still light enough to show that, judging by his costume, he was of the well-to-do farmer class. This was proclaimed by his broad, coarse, bonnet and the grey check plaid which he wore, not looped to the shoulder and pinned there by a brooch, Highland fashion, but wrapped round his middle, with the two ends brought over the shoulders and tucked under the wide belt which the plaid itself made, the fringes hanging down at each knee, as a Lowland shepherd might have worn the garment. As he threaded his way through the tortuous streets, ever descending, he heard the clatter of a troop of horse coming up, and paused, looking to the right and left, as if desirous of escaping an encounter which seemed inevitable. But if such were his object, the stoppage, although momentary, was already too long, for ere he could deflect his course, the foremost of the horsemen was upon him, a well known noble of the Scottish Court.

"Out of the way, fellow!" cried the rider, and, barely giving him time to obey, the horseman struck at the pedestrian fiercely with his whip. The young man's agility saved him. Nimbly he placed his back against the wall, thus avoiding the horse's hoof and the rider's lash. The victim's right hand made a swift motion to his left hip, but finding no weapon of defence there, the arm fell back to his side again, and he laughed quietly to himself. The next motion of his hand was more in accordance with his station, for it removed his bonnet, and he stood uncovered until the proud cavalcade passed him.

When the street was once more clear and the echoing sounds had died away in the direction of the castle, the youth descended and descended until he came to the lower part of the town where, turning aside up a narrow lane, he knocked at the door of a closed and shuttered building, evidently an abiding place of the poorer inhabitants of Stirling. With some degree of caution the door was slightly opened, but when the occupant saw, by the flash of light that came from within, who his visitor was, he threw the portal wide and warmly welcomed the newcomer.

"Hey, guidman!" he cried, "ye're late the night in Stirling."

"Yes," said the young man stepping inside, "but the farm will see nothing of me till the morning. I've a friend in town who gives me a bed for myself and a stall for my horse, and gets the same in return when he pays a visit to the country."

"A fair exchange," replied the host as he closed and barred the door.

The low room in which the stranger found himself was palpably a cobbler's shop. Boots and shoes of various sizes and different degrees of ill repair strewed the floor, and the bench in the corner under a lighted cruzie held implements of the trade, while the apron which enveloped the man of the door proclaimed his occupation. The incomer seated himself on a stool, and the cobbler returned to his last, resuming his interrupted work. He looked up however, from time to time, in kindly fashion at his visitor, who seemed to be a welcome guest.

"Well," said the shoemaker with a laugh, "what's wrong with you?"

"Wrong with me? Nothing. Why do you think there is anything amiss?"

"You are flushed in the face; your breath comes quick as if you had been running, and there's a set about your lips that spells anger."

"You are a very observing man, Flemming," replied he of the plaid. "I have been walking fast so that I should have little chance of meeting any one. But it is as well to tell the whole truth as only part of it. I had a fright up the street. One of those young court sprigs riding to the castle tried to trample me under the feet of his horse, and struck at me with his whip for getting into his road, so I had just to plaster my back against somebody's front door and keep out of the way."

"It's easy to see that you live in the country, Ballengeich," replied the cobbler, "or you would never get red in the face over a little thing like that."

"I had some thought of pulling him off his horse, nevertheless," said the Laird of Ballengeich, whose brow wrinkled into a frown at the thought of the indignity he had suffered.

"It was just as well you left him alone," commented the cobbler, "for an unarmed man must even take whatever those court gallants think fit to offer, and if wise, he keeps the gap in his face shut, for fear he gets a bigger gap opened in his head. Such doings on the part of the nobles do not make them exactly popular. Still, I am speaking rather freely, and doubtless you are a firm friend of the new king?" and the shoemaker cast a cautious sidelong glance at his visitor.

"A friend of the king? I wonder to hear you! I doubt if he has a greater enemy than myself in all Scotland."

"Do you mean that, Ballengeich?" inquired the shoemaker, with more of interest than the subject appeared to demand, laying down his hammer as he spoke, and looking intently at his guest.

"I'd never say it, if it wasn't true," replied the laird.

It was some moments before the workman spoke, and then he surprised the laird by a remark which had apparently nothing to do with what had been said before.

"You are not a married man, I think you told me?"

"No, I am not. There's time enough for that yet," returned the other with a smile. "You see, I am new to my situation of responsibility, and it's as well not to take in the wife till you are sure you can support her."

"What like a house have you got, and how far is it from Stirling?"

"The house is well enough in its way; there's more room in it than I care to occupy. It's strongly built of stone, and could stand a siege if necessary, as very likely it has done in days long past, for it's a stout old mansion. It's near enough to Stirling for me to come in and see my friend the cobbler in the evening, and sleep in my own bed that night, if I care to do so."

"Is it in a lonely place?"

"I can hardly say that. It is at the top of a bit hill, yet there's room enough to give you rest and retirement if you should think of keeping retreat from the busy world of the town. What's on your mind, Flemming? Are you swithering whether you'll turn farmer or no? Let me inform you that it's a poor occupation."

"I'll tell you what's on my mind, Ballengeich, if you'll swear piously to keep it a secret."

"Indeed, I'll do nothing of the sort," replied the young man decisively. "An honest man's bare word is as good as his bond, and the strongest oath ever sworn never yet kept a rascal from divulging a secret intrusted to him."

"You're right in that; you're right in that," the cobbler hastened to add, "but this involves others as well as myself, and all are bound to each other by oaths."

"Then I venture to say you are engaged in some nefarious business. What is it? I'll tell nobody, and mayhap, young as I am, I can give you some plain, useful advice from the green fields that will counteract the pernicious notions that rise in the stifling wynds of the crowded town."

"Well, I'm not at all sure that we don't need it, for to tell the truth I have met with a wild set of lads, and I find myself wondering how long my head will be in partnership with my body."

"Is the case so serious as that?"

"Aye, it is."

"Then why not withdraw?"

"Ah, that's easier said than done. When you once shut a spring door on yourself, it isn't by saying 'I will' that you get out. You'll not have forgotten the first night we met, when you jumped down on my back from the wall of the Grey Friars' Church?"

"I remember it very distinctly, but which was the more surprised, you or I, I have never yet been able to settle. I know I was very much taken aback."

"Not so much as I," interrupted the cobbler dryly, "when you came plump on my shoulders."

"I was going to say," went on Ballengeich, "that I'm afraid my explanation about taking a short cut was rather incoherent."

"Oh, no more than mine, that I was there to catch a thief. It was none of my business to learn why you were in the kirkyard."

"By the way, did you ever hear any more of the thief you were after?"

"That's just the point I am coming to. The man we were after was his youthful majesty, James the Fifth, of Scotland."

"What, the king!" exclaimed the amazed laird.

"Just him, and no other," replied the cobbler, "and very glad I am that the ploy miscarried, although I fear it's to come on again."

"I never heard the like of this!"

"You may well say that. You see it is known that the king in disguise visits a certain house, for what purpose his majesty will be able to tell you better than I. He goes unattended and secretly, and this gives us our chance."

"But what in the name of the god of fools whoever he happens to be, would you do with Jamie once you got him?"

"'Deed there's many things that might be mended in this country, as you very well know, and the king can mend them if he likes, with a word. Now rather than have his throat cut, our leader thinks he will agree to reasonable reform."

"And supposing he doesn't agree, are you going to cut his throat?"

"I don't know what would happen if he proved stubborn. The moderate section is just for locking him by somewhere until he listens to wisdom."

"And it is in your mind that my house should become a prison for the king?"

"It seems to me worth considering."

"There seems to me very little worth considering in the matter. It is a mad scheme. Supposing the king promised under compulsion, what would be his first action the moment he returned to Stirling Castle? He would scour the country for you, and your heads would come off one by one like buttons from an old coat."

"That's what I said. 'Trust the word of a Stuart,' says I, 'it's pure nonsense!'"

"Oh I'm not sure but the word of a Stuart is as good as the word of any other man," replied Ballengeich with a ring of anger in his voice, at which the cobbler looked up surprised.

"You're not such an enemy of the king as you let on at first," commented the mender of shoes. "I doubt if I should have told you all this."

"Have no fear. I can pledge you that my word is as good as a Stuart's at least."

"I hope it's a good deal better."

"Your plan is not only useless, but dangerous, my friend. I told you I would give you my advice, and now you have it. Do you think James is a lad that you can tie to your bench stool here, lock your door, and expect to find him when you came back? You must remember that James has been in captivity before, when the Earl of Angus thought he had him secure in the stronghold of Falkland, and yet, Jamie, who was then but a lad of sixteen, managed to escape. Man Flemming, I must tell you about that some day."

"Tell me about what?" inquired the shoemaker.

"Oh well, it may not be true after all," said young Ballengeich in confusion, "but a friend of mine was gardener at Falkland and knew the

18

whole story about James's escape. Never mind that; my advice to you is to shake hands with all such schemes, and turn your back on them."

"Oh, that's soon said," cried the cobbler with some impatience. "'Keep out of the fire and ye'll not be burnt,' says the branch on the tree to the faggot on the woodman's back. You see, Ballengeich, in this matter I'm between the cart-wheel and the hard road. My head's off if this ploy miscarries, as you've just told me, and my throat's cut if I withdraw from the secret conclave. It's but a choice between two hashings. There's a dead cobbler in any event."

"I see your difficulty," said the laird; "do you want to be helped out of it?"

"Does the toad want to get from under the harrow?"

"When is your next meeting, and where?"

"The meetings are held in this room, and the next will be on Wednesday night at eleven o'clock."

"Bless my soul!" cried Ballengeich. "Would nothing content you but to drink the whole bucketful? The rendezvous in your shop! Then whoever escapes, your head's on a pike."

"Aye," murmured the shoemaker dismally.

"It isn't taking very many of you to overturn the House of Stuart," said the laird, looking about the room, which was small.

"There's just one less than a dozen," replied the cobbler.

"Then we'll make up the number to the even twelve, hoping good luck will attend us, for we will be as many as the Apostles. Between now and Wednesday you might confer with your leaders, Flemming. Tell them you know a young man you can trust, who owns exactly the kind of house that James can be kept fast in, if he is captured. Say that your new conspirator will take the oath, or anything else they like to give, and add, what is more to the purpose, that he has a plot of his own which differs from theirs, in giving at least as much chance of success, and possesses the additional advantage of being safe. Whether his plan miscarries or not, there will be no need to fear a reprisal, and that is much to say in its favour."

"It is everything in its favour," said the shoemaker with a sigh of relief.

"Very well, then, I will meet you here on Wednesday night at this time, and learn whether or no they agree to have me as one of their number. If they refuse, there's no harm done; I shall say nothing, and the king will know no more about the matter than he does now."

"I could not ask better assurance than that," said the host cordially as his guest rose.

They shook hands, and the guidman of Ballengeich, after peering out into the darkness to see that the way was clear, took his leave.

The laird was prompt in keeping his appointment on the following Wednesday, and learned that the conspirators were glad of his assistance. The cobbler's tool-box had been pushed out of the way, and a makeshift table, composed of three boards and two trestles, occupied the centre of the room. A bench made up in similar fashion ran along the back wall, and there were besides, half a dozen stools. A hospitable pitcher of strong drink stood on the rude table, with a few small measures, cups and horns.

As if the weight of conspiracy had lain heavy on his shoulders, the young Laird of Ballengeich seemed older than he had ever looked before. Lines of care marked his brow, and his distraught manner proclaimed the plot-monger new to a dangerous business. The lights, however, were dim, and Ballengeich doubted if any there present would recognise him should they meet him in broad day, and this, in a measure, was comforting. The cobbler sat very quiet on his accustomed bench, the others occupying the stools and the board along the wall.

"We have been told," began the leader, who filled the chair at the head of the table, where he had administered the oath with much solemnity to their new member, "we have been told that you own a house which you will place at our disposal should the purpose for which we are gathered here together, succeed."

"I have such a house," said the laird, "and it is of course, placed freely at your service. But the plan you propose is so full of danger that I wondered if you have given the project the deep consideration it deserves. It will be a hazardous undertaking to get the king safely into my house, but let us suppose that done. How are you going to keep him there?"

"We will set a guard over him."

"Very good. Which of you are to be the guardsmen, and how many?"

The conspirators looked one at another, but none replied. At last the leader said,—

"It will be time to settle that when we have him safely under bolt."

"Pardon me, not so. The time to arrange all things is now. Everything must be cut and dried, or failure is certain. The moment the king is missing the country will be scoured for him. There will be no possible place of refuge for miles round that will not be searched for the missing monarch. We will suppose that four of you are guarding the king, two and two, turn about. What are the four, and myself, to say to the king's soldiers when they demand entrance to my house?"

"The king is but a boy, and when he sees death or compliance before him he will accede to our demands."

"He is a boy, it is true," agreed the laird, "but he is a boy, as I pointed out to my friend Flemming, who escaped from the clutches of the Earl of Angus, out of the stronghold of Falkland Palace, and who afterwards drove the earl and many of the Douglas leaders into English exile. That is the kind of boy you have to deal with. Suppose then, he gives consent to all you place before him? Do you think he will keep his word?"

"I doubt it," said the cobbler, speaking for the first time. "The word of a Stuart is not worth the snap of my finger."

"On the other hand, if he does not accede," continued Ballengeich, "what are we to do with him?"

"Cut his throat," replied the leader decisively.

"No, no," cried several others, and for a moment there was a clamour of discussion, all speaking at once, while the laird stood silently regarding the vociferous disputants. Finally their leader said,—

"What better plan have you to propose?"

"The king is a boy," spoke up Ballengeich, "as you have said." At the sound of his voice instant silence reigned. "But he is a boy, as I have told you, extremely difficult to handle with violence. I propose then to approach him peaceably. The fact that he is a boy, or a very young man at least, implies that his mind will be more impressionable than that of an older person whose ideas are set. I propose then that a deputation wait upon his majesty and place before him the evils that require remedying, being prepared to answer any question he may ask regarding the method of their amendment. If peaceable means fail, then try violence, say I, but it is hardly fair to the young man to approach him at the beginning of his reign with a dirk in the hand. His answer would likely be a reference to his headsman; that is a favourite Stuart mode of argument. I have some friends about the castle," continued the laird. "I supply them with various necessaries from the farm; and if I do say it myself, I am well thought of by some in authority. I can guarantee you, I am sure, a safe conduct for your mission."

"But if safe conduct be refused?" said the leader.

"In that case, no harm's done. I shall divulge the names of none here present, for indeed I know the name of none, except of my friend the cobbler."

"Will you head the delegation, and be its spokesman?"

"No. My power to serve you lies in the fact that I am well thought of in the palace. This power would be instantly destroyed were I known as disaffected. I would put it on this basis. My friend, Flemming, is the spokesman of ten others who have grievances to place before his majesty. Therefore, as a matter of friendship between Flemming and myself, I ask safe conduct for the eleven."

"Indeed," cried the cobbler, "I wish you would leave my name out of the affair, since no one else seems eager to put his own forward."

"I put mine forward in making the request," said Ballengeich.

"Aye, but not as one of the deputation."

"Very well," agreed the laird in an offhand manner, "if you make a point of it, I have no objection to saying that I shall make one of the concert. I only proposed to keep out of it, because it is always wise to have an unbiased person to put in his word at a critical moment, and it seems to me important to have such a person on the outside. But it shall be exactly as you please; I care little one way or the other. I have made my proposal, and with you rests the acceptance or the rejection of it. If you think it safer to kidnap a king than to have a friendly chat with him, amicably arranged beforehand, then all I can say is, that I don't in the least agree with you. Please yourselves; please yourselves. We have but one neck apiece, and surely we can risk it in the manner that brings us most content."

"There is wisdom in what the laird says," cried one of the more moderate party. "I never liked the kidnapping idea."

"Nor I," said the cobbler. "It was but a wild Hielan' notion."

"My project has this advantage," continued Ballengeich with nonchalant impartiality, "that if it does not succeed, you can then fall back upon abduction. Nothing in this proposal interferes with the ultimate carrying out of your first plan."

"It is putting our heads in the lion's mouth," objected the leader, but in the discussion that followed he was outvoted. Then came the choosing of the delegates, on which rock the enterprise was nearly wrecked, for there seemed to be no anxiety on the part of any four present to form the committee of expostulation which was to meet the monarch. At last it was decided that all should go, if Ballengeich could produce a written safe-conduct signed by the king, which would include eleven persons.

Within three days this document was placed in the hands of the cobbler by Ballengeich, who told him that it had been signed that morning. And he added that the king had expressed himself as well pleased to receive a deputation of his loyal subjects.

The cobbler handled the passport gingerly, as if he were not altogether assured of its potency to protect him.

"The conference is for Wednesday at midday," said Ballengeich. "Assemble some minutes before that hour in the courtyard of the castle, and you will be conducted to the Presence."

"Wednesday!" echoed the cobbler, his face turning pale. "Why Wednesday, the day of our weekly meetings? Did you suggest it?"

"It was the king's suggestion, of course," replied Ballengeich. "It is merely a coincidence, and is, I think, a good omen."

"I wish I were sure of it," moaned the cobbler.

Before the bell rang twelve the conspirators were gathered together in the courtyard of Castle Stirling; huddled would perhaps be the more accurate word, for they were eleven very frightened men. More than one cast longing looks towards the gate by which they had come in, but some places are easier to enter than to leave, and the portal was well guarded by stalwart soldiers.

As the bell slowly tolled twelve, an official came from the palace into the courtyard, searched the delegation for concealed weapons, and curtly commanded them to follow him. Climbing the stone stairway they were ushered into a large room containing a long oaken table with five chairs on one side and six on the other. At the head of the table was a high-backed seat resembling a throne. The official left them standing there alone, and after he had closed the door they heard the ominous sound of bolts being thrust into their places. The silence which followed seemed oppressive; almost suffocating. No man spoke, but each stood like a statue holding his cap in his hand. At last the tension was broken, but it would scarcely be correct to say that it was relieved. The heavy curtains parted and the king entered the room, clad in the imposing robes of his high state. A frown was on his brow, and he advanced straight from the doorway to the throne at the head of the table, without speaking or casting a glance at any one of the eleven. When he had seated himself he said gruffly,—

"There is a chair for each of you; sit down."

It is doubtful if any of the company, except the cobbler, at first recognised their ruler as the alleged Laird of Ballengeich; but at the sound of the monarch's voice several started and looked anxiously one at another. Again the king addressed them,—

"A week ago to-night I met you in Flemming's room. I appointed this day for the conference that the routine of your meetings might not be disturbed, as I thought it well that the last of your rebellious gatherings should be held in the Castle of Stirling, for I am resolved that this conclave shall be your final effort in treason. One of your number has stated that the word of a Stuart is not to be trusted. This reputation appears to have descended to me, and it is a pity I should not take advantage of it."

When the king ceased speaking he lifted a small mallet and smote a resounding bell, which was on the table before him. A curtain parted and two men entered bearing between them a block covered with black cloth; this they placed silently in the centre of the floor and withdrew. Again the king smote the bell and there entered a masked executioner with a gleaming axe over his shoulder. He took his place beside the block, resting the head of his axe on the floor.

"This," continued the king, "is the entertainment I have provided for you. Each of you shall taste of that," and he pointed to the heading block.

The cobbler rose unsteadily to his feet, drawing from his bosom with trembling fingers the parchment bearing the king's signature. He moistened his dry lips with his tongue, then spoke in a low voice.

"Sir," he said, "we are here under safe conduct from the king."

"Safe conduct to where?" cried James angrily, "that is the point. I stand by the document; read it; read it!"

"Sir, it says safe conduct for eleven men here present, under protection of your royal word."

"You do not keep to the point, cobbler," shouted the king bringing his fist down on the table. "Safe conduct to where? I asked. The parchment does not say safe conduct back into Stirling again. Safe conduct to Heaven, or elsewhere, was what I guaranteed."

"That is but an advocate's quibble, your majesty. Safe conduct is a phrase well understood by high and low alike. But we have placed our heads in the lion's mouth, as our leader said last Wednesday night, and we cannot complain if now his jaws are shut. Nevertheless I would respectfully submit to your majesty that I alone of those present doubted a Stuart's word, and am like to have my doubts practically confirmed. I would also point out to your majesty that my comrades would not have been here had I not trusted the Master of Ballengeich, and through him the king, therefore, I ask you to let me alone pay the penalty of my error, and allow my friends to go scatheless from the grim walls of Stirling."

"There is reason in what you say," replied the king. "Are you all agreed to that?" he asked of the others.

"No, by God," cried the leader springing to his feet and smiting the table with his fist as lustily as the king had done. "We stand together, or fall together. The mistake was ours as much as his, and we entered these gates with our eyes open."

"Headsman," said the king, "do your duty."

The headsman whipped off the black cloth and displayed underneath it a box containing a large jug surrounded by eleven drinking-horns. Those present, all now on their feet, glanced with amazement from the masked man to the king. The sternness had vanished from his majesty's face, as if a dark cloud had passed from the sun and allowed it to shine again. There sparkled in the king's eye all the jubilant mischief of the incorrigible boy, and his laughter rang to the ceiling. Somewhat recovering his gravity he stretched out his hand and pointed a finger at the cobbler.

"I frightened you, Flemming," he cried. "I frightened you; don't deny it. I'll wager my gold crown against a weaver's woollen bonnet, I frightened the whole eleven of you."

"Indeed," said the cobbler with an uneasy laugh, "I shall be the first to admit it."

"Your face was as white as a harvest moon in mid-sky, and I heard somebody's teeth chatter. Now the drink we have had at our meetings heretofore was vile, and no more fitted for a Christian throat than is the headsman's axe; but if you ever tasted anything better than this, tell me where to get a hogshead of it."

The headsman having filled their horns, the leader raised the flagon above his head and said,—

"I give you the toast of The King!"

"No, no," proclaimed the boyish monarch, "I want to drink this myself. I'll give you a toast. May there never come a time when a Scotchman is afraid to risk his head for what he thinks is right."

And this toast they drank together.

The King Dines

"When kings frown, courtiers tremble," said Sir Donald Sinclair to the Archbishop of St. Andrews, "but in Stirling the case seems reversed. The courtiers frown, and the king looks anxiously towards them."

"Indeed," replied the prelate, "that may well be. When a man invites a company to dine with him, and then makes the discovery that his larder is empty, there is cause for anxiety, be he king or churl. In truth my wame's beginning to think my throat's cut." And the learned churchman sympathetically smoothed down that portion of his person first named, whose rounded contour gave evidence that its owner was accustomed to ample rations regularly served.

"Ah well," continued Sir Donald, "his youthful majesty's foot is hardly in the stirrup yet, and I'm much mistaken in the glint of his eye and the tint of his beard, if once he is firmly in the saddle the horse will not feel the prick of the spur, should it try any tricks with him."

"Scotland would be none the worse of a firm king," admitted the archbishop, glancing furtively at the person they were discussing, "but James has been so long under the control of others that it will need some force of character to establish a will of his own. I doubt he is but a nought posing as a nine," concluded his reverence in a lower tone of voice.

"I know little of mathematics," said Sir Donald, "but yet enough to tell me that a nought needs merely a flourish to become a nine, and those nines among us who think him a nought, may become noughts should he prove a nine. There's a problem in figures for you, archbishop, with a warning at the end of it, like the flourish at the tail of the nine."

The young man to whom they referred, James, the fifth of that name, had been pacing the floor a little distance from the large group of hungry men who were awaiting their dinner with some impatience. Now and then the king paused in his perambulation, and gazed out of a window overlooking the courtyard, again resuming his disturbed march when his brief scrutiny was completed. The members of the group talked in whispers, one with another, none too well pleased at being kept waiting for so important a function as a meal.

Suddenly there was a clatter of horse's hoofs in the courtyard. The king turned once more to the window, glanced a moment at the commotion below, then gave utterance to an exclamation of annoyance, his right hand clenching angrily. Wheeling quickly to the guards at the door he cried,—

"Bring the chief huntsman here at once, and a prod in the back with a pike may make up for his loitering in the courtyard."

The men, who stood like statues with long axes at the doorway, made no move; but two soldiers, sitting on a bench outside, sprang to their feet and ran clattering down the stair. They returned presently with the chief huntsman, whom they projected suddenly into the room with a violence little to the woodman's taste, for he neglected to remove his bonnet in the royal presence, and so far forgot himself as to turn his head when he recovered his equilibrium, roundly cursing those who had made a projectile of him.

"Well, woodlander!" cried the king, his stern voice ringing down again from the lofty rafters of the great hall. "Are there no deer in my forests of the north?"

"Deer in plenty, your majesty," answered the fellow with a mixture of deference and disrespect, which in truth seemed to tinge the manners of all present. "There are deer in the king's forest, and yet a lack of venison in the king's larder!"

"What mean you by that, you scoundrel?" exclaimed the king, a flush overspreading his face, ruddy as his beard. "Have your marksmen lost their skill with bow and arrow, that you return destitute to the castle?"

"The marksmen are expert as ever, your majesty, and their arrows fly as unerringly to their billet, but in these rude times, your majesty, the sting of an arrow may not be followed by the whetting of a butcher's knife."

The king took an impatient step forward, then checked himself. One or two among the group of noblemen near the door laughed, and there was a ripple of suppressed merriment over the whole company. At first the frown on the king's brow deepened, and then as suddenly it cleared away, as a puff of wind scatters the mist from the heights of Stirling. When the king spoke again it was in a calm, even voice. "As I understand you, there was no difficulty in capturing the deer, but you encountered some obstacle between the forest and Stirling which caused you to return empty-handed. I hope you have not added the occupation of itinerant flesher to the noble calling of forest huntsman?"

"Indeed, your majesty," replied the unabashed hunter, "the profession of flesher was forced upon me. The deer we had slaughtered found it impossible to win by the gates of Arnprior."

"Ah! John Buchanan then happened to need venison as you passed?"

"Your majesty has hit the gold there. Buchanan not only needed it but took it from us."

"Did you inform him that your cargo was intended for the larder of the king?"

"I told him that in so many words, your majesty; and he replied that if James was king in Stirling, John was king in Kippen, and having the shorter name, he took the shorter method of supplying his kitchen."

"Made you any effort to defend your gear?"

"Truth to say, your majesty, that were a useless trial. The huntsman who will face the deer thinks no shame to turn his back on the wild boar, and Buchanan, when he demanded your majesty's venison, was well supported by a number of mad caterans with drawn swords in their hands, who had made up for a lack of good meat with a plentitude of strong drink. Resistance was futile, and we were fain to take the bannock that was handed to us, even though the ashes were upon it. Ronald of the Hills, a daft Heilan'man who knew no better, drew an arrow to his ear and would have pinned Buchanan to his own gate, resulting in the destruction of us all, had I not, with my stave, smote the weapon from his hand. Then the mad youth made such to-do that we had just to tie him up and bring him to Stirling on the horse's back like a sack of fodder."

"Your caution does credit to your Lowland breeding, Master huntsman, and the conduct of Ronald cannot be too severely condemned. Bring him here, I beg of you, that he may receive the king's censure."

Ronald was brought in, a wild, unkempt figure, his scanty dress disordered, bearing witness to the struggle in which he had but lately been engaged. His elbows were pinioned behind him, and his shock of red hair stood out like a heather broom. He scowled fiercely at the huntsman, and that cautious individual edged away from him, bound as he was.

"By my beard! as the men of the heathen East swear," said the king, "his hair somewhat matches my own in hue. Ronald, what is the first duty of a huntsman?"

"He speaks only the Gaelic, your majesty," explained the royal ranger.

"You have the Gaelic, MacNeish," continued the king, addressing one of his train. "Expound to him, I beg of you, my question. What is the first duty of a huntsman?"

MacNeish, stepping forward, put the question in Gaelic and received Ronald's reply.

"He says, your majesty, that a huntsman's first duty is to kill the game he is sent for."

"Quite right," and the king nodded approval. "Ask him if he knows as well the second duty of a huntsman."

Ronald's eye flashed as he gave his answer with a vehemence that caused the chief huntsman to move still farther away from him.

"He says, your majesty," translated MacNeish, "that the second duty of a huntsman is to cut the throat of any cateran who presumes to interfere with the progress of the provender from the forest to his master's kitchen."

"Right again," cried the king, smiting his thigh, "and an answer worthy of all commendation. Tell him this, MacNeish, that hereafter he is the chief huntsman to the Castle of Stirling. We will place this cowardly hellion in the kitchen where he will be safe from the hungry frenzy of a Buchanan, drunk or sober."

"But, your majesty—" protested the deposed ranger.

"To the kitchen with him!" sternly commandedry. "Strip off the woodlander's jacket he has disgraced and tie round him the strings of a scullion's apron, which will suit his middle better than the belt of a sword." Then the king, flashing forth his own weapon and stepping aside, swung it over the head of the Highlander, who stood like a statue in spite of the menace, and the sword came down with a deft accuracy which severed the binding cords without touching the person of the prisoner, freeing him at a stroke. A murmur of admiration at the dexterity of the king went up from the assemblage, every member of which was himself an expert with the weapon. The freed Highlander raised his brawny arms above his head and gave startling vent to the war-cry of his clan, "Loch Sloy! Loch Sloy!" unmindful of the presence in which he stood. Then he knelt swiftly and brought his lips to the buckle of the king's shoe.

"Gratitude in a MacFarlane!" sneered MacNeish.

"Aye," said the king, "and bravery too, for he never winked an eyelash when the sword swung above him; an admirable combination of qualities whether in a MacFarlane or a MacNeish. And now, gentlemen," continued his majesty, "although the affair of the huntsman is settled, it brings us no nearer our venison. If the cook will not to the king, then must the king to the cook. Gentlemen, to your arms and your horses! They say a Scotsman fights well when he is hungry; let us put the proverb to the test. We ride and dine with his majesty of Kippen."

A spontaneous cheer burst from every man in the great hall to the accompaniment of a rattle of swords. Most of those present were more anxious to follow the king to a contest than into a council chamber. When silence ensued, the mild voice of the archbishop, perhaps because it was due to his profession, put in a seasonable word; and the nobles scowled for they knew he had great influence with the king.

"Your majesty, if the Buchanans are drunk——"

"If they are drunk, my lord archbishop," interrupted James, "we will sober them. 'Tis a duty even the Church owes to the inebriate." And with that he led the way out of the hall, his reply clearing the brows of his followers.

A few minutes later a clattering cavalcade rode forth from the Castle of Stirling, through the town and down the path of Ballengeich, a score of soldiers bringing up the tail of the procession; and in due time the company came to the entrance of Arnprior Castle. There seemed like to be opposition at the gate, but Sir Donald, spurring his horse forward among the guard, scattered the members of it right and left, and, raising both voice and sword, shouted,—

"The king! The king! Make way for the King of Scotland!"

The defenders seeing themselves outnumbered, as the huntsmen had been in that locality a short time before, gave up their axes to the invaders as meekly as the royal rangers had given up their venison.

The king placed his own guard at the gate. Springing from his horse he entered the castle door, and mounted the stone steps, sword in hand, his retinue close at his heels. The great hall to which they ascended was no monk's chapel of silence. There was wafted to them, or rather blown down upon them like a fierce hurricane, the martial strains of "Buchanan for ever," played by pipers anything but scant of wind; yet even this tornado was not sufficient to drown the roar of human voices, some singing, others apparently in the heat of altercation, and during the height of this deafening clamour the king and his followers entered the dining-hall practically unobserved.

On the long oaken table, servitors were busily placing smoking viands soon to be consumed; others were filling the drinking-horns, while some of the guests were engaged in emptying them, although the meal had not yet begun. Buchanan, his back towards the incomers, his brawny hands on the table, leaning forward, was shouting to the company, commanding his guests to seat themselves and fall to while the venison was hot. There seemed to be several loud voiced disputes going on regarding precedence. The first intimation that the bellowing laird had of the intruder's presence was the cold touch of steel on his bare neck. He sprang round as if a wasp had stung him, his right hand swinging instinctively to the hilt of his sword, but the point of another was within an inch of his throat, and his hand fell away from his weapon.

"The fame of your hospitality has spread abroad, Buchanan," spoke the clear voice of the king, "so we have come to test its quality."

The pipers had stopped in their march, and with the ceasing of the music, the wind from the bags escaped to the outer air with a long wailing groan. The tumult of discussion subsided, and all eyes turned towards the speaker, some of the guests hastily drawing swords but returning them again to the scabbards when they saw themselves confronted by the king. Buchanan steadied himself with his back against the table, and in the sudden silence it seemed long ere he found his tongue. At last he said,—

"Does the king come as a guest with a drawn sword in his hand?"

"As you get north of Stirling, Buchanan,' replied James with a smile, "it is customary to bring the knife with you when you go out to dine. But I am quite in agreement with the Laird of Arnprior in thinking the sword an ill ornament in a banqueting-hall, therefore bestow your weapons on Sir Donald here, and command your clan now present to disarm."

With visible reluctance Buchanan divested himself of sword and dirk, and his comrades, now stricken dumb, followed his example. The weapons were thrown together in a corner of the hall where some of the king's soldiers stood guard over them. His majesty's prediction regarding the sobering effect of his advent was amply fulfilled. The disarmed men looked with dismay on one another, for they knew that such a prelude might well have its grand finale at the block or the gibbet. The king, although seemingly in high spirits, was an unknown quantity, and before now there had been those in power who, with a smile on their lips, had sent doomed men to a scaffold.

"In intercepting my venison, Buchanan," continued the king with

34

the utmost politeness, "you were actuated by one of two motives. Your intervention was either an insult to the king, or it was an intimation that you desired to become his cook. In which light am I to view your action, Buchanan?"

There was in the king's voice a sinister ring as he uttered this sentence that belied the smile upon his lips, and apprehension deepened as all present awaited Buchanan's reply. At the word "cook," he had straightened himself, and a deeper flush than the wine had left there, overspread his countenance; now he bowed with deference and said,—

"It has ever been my ambition to see your majesty grace with his presence my humble board."

"I was sure of it," cried James with a hearty laugh which brought relief to the anxious hearts of many standing before him. The king thrust his sword into a scabbard, and, with a clangour of hilt on iron, those behind him followed his example.

"And now," cried James, "let the king's men eat while the laird's men wait upon them. And as for you, John Buchanan, it is to-day my pleasure that you have the honour of being my cup-bearer."

Whether the honour thus thrust upon the Laird of Arnprior was as much to his liking as an invitation to sit down with his guest would have been, is questionable, but he served his majesty with good grace, and the king was loud in his praise of the venison, although his compliments fell sadly on the ears of the hungry men who watched it disappear so rapidly. At the end of the feast James rose with his flagon in his hand.

"I give you the king," he cried, "the King of Kippen. When I left Stirling I had made up my mind that there could be but one king in a country, but glorious Scotland shall have no such restriction, and I bestow upon Buchanan, whose ample cheer we have done justice to, the title of King of Kippen, so long as he does not fall into the error of supposing that Kippen includes all of Scotland, instead of Scotland including Kippen. And so, Laird of Arnprior, King of Kippen, we drink your good health, and when next my venison passes your door, take only that portion of it which bears the same relation to the whole, as the district of Kippen does to broad Scotland."

The toast was drunk with cheers, and when silence came, the King of Kippen, casting a rueful glance along the empty board, said,—

"I thank your majesty for your good wishes, but in truth the advice you give will be hard to follow, for I see I should have stolen twice the quantity of venison I did, because as I have not done so, I and my men are like to go hungry."

And thus Buchanan came into his title of King of Kippen, although he had to wait some time for his dinner on the day he acquired the distinction.

The King's Tryst

The king ruled. There was none to question the supremacy of James the Fifth. At the age of twenty-two he now sat firmly on his throne. He was at peace with England, friendly with France, and was pledged to take a wife from that country. His great grandfather, James the Second, had crushed the Black Douglas, and he himself had scattered the Red Douglas to exile. No Scottish noble was now powerful enough to threaten the stability of the throne. The country was contented and prosperous, so James might well take his pleasure as best pleased him. If any danger lurked near him it was unseen and unthought of.

The king, ever first in the chase, whether the quarry ran on four legs or on two, found himself alone on the road leading north-west from Stirling, having outstripped his comrades in their hunt of the deer. Evening was falling and James being some miles from Stirling Castle, raised his bugle to his lips to call together his scattered followers, but before a blast broke the stillness, his majesty was accosted by a woman who emerged suddenly and unnoticed from the forest on his left hand.

"My lord, the king;" she said, and her voice, like the sound of silver bells, thrilled with a note of inquiry.

"Yes, my lassie," answered the young man, peering down at his questioner, lowering his bugle, and reining in his frightened horse, which was startled by the sudden apparition before him. The dusk had not yet so far thickened but the king could see that his interlocutor was young and strikingly beautiful. Although dressed in the garb of the lower orders, there was a quiet and imposing dignity in her demeanour as she stood there by the side of the road. Her head was uncovered, the shawl she wore over it having slipped down to her shoulders, and her abundant hair, unknotted and unribboned, was ruddy as spun gold. Her complexion was dazzlingly fair, her eyes of the deepest blue, and her features perfection, except that her small mouth showed a trifle too much firmness, a quality which her strong but finely moulded chin corroborated and emphasised. The king, ever a connoisseur of womanly loveliness, almost held his breath as he gazed down upon the comely face upturned to him.

"They told me at Stirling," she said, "that you were hunting through this district, and I have been searching for you in the forest."

"Good heavens, girl!" cried the king; "have you walked all the way from Stirling?"

"Aye, and much further. It is nothing, for I am accustomed to it. And now I crave a word with your majesty."

"Surely, surely!" replied the king with enthusiasm, no thought of danger in this unconventional encounter even occurring to him. The natural prudence of James invariably deserted him where a pretty woman was concerned. Now, instead of summoning his train, he looked anxiously up and down the road listening for any sound of his men, but the stillness seemed to increase with the darkness, and the silence was profound, not even the rustle of a leaf disturbing it.

"And who, my girl, are you?" continued the king, noticing that her eyes followed his glance up and down the road with some trace of apprehension in them, and that she hesitated to speak.

"May it please your gracious majesty, I am humble tirewoman to that noble lady, Margaret Stuart, your honoured mother."

The king gave a whistle of astonishment.

"My mother!" he exclaimed. "Then what in the name of Heaven are you doing here and alone, so far from Methven?"

"We came from Methven yesterday to her ladyship's castle of Doune."

"Then her ladyship must have come to a very sudden resolution to travel, for the constable of Doune is in my hunting-party, and I'll swear he expected no visitors."

"My gracious lady did not wish Stuart the constable to expect her, nor does she now desire his knowledge of her presence in the castle. She commanded me to ask your majesty to request the constable to remain in Stirling, where, she understands, he spends most of his time. She begs your majesty to come to her with all speed and secrecy."

"I wonder what is wrong now?" mused the king. "I have not heard from her for nearly a year. She has quarrelled with her third husband, I suppose, for the Tudors are all daft where matrimony is concerned."

"What does your majesty say?" asked the girl.

"I was speaking to myself rather than to you, but I may add that I am ready to go anywhere if you are to be my guide. Lend me your hand and spring up here behind me. We will gallop to Doune at once."

The young woman drew back a step or two.

"No, no," she said. "The Lady Margaret is most anxious that your visit should be unknown to any but herself, so she begs you to dismiss your followers and lay your commands upon Constable Stuart of Doune."

"But my followers are all of them old enough to look after themselves," objected the king, "and the constable is not likely to leave Stirling where he has remained these many months."

"The Lady Margaret thought," persisted the girl, "that if your retinue returned to Stirling and learned of your continued absence, anxiety would ensue, and a search might be undertaken that would extend to Doune."

"How did my lady mother know I was hunting when you could not have learned of my excursion until you reached Stirling?" asked the king, with a glimmer of that caution which appeared to have deserted him.

The girl seemed somewhat nonplussed by the question, but she answered presently with quiet deliberation,—

"Her ladyship was much perturbed and feared I should not find you at the castle. She gave me various instructions, which she trusted I could accommodate to varying contingencies."

"My girl," said the king leaning towards her, "you do not speak like a serving-maid. What is your name?"

"I have been a gentlewoman, sire," she answered simply, "but women, alas, cannot control their fortunes. My name is Catherine. I will now forward to Doune, and wait for you at the further side of the new bridge the tailor has built over the Teith. If you will secure your horse somewhere before coming to the river, and meet me there on foot, I will conduct you to the castle. Will you come?"

"Of a surety," cried the king, in a tone that left no doubt of his intentions. "I shall overtake you long before you are at the bridge!" As he said this the girl fled away in the darkness, and then he raised his bugle to his lips and blew a blast that speedily brought answering calls.

James's unexplained absences were so frequent that his announcement of an intention not to return home that night caused no surprise among his company; so, bidding him good-night, they cantered off towards Stirling, while he, unaccompanied, set his face to the north-west, and his spurs to the horse's flanks, but his steed was already tired out and could not now keep pace with his impatience. To his disappointment, he did not overtake the girl, but found her waiting for him at the new bridge, and together they walked the short half mile to the castle. The young man was inclined to be conversational, but the girl made brief replies and finally besought his silence.

The night had proved exceedingly dark, and they were almost at the castle before its huge bulk loomed blackly before them. There was something so sinister in its dim, grim contour that for the first time since he set out on this night adventure, a suspicion that he was acting unwisely crossed the king's mind.

Still, he meditated, it was his mother's own castle, the constable of which was a warm friend of his—almost, as one might say, a relative, for Stuart was the younger brother of his mother's husband, so what could be amiss with this visit?

"You are not taking me to the main entrance," he whispered.

"No, to the postern door."

"But the postern door is situated in the wall high above my reach; it is intended for the exit of a possible messenger during a siege and not for the entrance of a guest."

"I am acting in accordance with my instructions," replied the girl. "A rope ladder descends from the postern door."

"A rope ladder! that sounds promising; will you ascend it?"

"Yes, sire, but meanwhile, I implore your majesty to be silent."

The king said no more until the rope ladder was in his hand.

"I hope it is strong," he murmured.

Then he mounted lightly up in the darkness, until he stood on the sill of the narrow doorway, when he reached forward his hand to assist his slower comrade in mounting, but she sprang past him without availing herself of his aid. In a low voice she begged pardon for preceding him. Then walked up and up a winding stone staircase, on whose steps there was barely room for two to pass each other. She pushed open a door and allowed some light to stream through on the turret stair, which disappeared in the darkness still further aloft.

The king found himself in a large square apartment either on the first or second story. It appeared in some sort to be a lady's boudoir, for the benches were cushioned and comfortable, and there were evidences, about on small tables, of tapestry work and other needle employment recently abandoned.

"Will your majesty kindly be seated," said the girl. "I must draw up the ladder, close the postern door, and then inform my lady that you are here."

She went out by the way they had entered and shut the door with a force that seemed to the king unnecessary, but he caught his breath an instant later as his quick ear seemed to tell him that a bolt had fallen. He rose at once, tried to open the door, and discovered it was indeed barred on the outside. One other exit remained to be tested; a larger door evidently communicating

41

with another room or passage; that also he found locked. He returned to the middle of the room and stood there for a few moments with knitted brow.

"Trapped, Jamie, my lad! Trapped!" he muttered to himself. "Now what object can my mother have in this? Does she expect by such childish means to resume her authority over me? Does she hope that her third husband shall rule Scotland in my name as did her second, with me a prisoner? By Saint Andrew, no!"

The king seized a bench, raised it over his head and crashed it in bits against the larger door with a noise that reverberated through the castle.

"Open!" he cried; "open instantly!"

Then he paused, awaiting the result of his fury. Presently he thought he heard light footsteps coming along the passage and an instant later the huge key turned slowly in the lock. The door opened, and to his amazement he saw standing before him with wide frightened eyes, his guide, but dressed now as a lady.

"Madam," said the king sternly, "I ask you the meaning of this pleasantry?"

"Pleasantry," echoed the girl, staring at him with her hand upon a huge iron key, alert to run if this handsome maniac, strewn round by the wreckage of the bench he had broken, attempted to lay hands on her.

"Pleasantry?" she repeated; "that is a question I may well ask you. Who are you, sir, and what are you doing here?"

"Who I am, and what I am doing here, you know very well, because you brought me here. A change of garb does not change a well-remembered face," and the king bowed to his visitor with a return of his customary courtliness, now that his suspicions were allayed, for he knew how to deal with pretty women. "Madam, there is no queen in Scotland, but you are queen by right of nature, and though you doff your gown, you cannot change your golden crown."

The girl's hand unconsciously went up to her ruddy hair, while she murmured more to herself than to him,—

"This is some of Catherine's work."

"Catherine was your name in the forest, my lady, what is your name in the castle?"

"Isabel is my name in castle and forest alike. You have met my twin sister, Catherine. Why has she brought you here?"

"Like an obedient son, I am here at the command of my honourable mother; and your sister—if indeed goddesses so strangely fair, and so strangely similar can be two persons—has gone to acquaint my mother of my arrival."

The girl's alarm seemed to increase as the king's diminished. Trouble, dismay, and fear marred her perfect face, and as the king scrutinised her more minutely, he saw that the firm mouth and the resolute chin of her sister had no place in the more softened and womanly features of the lady before him.

"Your mother? Who is she?"

"First, Margaret Tudor, daughter of the King of England, second, Margaret Stuart, wife of the King of Scotland, third, Margaret Douglas, ill mate of the Earl of Angus; fourth, and let us hope finally, Margaret Stuart again, spouse of Lord Methven, and owner of this castle."

The girl swayed as if she would fall, all colour struck suddenly from her face. She leaned, nearly fainting, against the stone wall, passing her hand once or twice across her terror-filled eyes.

"Great God," she moaned, "do not tell me that you are James, King of Scotland, here, and alone, in this den of Douglases!"

"Douglas!" cried the king roused at the hated name. "How can there be Douglases in the Castle of Doune; my mother's house, constabled by my friend, young Stuart."

"Your mother's house?" said the girl with an uncanny laugh. "When has the Lady Margaret set foot in Doune? Not since she was divorced from my uncle, Archibald Douglas, Earl of Angus! And the constable? Aye, the constable is in Stirling. Doune Castle stands gloomy and alone, but in Stirling with the young king, there are masques, and hunting and gaiety. Young Stuart draws the revenues of his charge, but pays slight attention to the fulfilment of his duty."

"You are then Isabel Douglas? And now, to echo your own question, how came you here? If this is a den of Douglases, as you say, how comes my mother's castle to be officered by the enemies of her son?"

"That you ask such a question shows little foresight or knowledge of men. When your first step-father, and my uncle, Archibald Douglas, had control of this castle through your mother's name, he filled it with his own adherents."

"Naturally; nepotism was a well-known trait of my domineering step-father, which did not add to his popularity in Scotland. Who can get office, or justice against a Douglas? was their cry. But did not young Stuart, when he was made constable, put in his own men?"

"The constable cares nothing for this stronghold so long as it furnishes money which he may spend gaily in Stirling."

"I see. So you and your sister found refuge among your underlings? and where so safe from search as within the king's mother's own fortress, almost under the shadow of Stirling? An admirable device. Why then do you jeopardise your safety by letting me into the secret?"

The girl sighed deeply with downcast eyes, then she flashed a glance at him which had something in it of the old Douglas hauteur.

"I fear," she said, "that it is not our safety which is jeopardised."

"You mean that I am in danger?"

"The same stronghold which gives immunity to a family of the Red Douglases can hardly be expected to confer security upon James the Fifth, their persecutor."

"No. Certainly that would be too much to expect. Are you then in this plot against me, my lady?"

"I have not heard of any plot. If there is one I know nothing of it. I merely acquaint you with some hint of my fears."

"Then I charge you as a loyal subject of the lawful king, to guide me from this stronghold, into which I have been cozened by treachery and falsehood."

Catherine, who had entered silently and unnoticed through the smaller door, now stepped forward, drew her sister into the room, took out the huge key, closed the door and locked it, then turned fiercely to the king. Her beautiful white right arm was bare to the elbow, the loose sleeve rolled up, and in her hand she held a dagger. With her back against the newly locked door, she said,—

"I'll be your majesty's guide from this castle, and your perjured soul shall find exit through a postern gate made by my dagger!"

"Oh, Catherine, Catherine," sobbed Isabel, weeping in fear and horror of the situation, "you cannot contemplate so awful a deed, a murder so foul, for however unworthy he may be, he is still the king."

"What is there foul in ridding the world of a reptile such as he? How many innocent lives has he taken to encompass his revenge? How many now of our name are exiled and starving because of his action? I shall strike the blow with greater surety, for in killing him I extinguish his treacherous race."

"No good can come from assassination, Catherine."

"What greater evil can spring from his death than from his life?"

"His killing will not bring back those whom he has slain; it will not cause our banished kinsmen to return. It will be a murder for revenge."

"And not the first in Scotland," said Catherine grimly.

The king had once more seated himself, and now, resting his chin on his open palm, listened to the discussion with the interested bearing of one who had little concern with its result. A half amused smile wreathed his lips, and once or twice he made a motion as if he would intervene, but on second thoughts kept silent.

"Do not attempt this fell deed, dear sister," pleaded Isabel earnestly. "Let us away as we intended. The horses are ready and waiting for us. Our mother is looking for our coming in her room. The night wears on and we must pass Stirling while it is yet dark, so there is no time to be lost. Dear sister, let us quit Scotland, as we purposed, an accursed land to all of our name, but let us quit it with unstained hands."

"Isabel, darling," said Catherine in a low voice that quavered with the emotion caused by her sister's distress and appeal, "what unlucky chance brought you to this fatal door at such a moment? Can you not understand that I have gone too far to retreat? Who, having caged the tiger, dare open again the gate and set him free? If for no other reason, the king must die because he is here and because I brought him here. Open the door behind you, Isabel, go down the circular stair, and at the postern step you will find the rope ladder by which I ascended. Get you to the courtyard and there wait for me, saying nothing."

"Catherine, Catherine, the king will pardon you. He will surely forgive what you have done in exchange for his life."

"Forgiveness!" cried Catherine, her eyes blazing again. "I want no forgiveness from the king of Scotland. Pardon! The tiger would pardon, till once he is free again. The king must die."

"I shall go as you have bid me, Catherine, but not to do your bidding. I shall arouse this castle and prevent an abominable crime."

Catherine laughed harshly.

"Whom would you call to your assistance? Douglases, Douglases, Douglases! How many of your way of thinking will you find in the castle? You know well, one only, and that is our mother, old and helpless. Rouse the castle, Isabel, if you will, and find a dead man, and perhaps a dead sister, when you break in this locked door."

The helpless Isabel sank her head against the wall and burst into a fury of weeping.

"Ladies," said the king soothingly, rising to his feet, "will you graciously condone my intervention in this dispute? You are discussing an important act, from the commission of which all sentiment should be eliminated; an act which requires the hard strong mind of a man brought to bear upon the pros and cons of its consummation. You are dealing with it entirely from the standpoint of the heart and not of the head, an error common with women, and one that has ever precluded their effective dealing with matters of State. You will pardon me, Lady Isabel, when I say that your sister takes a much more practical view of the situation than you do. She is perfectly right in holding that, having me prisoner here, it is impossible to allow me to go scatheless. There is no greater folly than the folly of half doing a thing."

"Does your majesty argue in favour of your own murder?" asked Isabel amazed, gazing at the young man through her tears.

"Not so, but still that is a consideration which I must endeavour to eliminate from my mind, if my advice is to be impartial, and of service to you. May I beg of you to be seated? We have the night before us, and may consider the various interesting points at our leisure, and thus no irremediable mistake need be made."

Isabel, wellnigh exhausted with the intensity of her feelings, sank upon the bench, but Catherine still stood motionless, dagger in hand, her back against the door. The king, seeing she did not intend to obey, went on suavely. There was a light of intense admiration in his eye as he regarded the standing woman.

"Ladies," he said, "can you tell me when last a King of Scotland—a James also—and a Catherine Douglas bore relation to each other in somewhat similar circumstances?"

The king paused, but the girl, lowering at him, made no reply, and after a few moments the young man went on.

"It was a year more than a century ago, when the life of James the First was not only threatened, but extinguished, not by one brave woman, but by a mob of cowardly assassins. Then Catherine Douglas nearly saved the life of her king. She thrust her fair young arm into the iron loops of a door, and had it shattered by those craven miscreants."

Isabel wept quietly, her face in her two open hands. But Catherine answered in anger,—

"Why did the Catherine Douglas of that day risk her life to save the king? Because James the First was a just monarch. Why does the Catherine Douglas of to-day wish to thrust her dagger into the false heart of James the Fifth? Because he has turned on the hand that nurtured him——"

"The hand that imprisoned him, Lady Catherine. Pardon my correction."

"He turned on the man who governed Scotland wisely and well."

"Again pardon me; he had no right to govern. I was the king, not Archibald Douglas. But all that is beside the question, and recrimination is as bad as sentiment for clouding cold reason. What I wished to point out is, that assassination of kings or the capture of them very rarely accomplishes its object. James the First was assassinated and as result two Stuarts, two Grahams and two Chamberses were tortured and executed; so his murderers profited little. My grandfather James the Third was carried off by the Boyds, but Sir Alexander Boyd was beheaded and his brother and nephew suffered forfeiture. I think I have shown then that violence is usually futile."

"Not so," answered Catherine; "your grandfather was assassinated, and the man who killed him is not known to this day. Your great-grandfather basely murdered the Black Douglas in Stirling, thus breaking his word of honour for he had given Douglas safe conduct, yet he profited by his act and crushed my kinsmen."

"I see, Lady Catherine, that you are too well versed in history for me to contend with you successfully on that subject," said the king with a silent laugh. "We will therefore restrict the inquiry to the present case, as wise people should. Tell me then, so that I may be the better able to advise you, what is your true object—revenge and my death, or the wringing from me of concessions for your family?"

"I could not wring concessions from you, because you could not make good those concessions unless I released you. I dare not release you, because I dare not trust you."

"I foresaw your difficulty, and so I told your sister that, having gone so far, you could not retreat. The issue is therefore narrowed down to death, and how it may best be accomplished. You have made the tactical mistake of forewarning me. I cannot understand why you did not mount my horse beside me and stab me in the back as we rode through the forest. Did this not occur to you, Lady Catherine?"

"It did, but there were objections. Your horse would doubtless have escaped me, and would have galloped riderless to Stirling; your body would have been found by break of day, and we but a few hours' march from Stirling. Here I expect you to lie undiscovered in this locked room till we are safe in England."

"That is clear reasoning," commented the king with impartiality, "but have you looked beyond? Who will be the successor of the throne? I have neither brother nor sister; my two uncles died before I was born, and I perish childless. I think you mentioned that you wished to extinguish our line. Very well; what follows? Who is heir to the throne?"

"It matters nothing to me," said Catherine firmly. "Whoever rules Scotland could not be a greater enemy to my race than you are."

"I am not so sure of that. I think your dagger-blow will bring consequences you do not look for, and that your kin, now exiled in England will find the stroke a savage one for them. You forget that the stern King of England is my uncle, and on this relationship may lay claim to the Scottish throne. Be that as it may, it will be no secret that a Douglas committed the murder; and think you Henry VIII will offer safe refuge to his nephew's assassins? You much misjudge him if you do. It would have been far better to have slain me in the forest. This castle business is but an ill-judged, ill thought-out plan. I am sorry to appear adversely critical, but such is my opinion, and it confirms me in the belief that women should leave steel and State alone."

"I dare not let you go," reiterated Catherine.

"Of a surety you dare not; that is what I have said from the beginning. On the other hand, I can make no concession, under coercion, that would save my life. You see we are both cowardly, each in a different way. And now having come to the absolutely logical conclusion that the king must die, you should turn your mind to the difficulties that confront you. I, you see, am also armed."

The king as he spoke took from his doublet a dagger almost similar to the one held by the girl. A gentle smile graced his lips as he ran his thumb along the edge, and then glanced up at the two in time to notice their consternation at this new element in the situation.

"If you enter a tiger's cage you should expect a touch of his claws, so, Lady Catherine, your task is more serious than you anticipated. There is furthermore another source of danger against you, and it is my sincere wish that in the struggle to come you may not be too severely handicapped. While the issue of our contest is still in doubt, your sister will assuredly unlock the door and give the alarm, hoping to prevent your contemplated crime, or my killing of you. I think it right that you should not be called upon to suffer this intervention, for, if you will permit me to say so, I admire your determination as much as I admire, in another way, the Lady Isabel's leaning towards mercy. I shall then, take this key from the larger door and place it, with your sister, outside on the narrow stairway. You have withdrawn the rope ladder so she cannot alarm the garrison."

"But I have not withdrawn it," said Catherine quickly. "My sister must not leave this room or she will bring interference."

"Then," said the king calmly, as he rose and took the key from the large door, "we shall at least make it impossible for her to open the way into the hall." And so saying, he stepped to the smaller door, which he opened, and before either of the women could prevent his action, or even grasp an inkling of his design, he stepped outside, key in hand, and thrust to their places the bolts of the stairway door.

The two girls looked at each other for a moment in silence, Isabel plainly panic-stricken, while in Catherine's face anger struggled with chagrin.

Each was quick to see the sudden consequences of this turning of the tables; the two were helpless prisoners in a remote portion of the castle, no one within its walls being acquainted with their whereabouts. The king, insulted, hoodwinked, and all but murdered, was now at liberty, free to ride the few short leagues that lay between Doune and Stirling, and before daybreak the fortress would be in the hands of an overwhelming force with the present garrison prisoners. In the awed stillness an unexpected sound came to them from the outside; the sound of a man endeavouring to suppress the hearty laughter that overmastered him. To be doomed is bad enough, but to be made the subject of levity was too much for the dauntless Catherine. She flung her dagger ringing to the stone floor with a gesture of rage, then sank upon a bench and gave way to tears; tears of bitter humiliation and rage.

"Ladies," said the king from the outside, "I beg that you will allow me to open the door." But, receiving no answer, the bolts were drawn once more; James again entered the apartment and gazed down upon two fair proud heads, crowned with ruddy hair.

"Dear ladies," said the king, "forgive me my untimely mirth. Both of you take matters much too seriously; a little laughter is necessary in this world. My Lady Catherine, I told you that I could grant no concessions under coercion, but now coercion has vanished and I enter this room a free man of my own will. Tell me, my girl, what is it you want? The rescinding of your father's exile? It is granted. The right to live unmolested in your own castle? It is granted. Safe conduct to England? It is granted. The privilege of remaining in Doune? It is granted. But do not ask me to rescind banishment against Archibald Douglas, Earl of Angus, for that I shall not concede. The Douglas ambition, and not the Scottish king, has wrecked the Douglas family, both Black and Red. But as far as concerns your own immediate kin, with one exception, I shall give anything you like to ask."

Catherine rose to her feet, threw back her auburn tresses, and said curtly,—

"We ask nothing but the privilege of leaving the country you rule."

The king bowed.

"And you, Lady Isabel?"

"I go with my sister and my mother."

"I grieve at your decision, ladies, and for the first time in my life envy England in getting an advantage over poor old Scotland, which I hope will not be irreparable, for I trust you will return. But if such be your determination, then go in peace, and in the daylight. Your journey shall not be molested by me. But, before you add finality to your intentions, I think it would be but fair to inform your lady mother that the king is anxious to be of service to her, and perhaps she may be content to accept what her daughters are apparently too proud to receive."

James placed the key once more in the lock, and turning to Catherine said,—

"My fair antagonist, I bid you good-night."

He stretched out his right hand, and she, with some hesitation and visible reluctance placed her palm in his. Then the king raised to his lips the hand which at one time seemed like to have stricken him.

"And you, sweet Isabel, whose gentle words I shall not soon forget, you will not refuse me your hand?"

"No, your majesty, if you will promise to think kindly of me."

The king, however, did not raise her hand to his lips, but placing an arm about her waist he drew her towards him and kissed her. Next moment he was hurrying down the stone steps, and the two were left alone together.

The King Investigates

The king, wishing to decide wisely, was troubled by a conflict of evidence, the bane of impartial judges all the world over. A courier from England had brought formal complaint that, while the two countries were ostensibly at peace, the condition along the border was practically a state of war. Raids were continually being made from the southern portion of Scotland across the boundary into England, and the robbers retreated unscathed to hide themselves among their hills, carrying their booty with them. These ruffians had long gone unpunished, and now England made friendly protest in the matter.

The king gathered his nobles about him and laid the case before them. Not a man among them but was older than himself, and therefore more experienced. James requested advice regarding the action it might be thought wise to take. Many of the nobles whose estates lay in the Lowlands of Scotland had themselves suffered from Highland cattle-lifters, and thus they were imbued with a fellow feeling for the raided English across the border. The English protest, they said, was courteously made. The evil was undoubted, and had existed unchecked for years, growing worse rather than better. Henry VIII, who now occupied the English throne, was a strong and determined man, and this continued source of irritation in the northern part of his realm might easily lead to a deplorable war between the two countries. In addition, James of Scotland was nephew to Henry of England, and the expostulation from uncle to nephew was of the mildest, without any threat even intimated.

The nobles thought that James might well put a stop to a state of things which no just man could approve, and thus do an act of justice which would at the same time please an august relative. James admitted that these were powerful arguments, but still if the Border robbers, who had many followers, resisted the Scottish force sent against them, there would be civil war, an outcome not to be looked forward to with light heart.

"In truth," said the king, "I would rather lead an army against England, with England in the right, than against my own countrymen, even if they were in the wrong."

This remark seemed to encourage certain gentlemen there present, who up to that moment had not spoken. The Earl of Bothwell, as the highest in rank among the silent phalanx, stepped forward and said,—

"Your majesty, there are always two sides to a question, and, with your permission, I should be glad to put in a word for those Border riders who have been so ruthlessly condemned by men who know nothing of them."

"It is for the purpose of hearing all there is to say that I called you together," rejoined the king. "Speak, my Lord of Bothwell."

"In the first place, your majesty, these Border men have had to stand the first brunt of all invasions into our country for centuries past. It is, therefore, little to be wondered at that they have small liking for the English. We are at peace with those to the south of us now, it is true; but how long that peace will remain unbroken, no man can say. There is, however, one thing certain, that if the King of Scotland exercises the power he undoubtedly possesses, and crushes the Border forces, he will have destroyed a staunch bulwark of his realm, and I quite agree with those gentlemen who have spoken so eloquently against the Borderers, that the King of England, and the people of England, will be well pleased."

This statement had a marked effect on King James, and it would have been well if those who agreed with the Earl of Bothwell had been as moderate in their denunciation. But some of them, apparently, could not forget the youth of the king, and, not having the sense to see that his majesty's desire was to render a just decision, thought he might be frightened by strong language.

"It is easy for those to speak well of the pike, who have not felt the prod of its point," cried Lord Maxwell angrily. "Few English invasions have reached Stirling, but every one of them have crossed the Border. What matters the lifting of some English cattle? The Southerners never scrupled to eat good Scottish beef whenever they set foot on Scottish soil. I would hang the English envoy for daring to come to a Scottish king with complaints of cattle lifting."

The king frowned slightly but said nothing, and then Adam Scott of Tushielaw had to thrust his bull neck into the noose.

"I give you fair warning," he cried, "that if the king's forces are turned against the Borderers, my sword helps my neighbours."

"And I say the same," shouted Cockburn of Henderland.

Some of the opposition were about to speak, but the king held up his hand for silence.

"That is treason," he said quietly. "Adam Scott, I have heard that you are called King of the Border. Scotland is blessed with a number of men who are king of this, or king of that, and I am sure I make no objection, as long as they do not forget the difference that exists between a king in name and a king in reality. I asked for advice, but not for threats."

Then to the whole assemblage he went on—

"Gentlemen, I thank you for your counsel. I shall give a soothing reply to my uncle's ambassador, keeping in mind the peace that exists between the two countries, and then I shall take what has been said on each side into consideration and let you know the result."

Accepting this as dismissal, those there congregated withdrew, save only Sir David Lyndsay, the king having made a sign for him to remain. "Well, Davie," he said, when they were alone, "what do you think of it all?"

"To tell truth, your majesty," answered the poet, "it's a knotty problem, not to be solved by rhyming brain. When the first spokesman finished I was entirely of his opinion, but, after that, the Earl of Bothwell's plea seemed equally weighty, and between the two I don't know what to think."

"That is the disadvantage of an unbiased mind, Davie. Now, with good, strong prejudices, one side or the other, the way would be clear, and yet I despise a man who doesn't know his own mind."

"Scott and Cockburn seemed to know their minds very well," ventured the poet, with a smile.

"Yes, and if one or two more of them had spoken as decidedly, I would have been off to the Border to-night at the head of my troops. It is a weakness of mine, but I can't put up with a threat very well."

"Kings are rarely called upon to thole a threat," said Sir David, with a laugh.

"I'm not so sure of that, Davie. Kings have to thole many things if they are to rule justly. Now, Davie, if you'll but tell me just what to do, it will be a great help, for then I can take the opposite direction with confidence."

But the poet shook his head.

"I cannot tell you," he said. "There seems much to be said for both sides."

"Then, Davie, send down to the town for the cobbler; send for Flemming, he is a common-sense, canny body; he shall be the Solomon of the occasion. That broad-faced hammer of his seems to rap out wisdom as well as drive pegs. Bring him up with you, and we'll place the case before him."

As the rhymster left the room, Sir Donald Sinclair came clanking in, seemingly in something of a hurry.

"Was it your majesty's pleasure," began Sir Donald, "to have detained Adam Scott and Cockburn?"

"No. Why do you ask?"

"Because they have mounted their horses and are off to the Border as fast as two good steeds can carry them."

"And where are Bothwell, Home, and Maxwell, and the Lairds of Fairniherst, Johnston and Buccleuch?"

"They are all closeted in the Earl of Bothwell's room, your majesty. Shall I take any action regarding them?"

"Oh no; do not meddle with them. You heard the opinions given a

56

while since, Donald? What conclusion did you arrive at?"

"I am scarcely an impartial judge, your majesty. A soldier is ever for fighting, and I fear he pays little attention to the right or wrong of it."

"You would try a fall with the Border kings perhaps?"

"Yes, your majesty, I would."

"Then I need have no fear but the troops will respond if I call on them?"

"None in the least, your majesty."

"Well, I am glad to hear that, Sir Donald, and, meanwhile, I can think of the project without any doubt regarding my army."

When the cobbler came to the castle with Sir David, the king led the way to one of his small private rooms, and there sketched out the argument on both sides of the question with great impartiality.

"Now, Flemming," he said, at the conclusion, "what is there to do?"

For a long time the shoemaker made no reply; then he scratched his head in perplexed fashion. At last he said:

"It gets beyond me, your majesty. Thieving is not right unless it's done under cover of law, which these reiving lads to the South seem to take small account of. On the other hand, to destroy them root and branch may be leaving Scotland naked to her enemy. I admit I'm fairly in a corner."

Sir David Lyndsay laughed.

"You're as bad as I am, cobbler," he said.

"There is one point," commented the king, "that no one seems to have taken any notice of, and that is this: Those who speak against the Border marauders are those who know little of them except by hearsay; while the lords in their neighbourhood, who should know them well, stand up for them, and even threaten to draw sword on their behalf."

"That certainly speaks well for the villains," admitted the cobbler.

"Then what is your verdict," demanded the king.

"Well, I kind of think I should leave them alone," said Flemming cautiously.

"Do you agree with him, David?"

"I'm not sure but I do. It seems a choice of two evils."

The king laughed riotously and smote his thigh.

"Well, of all half-hearted counsellors, King James has the champion pair; and yet I had made up my mind before I asked the advice of either of you."

"And what was that?" inquired Sir David, "to attack them?"

"No."

"To leave them alone?" suggested the cobbler.

"No."

"What then?" cried both together.

"What then? Why, just to get a little surer information. Here are three men of open minds. I propose that for the next week, or thereabouts, we three shall be honest cattle merchants, who will mount our honest horses and take a quiet bit journey along the Border. The scenery, they tell me, is grand, and David here will make poems on it. It's a healthy country, and the cobbler has been bending too assiduously over broken shoes of late, so the fresh air and the exercise will do him good."

"Losh, your majesty!" cried the cobbler, in dismay, "I'm no horseman. I never rode any four-legged thing but a cobbler's bench, and that side-saddle fashion."

"Oh, you'll have learnt when we reach the Border," said the king, with a laugh. "Before two days are past you'll be riding as well as Sir David, who is at present the worst horseman in all Scotland."

"Pegasus is the steed I yearn to ride," returned the poet, with a wry face.

"Yes, and even it sometimes throws you, David. You'll never be the Psalmist your namesake was. Well, we'll look on it as agreed. Flemming shall be purse-bearer, and so our tour will be an economical one. Here is a purse well filled. You will look after the drover's costumes, make all disbursements, and take care that you do not betray us by undue lavishness."

Thus it came about that three supposed drovers took their way to the Border by a route which drovers were never known to travel before, and, besides this, they were travelling empty-handed towards England, whereas, real drovers faced the south with their herds before them, and the north with those herds sold or stolen. Not one of the three had in his vocabulary a single word pertaining to the cattle trade, and every man with whom they spoke knew at once that, whatever else they might be, they were not drovers, and so the ill-fated three went blundering through the free-booters' country, climbing hills and descending dales, and frightening honest folk with the questions they asked; questions about men whose names should be spoken in a whisper, and even then with a look of fear over the shoulder. Innkeepers who saw them approach with delight, watched them leave with relief, thanking God that no raider had happened inside to hear their innocent inquiries; yet the three themselves were enjoying an interesting and instructive journey, and the king had come to the conclusion that the devil was not so black as he was painted.

At last, they stumbled into a hostelry kept by a man whose name was Armstrong. Their horses were taken care of and the trio sat down to a hearty meal, as had been their luck all along the Border.

"Landlord, does this meat come from England?" asked the king.

The landlord caught his breath. He stood stock still for a moment and then replied,—

"I hope it is to your lordship's liking."

"Oh! I'm no lordship," said James, "but an honest drover body, trying to find new markets for my stock."

"I can see that," replied the landlord; "then you will know that this meat's raised by Scotchmen."

"Raised!" laughed the king. "Raised where? In Northumberland? Are you sure 'lift' is not the word you mean?"

"Sir," said the landlord, gravely, "there's no lifting of cattle hereabout. This is not the Highlands. All in the neighbourhood are honest farmers or foresters."

"Earning their bread by the sweat of their brow," put in Sir David Lyndsay.

"Doubtless, when the English are after them," suggested the cobbler.

The landlord did not join in their mirth, but merely said,—

"If your dinner is to your liking, my duty is done."

"Quite so," answered the king. "We were merely curious regarding the origin of your viands; but the question seems to be a ticklish one in this district."

"Oh, not at all," replied the innkeeper grimly. "If you question enough, you are sure to meet some one who will make you a suitable answer."

The landlord, seemingly not liking the turn of the conversation, disappeared, and during the rest of the meal they were waited upon by a lowering, silent woman, who scowled savagely at them, and made no reply to the raillery of the king, who was in the highest spirits. They had ridden far that morning since breakfasting, and it was well after midday when they drew away from a table that had been devoted to their satisfying. Sir David and Flemming showed little inclination to proceed with their journey.

"The poor beasts must have a rest," said the poet, although none of the three were horsemen enough to go out and see how the animals fared at the hands of the stableman. The king was accustomed to be waited upon, and the other two knew little and cared less about horses. As they sat there in great content they heard suddenly a commotion outside and the clatter of many hoofs on the stone causeway. The door burst in, and there came, trampling, half a dozen men, who entered with scant ceremony, led by a stalwart individual who cast a quick glance from one to the other of the three who were seated. His eye rested on the king, whom, with quick intuition, he took to be the leader of the expedition and, doffing his feathered bonnet in a salutation that had more of mockery than respect in it, he said: "I hear that, like myself, you're in the cattle trade, and that you're anxious to learn the prospect of doing business in this mountainous locality."

"You are quite right," replied the king.

"I have in my byres near by," continued the man, "some of the finest stirks that ever stood on four hoofs. Would you be willing to come and give me your opinion of them, and say how much you care to pay for as many as you need?"

Again the man swept his bonnet nearly to the floor, and his six men, who stood back against the wall, as if to give the speaker the stage in the centre of the floor, glanced one at another. The king, however, was unruffled, and he replied with a twinkle in his eye,—

"My good sir, you are mistaken, we are on the other side of the market. We are sellers and not buyers."

"So was Judas," said the incomer, his politeness giving way to an expression of fierceness and cruelty which went far to terrify two of the seated men. "Are you sure, sir, that the cattle you sell have not two legs instead of four?"

"I don't understand you," replied the king.

"Is it men or stirks, you would give to the butcher?"

"Still I do not understand you," repeated the king.

"Oh, very well. How much are you asking for your cattle?"

"We are here rather to see how much may be offered."

"I can well believe you. Still, you must know something of the price of beasts on hoofs. How much would you want for a good, fat stirk? Answer me that!"

The king glanced at his two companions, and his glance said as plainly as words, "Give me a hint, in heaven's name, regarding the cost of a beast;" but in all Scotland he could not have found two men who knew less about the subject.

"Oh, well," said the king, nonchalantly, not at all liking the turn affairs had taken, "I suppose we would be satisfied with twenty pounds," and this being received with a roar of laughter, he added hastily, "twenty pounds Scots."

"Oh," said the big man, "I was afraid you were going to demand that amount in English currency. It is evident you will do well at the trade, if you can find such buyers."

"Then make us an offer," suggested the king, with the air of a man willing to listen to reason.

"Where are your cattle?"

"They're in the north."

"What part of the north?"

"My good fellow," cried the king, his temper rising, "you have asked many questions and answered none. Who are you, and what right have you to make your demands in such a tone?"

"Ah, then there's some spirit among the three of you. I am glad to see that. Who am I? I am Johnny Armstrong. Did you ever hear tell of him? And I suspect that your cattle are grown in the high town of Stirling. Am I right in that? It is in Stirling that you can sell what you may lift on the Border, and your cattle will be paid for in king's gold. You are spies, my fine gentlemen, and know as little of cattle as I know of the king and the court."

The king rejoined calmly,—

"The country is at peace. There can be no spies except in a time of war."

"Is it even so? Then what are you three doing rampaging up and down my land on the Border?"

"That the lands may be yours we do not dispute, nor have we interfered

62

with them. The highways are the king's, and we three are peaceful subjects of his, claiming, therefore, the right to travel on them as we will, so long as we infringe not his peace or the liberty of any man."

"Stoutly spoken and bravely, considering in what king's dominion you now find yourself. You have to learn that Johnny, and not Jamie, is king of the Border. And when you're in the hands of a man named Armstrong, you'll find how little a boy named Stuart can do for you. Tie them up!"

Before one of the three could move from the stool he occupied, they were set upon by the ruffians, and each Stirling man found his ankles fastened together and his elbows tied behind his back with a speed that amazed him.

"Bless my soul," moaned the poet, "all this in broad daylight, and in the king's dominion."

They were carried outside and flung thus helpless, face downward on horses, like so many sacks of corn, each before a mounted man. Armstrong sprung upon his horse and led his men from the high road into the forest, his followers numbering something like a score. The captives, from their agonising position on the horses, could see nothing of the way they were being taken, except that they journeyed on and on through dense woodland. They lost all knowledge of direction, and, by and by, came to the margin of a brawling stream, arriving at last, much to their relief, at a stronghold of vast extent, situated on a beetling rock that overhung the river. Here the three were placed on their feet again, and chattering women and children crowded round them, but, in no case, was there a word of pity or an expression of sympathy for their plight.

The striking feature of the castle was a tall square tower, which might be anything from seventy to a hundred feet in height; and connected with it were several stone buildings, some two stories and some three stories high. Round the castle, in a wide, irregular circle, had been built a stout stone wall, perhaps twenty feet high, wide enough on the top for half a dozen men to walk abreast. The space enclosed was tolerably flat, and large enough for a small army to exercise in. Leaning against the inside of this wall was an array of sheds, which provided stabling for the horses, and numerous stalls in which many cattle were lowing. The contour of the wall was broken by a gateway, through which the troop and their captives had entered. The inlet could be closed by a massive gate, which now stood open, and by a stout portcullis that hung ready to drop when a lever was pulled. But the most gruesome feature of this robber's lair was a stout beam of timber, which projected horizontally from the highest open window of the square tower. Attached to the further end of the beam was a thick rope, the looped end of which encircled the drawn neck of a man, whose lifeless body swayed like a leaden pendulum, helpless in the strong breeze. Seeing the eyes of the three directed to this pitiful object, Armstrong said to one of his men,—

"Just slip that fellow's head from the noose, Peter; we may need the rope again to-night." Then turning to his prisoners, Armstrong spoke like a courteous host anxious to exhibit to a welcome guest the striking features of his domain.

"That's but a grisly sight, gentlemen, to contemplate on a lowering evening."

The day was darkening to its close, and a storm, coming up out of the west, was bringing the night quicker than the hour sanctioned.

"But here is an ingenious contrivance," continued the freebooter, cheerfully, "which has commanded the admiration of many a man we were compelled to hang. You see there are so many meddlesome bodies in this world that a person like myself, who wishes to live in peace with all his fellows, must sometimes give the interferers a sharp bit lesson."

"I can well believe it," answered the king.

"An Englishman of great ingenuity had a plan for capturing us, but, as it stands, we captured him; and being a merciful man, always loth to hang, when anything else can be done, I set him at work here, and this is one of his constructions. As it's growing dark, come nearer that you may see how it works."

At the bottom of the tower, and close to it, there lay a wooden platform which afforded standing room for six or seven men. Peter got up on this platform and pulled a cord, which opened a concealed sluice-gate and resulted in a roar of pouring water. Gradually the platform lifted, and the king saw that it was placed on top of a tall pine-tree that had been cut in the form of a screw, the gigantic threads of which were well oiled. A whirling horizontal water-wheel, through the centre of which the big screw came slowly upwards, with Peter on the gradually elevating platform, formed the motive power of the contrivance.

"You understand the mechanism?" said Armstrong. "By pulling one cord, the water comes in on this side of the wheel and the platform ascends. Another cord closes the sluice and everything is stationary. A third cord opens the gate which lets the water drive the wheel in the opposite direction and then the platform descends. You see, I have taken away the old lower stairway that was originally built for the tower, and this is the only means of getting up and down from the top story. It does not, if you will notice, go entirely to the top, but stops at that door, fifty feet from the rock, into which Peter is now entering."

"It is a most ingenious invention," admitted the king. "I never saw anything like it before."

"It would be very useful in a place like Stirling," said Johnny, looking hard at his prisoner.

"I suppose it would," replied the king, in a tone indicating that it was no affair of his, "but you see I'm not a Stirling man myself. I belong rather to all Scotland; a man of the world, as you might say."

By this time Peter had climbed to the highest room of the tower, worked his way on hands and knees out to the end of the beam, and had drawn up to him the swaying body. With the deftness of expert practice, he loosened the noose and the body dropped like a plummet through the air, disappearing into the chasm below. Peter, taking the noose with him, crawled backward, like a crab, out of sight, and into the tower again. Armstrong, from below, had opened the other sluice, and the empty platform descended as leisurely and as tremblingly as it had risen. Armstrong himself cut the cords that bound the ankles of his captives.

"Now, gentlemen," he said, "if you will step on the platform I shall have the pleasure of showing you to your rooms."

Three armed men and the three prisoners moved upwards together.

"A fine sylvan view you have," said the king.

"Is it not!" exclaimed Armstrong, seemingly delighted that it pleased his visitor.

After the mechanical device had landed them some fifty feet above the rocks, they ascended several flights of stairs, a man with a torch leading the way. The prisoners were conducted to a small room, which had the roof of the tower for its ceiling. In a corner of the cell cowered a very abject specimen of the human race, who, when the others came, seemed anxious to attract as little attention as possible.

Armstrong, again, with his own hands removed the remaining cords from the prisoners, and the three stretched up their arms, glad to find them at liberty once more.

"Place the torch in its holder," said Johnny. "Now, gentlemen, that will last long enough to light you to your supper, which you will find on the floor behind you. I'm sure you will rest here comfortably for the night. The air is pure at this height, and I think you'll like this eagle's nest better than a dungeon under the ground. For my own part, I abhor a subterranean cell, and goodness knows I've been in many a one, but we're civilised folk here on the Border and try to treat our prisoners kindly."

"You must, indeed, earn their fervent gratitude," said the king.

"We should, we should," returned Johnny, "but I'm not certain that we do. Man is a thrawn beast as a rule. And now, you'll just think over your situation through the night, and be ready to answer me in the morning all the questions I'll ask of you. I'll be wanting to know who sent you here, and what news you have returned to him since you have been on the Border."

"We will give your request our deep consideration," replied the king.

"I'm glad to hear that. You see, we are such merciful people that we have but one rope to hang our enemies with, while we should have a dozen by rights. Still, I think we could manage three at a pinch, if your answers should happen to displease me. You will excuse the barring of the door, but the window is open to you if your lodgings are not to your liking. And so, good-night, the three of you."

"Good-night to you, Mr. Armstrong," said the king.

Peter had drawn in the rope, and its sinister loop lay on the floor, its further length resting on the window sill, and extending out to the end of the beam. The cobbler examined it with interest. "Come," cried the king, "there is little use letting a supper wait for the eating merely because we seem to have gone wrong in our inquiries about the cattle."

Neither the poet nor the cobbler had any appetite for supper, but the king was young and hungry, and did justice to the hospitality of the Armstrongs.

"Have you been here long?" he asked of the prisoner in the corner.

"A good while," answered the latter despondently. "I don't know for how long. They hanged my mate."

"I saw that. Do they hang many here about?"

"I think they do," replied the prisoner. "Some fling themselves down on the rocks, and others are starved to death. You see, the Armstrongs go off on a raid, and there's no one here to bring us food, for the women folk don't like to tamper with that machine that comes to the lower stair. I doubt if Johnny starves them intentionally, but he's kept away sometimes longer than he expects."

"Bless me," cried the king, "think of this happening in Scotland. And now, cobbler, what are we to do?"

"I'm wondering if this man would venture out to the end of the beam and untie the rope," suggested Flemming.

"Oh, I'll do that, willingly," cried the prisoner. "But what is the use of it;

it's about ten times too short, as the Armstrongs well know."

"Are we likely to be disturbed here through the night?" asked Flemming.

"Oh no, nor till late in the day to-morrow; they'll be down there eating and drinking till all hours, then they sleep long."

"Very well. Untie the other end of the rope, and see you crawl back here without falling."

As the prisoner obeyed instructions, Flemming rose to his feet and began feeling in his pockets, drawing forth, at last, a large brown ball.

"What is your plan, cobbler?" asked the king, with interest.

"Well, you see," replied Flemming, "the rope's short, but it's very thick."

"I don't see how that is to help us."

"There are nine or ten strands that have gone to the making of it, and I'm thinking that each of those strands will bear a man. Luckily, I have got a ball of my cobbler's wax here, and that will strengthen the strands, keep the knots from slipping, and make it easier to climb down."

"Cobbler!" cried the king, "if that lets us escape, I'll knight you."

"I care little for knighthood," returned the cobbler, "but I don't want to be benighted here."

"After such a remark as that, your majesty," exclaimed the poet, "I think you should have him beheaded, if he doesn't get us out of this safely."

"Indeed, Sir David," said the cobbler, as he unwound the rope, "if I don't get you out of here, the Armstrongs will save his majesty all trouble on the score of decapitation."

There was silence now as the three watched the deft hands of the cobbler, hurrying to make the most of the last rays of the flickering torch in the wall. He tested the strands and proved them strong, then ran each along the ball of wax, thus cementing their loose thread together. He knotted the ends with extreme care, tried their resistance thoroughly, and waxed them unsparingly.

It was a business of breathless interest, but at last the snake-like length of thin rope lay on the floor at his disposal. He tied an end securely to the beam just outside the window-sill so that there would be no sharp edge to cut the cord, then he paid out the line into the darkness, slowly and carefully that it might not became entangled.

"There," he said at last, with a sigh of satisfaction, "who's first for the rope. We three await your majesty's commands."

"Do you know the country hereabout?" asked the king of the man who had been prisoner longest.

"Every inch of it."

"Can you guide us safely to the north in the darkness?"

"Oh, yes, once I am down by the stream."

"Then," said the king, "go down by the stream. When you are on firm footing say no word, but shake the rope. If you prove a true guide to us this night we will pay you well."

"I shall be well paid with my liberty," replied the prisoner, crawling cautiously over the stone sill and disappearing in the darkness. The cobbler held the taut line in his hand. No man spoke, they hardly seemed to breathe until the cobbler said:

"He's safe. Your majesty should go next."

"The captain is the last to leave the ship," said the king; "over you go, Flemming." After the cobbler, Sir David descended, followed by the king; and they found at the bottom of the ravine some yards of line to spare.

Their adventures through that wild night and the next day, until they came to a village where they could purchase horses, form a story in themselves.

When the king reached Stirling, and was dressed once more in a costume more suited to his station than that which had been torn by the brambles of the Border, he called to him the chief minister of his realm.

"You will arrest immediately," he said, "Cockburn of Henderland, and

69

Adam Scott of Tushielaw, and have them beheaded."

"Without trial, your majesty?" asked the minister in amazement.

"Certainly not without trial, but see that the trial is as short as possible. Their crime is treason; the witnesses as many as you like to choose from our last council meeting. I love and adhere to the processes of law, but see that there is no mistake about the block being at the end of your trial." The minister made a note of this and awaited further instructions. "Place the Earl of Bothwell in the strongest room that Edinburgh Castle has vacant. Imprison Lord Maxwell and Lord Home and the Lairds of Fairniherst, Johnston and Buccleuch, in whatever stronghold is most convenient. Let these orders be carried out as speedily as possible."

The next man called into the royal presence was Sir Donald Sinclair.

"Have you five hundred mounted men ready for the road, Sir Donald?"

"Yes, your majesty, a thousand if you want them."

"Very well, a thousand I shall have, and I shall ride with you to the Border."

Nevertheless, when the king came to the inn where he had been captured, there were but twenty troopers with him. Sir Donald was the spokesman on that occasion. He said to the landlord, whose roving eye was taking count of the number of horses,—

"Go to Johnny Armstrong and tell him that the king, with twenty mounted men at his back, commands his presence here, and see that he comes quickly."

Johnny was not slow in replying to the invitation, and forty troopers rode behind him. The king sat on his horse, a little in advance of his squadron. As a mounted man, James looked well, and there was but little resemblance between him and the unfortunate drover, who had been taken prisoner at that spot two short weeks before.

"I have come promptly in answer to your majesty's call," said Armstrong, politely removing his bonnet, but making no motion to pay further deference to the King of Scotland.

"It gives me great pleasure to see you," replied the king, suavely. "You travel with a large escort, Mr. Armstrong?"

"Yes, your majesty, I am a sociable man and I like good company. The more stout fellows that are at my back, the better I am pleased."

"In this respect we are very much alike, Mr. Armstrong, as you will admit if you but cast your eyes to the rear of your little company."

At this, Johnny Armstrong violated a strict rule of royal etiquette and turned the back of his head to his king. He saw the forest alive with mounted men, their circle closing in upon him. He muttered the word: "Trapped!" and struck the spurs into his horse's flank. The stung steed pranced in a semi-circle answering his master's rein, but the fence of mounted steel was complete, every drawn sword a picket. Again Armstrong, laughing uneasily, faced the king, who still stood motionless.

"Your majesty has certainly the advantage of me as far as escort is concerned."

"It would seem so," replied James. "You travel with twoscore of men; I with a thousand."

"I have ever been a loyal subject of your majesty," said Armstrong, moistening his dry lips. "I hope I am to take no scathe for coming promptly and cordially to welcome your majesty to my poor district."

"You will be better able to answer your own question when you have replied to a few of mine. Have you ever met me before, Mr. Armstrong?"

The robber looked intently at the king.

"I think not," he said.

"Have you ever seen this man before?" and James motioned Sir David Lyndsay from the troop at his side.

Armstrong drew the back of his hand across his brow.

"I seem to remember him," he said, "but cannot tell where I have met him."

"Perhaps this third man will quicken your memory," and the cobbler came forward, dressed as he had been the night he was captured.

Armstrong gasped, and a greenish pallor overspread his face.

"What is your answer, Armstrong?" asked the king.

"I and my forty men will serve your majesty faithfully in your army if you grant us our lives."

"No thieves ride with any of Scotland's brigade, Armstrong."

"I will load your stoutest horse with gold until he cannot walk, if you spare our lives."

"The revenues of Scotland are sufficient as they are, Armstrong," replied the king.

"Harry of England will be glad to hear that the King of Scotland has destroyed twoscore of his stoutest warriors."

"The King of England is my relative, and I shall be happy to please him. The defence of Scotland is my care, and I have honest men enough in my army to see that it is secure. Have you anything further to say, Armstrong?"

"It is folly to seek grace at a graceless face. If we are for the tree, then to the tree with us. But if you make this fair forest bear such woeful fruit, you shall see the day when you shall die for lack of stout hearts like ours to follow you, as sure as this day is the fatal thirteenth."

The forty-one trees bore their burden, and thirteen years from that time the outlaw's prophecy was fulfilled.

The King's Gold

It is strange to record that the first serious difficulty which James encountered with the nobles who supported him, arose not over a question of State, but through the machinations of a foreign mountebank. The issue came to a point where, if the king had proceeded to punish the intriguer, his majesty might have stood alone while the lords of his court would have ranged themselves in support of the charlatan—a most serious state of things, the like of which has before now overturned a throne. In dealing with this unexpected crisis, the young king acted with a wisdom scarcely to be expected from his years. He directed the nobility as a skilful rider manages a mettlesome horse, sparing curb and spur when the use of the one might have unseated him, or the use of the other resulted in a frenzied bolt. Thus the judicious horseman keeps his saddle, yet arrives at the destination he has marked out from the beginning.

In the dusk of the evening, James went down the high street of Stirling, keeping close to the wall as was his custom when about to pay a visit to his friend the cobbler, for although several members of the court knew that he had a liking for low company, the king was well aware of the haughty disdain with which the nobles regarded those of the mechanical or trading classes. So he thought it best not to run counter to a prejudice so deeply rooted, and for this reason he restricted the knowledge of his visits to a few of his more intimate friends.

As the king was about to turn out of the main street he ran suddenly into the arms of a man coming from the shop of a clothier who made costumes for the court. As each started back from the unexpected encounter, the light from the mercer's shop window lit up the face of his majesty's opponent, and the latter saw that he had before him his old friend, Sir David Lyndsay.

"Ha, Davie!" cried the king, "it's surely late in the day to choose the colours for a new jacket."

"Indeed your majesty is in the right," replied Sir David, "but I was not selecting cloth; I was merely enacting the part of an honest man, and liquidating a reckoning of long standing."

"What, a poet with money!" exclaimed the king. "Who ever heard of such a thing? Man Davie, you might share the knowledge of your treasure-house with a friend. Kings are always in want of money. Is your gold mine rich enough for two?"

The king spoke jocularly, placing no particular meaning upon his words, and if Sir David had answered in kind, James would doubtless have thought no more about the matter, but the poet stammered and showed such evident confusion that his majesty's quick suspicions were at once aroused. He remembered that of late a change had come over the court. Scottish nobles were too poor to be lavish in dress, and frequently the somewhat meagre state of their wardrobe had furnished a subject for jest on the part of ambassadors from France or Spain. But when other foreigners less privileged than an ambassador had ventured to make the same theme one for mirth, they speedily found there was no joke in Scottish steel, which was ever at an opponent's service, even if gold were not. So those who were wise and fond of life, became careful not to make invidious comparisons between the gallants of Edinburgh and Stirling, and those of Paris and Madrid. But of late the court at Stirling had blossomed out in fine array, and although this grandeur had attracted the notice of the king and pleased him, he had given no thought to the origin of the new splendour.

The king instantly changed his mind regarding his visit to the cobbler, linked arm with the poet, and together they went up the street. This sudden reversion of direction gave the royal wanderer a new theme for thought and surmise. It seemed as if all the town was on the move, acting as surreptitiously as he himself had done a few moments previously. At first he imagined he had been followed, and the suspicion angered him. In the gloom he was unable to recognise any of the wayfarers, and each seemed anxious to avoid detection, passing hurriedly or slipping quietly down some less frequented alley or lane. Certain of the figures appeared familiar, but none stopped to question the king.

"Davie," cried James, pausing in the middle of the street, "you make a very poor conspirator."

"Indeed, your majesty," replied the poet earnestly, "no one is less of a conspirator than I."

"Davie, you are hiding something from me."

"That I am not, your majesty. I am quite ready to answer truly any question your majesty cares to ask."

"The trouble is, Davie, that my majesty has not yet got a clue which will lead to shrewd questioning, but as a beginning, I ask you, what is the meaning of all this court stir in the old town of Stirling?"

"How should I know, your majesty?" asked the poet in evident distress.

"There now, Davie, there now! The very first question I propound gets an evasive answer. The man who did not know would have replied that he did not. I dislike being juggled with, and for the first time in my life, Sir David Lyndsay, I am angered with you."

The knight was visibly perturbed, but at last he answered,—

"In this matter I am sworn to secrecy."

"All secrets reveal themselves at the king's command," replied James sternly. "Speak out; speak fully, and speak quickly."

"There is no guilt in the secret, your majesty. I doubt if any of your court would hesitate to tell you all, were it not that they fear ridicule, which is a thing a Scottish noble is loth to put up with whether from the king or commoner."

"Get on, and waste not so much time in the introduction," said his majesty shortly.

"Well, there came some time since to Stirling, an Italian chemist, who took up his abode and set up his shop in the abandoned refectory of the old Monastery. He is the author of many wonderful inventions, but none interests the court so much as the compounding of pure gold in a crucible from the ordinary earth of the fields."

"I can well believe that," cried the king. "I have some stout fighters in my court who fear neither man nor devil in battle, yet who would stand with mouth agape before a juggler's tent. But surely, Davie, you, who have been to the colleges, and have read much from learned books, are not such a fool as to be deluded by that ancient fallacy, the transmutation of any other metals into gold?"

Sir David laughed uneasily.

"I did not say I believed it, your majesty, still, a man must place some credence in what his eye sees done, as well as in what he reads from books; and after all, the proof of the cudgel is the rap on the head. I have beheld the contest, beginning with an empty pot and ending with a bar of gold."

"Doubtless. I have seen a juggler swallow hot iron, but I have never believed it went down his throttle, although it appeared to have done so. Did you get any share of the transmuted gold? That's the practical test, my Davie."

"That is exactly the test your barons applied. I doubt if their nobilities would take much interest in a scientific experiment were there no profit at the end of it. Each man entering the laboratory pays what he pleases to the money taker at the table, but it must not be less than one gold bonnet-piece. When all have entered, the doors are closed and locked. The amount of money collected is weighed against small bars of gold which the alchemist places in the opposite scale until the two are equally balanced. This bar of gold he then throws into the crucible."

"Oh, he puts gold into the crucible, does he? Where then is the profit? I thought these necromancers made gold from iron."

"Signor Farini's method is different, your majesty. He asserts that like attracts like, and that the gold in the crucible will take to itself the minute unseen particles which he believes exists in all soils; the intense heat burning away the dross and leaving the refined gold."

"I see; and how ends this experiment?"

"The residue is cooled and weighed. Sometimes it is double the amount of gold put in, sometimes treble; and I have known him upon occasion take from the crucible quadruple the gold of the bar, but never have I known a melting fall below double the amount collected by the man at the table. At the final act each noble has returned to him double or treble the gold he relinquished on entering."

"Where then arises the profit to your Italian? I never knew these foreigners to work for nothing."

"He says he does it for love of Scotland and hatred of England; an ancient enemy. Were but the Scottish nation rich, he thinks they could the better withstand incursions from the south."

"Well, Davie, that seems to me a most unsubstantial reason. Scotland's protection has been her poverty in all except hard knocks. Were she as wealthy as France it would be the greater temptation for Englishers to overrun the country. My grandfather, James the Third, had a black chest full of gold and jewels, yet he was murdered flying from defeat in battle. When does this golden wizard fire his cauldron, Davie?"

"To-night, your majesty. That is the reason the nobles of your court were making sly haste to his domicile."

"Ah, and Sir David Lyndsay was hurrying to the same spot so blindly that he nearly overran his monarch."

"It is even so, your majesty."

"Then am I hindering you from much profit, and you must even blame yourself for being so long in the telling. However, it is never too late to turn one bonnet-piece into two. So, Davie, lead the way, for I would see this alchemist turn out gold from a pot as a housewife boils potatoes."

"I fear, your majesty, that the doors will be shut."

"If they are, Davie, the king's name will open them. Lead the way; lead the way."

The doors were not shut but were just on the point of closing when Sir

David put his shoulder to them and forced his way in, followed closely by his companion. The king and his henchman found themselves in a small ante-room, furnished only with a bench and a table; on the latter was a yellow heap of bonnet-pieces of the king's own coinage. Beside this heap lay a scroll with the requisites for writing. The money-taker, a gaunt foreigner clad in long robes like a monk, closed the door and barred it securely, then returned to the table. He nodded to Sir David, and glanced with some distrust upon his plaid-covered companion.

"Whom have you brought to us, Sir Lyndsay?" asked the man suspiciously.

"A friend of mine, the Master of Ballengeich; one who can keep his own counsel and who wishes to turn an honest penny."

"We admit none except those connected with the court," demurred the money-taker.

"Well, in a manner, Ballengeich is connected with the court. He supplies the castle with the products of his farm."

The man shook his head.

"That will not do," he said, "my orders are strict. I dare not admit him."

"Is not my money as good as another's?" asked Ballengeich, speaking for the first time.

"No offence is meant to you, sir, as your friend Sir Lyndsay knows, but I have my orders and dare not exceed them."

"Do you refuse me admittance then?"

"I am compelled to do so, sir, greatly to my regret."

"Is not my surety sufficient?" asked Sir David.

"I am deeply grieved to refuse you, sir, but I cannot disobey my strict instructions."

"Oh, very well then," said the king impatiently, "we will stay no further

78

question. Sir David here is a close friend of the king, and a friend of my own, therefore we will return to the castle and get the king's warrant, which, I trust, will open any door in Stirling."

The warder seemed nonplussed at this and looked quickly from one to the other; finally he said,—

"Will you allow me a moment to consult with my master?"

"Very well, so that you do not hold us long," replied the Master of Ballengeich.

"I shall do my errand quickly, for at this moment I am keeping the whole nobility of Scotland waiting."

The man disappeared, taking, however, the gold with him in a bag. In a short space of time he returned and bowing to the two waiting men he said,—

"My master is anxious to please you, Sir Lyndsay, and will accept the money of your friend." Whereupon the two placed upon the table five gold pieces each, and the amount was credited opposite their names upon the parchment.

Sir David, leading the way, drew aside one heavy curtain and then a second one, which allowed them to enter a long low-roofed room almost in total darkness, as far as the end to which they were introduced was concerned; but the upper portion of the hall was lit in lurid fashion. At the further end of the Refectory was a raised platform on which the heads of the Order had dined, during the prosperous days of the edifice, while the humbler brethren occupied, as was customary, the main body of the lower floor. Upon this platform stood a metal tripod, which held a basket of dazzling fire, and in this basket was set a crucible, now changing from red to white, under the constant exertions of two creatures who looked like imps from the lower regions rather than inhabitants of the upper world. These two strove industriously with a huge bellows which caused the fire to roar fiercely, and this unholy light cast its effulgence upon the faces of many notable men packed closely together in the body of the hall; it also shone on the figure of a tall man, the ghastly pallor of whose countenance was enhanced by a fringe of hair black as midnight. He had a nose like a vulture's beak, and eyes piercing in their intensity, as black as his midnight hair. His costume also resembled that of a monk in cut, but it was scarlet in hue; and the radiance of the furnace caused it to glow as if illumined by some fire from within.

At the moment the last two entered, Farini was explaining to his audience, in an accent palpably foreign, that he was a man of science, and that the devil gave him no aid in his researches, an assertion doubtless perfectly accurate. His audience listened to him with visible impatience, evidently anxious for talk to cease and practical work to begin.

The wizard held in his right hand the bag of gold that the king had seen taken from the outer room. Presently there entered through another curtained doorway, on what might be called the stage, the money-taker in the monk's dress, who handed to the necromancer the coins given him by Lyndsay and Ballengeich, which the wizard tossed carelessly into the bag. The attendant placed the scroll upon a table and then came forward with a weighing-machine held in his hand. The alchemist placed the gold from the bag upon one side of the scale, and threw into the other, bar after bar of yellow metal until the two were equal. Then the bag of gold was placed on the table beside the scroll, and the wizard carefully deposited the yellow bars within the crucible, the two imps now working the bellows more strenuously than ever.

The experiment was carried on precisely as Sir David had foretold, but there was one weird effect which the poet had not mentioned. When the necromancer added to the melting-pot huge lumps of what appeared to be common soil from the field, the mixture glared each time with a new colour. Once a vivid violet colour flamed up, which cast such a livid death-like hue on the faces of the knights there present, that each looked upon the other in obvious fear. Again the flame was pure white; again scarlet; again blue; again yellow. When at last the incantation was complete, the bellows-work was stopped. The coruscating caldron was lifted from the fire by an iron hook and chain, and set upon the stone floor to cool, bubbling and sparkling like a thing of evil; but the radiance became duller and duller as time went on, and finally its contents were poured out into a mould of sand, and there congealing, the result was lifted by tongs and laid upon the scale. The bag of gold was placed again in the opposite disc, but the heated metal far outweighed it. The wizard then unlocked a desk and threw coin after coin in the pan that held the bag, until at last the beam of the scale hung level. The secretary now pushed forward a table to the edge of the platform, and on the table placed a rush-light which served but to illuminate the parchment before him. With great rapidity he counted the gold pieces which were not in the bag, then whispered to his master.

The room was deathly still as the man in scarlet stepped forward to make his announcement.

"I regret," he said, "that our experiment has not been as successful as I had hoped. This doubtless has been caused by the poverty of the earth from which I took my material. I shall dig elsewhere against our next meeting, and then we may look for better results. To-night I can return to you but double the money you gave to my treasurer."

At this there went up what seemed to be a sigh of relief from the audience, which had been holding its breath with all the eagerness of a gambler, who had made a stake and awaited the outcome of the throw.

The necromancer, taking the parchment, called out name after name, and as each title was enunciated the bearer of it came to the edge of the platform and received from the secretary double the amount of gold pieces set down on the parchment. As each man secreted his treasure he passed along out of the hall; and so it came about that Sir David and Ballengeich, being the last on the list, received the remaining coins on the table, and silently took their departure.

The king spoke no word until they had entered the castle and were within his private room. Once there, the first thing he did was to pull from his pouch the coins he had received and examine them carefully one by one. There was no doubt about them, each was a good Scottish gold piece, with the king's profile and bonnet stamped thereon.

"You will find them genuine," said Sir David. "I had my own fears regarding them at first, thinking that this foreigner was trying the trick which Robert Cockran, the mason, accomplished so successfully during the reign of your grandfather, mixing the silver coins with copper and lead; but I had them tested by a goldsmith in Edinburgh and was assured the pieces are just what they claim to be."

"Prudent man!" exclaimed the king, throwing himself down on a seat and jingling the gold pieces. "Well, Davie, what do you think of it all? Give me an opinion as honest as the coin."

"Truth to tell, your majesty, I do not know what to think of it. It may be as he says, that the earth here contains particles of gold, that are drawn to the bars he throws in the melting-pot. If the man is a cheat, where can he hope for his profit?"

"Where indeed? I mind you told me he had other marvellous inventions; what are they?"

"He has a plan by which a man in full armour can enter the water and walk beneath it for any length of time without suffocating."

"Have you seen this tried?"

"No, your majesty; there has been no opportunity."

"What an admirable contrivance for invading Ireland! What are his plans as far as England is concerned? He seems, if I remember your tale aright, to have some animosity in that direction."

"He has constructed a pair of wings, and each soldier being provided with them can sail through the air across the Border."

"Admirable, admirable!" exclaimed the king nodding his head. "Now indeed is England ours, and France too for that matter, if his wings will carry so far. Have you seen these wings?"

"Yes, your majesty, but I have not seen them tried. They seem to be made of fine silk stretched on an extremely light framework, and are worked by the arms thrust up or down; thus, he says, a man may rise or fall at will."

"As to the falling, I believe him, and the rising I shall believe when I see it. Has our visit to-night then taught you nothing, David?"

"Nothing but what I knew before. What has it taught your majesty?"

"In the first place our charlatan does not want the king to know what he is doing, because when his subordinate refused me admittance and I said to him I would appeal to the king, he saw at once that this was serious, and wished to consult his master. His master was then willing to admit anyone so long as there was no appeal to the king. I therefore surmise he is most anxious to conceal his operations from me. What is your opinion, Davie?"

"It would seem that your majesty is in the right."

"Then again if he is a real scientist and has discovered an easy method of producing gold and is desirous to enrich Scotland, why should he object to a plain farmer like the Guidman of Ballengeich profiting by his production?"

"That is quite true, your majesty; but I suppose the line must be drawn somewhere, and I imagine he purposes to enrich only those of the highest rank, as being more powerful than the yeomen."

"Then we come back, Davie, to what I said before; why exclude the king who is of higher rank than any noble?"

"I have already confessed, your majesty, that I cannot fathom his motives."

"Well, you see at what we have arrived. This foreigner wishes to influence those who can influence the king. He wishes to have among his audience none but those belonging to the court. He has some project that he dare not place before the king. We will now return to the consideration of that project. In the first place, the man is not an Italian. Did a scholar like you, Davie, fail to notice that when he was in want of a word, it was a French word he used? He is therefore no Italian, but a Frenchman masquerading as an Italian. Therefore, the project, whatever it is, pertains to France, and it is his desire that this shall not be known. Now what does France most desire Scotland to do at this moment?"

"It thinks we should avenge Flodden; and many belonging to the court are in agreement with France on this point."

"Has your necromancer ever mentioned Flodden?"

"Once or twice he spoke of it with regret."

"I thought so," continued the king; "and now I hope you are beginning to see his design."

"What your majesty says is very ingenious; but if I may be permitted to raise an objection to the theory, I would ask your majesty why this was not done through the French ambassador? French gold has been used before now in the Scottish Court; and it seems to me that a great nation like France would not stoop to enlist the devices of a charlatan, if this man be a charlatan."

"Ah, now we enter the domain of State secrets, Davie, and there is where a king has an advantage over the commoner. Of course I know many things hidden from you which give colour to my surmise. Some while ago the French ambassador offered me a subsidy. Now I am not so avaricious as my grandfather, nor so lavish as my father, and I told the ambassador that I would depend on Scottish gold. I acquainted him with the success of my German miners in extracting gold from Leadhills in the Clydesdale, and I showed him my newly coined pieces. He was so condescendingly pleased and interested that he begged the privilege of having his own bars of metal coined in my mint, in order to disburse his expenses in the coin of the realm, and also to send some of our bonnet-pieces as specimens to France itself. This right of coinage I willingly bestowed upon him; firstly, because he asked it; secondly, I was glad to have some account of his expenditure. When I came in just now I examined these coins closely, and you imagined that I was suspicious of the purity of the metal. This was not so. I told my mint-master to coin all the bars the ambassador gave him, to keep a strict account of the issue, and to mark each piece with the letter 'F' on the margin. I find three of the coins which we received to-night bearing this private mark; therefore, they have passed through the hands of the French ambassador to the alchemist."

Sir David gave forth an exclamation of surprise. He left his seat, took the bonnet-pieces from his pocket and placed them under the lamp.

"Now," said the king, "you need sharp eyes to detect this mark, but there it is, and there, and there. Let us look a little closer into the object of France. The battle of Flodden was fought when I was little more than a year old; it destroyed the king, the flower of Scottish nobility, and ten thousand of her common soldiers. Who was responsible for this frightful calamity? My mother was strongly against the campaign, which was to bring the forces of her husband in contention with the forces of her brother, at that moment absent in France. The man who urged on the conflict was De la Motte, the French ambassador, standing ever at my father's side, whispering his treacherous, poisonous advice into an ear too willing to listen. England was not a bitter enemy, for England did not follow up her victory and march into Scotland, where none were left to command a Scottish army, and no Scottish army was left to obey. Scotland, on this occasion, was merely the catspaw of France. Now I am the son of an Englishwoman. The English king is my uncle, and France fears that I will keep the peace with my neighbour; so through his ambassador, he sounds me, and learns that such indeed is my intention. France resolves to leave me alone and accomplish its object by corrupting, with gold coined in my own mint, the nobles of my court, and, by God!" cried James in sudden anger, bringing his fist down on the table and making the coins jingle, "France is succeeding, through the blind stupidity of men who might have been expected to know their right hand from their left. The greatest heads of my realm are being cozened by a trickster; befooled in a way that any humble ploughman should be ashamed of. You see now why they wish to keep the silly proceedings from the king. I tell you, Davie, that Italian's head comes off, and thus in some small measure will I avenge Flodden."

Sir David Lyndsay sat meditatively silent for some moments while the king in angry impatience strode up and down the small limits of the room. When the heat of his majesty's temper had partially cooled, Sir David spoke with something of diplomatic shrewdness.

"I never before realised the depth and penetration of your majesty's mind. You have gone straight to the heart of this mystery, and have thrown light into

85

its obscurest corner, as a dozen flaming torches would have illumined that dark laboratory in the Monastery. I have shared the stupidity of your nobles, which the clarity of your judgment now exposes so plainly; therefore, I feel that it would be presumption on my part to offer advice to your majesty in the further prosecution of this affair."

"No, Davie, no," said the king, stopping in his march and speaking with pleased cordiality, "no, I value your advice; you are an honest man, and it is not to be expected that the subtilty and craftiness of these foreigners should be as clear to you as the sunshine on a Highland hill. Speak out, Davie, and if you give me your counsel, I know it will be as wholesome as oatmeal porridge."

"Well, your majesty, you must meet subtilty with subtilty."

"I am not sure that the adage holds good, Davie," demurred the king. "You cannot outrace a Highlandman in his own glen, although you may fight him fairly in the open. Once this Frenchman's head is off, you stop his boiling-pot."

"That is quite true, your majesty, but if the French ambassador should put in a claim for his worthless carcass, you will find yourself on the eve of a break with France, if you proceed to his execution."

"But I shall have made France throw off its mask."

"It is not France I am thinking about, your majesty. Your own nobles have gone clean daft over this Italian. He is their goose that lays the golden eggs, and you saw yourself to-night with what breathless expectation they watched his experimenting. I am sure, your majesty, that they will stand by him, and that you will find not only France but Scotland arrayed against you. A moment's reflection will show you the danger. These meetings have been going on for months past, yet no whisper of their progress has reached your majesty's ears."

"That is true; even you yourself, Davie, kept silent."

"I swore an oath of silence, and honestly, I did not think that this gold-making was an affair of State."

"Very well. I will act with caution. The breath of the money-getter tarnishes the polish of the sword; and in my dealings I shall try to recollect that I have to do with men growing rapidly rich, as well as with nobles who should be too proud to accept unearned gold from any man. Now, Davie, I'll need your help in this, and in aiding me you will assist yourself, thus will virtue be its own reward, as is preached to us. I will give you as many gold pieces as you need, and instead of paying three pieces at the entrance, give the man three hundred. Urge all the nobles to increase their wagers; for thus we shall soon learn the depths of this yellow treasury. If I attempt to wring the neck of the goose before the eggs are laid, my followers would be justified in saying that the English part of my nature had got the better of the Scotch. Meanwhile, I will know nothing of this man's doings, and I hope for your sake, Davie, that the gold mine will prove as prolific as my own in the Clydesdale."

The nobles followed the example set to them by the lavish Sir David. They needed no urging from him to increase their stakes. The fever of the gambler was on each of them, and soon the alleged Italian began to be embarrassed in keeping up the pace he had set for himself. It required now an enormous sum to pay even double the amount taken at the door. The necromancer announced that the meetings would be held less often, but the nobles would not have it so. Then his experiments became less and less successful. One night the bonus amounted only to half the coins given to the treasurer, and then there were ominous grumblings. At the next meeting the bare amount paid in was given back, and the deep roar of resentment which greeted this proclamation made the foreigner tremble in his red robe. The ambassador was sending messenger after messenger to France, and looked anxiously for their return, while the necromancer did everything to gain time. At last there came an experiment which failed entirely; no gold was produced in the crucible. The alchemist begged for a postponement, but swords flashed forth and he was compelled on the spot to renew his incantation. If gold could be made on one occasion why not on another? cried the barons with some show of reason. The conjurer had conjured up a demon he could not control; the demon of greed.

The only man about the court who seemed to know nothing of what was going forward was the king himself. The French ambassador narrowly watched his actions, but James was the same free-hearted, jovial, pleasure-seeking monarch he had always been. He hunted and caroused, and was the life of any party of pleasure which sallied forth from the castle. He disappeared now and then, as was his custom, and could not be found, although his nobles winked at one another, while the perturbed French ambassador looked anxiously for the treasure ship that never came.

At last the nobles, who, in spite of their threatenings, had too much shrewdness to kill the gold-maker, hoping his lapse of power was only temporary, forced the question to a head and made appeal to the astonished king himself. Here was a man, they said, who could make gold and wouldn't. They desired a mandate to go forth, compelling him to resume the lucrative occupation he had abandoned.

The king expressed his amazement at what he heard, and summoned the mountebank before him. The gold-maker abandoned his robe of scarlet and appeared before James dressed soberly. He confessed that he knew the secret of extracting gold from ordinary soil, but submitted that he was not a Scottish citizen and therefore could not properly be coerced by the Scottish laws so long as he infringed none of the statutes. The king held that this appeal was well founded, and disclaimed any desire to coerce a citizen of a friendly state. At this the charlatan brightened perceptibly, and proportionately the gloom on the brows of the nobles deepened.

"But if you can produce gold, as you say, why do you refuse to do so?" demanded the king.

"I respectfully submit to your majesty," replied the mountebank, "that I have now perfected an invention of infinitely greater value than the gold-making process; an invention that will give Scotland a power possessed by no other nation, and which will enable it to conquer any kingdom, no matter how remote it may be from this land I so much honour. I wish, then, to devote the remaining energies of my life to the enlarging of this invention, rather than waste my time in what is, after all, the lowest pursuit to which a man may demean himself, namely, the mere gathering of money," and the speaker cast a glance of triumph at the disgruntled barons.

"I quite agree with you regarding your estimation of acquisitiveness," said the king cordially, giving no heed to the murmurs of his followers. "In what does this new invention consist?"

"It is simply a pair of wings, your majesty, made from the finest silk which I import from France. They may be fitted to any human being, and they give that human being the power which birds have long possessed."

"Well," said the king with a laugh, "I should be the last to teach a Scottish warrior to fly; still the ability to do so would have been, on several occasions, advantageous to us. Have you your wings at hand?"

"Yes, your majesty."

"Then you yourself shall test them in our presence."

"But I should like to spend, your majesty, some further time on preparation," demurred the man uneasily.

"I thought you said a moment ago that the invention was perfect."

"Nothing human is perfect, your majesty, and if I said so I spoke with the over-confidence of the inventor. I have, however, succeeded in sailing through the air, but cannot yet make way against a wind."

"Oh, you have succeeded so far as to interest us in a most attractive experiment. Bid your assistant bring them at once, and let us understand their principle. I rejoice to know that Scotland is to have the benefit of your great genius."

Farini showed little enthusiasm anent the king's confidence in him. He had, during the colloquy, cast many an anxious glance towards the French ambassador, apparently much to the annoyance of that high dignitary, for now the Frenchman, seeing his continued hesitation, said sharply,—

"You have heard his majesty's commands; get on your paraphernalia."

When the Italian was at last equipped, looking like a demon in a painting that hung in the chapel, the king led the way to the edge of Stirling cliff.

"There," he said, indicating a spot on the brow of the precipice, "you could not find in all Scotland a better vantage-point for a flight."

The terrified man stood for a moment on the verge of the appalling precipice; then he gave utterance to a remarkable pronouncement, the import of which was perhaps misunderstood because of the chattering of his teeth.

"Oh, not here, your majesty! Forgive me, and I will confess everything. The gold which I pretended to——"

"Fly, you fool!" cried the French ambassador, pushing the Italian suddenly between the shoulders and launching him into space. With a wild scream Farini endeavoured to support himself with his gauze-like wings, and for a moment seemed to hover in mid-air; but the framework cracked and the victim, whirling head over heels, fell like a plummet to the bottom of the cliff.

"I fear you have been too impetuous with him," said the king severely, although as his majesty glanced at Sir David Lyndsay the faint suspicion of a wink momentarily obscured his eye,—a temporary veiling of the royal refulgence, which passed unnoticed as every one else was gazing over the cliff at the motionless form of the fallen man.

"I am to blame, sire," replied the ambassador contritely, "but I think the villain is an impostor, and I could not bear to see your royal indulgence trifled with. However, I am willing to make amends for my imprudence, and if the scoundrel lives, I shall, at my own expense, transport him instantly to France, where he shall have the attendance of the best surgeons the country affords."

"That is very generous of you," replied the king.

And the ambassador, craving permission to retire, hastened to translate his benevolence into action.

Farini was still unconscious when the ambassador and his attendants reached him; but the French nobleman proved as good as his word, for he had the injured man, whose thigh-bone was broken, conveyed in a litter to Leith, and from there shipped to France. But it was many a day before the Scottish nobles ceased to deplore the untimely departure of their gold-maker.

The King A-Begging

Literary ambition has before now led men into difficulties. The king had completed a poem in thirteen stanzas entitled "The Beggar Man," and the prime requisite of a completed poem is an audience to listen to it. In spite of the fact that he wrote poetry, the king was a sensible person, and he knew that if he read his verses to the court, the members thereof were not the persons to criticise adequately the merits of such a composition; for you cannot expect a high noble, who, if he ever notices a beggar, merely does so to throw a curse at him, or lay the flat of his sword over his shoulders, to appreciate an epic which celebrates the free life led by a mendicant.

The king was well aware that he would receive ample praise for his production; king's goods are ever the best in the market, and though, like every other literary man, it was praise and not criticism that James wanted, still he preferred to have such praise from the lips of one who knew something of the life he tried to sing; therefore, as evening came on, the monarch dressed himself in his farmer costume, and, taking his thirteen stanzas with him, ventured upon a cautious visit to his friend the cobbler in the lower town of Stirling.

The cobbler listened with an attention which was in itself flattering, and paid his royal visitor the additional compliment of asking him to repeat certain of the verses, which the king in his own heart thought were the best. Then when the thirteenth stanza was arrived at, with the "No-that-bad" commendation, which is dear to the heart of the chary Scotchman, be he of high or low degree, Flemming continued,—

"They might be worse, and we've had many a poet of great reputation in Scotland who would not be ashamed to father them. But I'm thinking you paint the existence of a beggar in brighter colours than the life itself warrants."

"No, no, Flemming," protested the king earnestly. "I'm convinced that only the beggar knows what true contentment is. You see he begins at the very bottom of the ladder and every step he takes must be a step upward. Now imagine a man at the top, like myself; any move I make in the way of changing my condition must be downward. A beggar is the real king, and a king is but a beggar, for he holds his position by the favour of others. You see, Flemming, anything a beggar gets is so much to the good; and, as he has nothing to lose, not even his head—for who would send a beggar to the block—he must needs be therefore the most contented man on the face of the footstool."

"Oh, that's maybe true enough," replied Flemming, set in his own notion notwithstanding it was the king who opposed him; "but look you, what a scope a beggar has for envy, for there's nobody he meets that's not better off than himself."

"You go to extremes, Flemming. An envious man is unhappy wherever you place him; but I'm speaking of ordinary persons like ourselves, with charity and good-will toward all their fellow-kind. That man, I say, is happier as a beggar than as a king."

"Well, in so far as concerns myself, your majesty, I'd like to be sure of a roof over my head when the rain's coming down, and of that a beggar never can be. A king or a cobbler has a place to lay his head, at any rate."

"Aye," admitted the king, "but sometimes that place is the block. To tell you the truth, Flemming, I'm thinking of taking a week at the begging myself. A poet should have practical knowledge of the subject about which he writes. Give me a week on the road, Flemming, and I'll pen you a poem on beggary that will get warmer praise from you than this has had."

"I give your rhyming the very highest praise, and say that Gavin Douglas himself might have been proud had he put those lines together."

To this the king made no reply, and the cobbler, looking up at him, saw that a frown marred his brow. Then he remembered, as usual a trifle late, James's hatred of the Douglas name; a hatred that had been honestly earned by the Earl of Angus, head of that clan. Flemming was learning that it was as dangerous to praise, as to criticise a king. With native caution however, the cobbler took no notice of his majesty's displeasure, but added an amendment to his first statement.

"It would perhaps be more truthful to say that the verses are worthy of Sir David Lyndsay. In fact, although Sir David is a greater poet than Gavin Douglas, I doubt very much if in his happiest moments he could have equalled 'The Beggar Man.'"

In mentioning Sir David Lyndsay, Flemming had named the king's greatest friend, and the cobbler's desire to please could not have escaped the notice of a man much less shrewd than was James the Fifth. The king rose to his feet, checking a laugh.

"Man Flemming," he said, "I wonder at you! Have you forgotten that Sir David Lyndsay married Janet Douglas?"

The palpable dismay on the cobbler's countenance caused the young man to laugh outright.

"The cobbler should stick to his honesty, and not endeavour to tread the slippery path of courtiership. Flemming, if I wanted flattery I could get that up at the castle. I come down here for something better. If anything I could write were half so good as Sir David's worst, I should be a pleased man. But I'm learning, Flemming, I'm learning. This very day some of my most powerful nobles have presented me with a respectful petition. A year ago I should have said 'No' before I had got to the signature of it. But now I have thanked them for their attention to affairs of State, although between me and you and that bench, Flemming, it's a pure matter of their own greed and selfishness. So I've told them I will give the subject my deepest consideration, and that they shall have their answer this day fortnight. Is not that the wisdom of the serpent combined with the harmlessness of the dove?"

"It is indeed," agreed the cobbler.

"Very well; to-morrow it shall be given out that this petition will occupy my mind for at least a week, and during that time the king is invisible to all comers, high or low. To-morrow, Flemming, you'll get me as clean a suit of beggar's rags as you can lay your hands on. I'll come down here as the Master of Ballengeich, and leave these farmer's clothes in your care. I shall pass from this door as a beggar, and come back to it in the same condition a week or ten days hence, so see that you're at hand to receive me."

"Does your majesty intend to go alone?"

"Entirely alone, Flemming. Bless me, do you imagine I would tramp the country as a beggar with a troop of horse at my back?"

"Your majesty would be wise to think twice of such a project," warned the cobbler.

"Oh, well, I've doubled the number; I've thought four times about it; once when I was writing the poem, and three times while you were raising objections to my assertion that the beggar is the happiest man on earth."

"If your majesty's mind is fixed, then there's no more to be said. But take my advice and put a belt round your body with a number of gold pieces in it, for the time may come when you'll want a horse in a hurry, and perhaps you may be refused lodgings even when you greatly need them; in either case a few gold rascals will stand your friend."

"That's canny counsel, Flemming, and I'll act on it."

"And perhaps it might be as well to leave with some one in whom you have confidence, instructions so that you could be communicated with if your presence was needed hurriedly at Stirling."

"No, no, Flemming. Nothing can go wrong in a week. A beggar with a string tied to his legs that some one in Stirling can pull at his pleasure, is not a real beggar, but a slave. If they should want me sorely in Stirling before I return, they'll think the more of me once I am back."

And thus it came about that the King of Scotland, with a belt of gold around his waist in case of need, and garments concealing the belt which gave little indication that anything worth a robber's care was underneath, tramped the high roads and byways of a part of Scotland, finding in general a welcome wherever he went, for he could tell a story that would bring a laugh, and sing a song that would bring a tear, and all such rarely starve or lack shelter in this sympathetic world.

Only once did he feel himself in danger, and that was on what he thought to be the last day of his tramp, for in the evening he expected to reach the lower town of Stirling, even though he came to it late in the night. But the weather of Scotland has always something to say to the pedestrian, and it delights in upsetting his plans.

He was still more than two leagues from his castle, and the dark Forest of Torwood lay between him and royal Stirling, when towards the end of a lowering day, there came up over the hills to the west one of the fiercest storms he had ever beheld, which drove him for shelter to a wayside inn on the outskirts of the forest. The place of shelter was low and forbidding enough, but needs must when a Scottish storm drives, and the king burst in on a drinking company, bringing a swirl of rain and a blast of wind with him; so fierce in truth was the wind that one of the drinkers had to spring to his feet and put his shoulder to the door before the king could get it closed again. He found but scant welcome in the company. Those seated on the benches by the fire scowled at him; and the landlord seeing he was but a beggar, did not limit his displeasure to so silent a censure.

"What in the fiend's name," he cried angrily, "does the like of you want in here?"

The king nonchalantly shook the water from his rags and took a step nearer the fire.

"That is a very unnecessary question, landlord," said the young man with a smile, "nevertheless, I will answer it. I want shelter in the first place, and food and drink as soon as you can bring them."

"Shelter you can get behind a stone dyke or in the forest," retorted his host; "food and drink are for those who can pay for it. Get you gone! You mar good company."

"In truth, landlord, your company is none to my liking, but I happen to prefer it to the storm. Food and drink, you say, are for those who can pay; you see one of them before you, therefore, sir, hasten to your duty, or it may be mine to hurry you unpleasantly."

This truculence on the part of a supposed beggar had not the effect one might have expected of increasing the boisterousness of the landlord. That individual well knew that many beggars were better able to pay their way than was he himself when he took to journeying, so he replied more civilly,—

"I'll take your order for a meal when I have seen the colour of your money."

"Quite right," said the king, "and only fair Scottish caution." Then with a lack of that quality he had just commended, he drew his belt out from under his coat, and taking a gold piece from it, threw the coin on the table.

The entrance of the king and the manner of his reception exposed him to the danger almost sure to attend the display of so much wealth in such forbidding company. A moment later he realised the jeopardy in which his rashness had placed him, by the significant glances which the half-dozen rough men there seated gave to each other. He was alone and unarmed in a disreputable bothy on the edge of a forest, well known as the refuge of desperate characters. He wished that he had even one of the sharp knives belonging to his friend the cobbler, so that he might defend himself. However, the evil was done, if evil it was, and there was no help for it. James was never a man to cross a bridge before he came to it; so he set himself down to the steaming venison brought for his refreshment, and made no inquiry whether it were poached or not, being well aware that any question in that direction was as unnecessary as had been the landlord's first query to himself. He was young. His appetite, at all times of the best, was sharpened by his journey, and the ale, poor as it was, seemed to him the finest brew he had ever tasted. The landlord was now all obsequiousness, and told the beggar he could command the best in the house.

When the time came to retire, his host brought the king by a ladder to a loft which occupied the whole length of the building, and muttered something about the others sleeping here as well, but thanked Heaven there was room enough for an army.

"This will not do for me," said the beggar, coming down again. "I'll take to the storm first. What is this chamber leading out from the tap-room?"

"That is my own," replied the landlord, with some return of his old incivility, "and I'll give it up to no beggar."

The king without answering opened the door of the chamber and found himself in a room that could be barricaded. Taking a light with him he examined it more minutely.

"Is this matchlock loaded?" he asked, pointing to a clumsy gun, which had doubtless caused the death of more than one deer in the forest.

The landlord answered in surly fashion that it was, but the king tested the point for himself.

"Now," he said, "I rest here, and you will see that I am not disturbed. Any man who attempts to enter this room gets the contents of this gun in him, and I'll trust to my two daggers to take care of the rest."

He had no dagger with him, but he spoke for the benefit of the company in the tap-room. Something in his resolute manner seemed to impress the landlord, who grumbled, muttering half to himself and half to his companions, but he nevertheless retired, leaving the king alone, whereupon James fortified the door, and afterward slept unmolested the sleep of a tired man, until broad day woke him.

Wonderful is the change wrought in a man's feelings by a fair morning. A new day; a new lease of life. The recurrent morning must have been contrived to give discouraged humanity a fresh chance. The king, amazed to find that he had slept so soundly in spite of the weight of apprehension on his mind the night before, discovered this apprehension to be groundless in the clear light of the new day. The sulky villains of the tap-room were now honest fellows who would harm no one, and James laughed aloud at his needless fears; the loaded matchlock in the corner giving no hint of its influence towards a peaceful night. The landlord seemed, indeed, a most civil person, who would be the last to turn a penniless man from his door. James, over his breakfast, asked what had become of the company, and his host replied that they were woodlanders; good lads in their way, but abashed before strangers. Some of them had gone to their affairs in the forest and others had proceeded to St. Ninians, to enjoy the hanging set for that day.

"And which way may your honour be journeying?" asked the innkeeper, "for I see that you are no beggar."

"I am no beggar at such an inhospitable house as this," replied the wayfarer, "but elsewhere I am a beggar, that is to say, the gold I come by is asked for, and not earned."

"Ah, that's it, is it?" said the other with a nod, "but for such a trade you need your weapons by your side."

"The deadliest weapons," rejoined the king mysteriously, "are not always those most plainly on view. The sting of the wasp is generally felt before it is seen."

The landlord was plainly disturbed by the intelligence he had received, and now made some ado to get the change for the gold piece, but his guest replied airily that it did not matter.

"With whatever's coming to me," he said, "feed the next beggar that applies to you on a rainy night with less at his belt to commend him than I have."

"Well, good-day to you, and thank you," said the innkeeper. "If you're going Stirling way, your road's straight through the forest, and when you come to St. Ninians you'll be in time to see a fine hanging, for they're throttling Baldy Hutchinson to-day, the biggest man between here and the Border, yes, and beyond it, I warrant."

"That will be interesting," replied the king. "Good-day to you."

At the side of the wall, which ran from the end of the hostel and enclosed a bit of ground appertaining to it, James stooped ostensibly to tie his shoe, but in reality to learn if his late host made any move, for he suspected that the sinister company of the night before might not be so far away as the landlord had intimated. His stratagem was not without its reward. The back door opened, and he heard the landlord say in a husky whisper to some one unseen,—

"Run, Jock, as fast's you can to the second turning in the road, and tell Steenie and his men they'd best leave this chap alone; he's a robber himself."

The king smiled as he walked slowly north towards the forest and saw a bare-legged boy race at great speed across the fields and disappear at their margin. He resolved to give time for this message to arrive, so that he might not be molested, and therefore sauntered at a more leisurely rate than that at which a man usually begins a journey on an inspiring morning.

Entering the forest at last, he relaxed no precaution, but kept to the middle of the road with his stout stick ready in his hand. Whether Jock found his men or not he never learned, but at the second turning five stalwart ruffians fell upon him; two armed with knives, and three with cudgels. The king's early athletic training was to be put to a practical test. His first action was to break the wrist of one of the scoundrels who held a knife, but before he could pay attention to any of the others he had received two or three resounding blows from the cudgels, and now was fully occupied warding off their strokes, backing down the road to keep his assailants in front of him. His great agility gave him an advantage over the comparative clumsiness of the four yokels who pressed him, but he was well aware that an unguarded blow might lay him at their mercy. He was more afraid of the single knife than of the three clubs, and springing through a fortunate opening was delighted to crack the crown of the man who held the blade, stretching him helpless in a cart rut. The three who remained seemed in no way disheartened by the discomfiture of their comrades, but came on with greater fury. The king retreated and retreated baffling their evident desire to get in his rear, and thus the fighting four came to the corner of the road that James had passed a short time previously. One of the trio got in a nasty crack on the top of the beggar's bonnet, which brought him to his knees, and before he could recover his footing, a blow on the shoulder felled him. At this critical juncture there rose a wild shout down the road, for the fighting party, in coming round the turn, had brought themselves within view of a sturdy pedestrian forging along at a great pace, which he nevertheless marvellously accelerated on seeing the mêlée. For a moment the dazed man on the ground thought that the landlord had come to his rescue, but it was not so. It seemed as if a remnant of the storm had swept like a whirlwind among the aggressors, for the newcomer in the fray, with savage exclamations, which showed his delight in a tumult, scattered the enemy as a tornado drives before it the leaves of a forest. The king raised himself on his elbow and watched the gigantic stranger lay about him with his stick, while the five, with cries of terror, disappeared into the forest, for the two that were prostrate had now recovered wind enough to run.

"Losh," panted the giant, returning to the man on the road, "I wish I'd been here at the beginning."

"Thank goodness you came at the end," said the king, staggering unsteadily to his feet.

"Are you hurt?" asked the stranger.

"I'm not just sure yet," replied the king, removing his bonnet and rubbing the top of his head with a circular movement of his hand.

"Just a bit cloor on the croon," said the other in broad Lowland Scotch. "It stunners a man, but it's nothin' ava when ye can stan' on your ain feet."

"Oh, it's not the first time I've had to fight for my crown," said James with a laugh, "but five to one are odds a little more heavy than I care to encounter."

"Are ye able to walk on, for I'm in a bit o' a hurry, as ye'd have seen if your attention hadna been turned to the north."

"Oh, quite able," replied the king as they strode along together.

"What's wrong wi' those scamps to lay on a poor beggar man?" asked the stranger.

"Nothing, except that the beggar man is not so poor as he looks, and has a belt of gold about him, which he was foolish enough to show last night at the inn where these lads were drinking."

"Then the lesson hasn't taught you much, or you wouldn't say that to a complete stranger in the middle of a black forest, and you alone with him, that is, unless they've succeeded in reiving the belt away from you?"

"No, they have not robbed me, and to show you that I am not such a fool as you take me for, I may add that the moment you came up I resolved to give to my rescuer every gold piece that is in my belt. So you see, if you thought of robbing me, there's little use in taking by force what a man is more than willing to give you of his own free will."

The giant threw back his head and the wood resounded with his laughter.

"What I have said seems to amuse you," said the king not too well pleased at the boisterous merriment of his companion.

"It does that," replied the stranger, still struggling with his mirth; then striking the king on the shoulder, he continued, "I suppose there is not another man in all broad Scotland to-day but me, that wouldn't give the snap of his fingers for all the gold you ever carried."

"Then you must be wealthy," commented the king. "Yet it can't be that, for the richest men I know are the greediest."

"No, it isn't that," rejoined the stranger, "but if you wander anywhere about this region you will understand what I mean when I tell you that I'm Baldy Hutchinson."

"Baldy Hutchinson!" echoed the king, wrinkling his brows, trying to remember where he had heard that name before, then with sudden enlightenment,—

"What, not the man who is to be hanged to-day at St. Ninians?"

"The very same, so you see that all the gold ever minted is of little use to a man with a tightening rope round his neck." And the comicality of the situation again overcoming Mr. Hutchinson, his robust sides shook once more with laughter.

The king stopped in the middle of the road and stared at his companion with amazement.

"Surely you are aware," he said at last, "that you are on the direct road to St. Ninians?"

"Surely, surely," replied Baldy, "and you remind me, that we must not stand yammering here, for there will be a great gathering there to see the hanging. All my friends are there now, and if I say it, who shouldn't, I've more friends than possibly any other man in this part of Scotland."

"But, do you mean that you are going voluntarily to your own hanging? Bless my soul, man, turn in your tracks and make for across the Border."

Hutchinson shook his head.

"If I had intended to do that," he said, "I could have saved myself many a long step yesterday and this morning, for I was a good deal nearer the Border than I am at this moment. No, no, you see I have passed my word. The sheriff gave me a week among my own friends to settle my worldly affairs, and bid the wife and the bairns good-bye. So I said to the sheriff, 'I'm your man whenever you are ready for the hanging.' Now, the word of Baldy Hutchinson has never been broken yet, and the sheriff knew it, although I must admit he swithered long ere he trusted it on an occasion like this. But at last he said to me, 'Baldy,' says he, 'I'll take your plighted word. You've got a week before you, and you must just go and come as quietly as you can, and be here before the clock strikes twelve on Friday, for folk'll want to see you hanged before they have their dinners.' And that's what way I'm in such a hurry now, for I'm feared the farmers will be gathered, and that it will be difficult for me to place myself in the hands of the sheriff without somebody getting to jalouse what has happened."

"I've heard many a strange tale," said the king, "but this beats anything in my experience."

"Oh there's a great deal to be picked up by tramping the roads," replied Hutchinson sagely.

"What is your crime?" inquired his majesty.

"Oh, the crime's neither here nor there. If they want to hang a man, they'll hang him crime or no crime."

"But why should they want to hang a man with so many friends?"

"Well, you see a man may have many friends and yet two or three powerful enemies. My crime, as you call it, is that I'm related to the Douglases; that's the real crime; but that's not what I'm to be hanged for. Oh no, it's all done according to the legal satisfaction of the lawyers. I'm hanged for treason to the king; a right royal crime, that dubs a man a gentleman as much as if the king's sword slaps his bended back; a crime that better men than me have often suffered for, and that many will suffer for yet ere kings are abolished, I'm thinking. You see, as I said, I married into the Douglas family, and when the Earl of Angus let this young sprig of a king slip through his fingers, it was as much as one's very life was worth to whisper the name of Douglas. Now I think the Earl of Angus a good man, and when he was driven to England, and the Douglases scattered far and wide by this rapscallion callant with a crown on his head, I being an outspoken man, gave my opinion of the king, damn him, and there were plenty to report it. I did not deny it, indeed I do not deny it to-day, therefore my neck's like to be longer before the sun goes down."

"But surely," exclaimed the beggar, "they will not hang a man in Scotland for merely saying a hasty word against the king?"

"There's more happens in this realm than the king kens of, and all done in his name too. But to speak truth, there was a bit extra against me as well. A wheen of the daft bodies in Stirling made up a slip of a plot to trap the king and put him in hiding for a while until he listened to what they called reason. There were two weavers among them and weavers are always plotting; a cobbler, and such like people, and they sent word, would I come and help them. I was fool enough to write them a note, and entrusted it to their messenger. I told them to leave the king alone until I came to Stirling, and then I would just nab him myself, put him under my oxter and walk down towards the Border with him, for I knew that if they went on they'd but lose their silly heads. And so, wishing no harm to the king, I made my way to Stirling, but did not get within a mile of it, for they tripped me up at St. Ninians, having captured my letter. So I was sentenced, and it seems the king found out all about their plot as I knew he would, and pardoned the men who were going to kidnap him, while the man who wanted to stop such foolishness is to be hanged in his name."

"That seems villainously unfair," said the beggar. "Didn't the eleven try to do anything for you?"

"How do you know there were eleven?" cried Hutchinson, turning round upon him.

"I thought you said eleven."

"Well, maybe I did, maybe I did; yes, there were eleven of them. They never got my letter. Their messenger was a traitor, as is usually the case, and merely told them I would have nothing to do with their foolish venture; and that brings me to the point I have been coming to. You see although I would keep my word in any case, yet I'm not so feared to approach St. Ninians as another man might be. Young Jamie, the king, seems to have more sense in his noodle than he gets credit for. Some of his forbears would have snapped off the heads of that eleven without thinking more of the matter, but he seems to have recognised they were but poor silly bodies, and so let them go. Now the moment they set me at liberty, a week since, I got a messenger I could trust, and sent him to the cobbler, Flemming by name. I told Flemming I was to be hanged, but he had still a week to get me a reprieve. I asked him to go to the king and tell him the whole truth of the matter, so I'm thinking that a pardon will be on the scaffold there before me; still, the disappointment of the hundreds waiting to see the hanging will be great."

"Good God!" cried the beggar aghast, stopping dead in the middle of the road and regarding his comrade with horror.

"What's wrong with you?" asked the big man stopping also.

"Has it never occurred to you that the king may be away from the palace, and no one in the place able to find him?"

"No one able to find the King of Scotland? That's an unheard-of thing."

"Listen to me, Hutchinson. Let us avoid St. Ninians, and go direct to Stirling; it's only a mile or two further on. Let us see the cobbler before running your neck into a noose."

"But, man, the cobbler will be at St. Ninians, either with a pardon or to see me hanged, like the good friend he is."

"There will be no pardon at St. Ninians. Let us to Stirling; let us to Stirling. I know that the king has not been at home for a week past."

"How can you know that?"

"Never mind how I know it. Will you do what I tell you?"

"Not I! I'm a lad o' my word."

"Then you are a doomed man. I tell you the king has not been in Stirling since you left St. Ninians." Then with a burst of impatience James cried, "You stubborn fool, I am the king!"

At first the big man seemed inclined to laugh, and he looked over the beggar from top to toe, but presently an expression of pity overspread his countenance, and he spoke soothingly to his comrade.

"Yes, yes, my man," he said, "I knew you were the king from the very first. Just sit down on this stone for a minute and let me examine that clip you got on the top of the head. I fear me it's worse than I thought it was."

"Nonsense," cried the king, "my head is perfectly right; it is yours that is gone aglee."

"True enough, true enough," continued Hutchinson mildly, in the tone that he would have used towards a fractious child, "and you are not the first that's said it. But let us get on to St. Ninians."

"No, let us make direct for Stirling."

"I'll tell you what we'll do," continued Hutchinson in the same tone of exasperating tolerance. "I'll to St. Ninians and let them know the king's pardon's coming. You'll trot along to Stirling, put on your king's clothes and then come and set me free. That's the way we'll arrange it, my mannie."

The king made a gesture of despair, but remained silent, and they walked rapidly down the road together. They had quitted the forest, and the village of St. Ninians was now in view. As they approached the place more nearly, Hutchinson was pleased to see that a great crowd had gathered to view the hanging. He seemed to take this as a personal compliment to himself; as an evidence of his popularity.

The two made their way to the back of the great assemblage where a few soldiers guarded an enclosure within which was the anxious sheriff and his minor officials.

"Bless me, Baldy!" cried the sheriff in a tone of great relief, "I thought you had given me the slip."

"Ye thought naething o' the kind, sheriff," rejoined Baldy complacently. "I said I would be here, and here I am."

"You are just late enough," grumbled the sheriff. "The people have been waiting this two hours."

"They'll think it all the better when they see it," commented Baldy. "I was held back a bit on the road. Has there no message come from the king?"

"Could you expect it, when the crime's treason?" asked the sheriff impatiently, "but there's been a cobbler here that's given me more bother than twenty kings, and cannot be pacified. He says the king's away from Stirling, and this execution must be put by for another ten days, which is impossible."

"Allow me a word in your ear privately," said the beggar to the sheriff.

"I'll see you after the job's done," replied the badgered man. "I have no more places to give away, you must just stand your chances with the mob."

Baldy put his open hand to the side of his mouth and whispered to the sheriff:

"This beggar man," he said, "has been misused by a gang of thieves in Torwood Forest."

"I cannot attend to that now," rejoined the sheriff with increasing irritation.

107

"No, no," continued Baldy suavely, "it's no that, but he's got a frightful dunner on the top o' the head, and he thinks he's the king."

"I am the king," cried the beggar, overhearing the last word of caution, "and I warn you, sir, that you proceed with this execution at your peril. I am James of Scotland, and I forbid the hanging."

At this moment there broke through the insufficient military guard a wild unkempt figure, whose appearance caused trepidation to the already much-tried sheriff.

"There's the crazy cobbler again," he moaned dejectedly. "Now the fat's all in the fire. I think I'll hang the three of them, trial or no trial."

"Oh, your majesty!" cried the cobbler,—and it was hard to say which of the two was the more disreputable in appearance,—"this man Hutchinson is innocent. You will surely not allow the hanging to take place, now you are here."

"I'll not allow it, if I can prevent it, and can get this fool of a sheriff to listen."

"Fool of a sheriff! say you," stuttered that official in rising anger. "Here, guard, take these two ragamuffins into custody, and see that they are kept quiet till this hanging's done with. Hutchinson, get up on the scaffold; this is all your fault. Hangman, do your duty."

Baldy Hutchinson, begging the cobbler to make no further trouble, mounted the steps leading to the platform, the hangman close behind him. Before the guard could lay hands on the king, he sprang also up the steps, and took a place on the outward edge of the scaffold. Raising his hand, he demanded silence.

"I am James, King of Scotland," he proclaimed in stentorian tones. "I command you as loyal subjects to depart to your homes. There will be no execution to-day. The king reprieves Baldy Hutchinson."

The cobbler stood at the king's back, and when he had ended, lifted his voice and shouted,—

"God save the King!"

The mob heard the announcement in silence, and then a roar of laughter followed, as they gazed at the two tattered figures on the edge of the platform. But the laughter was followed by an ominous howl of rage, as they understood that they were like to be cheated of a spectacle.

"Losh, I'll king him," shouted the indignant sheriff, as he mounted the steps, and before the beggar or his comrade could defend themselves, that official with his own hands precipitated them down among the assemblage at the foot of the scaffold. And now the spirit of a wild beast was let loose among the rabble. The king and his henchman staggered to their feet and beat off, as well as they could, the multitude that pressed vociferously upon them. A soldier, struggling through, tried to arrest the beggarman, but the king nimbly wrested his sword from him, and circled the blade in the air with a venomous hiss of steel that caused the nearer portion of the mob to press back eagerly, as, a moment before, they had pressed forward. The man who swung a blade like that was certainly worthy of respect, be he beggar or monarch. The cobbler's face was grimed and bleeding, but the king's newly won sword cleared a space around him. And now the bellowing voice of Baldy Hutchinson made itself heard above the din.

"Stand back from him," he shouted. "They're decent honest bodies, even if they've gone clean mad."

But now these at the back of the crowd were forcing the others forward, and Baldy saw that in spite of the sword, his old and his new friend would be presently engulfed. He turned to one of the upright posts of the scaffold and gave it a tremendous shuddering kick; then reaching up to the cross-bar and exerting his Samson-like strength, he wrenched it with a crash of tearing wood down from its position, and armed with this formidable weapon he sprung into the mob, scattering it right and left with his hangman's beam.

"A riot and a rescue!" roared the sheriff. "Mount, Trooper MacKenzie, and ride as if the devil were after you to Stirling; to Stirling, man, and bring back with you a troop of the king's horse."

"We must stop that man getting to Stirling," said Baldy, "or he'll have the king's men on you. I'll clear a way for you through the people, and then you two must take leg bail for it to the forest."

"Stand where you are," said the beggar. "The king's horse is what I want to see."

"Dods, you'll see them soon enough. Look at that gallop!"

MacKenzie indeed had lost no time in getting astride his steed, and was now disappearing towards Stirling like the wind. The more timorous of the assemblage, fearing the oncoming of the cavalry, which usually made short work of all opposition, caring little who was trampled beneath horses' hoofs, began to disperse, and seek stations of greater safety than the space before the scaffold afforded.

"Believe me," said Baldy earnestly to his two friends, "you'd better make your legs save your throttle. This is a hanging affair for you as well as for me, for you've interfered with the due course of the law."

"It's not the first time I've done so," said the beggar with great composure, and shortly after they heard the thunder of horses' hoofs coming from the north.

"Thank God!" said the sheriff when he heard the welcome sound. The mob dissolved and left a free passage for the galloping cavalcade. The stout Baldy Hutchinson and his two comrades stood alone to receive the onset.

The king took a few steps forward, raised his sword aloft and shouted,—

"Halt, Sir Donald!"

Sir Donald Sinclair obeyed the command so suddenly that his horse's front feet tore up the turf as he reined back, while his sharp order to the troop behind him brought the company to an almost instantaneous stand.

"Sir Donald," said the king, "I am for Stirling with my two friends here. See that we are not followed, and ask this hilarious company to disperse quietly to their homes. Do it kindly, Sir Donald. There is no particular hurry, and they have all the afternoon before them. Bring your troop back to Stirling in an hour or two."

"Will your majesty not take my horse?" asked Sir Donald Sinclair.

"No, Donald," replied the king with a smile, glancing down at his rags. "Scottish horsemen have always looked well in the saddle; yourself are an example of that, and I have no wish to make this costume fashionable as a riding suit."

The sheriff who stood by with dropped jaw, now flung himself on his knees and craved pardon for laying hands on the Lord's anointed.

"The least said of that the better," remarked the king drily. "But if you are sorry, sheriff, that the people should be disappointed at not seeing a man hanged, I think you would make a very good substitute for my big friend Baldy here."

The sheriff tremulously asserted that the populace were but too pleased at this exhibition of the royal clemency.

"If that is the case then," replied his majesty, "we shall not need to trouble you. And so, farewell to you!"

The king, Baldy, and the cobbler took the road towards Stirling, and Sir Donald spread out his troop to intercept traffic in that direction. Advancing toward the bewildered crowd, Sir Donald spoke to them.

"You will go quietly to your homes," he said. "You have not seen the hanging, but you have witnessed to-day what none in Scotland ever saw before, the king intervene personally to save a doomed man; therefore, be satisfied, and go home."

Some one in the mob cried,—

"Hurrah for the poor man's king! Cheer, lads, cheer!" A great uproar was lifted to the skies; afar off the three pedestrians heard it, and Baldy, the man of many friends, taking the clamour as a public compliment to himself, waved his bonnet at the distant vociferous multitude.

The King's Visit

"No, no," said the king decisively, "Bring them in, bring them in. I'll have none cast into prison without at least a hearing. Have any of your men been killed?"

"No, your majesty," replied Sir Donald, "but some of them have wounds they will not forget in a hurry; the Highlandmen fought like tiger-cats."

"How many are there of them?" asked the king.

"Something more than a score, with a piper that's noisier than the other twenty, led by a breechless ruffian, although I must say he knows what to do with a sword."

"All armed, you say?"

"Every one of them but the piper. About half an hour ago they came marching up the main street of Stirling, each man with his sword drawn, and the pipes skirling death and defiance. They had the whole town at their heels laughing and jeering at them and imitating the wild Highland music. At first, they paid little attention to the mob that followed them, but in the square their leader gave a word in Gaelic, and at once the whole company swerved about and charged the crowd. There was instant panic among the townspeople, who fled in all directions out-screaming the pibroch in their fright. No one was hurt, for the Highlandmen struck them with the flat of their swords, but several were trampled under foot and are none the better for it."

"It serves them right," commented the king. "I hope it will teach them manners, towards strangers, at least. What followed?"

"A whistle from their leader collected his helots again, and so they marched straight from the square to the gates of the castle. The two soldiers on guard crossed pikes before them, but the leader, without a word, struck down their weapons and attempted to march in, brave as you please; who but they! There was a bit of a scuffle at the gate, then the bugle sounded and we surrounded them, trying to disarm them peaceably at first, but they fought like demons, and so there's some sore heads among them."

"You disarmed them, of course?"

"Certainly, your majesty."

"Very well; bring them in and let us hear what they have to say for themselves."

The doors were flung open, a sharp command was given, and presently there entered the group of Highlanders, disarmed and with their elbows tied behind their backs. A strong guard of the soldiery accompanied them on either side. The Highlanders were men of magnificent physique, a quality that was enhanced by the picturesque costume they wore, in spite of the fact that in some instances, this costume was in tatters, and the wearers cut and bleeding. But, stalwart as his followers were, their leader far outmeasured them in height and girth; a truly magnificent specimen of the human race, who strode up the long room with an imperial swagger such as had never before been seen in Stirling, in spite of the fact that his arms were pinioned. He marched on until he came before the king, and there took his stand, without any indication of bowing his bonneted head, or bending his sturdy bare knees. The moment the leader set his foot across the threshold, the unabashed piper immediately protruded his chest, and struck up the wild strain of "Failte mhic an Abba," or the Salute to the Chief.

"Stop it, ye deevil!" cried the captain of the guard. "How dare you set up such a squawking in the presence of the king?" and as the piper paid not the slightest attention to him, he struck the mouth-piece from the lips of the performer. This, however, did not cause a cessation of the music, for the bag under the piper's elbow was filled with wind and the fingers of the musician bravely kept up the strain on the reed chanter with its nine holes, and thus he played until his chief came to a stand before the king. The king gazed with undisguised admiration upon the foremost Highlander, and said quietly to the captain of the guard,—

"Unbind him!"

On finding his arms released, the mountaineer stretched them out once or twice, then folded them across his breast, making no motion however to remove his plumed bonnet, although every one else in the room except himself and his men were uncovered.

"You have come in from the country," began the king, a suspicion of a smile hovering about his lips, "to enjoy the metropolitan delights of Stirling. How are you satisfied with your reception?"

The big Highlandman made no reply, but frowned heavily, and bestowed a savage glance on several of the courtiers, among whom a light ripple of laughter had run after the king put his question.

"These savages," suggested Sir Donald, "do not understand anything but the Gaelic. Is it your majesty's pleasure that the interpreter be called?"

"Yes, bring him in."

When the interpreter arrived, the king said,—

"Ask this man if his action is the forefront of a Highland invasion of the Lowlands, or merely a little private attempt on his own part to take the castle by assault?"

The interpreter put the question in Gaelic, and was answered with gruff brevity by the marauder. The interpreter, bowing low to the king, said smoothly,—

"This man humbly begs to inform your majesty—"

"Speak truth, MacPherson!" cautioned the king. "Translate faithfully exactly what he says. Our friend here, by the look of him, does not do anything humbly, or fawn or beg. Translate accurately. What does he say?"

The polite MacPherson was taken aback by this reproof, but answered,—

"He says, your majesty, he will hold no communication with me, because I am of an inferior clan, which is untrue. The MacPhersons were a civilised clan centuries ago, which the MacNabs are not to this day, so please your majesty."

The MacNab's hand darted to his left side, but finding no sword to his grasp, it fell away again.

"You are a liar!" cried the chief in very passable English which was not to be misunderstood. "The MacPhersons are no clan, but an insignificant branch of the Chattan. 'Touch not the Cat' is your motto, and a good one, for a MacPherson can scratch but he cannot handle the broadsword."

MacPherson drew himself up, his face reddening with anger. His hand also sought instinctively the hilt of his sword, but the presence in which he stood restricted him.

"It is quite safe," he said with something like the spit of a cat, "for a heathen to insult a Christian in the presence of his king, and the MacNabs have ever shown a taste for the cautious cause."

"Tut, tut," cried the king with impatience, "am I to find myself involved in a Highland feud in my own hall? MacPherson, it seems this man does not require your interpreting, so perhaps it will further the peace of our realm if you withdraw quietly."

MacPherson with a low obeisance, did so; then to MacNab the king spoke,—

"Sir, as it appears you are acquainted with our language, why did you not reply to the question I put to you?"

"Because I would have you know it was not the proper kind of question to ask the like of me. I am a descendant of kings."

"Well, as far as that goes, I am a descendant of kings myself, though sorry I should be to defend all their actions."

"Your family only began with Robert the Bruce; mine was old ere he came to the throne."

"That may well be, still you must admit that what Robert lacked in ancestry, he furnished forth in ability."

"But the Clan MacNab defeated him at the battle of Del Rhi."

"True, with some assistance, which you ignore, from Alexander of Argyll. However, if this discussion is to become a competition in history, for the benefit of our ignorant courtiers, I may be allowed to add that my good ancestor, Robert, did not forget the actions of the MacNabs at Del Rhi, and later overran their country, dismantled their fortresses, leaving the clan in a more sane and chastened condition than that in which he found it. But what has all this to do with your coming storming into a peaceable town like Stirling?"

"In truth, your majesty," whispered Sir David Lyndsay, "I think they must have come to replenish their wardrobe, and in that they are not a moment too soon."

"I came," said the chief, who had not heard this last remark, "because of the foray you have mentioned. I came because Robert the Bruce desolated our country."

"By my good sword!" cried James, "speaking as one king to another, your revenge is somewhat belated, a lapse of two centuries should have outlawed the debt. Did you expect then to take Stirling with twenty men?"

"I expected King James the Fifth to rectify the wrong done by King Robert the First."

"Your expectation does honour to my reputation as a just man, but I have already disclaimed responsibility for the deeds of ancestors less remote than good King Robert."

"You have made proclamation in the Highlands that the chieftains must bring you proof of their right to occupy their lands."

"I have, and some have preferred to me their deeds of tenure, others prepared to fight; the cases have been settled in both instances. To which of these two classes do you belong, Chief of the Clan MacNab?"

"To neither. I cannot submit to you our parchments because Robert, your ancestor, destroyed them. I cannot fight the army of the Lowlands because my clan is small, therefore I, Finlay MacNab, fifth of my name, as

116

you are fifth of yours, come to you in peace, asking you to repair the wrong done by your ancestor."

"Indeed!" cried the king. "If the present advent typifies your idea of a peaceful visit, then God forfend that I should ever meet you in anger."

"I came in peace and have been shamefully used."

"You must not hold that against us," said James. "Look you now, if I had come storming at your castle door, sword in hand, how would you have treated me, Finlay the Fifth?"

"If you had come with only twenty men behind you, I should treat you with all the hospitality of Glendochart, which far exceeds that of Stirling or any other part of your money-making Lowlands, where gold coin is valued more than a steel blade."

"It has all been a mistake," said the king with great cordiality. "The parchment you seek shall be given you, and I trust that your generosity, Lord of Glendochart, will allow me to amend your opinion of Stirling hospitality. I shall take it kindly if you will be my guests in the castle until my officers of law repair the harshness of my ancestor, Robert." Then, turning to the guard the king continued,—

"Unbind these gentlemen, and return to them their arms."

While the loosening of the men was rapidly being accomplished, the captain of the guard brought the chief his sword, and would have presented it to him, but the king himself rose and took the weapon in his own hand, tendering it to its owner. The chieftain accepted the sword and rested its point on the floor, then in dignified native courtesy, he doffed his broad, feathered bonnet.

"Sire," he said, with slow deliberation, "Scotland has a king that this good blade shall ever be proud to serve."

For three days, the MacNabs were the guests of the king in the castle, while the legal documents were being prepared. King and chieftain walked the town together, and all that Stirling had to show, MacNab beheld. The king was desirous of costuming, at his own expense, the portion of the clan that was now in his castle, whose disarray was largely due to his own soldiers, but he feared the proposal might offend the pride of Finlay the Fifth.

James's tact, however, overcame the difficulty.

"When I visit you, MacNab, over by Loch Tay, there is one favour I must ask; I want your tailors to make for me and the men of my following, suits of kilts in the MacNab tartan."

"Surely, surely," replied the chief, "and a better weaving you will get nowhere in the Highlands."

"I like the colour of it," continued the king. "There is a royal red in it that pleases me. Now there is a good deal of red in the Stuart tartan, and I should be greatly gratified if you would permit your men to wear my colours, as my men shall wear yours. My tailors here will be proud to boast that they have made costumes for the Clan MacNab. You know what tradesmen bodies are, they're pleased when we take a little notice of them."

"Surely," again replied MacNab, more dubiously, "and I shall send them the money for it when I get home."

"Indeed," said the king, "if you think I am going to have a full purse when I'm in the MacNab country, you're mistaken."

"I never suggested such a thing," replied the chief indignantly. "You'll count nane o' yer ain bawbees when you are with me."

"Ah, well," rejoined the king, "that's right, and so you will just leave me to settle with my own tailors here."

Thus the re-costuming came about, and all in all it was just as well that MacNab did not insist on his own tartan, for there was none of it in Stirling, while of the Stuart plaid there was a sufficiency to clothe a regiment.

On the last night, there was a banquet given which was the best that Stirling could bestow, in honour of the Clan MacNab. The great hall was decorated with the colours of the clan, and at the further end had been painted the arms of the MacNab—the open boat, with its oars, on the sea proper, the head of the savage, the two supporting figures and the Latin motto underneath, "Timor omnis abseto". Five pipers of the king's court had learned the Salute to the Chief, and now, headed by MacNab's own, they paced up and down the long room, making it ring with their war-like music. The king and the chieftain came in together, and as the latter took his place at his host's right hand, his impassive face betrayed no surprise at the splendid preparations which had been made for his reception. Indeed, the Highlanders all acted as if they had been accustomed to sit down to such a banquet every night. Many dainties were placed on the ample board cunningly prepared by foreign cooks, the like of which the Highlanders had never before tasted; but the mountaineers ate stolidly whatever was set in front of them, and if unusual flavours saluted their palates, the strangers made no sign of approval or the reverse. The red wine of Burgundy, grown old in the king's cellars, was new to most of them, and they drank it like water, emptying their tankards as fast as the attendant could refill them. Soon the ruddy fluid, whose potency had been under-estimated, began to have its effect, and the dinner table became noisy as the meal progressed, songs bursting forth now and then, with strange shouts and cries more familiar to the hills of Loch Tay than to the rafters of Stirling. The chief himself, lost the solemn dignity which had at first characterised him, and as he emptied flagon after flagon he boasted loudly of the prowess of his clan; foretold what he would do in future fields now that he was allied with the King of Scotland. Often forgetting himself, he fell into the Gaelic, roaring forth a torrent of words that had no meaning for many there present, then remembering the king did not understand the language, he expressed his pity for a man in such condition, saying the Gaelic was the oldest tongue in existence, and the first spoken by human lips upon this earth. It was much more expressive, he said, than the dialect of the Lowlands, and the only language that could fittingly describe war and battle, just as the pibroch was the only music suitable to strife, to all of which the smiling king nodded approval. At last MacNab sprang to his feet, holding aloft his brimming flagon, which literally rained Burgundy down upon him, and called for cheers for the King of Scotland, a worthy prince who knew well how to entertain a brother prince. Repeating this in Gaelic, his men, who had also risen with their chief, now sprang upon the benches, where standing unsteadily, they raised a series of yells so wild that a shudder of fear passed through many of the courtiers there present. The chief, calling to his piper, commanded him instantly to compose a pibroch for the king, and that ready musician, swelling with pride, marched up and down and round and round the great hall pouring forth a triumphal quickstep, with many wonderful flourishes and variations. Then at a word from the chief, each man placed his flagon on the table, whipped out his sword, swung it overhead, to the amazement of the courtiers, for it is not in accord with etiquette to show cold steel to the eyes of the king. Down came the blades instantly and together, each man splitting in two the goblet he had drunk from.

"You must all come to Loch Tay," cried the chief, "and I will show you a banqueting hall in honour of James the Fifth, such as you have never before seen." Then to the horror of the courtiers, he suddenly smote the king on the back with his open palm and cried, "Jamie, my lad, you'll come and visit me at Loch Tay?"

The smitten king laughed heartily and replied,—

"Yes, Finlay, I will."

The next day the MacNabs marched from the castle and down through the town of Stirling with much pomp and circumstance. They were escorted by the king's own guard, and this time the populace made no sneering remarks but thronged the windows and the roofs, cheering heartily, while the Highlanders kept proud step to the shrill music of the pipes. And thus the clansmen set faces towards the north on their long tramp home.

"What proud 'deevils' they are," said Sir David Lyndsay to the king after the northern company had departed. "I have been through the MacNab country from one end of it to the other, and there is not a decent hut on the hillside, let alone a castle fit to entertain a king, yet the chief gives an invitation in the heat of wine, and when he is sobered, he is too proud to admit that he cannot make good the words he has uttered."

"That very thing is troubling me," replied the king, "but it's a long time till July, and between now and then we will make him some excuse for not returning his visit, and thus avoid putting the old man to shame."

"But that too will offend him beyond repair," objected the poet.

"Well, we must just lay our heads together, Davie," answered the king, "and think of some way that will neither be an insult nor a humiliation. It might not be a bad plan for me to put on disguise and visit Finlay alone."

"Would you trust yourself, unaccompanied, among those wild caterans? One doesn't know what they might do."

"I wish I were as safe in Stirling as I should be among the MacNabs," replied the king.

However, affairs of state did not permit the carrying out of the king's intention. Embassies came from various countries, and the king must entertain the foreigners in a manner becoming their importance. This, however, gave James the valid excuse he required, and so he sent a commission to the chief of the MacNabs. "His majesty," said the head commissioner, "is entertaining the ambassadors from Spain and from France, and likewise a legate from the Pope. If he came north, he must at least bring with him these great noblemen with their retinues; and while he would have been glad to visit you with some of his own men, he could not impose upon the hospitality thus generously tendered, by bringing also a large number of strangers and foreigners."

"Tell his majesty," replied MacNab with dignity, "that whether he bring with him the King of Spain, the Emperor of France, or even the Pope himself, none of these princes is, in the estimation of MacNab, superior to James the Fifth, of Scotland. The entertainment therefore, which the king graciously condescends to accept, is certainly good enough for any foreigners that may accompany him, be their nobility ever so high."

When this reply was reported to the king he first smiled and then sighed.

"I can do nothing further," he said. "Return to MacNab and tell him that the Pope's legate desires to visit the Priory on Loch Tay. Tell the chief that we will take the boat along the lake on the day arranged. Say that the foreigners are anxious to taste the venison of the hills, and that nothing could be better than to give us a dinner under the trees. Tell him that he need not be at any trouble to provide us lodging, for we shall return to the Island Priory and there sleep."

In the early morning the king and his followers, the ambassadors and their train embarked on boats that had been brought overland for their accommodation, and sailed from the Island Priory the length of the beautiful lake; the numerous craft being driven through the water by strong northern oarsmen, their wild chaunting choruses echoing back from the picturesque mountains as they bent to their work. The evening before, horses for the party had been led through forests, over the hills, and along the strand, to the meeting-place at the other end of the lake. Here they were greeted by the MacNabs, pipers and all, and mounting the horses the gay cavalcade was led up the valley. The king had warned their foreign Highnesses that they were not to expect in this wilderness the niceties of Rome, Paris or Madrid, and each of the ambassadors expressed his delight at the prospect of an outing certain to contain so much that was novel and unusual to them.

A summer haze hung in the valley, and when the king came in sight of the stronghold of the MacNabs he rubbed his eyes in wonder, thinking the misty uncertainty of the atmosphere was playing wizard tricks with his vision. There, before them, stood the most bulky edifice, the most extraordinary pile he had ever beheld. Tremendous in extent, it seemed to have embodied every marked feature of a mediæval castle. At one end a great square keep arose, its amazing height looming gigantically in the gauze-like magic of the mist. A high wall, machicolated at the top, connected this keep with a small octagonal tower, whose twin was placed some distance to the left, leaving an opening between for a wide entrance. The two octagonal towers formed a sort of frame for a roaring waterfall in the background. From the second octagonal tower another extended lofty wall connected it with a round peel as high as the keep. This castle of a size so enormous that it made all others its beholders had ever seen shrink into comparative insignificance, was surrounded by a bailey wall; outside of that was a moat which proved to be a foaming river, fed by the volume of water which came down the precipice behind the castle. The lashing current and the snow-white cascade formed a striking contrast to the deep moss-green hue of the castle itself.

"We have many great strongholds in Italy," said the Pope's legate, "but never have I seen anything to compare with this."

"Oh," said MacNab slightingly, "we are but a small clan; you should see the Highland castles further north; they are of stone; indeed our own fortresses, which are further inland, are also of stone. This is merely our pleasure-house built of pine-trees."

"A castle of logs!" exclaimed the Pope's legate. "I never before heard of such a thing."

They crossed the bridge, passed between the two octagonal towers and entered the extensive courtyard, surrounded by the castle itself; a courtyard broad enough to afford manoeuvring ground for an army. The interior walls were as attractive as the outside was grim and forbidding. Balconies ran around three sides of the enclosure, tall thin, straight pine poles, rising three stories high, supporting them, each pole fluttering a flag at the top. The balconies were all festooned with branches of living green.

The air was tremulous with the thunder of the cataract and the courtyard was cut in two by a rushing torrent, spanned by rustic bridges. The walls were peopled by cheering clansmen, and nearly a score of pipers did much to increase the din. Inside, the king and his men found ample accommodation; their rooms were carpeted with moss and with flowers, forming a variety of colour and yielding a softness to the foot which the artificial piles of Eastern looms would have attempted to rival in vain. Here for three days the royal party was entertained. Hunting in the forest gave them prodigious appetites, and there was no criticism of the cooking. The supply of food and drink was lavish in the extreme; fish from the river and the loch, game from the moors and venison from the hills.

It was evening of the third day when the cavalcade set out again for the Priory; the chief, Finlay MacNab, accompanied his guests down the valley, and when some distance from the castle of logs, James smote him on the shoulder, copying thus his own astonishing action. "Sir Finlay," he cried, "a king's hand should be no less potent than a king's sword, and thus I create thee a knight of my realm, for never before has monarch been so royally entertained, and now I pause here to look once more on your castle of pine."

So they all stayed progress and turned their eyes toward the wooden palace they had left.

"If it were built of stone," said the Pope's legate, "it would be the strongest house in the world as it is the largest."

"A bulwark of bones is better than a castle of stones," said Sir Finlay. "That is an old Highland saying with us, which means that a brave following is the best ward. I will show you my bulwark of bones."

And with that, bowing to the king as if to ask permission, he raised his bugle to his lips and blew a blast. Instantly from the corner of the further bastion a torch flamed forth, and that torch lighted the one next it, and this its neighbour, so that speedily a line of fire ran along the outlines of the castle, marking out the square towers and the round, lining the curtain, the smaller towers, turrets and parapets. Then at the top of the bailey wall a circle of Highlanders lit torch after torch, and thus was the whole castle illumined by a circle of fire. The huge edifice was etched in flame against the sombre background of the high mountain.

"Confess, legate," cried the king, "that you never saw anything more beautiful even in fair Italy."

"I am willing to admit as much," replied the Roman.

Another blast from the bugle and all the torches on the castle itself disappeared, although the fire on the bailey wall remained intact, and the reason for this soon became apparent. From machicolated tower, keep, peel and curtain, the nimble Highlanders, torchless, scrambled down, cheering as they came. It seemed incredible that they could have attained such speed, picking their precarious way by grasping protruding branch or stump or limb, or by thrusting hand between the interstices of the timber, without slipping, falling and breaking their necks.

For a moment the castle walls were alive with fluttering tartans, strongly illuminated by the torches from the outer bailey. Each man held his breath while this perilous acrobatic performance was being accomplished, and silence reigned over the royal party until suddenly broken by the Italian.

"Highlander!" he cried, "your castle is on fire."

"Aye," said the Highlander calmly, raising his bugle again to his lips.

At the next blast those on the bailey wall thrust their torches, still burning among the chinks of the logs, and swarmed to the ground as speedily and as safely as those on the main building had done. Now the lighted torches that had been thrown on the roof of the castle, disappearing a moment from sight, gave evidence of their existence. Here and there a long tongue of flame sprung up and died down again.

"Can nothing be done to save the palace?" shouted the excitable Frenchman. "The waterfall; the waterfall! Let us go back, or the castle will be destroyed."

"Stand where you are," said the chief, "and you will see a sight worth coming north for."

Now almost with the suddenness of an explosion, great sheets of flame rose towering into a mountain of fire, as if this roaring furnace would emulate in height the wooded hills behind it. The logs themselves seemed to redden as the light glowed through every crevice between them. The bastions, the bailey walls, were great wheels of flame, encircling a palace that had all the vivid radiance of molten gold. The valley for miles up and down was lighter than the sun ever made it.

"Chieftain," said the legate in an awed whisper, "is this conflagration accident or design?"

"It is our custom," replied MacNab. "A monarch's pathway must be lighted, and it is not fitting that a residence once honoured by our king should ever again be occupied by anyone less noble. The pine tree is the badge of my clan. At my behest the pine tree sheltered the king, and now, at the blast of my bugle, it sends forth to the glen its farewell of flame."

The King Explores

James was pleased with himself. He had finished a poem, admitted by all the court to excel anything that Sir David Lyndsay ever wrote, and he had out-distanced James MacDonald, son of the Laird of Sleat, in a contest for the preference of the fairest lady in Stirling, and young MacDonald was certainly the handsomest sprig about the palace. So the double victory in the art of rhythm and of love naturally induced the king to hold a great conceit of himself. Poor Davie, who was as modest a man regarding his own merits as could be found in the realm, quite readily and honestly hailed the king his superior in the construction of jingling rhyme, but the strapping young Highlander was proud as any scion of the royal house, and he took his defeat less diffidently.

"If the king," he said boldly, "was plain Jamie Stuart, as I am Jamie MacDonald, we would soon see who was winner of the bonniest lass, and if he objected to fair play I'd not scruple to meet him sword in hand on the heather of the hills, but not on the stones of Stirling. It is the crown that has won, and not the face underneath it."

Now this was rank treason, for you must never talk of swords in relation to a king, except that they be drawn in his defence. The inexperienced young man made a very poor courtier, for he spoke as his mind prompted him, a reckless habit that has brought many a head to the block. Although MacDonald had a number of friends who admired the frank, if somewhat hot-headed nature of the youth, his Highland swagger often earned for him not a few enemies who would have been glad of his downfall. Besides this, there are always about a court plenty of sycophants eager to curry favour with the ruling power; and so it was not long after these injudicious utterances had been given forth that they were brought, with many exaggerations, to the ears of the king.

"You think, then," said his majesty to one of the tale-bearers, "that if Jamie had the chance he would run his iron through my royal person?"

"There is little doubt of it, your majesty," replied the parasite.

"Ah, well," commented James, "kings must take their luck like other folk, and some day Jamie and I may meet on the heather with no other witnesses than the mountains around us and the blue sky above us, and in that case I shall have to do the best I can. I make no doubt that MacDonald's position in Stirling is less pleasant than my own. He is practically a prisoner, held hostage here for the good conduct of his father, the firebrand of Sleat, so we must not take too seriously the vapouring of a youth whose leg is tied. I was once a captive myself to the Douglas, and I used words that would scarcely have been pleasant for my gaoler to hear had some kind friend carried them, so I have ever a soft side for the man in thrall."

To the amazement of the courtiers, who had shown some inclination to avoid the company of MacDonald after he had unburdened his soul, the king continued to treat the Highlander as affably as ever, but many thought his majesty was merely biding his time, which was indeed the case. The wiser heads about the court strongly approved of this diplomacy, as before they had looked askance at the king's rivalry with the irascible youth. They knew that affairs were not going well in the north, and so loose were the bonds restraining MacDonald, that at any moment he might very readily have escaped, ridden to the hills, and there augmented the almost constant warfare in those mountainous regions. Every clan that could be kept quiet was so much to the good, for although they fought mostly among themselves, there was ever a danger of a combination which might threaten the throne of Scotland. Very often the king recklessly offended those whom he should conciliate, but even the wiseacres were compelled to admit that his jaunty kindness frequently smoothed out what looked like a dangerous quarrel. The sage counsellors, however, thought the king should keep a closer watch on those Highland chieftains who were practically hostages in his court. But to this advice James would never listen. Having been a captive himself not so very long before, as he frequently remarked, he thus felt an intense sympathy for those in like condition, even though he himself kept them so through the necessity of internal politics, yet he always endeavoured to make the restraint sit as lightly as possible on his victims.

Some weeks after the ill-considered anti-royal threats had been made, their promulgator was one of a group in the courtyard of the castle, when the captain of the guard came forward and said the king wished to see him in his private chamber. MacDonald may have been taken aback by the unexpected summons, but he carried the matter off nonchalantly enough, with the air of one who fears neither potentate nor peasant, and so accompanied the captain; but the gossips nodded their heads sagely at one another, whispering that it would be well to take a good view of MacDonald's back, as they were little likely to see him soon again, and this whisper proved true, for next day MacDonald had completely disappeared, no one knew whither.

When James the laird's son, entered the presence of James the king, the latter said as soon as the captain had left them alone together,—

"Jamie, my man, you understand the Gaelic, so it is possible you understand those who speak it."

"If your majesty means the Highlanders, they are easily enough understood. They are plain, simple, honest bodies who speak what's on their minds, and who are always willing, in an argument, to exchange the wag of the tongue for a swoop of the black knife."

"I admit," said the king with a smile, "that they are a guileless pastoral people, easy to get on with if you comprehend them, but that is where I'm at a loss, and I thought your head might supplement my own."

"I am delighted to hear you want my head for no other purpose but that of giving advice," returned the Highlander candidly.

"Truth to tell, Jamie, your head would be of little use to me were it not on your shoulders. If the head were that of a winsome lassie I might be tempted to take it on my own shoulder, but otherwise I am well content to let heads remain where Providence places them."

Whether intentional or not, the king had touched a sore spot when he referred to the laying of a winsome lassie's head on his shoulder, and MacDonald drew himself up rather stiffly.

"In any ploy with the ladies," he said, "your majesty has the weight of an ermine cloak in your favour, and we all know how the lassies like millinery."

"Then, Jamie, in a fair field, you think you would have the advantage of me, as for example if our carpet were the heather instead of the weaving of an Eastern loom?"

"I just think that," said MacDonald stoutly.

The king threw back his head and laughed the generous laugh of the all-conquering man.

"E-god, Jamie, my man, we may put that to the test before long, but it is in the high realms of statesmanship I want your advice, and not in the frivolous courts of love. You may give that advice the more freely when I tell you that I have made up my mind what to do in any case, and am not likely to be swayed one way or other by the counsel I shall receive."

"Then why does your majesty wish to have my opinion?" asked the Highlander.

"Lord, I'll want more than your opinion before this is done with, but I may tell you at once that there's troublesome news from Skye."

"Are the MacLeods up again?"

"Aye, they're up and down. They're up in their anger and down on their neighbours. I cannot fathom the intricacies of their disputes, but it may interest you to know that some of your clan are engaged in it. I suspect that Alexander MacLeod of Dunvegan is behind all this, although he may not be an active participant."

"Ah, that is Allaster Crottach," said the young man, knitting his brows.

"Allaster, yes, but what does Crottach mean?" asked the king.

"It means the humpback."

"Yes, that's the man, and a crafty plausible old gentleman he is. He got a charter under the Great Seal, of all his lands, from my father, dated the fifteenth of June, 1468. This did not satisfy him, and when I came to the throne he asked for a similar charter from me, which I signed on the thirteenth of February last. Its conditions seemed to be most advantageous to him, for all that was required of him was that he should keep for my use a galley of twenty-six oars, and likewise keep the peace. I am not aware whether the galley has been built or not, but there is certainly very little peace where a MacLeod has a claymore in his hand. Now, Jamie, the MacLeods are your neighbours in Sleat, so tell me what you would do were the king's crown on your head?"

"I should withdraw their charter," said MacDonald.

"That seems but just," concurred the king, "still, I doubt if our friend the humpback places very much value on the writing of his august sovereign. He knows he holds his lands as he holds his sword, his grip on the one relaxing when he loses his grip on the other. We will suppose, however, the charter withdrawn and the MacLeod laughing defiance at us. What next, MacDonald?"

"Next! I would raise an army and march against him and make him laugh on the other side of his crooked mouth."

"Hum," said the king, "that means traversing the country of the Grahams, who would probably let us by; then we next meet the Stewarts, and for my name's sake perhaps they might not molest us. We march out of their country into the land of the MacNabs, and the chief is an old friend of mine, so we need fear no disturbance there. After that we must trust ourselves to the tender mercies of the Campbells, and the outcome would depend on what they could make by attacking us or by leaving us alone. Next the Clan Cameron confronts us, and are more likely than not to dispute our passage. After them the MacDonalds, and there, of course, you stand my friend. When at last we reached the Sound of Sleat, how many of us would be left, and how are we to get across to Skye with the MacLeods on the mainland to the north of us? I am thinking, Jamie, there are lions in that path."

"The lions are imaginary, your majesty. The Grahams, the Stewarts, the MacNabs would rise not against you, but for you, delighted to be led by their king. The Campbells themselves must join you, if your force were large enough to do without them. Among the MacDonalds alone I could guarantee you an army. You forget that the Highlandman is always anxious for warfare. Leave Stirling with a thousand men and you will have ten thousand before you are at the shores of Sleat."

The king meditated for a few moments, then he looked up at his comrade with that engaging smile of his.

"It may all be as you say, Jamie. Perhaps the Highlands would rise with me instead of against me, but a prudent commander must not ignore the possibility of the reverse. However, apart from all this I am desirous of quelling the military ardour of the Highlands, not of augmenting it. It's easy enough setting the heather on fire in dry weather, but he is a wise prophet who tells where the conflagration ends. I would rather carry a bucket of water than a sword, even though it may be heavier."

"If your majesty will tell me what you have resolved upon, then I shall very blithely give you my opinion on it. It is always easier to criticise the plans of another than to put forward sensible plans of one's own."

"You are right in that, Jamie, and the remark shows I have chosen a wise counsellor. Very well, then. I have never seen the renowned island of Skye. They tell me it is even more picturesque than Stirling itself. I propose then to don a disguise, visit Skye, and find out if I can what the turbulent islanders want. If I am not able to grant their desire, I can at least deal the better with them for being acquainted."

"Your majesty does not purpose going alone?" cried MacDonald in amazement.

"Certainly not. I shall be well guarded."

"Ah, that is a different matter, and exactly what I advised."

"You advised an army, which I shall not take with me. I shall be well guarded by my good right arm, and by the still more potent right arm, if I may believe his own statement, of my friend, Jamie MacDonald of Sleat."

With bent brows MacDonald pondered for a few moments, then

looking up, said,—

"Will your majesty trust yourself in the wilderness with a prisoner?"

"There is no question of any prisoner. If you refer to yourself, you have always been at liberty to come and go as pleased you. As for trusting, I trust myself to a good comrade, and a Highland gentleman."

The king rose as he spoke and extended his hand, which the other grasped with great cordiality.

"You will get yourself out of Stirling to-night," continued the king, "as quietly as possible, and hie you to my Castle of Doune, and there wait until I come, which may be in a day, or may be in a week. I will tell the court that you have gone to your own home, which will be true enough. That will keep the gossips from saying we have each made away with the other if we both leave together. You see, Jamie, I must have some one with me who speaks the Gaelic."

"My advice has been slighted so far," said MacDonald, "yet I must give you another piece of it. We are going into a kittleish country. I advise you to order your fleet into some safe cove on the west coast. It will do the west Highlanders good to see what ships you have, for they think that no one but themselves and Noah could build a boat. When we come up into my own country we'll get a gillie or two that can be depended on to wait on us, then if we are nipped, one or other of these gillies can easily steal a boat and make for the fleet with your orders to the admiral."

"That is not a bad plan, Jamie," said the king, "and we will arrange it as you suggest."

The court wondered greatly at the sudden disappearance of James MacDonald, but none dared to make inquiry, some thinking he had escaped to the north, others, that a dungeon in Stirling Castle might reveal his whereabouts. The king was as genial as ever, and the wiseacres surmised from his manner that he meditated going off on tramp again. The fleet was ordered to Loch Torridon, where it could keep a watchful eye on turbulent Skye. The king spent three days in settling those affairs of the realm which demanded immediate attention, left Sir Donald Sinclair in temporary command, and rode off to Doune Castle.

From this stronghold there issued next morning before daylight, two well-mounted young men, who struck in a northwesterly direction for the wild Highland country. Their adventures were many and various, but MacDonald's Gaelic and knowledge of the locality carried them scatheless to the coast, although much of the journey was done on foot, for before half the way was accomplished the insurmountable difficulty of the passes compelled them to relinquish their horses. As it was unadvisable for them to enter Skye in anything like state, the two travellers contented themselves with an ordinary fishing-boat, which spread sail when the winds were fair, and depended on the oars of the crew when the sea was calm. They were accompanied by two gillies, who were intended to be useful on any ordinary occasion, and necessary in case of emergency, for the boat and its crew were to wait in any harbour of Skye that was determined upon and carry news to Loch Torridon if the presence of the fleet was deemed necessary.

It was a beautiful evening, with the sea as smooth as glass, when the fishing-boat, with sails folded, propelled by the stalwart arms of the rowers, entered a land-locked harbour, guarded by bold headlands. The name given to the place by MacDonald was so unpronounceable in Gaelic that it completely baffled the Saxon tongue of the king, but although his majesty was not aware of the fact, his own presence was to remedy that difficulty, because the place was ever afterwards known as the Haven of the King—Portree.

The scattered village climbed up the steep acclivity, and as the royal party rounded the headland and came in sight of the place, it seemed as if the inhabitants knew a distinguished visitor was about to honour them with his presence, for the whole population, cheering and gesticulating, was gathered along the shore. The gillie, however, informed his master that the demonstration was probably on the occasion of the launch of the handsome ship which they now saw, covered with flags, riding placidly on the surface of the bay. She was evidently new for her sides were fresh from the axe, without stain of either weather or wave.

"It seems the boat is yours," said MacDonald to the king in English.

"It is the twenty-six oared galley that Allaster Crottach was bound by his agreement to build for you. My man tells me that it is to be taken to-morrow to Dunvegan Castle, so it is likely to be used by Allaster Crottach himself before your majesty sets foot in it, for if it had been intended only for the king it would have been left here so that it might be convenient to the mainland. It has been built by Malcolm MacLeod, the leader of all the people in these parts. He thinks himself the most famous boat-builder in the world, so Allaster has at least fulfilled one part of his agreement, and doubtless believes this to be the finest craft afloat."

"It is indeed a beautiful barge," assented the king, admiring the graceful lines of the ship. "But what is that long-haired, bare-legged cateran screaming about with his arms going like a windmill? The crowd evidently appreciates his efforts, for they are rapturous in their applause."

MacDonald held up his hand and the oarsmen paused, while the boat gently glided towards the shore. In the still air, across the water, the impassioned Gaelic words came clearly to the voyagers.

"He is saying," translated MacDonald, after a few moments listening, "that the MacLeods are like the eternal rocks of Skye, and their enemies like the waves of the sea. Their enemies dash against them and they remain unmoved, while the wave is shattered into infinitesimal spray. So do the MacLeods defy and scorn all who come against them."

The king shrugged his shoulders.

"The man forgets that the sea also is eternal, and that it ultimately wears away the cliff. This appears to be an incitement towards war, then?"

"Oh, not so," replied MacDonald. "The man is one of their poets, and he is reciting an epic he has written, doubtless in praise of Malcolm's boat-building."

"God save us!" cried the king. "Have we then poets in Skye?"

"The whole of the Highlands is a land of poetry, your majesty," affirmed MacDonald drawing himself up proudly, "although the very poor judges of the art in Stirling may not be aware of the fact."

The king laughed heartily at this.

"I must tell that to Davie Lyndsay," he said. "But here we have another follower of the muse who has taken the place of the first. Surely nowhere else is the goddess served by votaries so unkempt. What is this one saying?"

"He says that beautiful is the western sky when the sun sinks beneath the wave, but more beautiful still is the cheek of the Rose of Skye, the daughter of their chieftain."

"Ah, that is better and more reassuring. I think either of us, Jamie, would rather be within sight of the smiles of the Rose of Skye than within reach of the claymores of her kinsmen."

By this time the assemblage on shore became aware that visitors were approaching, and the declamation ceased. Malcolm MacLeod himself came forward on the landing to greet the newcomers. He was a huge man of about fifty, tall and well proportioned, with an honest but masterful face, all in all a magnificent specimen of the race, destined by nature to be a leader of men. He received his visitors with dignified courtesy.

"I am James MacDonald," explained that young man by way of introduction, "son of the Laird of Sleat. We heard you had built a boat for the king, and so have come to see it. This is James Stuart, a friend of mine from the Lowlands, and I have brought him with me that he may learn what boat-building really is."

"You are very welcome," said MacLeod, "and just in time, for they are taking her round the headland to Dunvegan to-morrow morning. Aye, she's a bonnie boat, if I do say it myself, for no one knows her and what she'll do better than I."

"The king should be proud of her," said MacDonald.

MacLeod tossed his shaggy head and replied with a sneer,—

"It's little the king knows about boats. He should be playing with a shallop in a tub of water, instead of meddling with men's affairs. Allaster Crottach is our king, and if he graciously pleases to tickle the lad in Stirling by saying he owns the boat, Allaster himself will have the using of her. I would not spike a plank for the king, but I'd build a fleet for Allaster if he wanted it. Has your friend the Gaelic? If he has, he may tell the king what I say, when he goes back to the Lowlands."

"No, he has no Gaelic, Malcolm, but I'll put into the English whatever you like to say."

And so he gave to the king a free rendition of MacLeod's remarks, toning them down a little, but James was shrewd enough to suspect from the manner of the man of Skye, that he held his nominal monarch in slight esteem.

Malcolm MacLeod took the strangers to his own house, which was the best in the village. Almost the entire population of the port had been working on the king's boat, and now that it was finished and launched, the place had earned a holiday. Malcolm was delighted to have visitors who could bear witness to the skill of his designing, appreciate the genius of the poets and listen to the skreigh of the piping. The strangers were most hospitably entertained and entered thoroughly into the spirit of the festivities. The morning after their arrival they cheered as lustily as the others when the twenty-six oars of the king's barge struck the water and the craft moved majestically out of the harbour. They seemed to have come into a land of good-will toward all mankind; high and low vying with each other to make their stay as pleasant as possible.

"Losh, Jamie," said the king to his friend two or three days after their arrival, "I might well have ignored your advice about the ships, as I did your base counsel about the army. I need no fleet here to protect me in Skye where every man is my friend."

"That is very true," replied MacDonald, "but you must not forget that no one has any suspicion who you are. Everyone is a friend of James Stuart of the Lowlands, but I hear nobody say a good word for the king."

"What have they against him?" asked the Guidman of Ballengeich with a frown, for it was not complimentary to hear that in a part of his own dominion he was thought little of.

"It isn't exactly that they have anything against the king," said MacDonald, perhaps not slow to prick the self-esteem of his comrade, "but they consider him merely a boy, of small weight in their affairs one way or another. They neither fear him nor respect him. The real monarch of these regions is the humpback in Dunvegan Castle; and even if they knew you were the king, your sternest command would have no effect against his slightest wish, unless you had irresistible force at the back of you."

"Ah, Jamie, you are simply trying to justify the bringing of the fleet round Scotland."

"Indeed and I am not. The only use to which you can put your fleet will be to get you away from here in case of trouble. As far as its force is concerned, these islanders would simply take to the hills and defy it."

"Ah, well," said the king, "I'll make them think better of me before I am done with them."

The week's festivities were to end with a grand poetical contest. All the bards of the island were scribbling; at any rate, those who could write. The poets who had not that gift were committing their verses to memory that they might be prepared to recite them before the judges, three famous minstrels, who were chosen from three districts on the island, thus giving variety and a chance of fairness to their decisions.

The king resolved to enter this competition, and he employed MacDonald every evening translating into the language of Skye, the poem which had been considered so good in Stirling, and MacDonald was to recite it for him at the contest. But this Homeric competition was endangered by disquieting news brought to the island by the fishermen. They reported that a powerful fleet had been seen rounding the northern coast of Scotland, and was now making towards the south. This unexpected intelligence seemed to change instantaneously the attitude of the islanders towards their two guests. Suspicion electrified the air. The news of the sighting of the fleet, coming so quickly on the advent of two strangers, who apparently had no particular business on the island, caused them to be looked upon as spies, and for a day or two they were in danger of being treated as such. The king's alertness of mind saved the situation. He had brought with him from Stirling, in case of emergencies, several sheets of blank parchment, each bearing the Great Seal of Scotland. Once more the useful MacDonald was his amanuensis. A proclamation in Gaelic was written and the signature of James the Fifth inscribed thereon. This document was enclosed with a communication, containing directions to the admiral of the fleet, and MacDonald entrusted the packet to one of his gillies, with orders that sail should be set for Loch Torridon, and the message given to the officer in command.

Three days later the ferment on the island was immeasurably increased when the guard on the headland reported that a ship of war was making direct for the harbour. A horseman was despatched full gallop to Dunvegan Castle to inform the head of the clan of the mysterious visit of the two men, followed so soon by the approach of a belligerent vessel. But before the messenger was ten miles on his way, the ceremony was over and done with. The big ship sailed majestically through the narrows, cast anchor and fired a salute. A well-manned boat was lowered and rowed to the shore. There stepped from the boat an officer in a splendid uniform, followed by a lieutenant and half a dozen men, one of whom carried the flag of Scotland. This company marched to the cross, which stood in the centre of the village, and the crowd sullenly followed, with Malcolm MacLeod at their head, not knowing what the action of the naval officer might portend, and in absence of definite orders from their chief, hesitating to oppose this inland march. Many of those on the fleet were Highlanders, and the second in command was one of them. This man mounted the three steps at the foot of the cross and stood with his back against the upright stone. His chief handed him a roll of parchment, and the subordinate officer in a loud voice, and in excellent Gaelic, cried,—

"A Proclamation from His Most Excellent Majesty, James the Fifth of Scotland! God save the King!"

At this the chief officer raised his sword in salute, and his men sent up a cheer, but the aggregation was not seconded by any of the large concourse there gathered together. Undaunted by this frigid reception the officer unrolled the manuscript and read its contents in a voice that reached to the furthest outskirts of the crowd:

"I, James of Scotland, lawful King of this realm, do proclaim to all loyal subjects, that the safety and liberty of my land depends on an unconquerable fleet, and that the merit of the fleet consists in stout well-built ships, therefore the man whom I, the King, delight to honour is he whose skill produces the best sea-going craft, so I hereon inscribe the name of Malcolm MacLeod, master shipbuilder, a man who has designed and constructed a boat of which all Scotland has reason to be proud. The King's barge of twenty-six oars, planned by Malcolm MacLeod and built for him by the people of Skye, will be used as a model for all ship-builders in the Scottish navy."

The reader now looked up from his parchment and gazed over the assemblage.

"Is Malcolm MacLeod here?" he asked. "Let him step forward."

The giant, somewhat dazed, walking like a man in a dream, approached the foot of the cross. The officer rolled the proclamation and presented it to the shipbuilder, saying:—

"From the hand of the king, to the hand of Malcolm MacLeod."

Malcolm accepted it, muttering half with a smile, half with a frown,—

"E-god, the king knows a good boat when he gets it."

Then the officer uplifted his sword and cried,—

"God save the king;" and now the hills around re-echoed with the cheering.

The little company without another word retraced their steps to the small boat, and made for the ship which was now facing outward, anchor hoisted and sails spread once more, so the watching Highlanders had a view of a large vessel superbly managed, as the west wind which brought her into the harbour took her safely out again.

The royal young man had a striking lesson on the fickleness of the populace. Heretofore as MacDonald had truly said, no one had a good word to say for the king; now it was evident that James V. of Scotland was the greatest and wisest monarch that ever sat on a throne.

Malcolm MacLeod had been always so proud of his skill that this proclamation could hardly augment his self-esteem, but it suddenly changed his views regarding his august overlord. In conversation ever after it became, "I and the king," and he was almost willing to admit that James was very nearly as great a man as Alexander MacLeod of Dunvegan.

The enthusiasm was so great that several bards composed special poems in honour of the king of Scotland, and next day the effusions were to be heard at the cross, and the prizes awarded. The first thing done, however, after the departure of the ship, was to send another mounted messenger to Dunvegan Castle, so that the lord of the island might learn that no invasion was to be feared from the fleet. The parchment proclamation was sent on to the chief, ostensibly in explanation of the ship's visit, but probably because Malcolm was not loth to let the head of the clan know what the head of the country thought of his workmanship.

It was early next morning that the reading and reciting of the poems began, and so lengthy were these effusions that it was well past noon before the last had been heard. To the chagrin of James he found himself fifteen on the list when the honours were awarded. MacDonald, endeavouring to keep a straight face, told the king of the judges' decision, adding,—

"It will be as well not to let Davie Lyndsay know of this."

"Oh, you may tell whom you please," cried the king. "I was sure you would bungle it in the Gaelic."

The king was pacing up and down the room in no very good humour, so the young Highlander thought it best not to reply. He was saved however, from the embarrassment of silence by the entrance of Malcolm MacLeod.

"You are in great good fortune," said Malcolm. "The messengers have returned with a score of horsemen at their backs, and Dunvegan himself invites you to the castle."

MacDonald seemed in no way jubilant over what his host considered the utmost honour that could be bestowed upon two strangers.

"What does he say?" demanded the king.

"He says that MacLeod of Dunvegan has invited us to his castle."

"Well, we will go then. I suppose we can get horses here, or shall we journey round by boat?"

"I understand," replied MacDonald, "that the chief has sent horses for us, and furthermore an escort of a score of men, so I'm thinking we have very little choice about the matter."

"Very well," returned the king with a shrug of indifference, "let us be off and see our new host. I wonder if he will be as easily flattered as the one we are leaving."

"I doubt it," said MacDonald seriously.

The King Drinks

The two young men mounted the small shaggy horses that had been provided for them by the forethought of their future host, MacLeod of Dunvegan. Apparently the king had forgotten all about his crushing defeat in the poetical contest of the day before, for he was blithe and gay, the most cheerful of those assembled, adventuring now and then scraps of Gaelic that he had picked up, and his pronunciation contributed much to the hilarity of the occasion.

MacDonald, on the other hand, was gloomy and taciturn, as if already some premonition of the fate that awaited him at Dunvegan cast its shadow before. The news of the great condescension of the laird in inviting two strangers to his castle had spread through all the land, and, early as was the hour, the whole population of the district had gathered to wish the travellers a cordial farewell. The escort, as the king called the score of men, who were to act as convoy from one port to the other; or the guard, as MacDonald termed them, sat on their horses in silence, awaiting the word of command to set forth.

At last this word was given, and the procession began its march amidst the cheers of the people and a skirling of the pipes. The distance was little more than seven leagues over a wild uninviting country. MacDonald sat his horse dejected and silent, for the prospect confronting him was far from alluring. The king was incognito, he was not; and he had begun to doubt the wisdom of having given his actual designation to the people of Skye, for the relations between this island and the mainland were at that time far from being of the most cordial description.

Dunvegan Castle was a grim stronghold in which the MacLeods sat so secure that all the efforts of all the MacDonalds, even if they were for once united, could not dislodge them. It was one of the most remote inhabited places in all Scotland, its next neighbour to the west being that new land of America discovered not yet fifty years. For the son of one Highland chieftain to come so completely into the power of another, his own people knowing practically nothing of his whereabouts, was a situation that did not commend itself to the young man. Allaster Crottach was celebrated more for craft than for violence. He had extended and consolidated his possessions with the skill of a diplomatist rather than by the arms of his soldiers, and MacDonald thought it quite likely that a slice of Sleat might be the ransom for his release. If through any incautious remark of his comrade the Crottach became aware that he held not only MacDonald of Sleat but also the King of Scotland, the fates only knew what might happen. The king, however, appeared to have no forebodings, but trotted along with great complacency, commenting now and then on the barrenness of the landscape.

The party had accomplished little more than half the distance, when, as they fronted a slight elevation, there came to them over the hills wild pipe music, louder than anything of that kind the king had ever heard.

"The MacLeod is evidently about to welcome us in state," said his majesty to MacDonald, "he must have the very monarch of pipers in his train."

"The MacRimmon," admitted MacDonald, "are acknowledged to be the best pipers in all the Highlands, and they are hereditary musicians to the MacLeod. The sounds we hear indicate that a number of pipers are playing in unison."

On reaching the brow of the hill they found this was indeed the case. There were from thirty to fifty pipers, but they evidently bore no greeting to the travellers, for the musical party was marching in the same direction as themselves, playing vigorously as they swung along. At the instance of the king, MacDonald made inquiries regarding this extraordinary spectacle. The taciturn commander of the guard answered briefly that it was the College of Pipers. The students were marching back to Bocraig on the other side of Loch Follart, where instruction in piping was bestowed by the MacRimmon; this excursion over the hills giving them training in piping and in tramping at the same time. The musical regiment took its way straight across the moors and so very soon was lost sight of by the two travellers, who kept to a track which

143

was more or less of a road.

In due time the cavalcade reached Dunvegan Castle, and even a man accustomed to so stout a fortress as that of Stirling could not but be struck by the size, the strength, and the situation of this frowning stronghold; yet, extensive as it was, its proprietor evidently found it inadequate for his ambitions, as he was now building a massive tower which added a further dignity to the structure.

The king and his companion were received at the front entrance by an old man, whom each at once knew could not be their host, for his back had originally been straight enough, though now slightly stooped through age. He led them within, and up a stair direct to the apartments reserved for them. Their aged conductor spoke no English, so the burden of conversation fell on MacDonald. As soon as the latter perceived that he and his friend were to be separated, the king lodged at one end of the castle, and himself at the other, he protested against this arrangement, demanding two adjoining rooms. The old man replied that he was following instructions given, and if the rooms assigned were not satisfactory, his master would doubtless change them on the morrow.

"But, my good man," expostulated MacDonald, "we expect to be leaving the castle to-morrow."

"In that case," replied their cicerone with a scarcely perceptible shrug of the shoulders, "it makes but little difference for one night." The king inquiring into the purport of the discussion, quite agreed with the elderly guide, that the matter was of small moment.

"If our genial innkeeper intends to murder us," he said, "we shall be quite as helpless together as separate, for he has irresistible force at his command. If we are in a trap there is little use in snarling at the bars. By all accounts Dunvegan is a shrewd man, and I can see no object which he can attain by doing harm to either of us. If he had a son who was next heir to the position I hold, I confess I might sleep uneasily to-night; but as he must know that the king's fleet is hovering about his coast, and that his castle would make a most excellent target for it, as he cannot transport his house to the hills should the ships sail up the loch, I don't see what he can gain by maltreating two men, whom he must suspect of having some connection with the advent of the fleet."

"Oh, I have no thought," replied MacDonald, "that the Eagle of Dunvegan would fly so high as you suggest, but there are lowlier perches on which he may like to fix his talons. He has long cast covetous eyes across the Sound of Sleat to the mainland, and, whatever he knows or suspects, he is sure of one thing, which is that he has the son of the Laird of Sleat safely landed in his own house."

"How distrustful you Highlanders are of each other!" cried the young monarch laughing. "Bless me, Jamie, no bargain made in durance will hold; then you must remember you have me behind you, and I have all the power in Scotland behind me."

"That is very true, but the power of nothing is behind either of us if we cannot get word to the outside world. Last night on learning we were invited to this place, I searched for my gillies, but without success. My boat and its crew have been taken elsewhere. So you see there is at least a design to cut our communications. I'm thinking we'll see more of Loch Follart from this window for a while than of the field of Bannockburn from Stirling Towers."

"I quite agree with you, Jamie, that we're fairly nabbed, but the old gentleman who has us in thrall can make nothing by ill-using us. Sooner or later he must divulge his plan, whatever it is, before he can benefit from it, and when he does that it will be time enough to consider what course we are to pursue." Then turning suddenly towards their guide, who had been standing motionless during this conversation, the king said sharply in English,—

"Is your master at home?"

The old man made no reply, but looked at MacDonald as if for translation. The latter repeated the question in Gaelic and received an affirmative answer.

"He says the laird is at home. He has no English."

"I wasn't just sure of that, so I tested it by an abrupt question, thus locking the door after the horse was stolen, for we have spoken rather plainly before him, and so have proved ourselves in the beginning very poor conspirators. However, I care little what the next move is so long as it brings us something to eat. Clear your gloomy brow, Jamie, and tell them in the most culinary Gaelic that this is not a fast-day with us, and the ride across the moors has increased our appetites."

MacDonald followed his custodian down the long corridor, and the king entered the apartment assigned to him.

After sufficient time had elapsed to allow the travellers to remove the traces of travel from their persons, they were summoned to a small room where they found a most welcome and substantial meal set out for them. A generous flagon of wine stood by each trencher; it was the first the king had had an opportunity of tasting since he left his capital, and he seized upon the measure with some eagerness.

"Here's to the MacLeod!" he cried.

"I drink to the king, and good luck to him!" said MacDonald.

"I drink to anything, so long as the wine is sound," rejoined his majesty, enjoying a deep draught. "E-god, Jamie," he cried setting the flagon down again, "that's better claret than we have in Stirling."

"There is no reason why it shouldn't be excellent," replied MacDonald, "for the laird's own ships bring it direct from the coast of France to the coast of Skye, and there's little chance of adulteration between the two."

When the repast was finished the aged man who had received them at the door entered and announced that MacLeod of MacLeod was ready to greet them in his study. They followed him and were ushered into an oblong room somewhat larger than the one they had left. The king was astonished to find the walls lined with numerous volumes, some of the tomes massive in heavy binding. As books were not over-plentiful even in the realms of civilisation, he had not expected to find them in a corner of the world so remote.

Allaster the Hunchback sat by the side of a huge oaken table, and he did not rise from his chair when his visitors were presented to him, either because he wished the better to conceal the deformity which gave him his nickname, or because he did not consider his guests of such importance as to deserve a more courteous reception. He addressed them in excellent English, and the king constituted himself spokesman for the occasion, MacDonald standing by taciturn, in spite of the excellence of the wine, which indeed he had consumed somewhat sparingly.

"I understand," began MacLeod, "that you have honoured my poor rugged island of Skye with your presence for some days."

"The honour, sir, has been ours," replied the king with an inclination of his head. "I was visiting my friend MacDonald in Sleat and heard of the king's barge, so we came over to see it."

"This is your friend MacDonald of Sleat then?"

"Yes. May I have the pleasure of presenting Mr. James MacDonald to the MacLeod?"

The two Highlanders, one sitting, one standing, bowed somewhat distantly to each other as the king, with a flourish of his hand, made the introduction.

"Perhaps," continued MacLeod suavely, "your friend from Sleat will do a like obligement for yourself."

"I shall not put him to that trouble," said the king airily. "I am of such small account that it would be a pity to put upon a Highland chieftain the task of pronouncing my name. I am called the Guidman of Ballengeich, very much at your service, sir."

"Guidman, meaning farmer of course?" asked Dunvegan.

"Meaning small farmer," said the king with a graceful inclination of the head.

The tones of the MacLeod had not been too cordial from the first, but they became less so at this confession of low quality on the part of his visitor.

147

"You will forgive my ignorance, but where is Ballengeich?"

"It is a little steading near Stirling, but of more value than its size would indicate, for I am fortunate in possessing the custom of the court."

"You cater for the castle then?" asked MacLeod frigidly.

"Yes, in various ways."

MacLeod turned from his loquacious guest as if he desired to hold no further converse with him, and thus, however crafty he might be, he convinced the king that the castle had no suspicion whom it held. MacLeod said abruptly to his other visitor, fastening his piercing eyes upon him,—

"I heard you were prisoner at Stirling?"

"Prisoner, sir!" cried MacDonald angrily, the red colour mounting to the roots of his hair. But before he could speak further his garrulous companion struck in.

"What an absurd rumour. MacDonald a prisoner! I assure you he was no more a prisoner at Stirling Castle than he is at this moment in Dunvegan Castle."

"Ah," said McLeod turning again to the farmer, his eyes partially closing, examining the other with more severe scrutiny than had previously been the case. "He was at liberty to come and go as he pleased, then?"

"As free as air, sir; otherwise how could he have visited my slight holding and thus become acquainted with me?"

"I thought perhaps he had met you in the courtyard of Stirling with a sack of corn on your shoulder."

The king laughed heartily at this.

"I said a small farmer certainly, but I am not quite so unimportant as you seem to imply. I have a better horse to carry my corn than the one that to-day carried me to Dunvegan."

The laird ignored this disparagement of his cattle.

148

"You came to Skye then to see the king's boat, of which you had heard favourable report? The news of her seems to have travelled very quickly."

"Indeed and that's true," said the king complacently. "Information spreads rapidly in the Highlands."

"It seems to spread to the Lowlands as well. You heard the king's proclamation perhaps?"

"Yes, we heard the pronouncement."

"It's possible you came from the fleet?"

"No. We came overland."

"Had you heard of the fame of Malcolm's boat before you left Stirling?"

"I did not say we left Stirling. As a matter of fact we left the small village of Doune some miles to the north of it, and at that time had heard nothing either of Malcolm or his boat."

"Hum," ejaculated the laird, rummaging among his papers on the table. The king glancing in the direction of MacLeod's hands saw spread out the charter which he himself had signed, giving MacLeod tenure of his land, and beside it, as if this island magnate had been comparing the signatures was the recent draft of the proclamation commending Malcolm MacLeod's boat. This document Dunvegan passed to the Guidman of Ballengeich.

"You know the king's writing perhaps? Will you tell me whether this is, as I suspect, a forgery?"

James wrinkled his brows and examined the signature with minute care. "I have seen the writing of his majesty," he said at last, "but MacDonald here knows it better than I. What do you think of it, Jamie?" he continued, passing on the parchment to his friend. "Is this the real Mackay, or is it not?"

"It is," said MacDonald shortly and definitely.

"You say that is the actual signature of the king?" inquired MacLeod.

"I could swear it is as genuine as the one on your charter," replied

MacDonald.

"Well, now," said MacLeod leaning back in his chair, "will you resolve a mystery for me? How is it likely that James Fifth ever heard of Malcolm MacLeod's boat? and if he did, do you consider it probable that an august monarch would compliment a Highland cateran's skill with the axe?"

"James is a douce body," said the king, "and knows more of what is going on in his realm than folk who think themselves wiser might imagine."

"You hint, then," said MacLeod, drawing down his black brows, "that his majesty may have spies in Skye?"

"Truth to tell, Laird of Dunvegan, it is more than likely," admitted the king, with an air of great candour.

The frown on MacLeod's countenance deepened, and he said harshly,—

"You two gentlemen probably know the fate of spies when they are captured. Their fate is a short shrift, and a long rope."

"And quite properly so," rejoined the king promptly.

"I am glad that you are so well informed, and need no instruction from me," commented the Crottach with menace in his tone.

Suddenly the king's manner changed, and the air of authority which was natural to him asserted itself.

"MacLeod of Skye," he cried, "this discussion and beating about the bush is interesting, but nothing at all to the purpose. You are hinting that we two are spies, and I tell you there are no spies, and can be no spies on this island."

"I have only your word to set against my own doubts," said the MacLeod.

"My word and your doubts are both aside from the purpose. Your mind has become confused. Unless you are at war with James of Scotland, there can be spies neither in the domain you hold under his hand, nor in the kingdom over which he rules. Are you a rebel against your king, MacLeod of Skye?"

"That I am not," answered Allaster hastily, and with evident discomposure.

"Very well then. You see the absurdity of an argument on espionage. MacDonald and I have as much right on the island of Skye as you have, because it is part of the Kingdom of Scotland, and we are loyal, if humble subjects of his majesty."

"You are not come here then to report on the condition of Skye?"

"We came here of our own free will; the messengers of no man, and we are to report to no man. If the king should ask me any question regarding my visit to Skye, I would answer him, that I had met with the utmost courtesy, except from its chief. I would say that MacLeod of MacLeod was so ignorant regarding the usages of good society that he received us sitting down, and never asked us to be seated, an error in politeness which I was myself forced to amend. MacDonald, plant yourself on that chair beside you. I will take this one."

MacDonald promptly obeyed the command, and the king seated himself, throwing one leg over the other and leaning back in comfort.

"Now, my Lord of Skye," he said, "have you any further questions to ask, or any additional hints to bestow upon your guests, at present in your sullen presence upon your own invitation?"

The chieftain regarded the king in silence for a few moments, then said without change of countenance,—

"By God! you may be a small farmer, but you are a brave man. You are the first who has questioned the authority of the MacLeod on his own ground. So the case being without precedent, one has to be made, and that will require some thought. We will postpone the question until later. I trust you will both honour me with your presence at dinner this evening, but if you prefer it, you may sup alone in your own apartments."

"We are sociable travellers," said the king rising, for the laird's words had in them an inflection of dismissal, "and we will have great pleasure in accepting seats at your table."

151

Then with a bow to the man who still remained in his chair, the king and his comrade withdrew. They consulted together for a time in the room of the former, but reached no definite decision. MacDonald urged that they should come to an understanding with their host at once, and learn whether they were prisoners or free men, but the king held that Allaster should have the time for thinking over the situation which had been practically agreed on.

"There is no hurry," he said. "Each of us is younger than Allaster and so there is time to bide."

On being summoned to the great dining-hall that night, they found a company awaiting dinner numbering perhaps a score, all men. A piper was marching up and down the room making the timbers ring with his martial music. The MacLeod stood at the head of his table, a stalwart man whose massive head seemed sunk rather deep between his broad shoulders, but otherwise, perhaps because his costume was cunningly arranged, there was slight indication of the deformity with which he was afflicted. He greeted his guests with no great show of affability, and indicated the bench at his right hand as the seat of MacDonald. The young Highlander hesitated to take the place of preference, and glanced uneasily at his comrade.

"I am slightly deaf in my right ear," said the king good naturedly, "and as I should be grieved to miss any observations you may make, I will, with your permission, occupy the place you would bestow upon my friend."

MacLeod looked sternly at the speaker for a moment, but seeing that MacDonald, without protest moved speedily round to the left, he said at last,—

"Settle it as pleases you, but I should have thought a Highland chieftain took precedence of a Lowland huckster."

"Not a huckster exactly," explained the king with a smile. "My patrimony of Ballengeich may be small, but such as it is, I am the undisputed laird of it, while at best MacDonald is but the son of a laird, so because of my deaf ear, and according to your own rules of precedence, I think I may claim the place of honour at your right." And as the MacLeod, with an angry growl sat down, the king and MacDonald followed his example. The others took their places in some haste, and with more or less of disorder. It was plain that MacLeod preferred the silent Highlander to the more loquacious farmer of Ballengeich, for during the meal he addressed most of his remarks to the man on his left, although his advances were not as cordially received as perhaps they might have been. The king showed no resentment at this neglect, but concentrated his attention on the business at hand.

When the eating was done with, the servants placed three large flagons before their master and the two who sat on either side of him. These they filled to the brim with wine.

"Gentlemen," said MacLeod, "it is a custom in this castle that our guests, to show they are good men and true, each empty one of these flagons at a draught, and without drawing breath. Will you then accompany me to any toast you may care to name?"

"The wine I have already consumed at your hospitable board," said the king, "is the best that ever ran down a thirsty man's throat; but if I supplement it with so generous and instant an addition, I fear my legs will refuse their service, even if my head retain sense enough to give the command."

"That need not trouble you," said MacLeod, "for in the last hundred years no man has insulted this vintage by leaving the hall on his own feet. There stand your legs against the wall, Guidman of Ballengeich."

The king, glancing over his shoulder, saw standing against the wall a row of brawny gillies, each two of whom supported a stretcher, whose use was at once apparent.

"Very well," cried the king to his host; "give you a suitable toast, MacLeod, and I will enter with you the rosy realms of the red wine."

MacLeod then stood up.

"I give you," he said, "the King of Scotland. May he be blest with more wisdom than were some of his ancestors!" This he repeated in Gaelic, and the sentiment was received uproariously, for the wine was already making itself felt in the great hall.

If MacLeod had any design in offering this toast it did not appear on the surface, and if he expected a hesitancy on the part of his guests to do honour to it, he was disappointed, for each young man rose with the rest.

"Here's to the king!" cried the one on his right, "and may he imbibe wisdom as I imbibe wine." Then raising the flagon to his lips he drained it dry and set it with a crash on the table again.

MacLeod and MacDonald drank more slowly, but they ultimately achieved the same end. Then all seated themselves once more, and the drinking continued without the useless intervention of further talk. One by one the revellers sank under the table unnoticed by their noisy comrades, to be quickly pounced upon by the watchful stretcher-bearers, who, with a deftness evidently the result of much practice, placed the helpless individual on the carrier and marched off with him. This continuous disappearance of the fallen rapidly thinned the ranks of the combatants struggling with the giant Bacchus.

The king had been reluctant to enter this contest, fearing the red wine would loosen his tongue, but as the evening wore on he found all his resolution concentrated in a determination to walk to his bed. MacDonald proved no protection. Early in the bout his unaccustomed head descended gently upon the table and he was promptly carried off to rest.

At last MacLeod and the king sat alone in the hall, that looked larger now it was so nearly empty; and James, as a test of what sense remained to him, set himself to count the torches burning more and more dimly in the haze of their own smoke. But he gave up the attempt when he saw that they had increased by hundreds and thousands, and were engaged in a wild pyrotechnic dance to the rhythm of the last march that had been played on the pipes. He swayed over towards his host and smote him uncertainly on the shoulder.

"MacLeod," he cried, "I challenge you to stand, and I'll wager you I can walk further down the corridor with fewer collisions against either wall than any man in Skye."

With difficulty the king rose to his feet, and as he did so the stool on which he sat, because of a lurch against it, fell clattering to the floor.

"The very benches are drunk, MacLeod, and the table sways like a ship at sea. That stool is as insecure as a throne. Rise up if you can and see if yours is any better."

But the MacLeod sat helpless, glaring at him from under his shaggy eyebrows. Seeing him stationary the king laughed so heartily that he nearly unbalanced himself, and was forced to cling for support to the edge of the table. Then straightening himself to excessive rigidity he muttered,—

"Good-night, MacLeod. Sit there and see the rule of your house broken by your——" If the next word were "monarch," or "king," it was never uttered, for as James made his uncertain way towards the door, the expert gillies, who knew their business, came up behind him, swooped the stretcher against his unreliant legs, and they failing instantly, he fell backward on the stoutly woven web between the two poles. There was a guttural laugh from MacLeod, and the prone man helplessly waving his hands, shouted,—

"Unfair, by Saint Andrew, unfair! Curse the foe who attacks a man from the rear."

The King Sails

The young men awoke somewhat late next day with heads reasonably clear, a very practical testimonial to the soundness of their previous night's vintage.

"What's to be done?" asked the king.

MacDonald proposed that they should repair instantly to MacLeod and demand of him conveyance and safe conduct to the mainland.

"We can scarcely do that," demurred the king, "until we are sure that detention is intended. Let us put the matter at once to a practical test, and see if we are prevented from leaving the castle. If we are, then is the time for protest."

Acting on this suggestion, the two went outside and took the road by which they had come. They found an agile young gillie at their heels before they were out of sight of Dunvegan.

"Why are you following us?" asked MacDonald, in Gaelic.

"I was told to wait on your lordships," returned the man.

"We need no waiting on; turn back."

But the gillie shook his shaggy uncovered head and patiently trod in their footsteps.

"Let us see how far he will follow," said the king as he strode on. The gillie accompanied them for half an hour or more without making any protest, but at last he said to MacDonald that he thought it was time to return.

"We are going through to the coast we came from," replied MacDonald, "and do not intend to return."

At this the gillie drew from his belt a short black tube that looked like a practising chanter, which indeed it was, and on this he blew a few shrill notes.

Up to that moment the way had been clear, but now there appeared over the hill in front of them a dozen armed men, who approached carelessly as if they had merely happened to be in the neighbourhood, or were journeying together toward the castle.

"I think it is time to go back," suggested the gillie in a dull, uninterested voice.

"I think it is myself," replied MacDonald.

And so the futile excursion came to an end.

Once more in the castle they were confronted again by the question, What next?

"I am certain," said the king, "that if MacLeod is attempting to hold us, there is little use in making appeal to him, and we have small chance of getting word to the fleet. I propose then to coerce him. He was alone in his study yesterday, and he may be alone there now. A sword's point at a man's throat is an irresistible argument."

"But will he keep his word if he gives it under distress?" objected MacDonald.

"I think he will, but it is better not to put too strong a temptation on him. If we come on him alone we will make him sign a pass for us. Then we will gag and tie him securely, convey him, when the way is clear, to this room, where he will be less likely to be looked for. We will then give him the consolation that if his pass proves useless we will return and finish the business by sending him into a less troublesome world."

This advice was no sooner promulgated than it was acted upon. The pair traversed the corridors unseen until they came to the door of the study, then, slipping out their swords, they entered quickly unannounced. The sight which confronted them was so unexpected that each stood there with drawn sword in hand as if stricken into stone.

MacLeod was not in the room, but in his stead, beside the wall of books, her hand upraised, taking down a small vellum-covered volume, was the most beautiful young girl, of perhaps nineteen or twenty, that either of them had ever looked upon. She seemed surprised at their abrupt entrance and remained statuesquely in her position, as motionless as they. The young woman was the first of the three to recover her composure. Relinquishing the book to the shelf, the hand came down to her side, and she said in most charming, liquid tones, but in broken English,—

"You are looking for my father perhaps?"

The king, ever gallant, swept his hat from his head and bowed low, his alertness of mind saving the situation, for he answered quickly,—

"Indeed no, my lady. We thought the room was empty, so I implore you to pardon our intrusion. We were here yesterday, and my friend and I have just had a dispute regarding the size of these gigantic tomes on the lower shelf; my friend insisting that they exceeded our sword blades in length. Pardon me madam?" and the king stepped briskly to the largest book, laying his sword down its back as if in measurement.

"There, Jamie," he cried, "I have won the wager. I knew it was not more than three quarters the length of my blade."

The glance of fear to which the young woman had treated them departed from her face, and she smiled slightly at the young man's eagerness.

"I gather from your remark," he said, "that you are Miss MacLeod of Dunvegan. May I introduce my friend, James MacDonald of Sleat. My own name is James Stuart, and for a time we are your father's guests at Dunvegan."

The young lady with inimitable grace bowed her queenly head to each of them in turn. The men slipped their swords quietly back into their scabbards.

"I give you good welcome to Dunvegan," said the girl. "I regret that I do not speak fair the English."

"Indeed, my lady," rejoined the susceptible king, "it is the most charming English I ever heard."

The fair stranger laughed in low and most melodious cadence, like a distant cathedral's chime falling on the evening air.

"I am thinking you will be flattering me," she said, "but I know my English is not good, for there are few in these parts that I can speak to in it."

"I shall be delighted to be your teacher," replied the king with his most courteous intonation. He knew from experience that any offer of tutorship from him had always proved exceedingly acceptable to the more dainty sex, and this knowledge gave him unbounded confidence while it augmented his natural self-esteem.

"It is perhaps that you already speak the Gaelic?" suggested the young woman.

"Alas! no madam. But I should be overjoyed to learn and there, it may be, you will accept me in the part of pupil. You will find me a devoted and most obedient scholar. I am in a way what you might call a poet, and I am told on every hand that Gaelic is the proper medium for that art."

A puzzled expression troubled the face of the girl as she endeavoured to follow the communication addressed to her, but MacDonald sprang somewhat eagerly to the rescue, and delivered a long harangue in her native language. Her delight was instant, the cloud on her brow disappearing as if by magic under the genial influence of the accustomed converse. The king's physiognomy also underwent a change but the transformation was not so pleasing as that which had illumined the countenance of the girl. His majesty distinctly scowled at the intrepid subject who had so impetuously intervened, but the pair paid slight attention to him, conversing amiably together, much to their mutual pleasure.

Now, it is nowhere considered polite to use a language not understood by some one person in the party. This fact MacDonald knew perfectly well, and he doubtless would have acted differently if he had taken the time to think, but he had become so engrossed by the beauty of the lady, that, for the moment, every other consideration seemed to have fled from his mind. Miss MacLeod is to be excused because she probably supposed a Stuart to be more or less acquainted with the language, in spite of his former disclaimer, which it is not likely she fully comprehended. So she talked fluently and laughed lightly, while one of her auditors was consumed by an anger he dared not show.

The tension of the situation was changed rather than relieved, by the silent opening of the door, and the pause of MacLeod himself on the threshold, gazing dubiously at the group before him. The animation of the girl fell from her the moment she beheld her father, and the young men, turning, were confronted by the gloomy features of the chieftain. The MacLeod closed the door softly, and, without a word, walked to his chair beside the table. The girl, bowing slightly, with visible restraint, quitted the room, and, as she did so, MacDonald's alertness again proved his friend, for he tip-toed quickly to the door, before the king, accustomed to be waited upon rather than waiting, recollected himself; and held it open for the lady, making a gallant sweep with his bonnet as she passed out.

When the supple young man returned to his place beside the king he said in a whisper,—

"No sword's point play with the father of such a beauty, eh?"

To this remark his majesty made no reply, but said rather gruffly and abruptly to his host,—

"Do you hold us prisoners in this castle, sir?"

"That will depend on the answers I get from you," replied the MacLeod slowly. "Are you two or either of you, emissaries of the king?"

"We are not."

"Does the king know you are here?"

"Regarding the king, his knowledge or his doings, you had better address your inquiries to him personally. We have no authority to speak for his majesty."

"You are merely two private gentlemen, then, come all this distance to satisfy a love of travel and a taste for scenery?"

"You have stated the case with great accuracy, sir."

"Yesterday you spoke of my lack of manners in failing to ask you to be seated; I shall now refer to a breach of politeness on your own part. It is customary when strangers visit a province under an acknowledged ruler, that they should make a formal call upon the ruler before betaking themselves to other portions of his territory. You remained for several days in Skye without taking the trouble to inform me of your arrival."

"Sir," replied James haughtily, "I dispute your contention entirely. You are not the ruler of Skye."

"Who is then?"

"The King of Scotland, of course."

The MacLeod laughed in a fashion that somewhat resembled the snarl of an angry dog.

"Of course, as you say. No one disputes that James is king of all Scotland, and I would be the last to question his right, because I hold my lands under charter bearing his signature, carrying the Great Seal of the kingdom; nevertheless, the MacLeods held Skye long before the present royal family of Scotland were heard of, and I would have been MacLeod of MacLeod although James had never put his hand to this parchment. Meanwhile, I take the risk of detaining you until I learn more about you, and if the king makes objection, I shall apologise."

"You will apologise," said James sternly.

"Oh, it is easily done, and fair words smooth many a difficulty. I shall write to him if he complain, that I asked especially if you were his men, that you denied it, and so, both for his safety and my own, I considered it well to discover whether or not you were enemies of the realm. If the father of MacDonald is offended I shall be pleased to meet him either on sea or land, in anger or in friendship, and as for you, who talk so glibly of the king, I would warn you that many things happen in Skye that the king knows nothing of, besides the making of strong drink."

The king made him a courtier-like bow for this long speech, and answered lightly,—

"The cock crows blithely on his own midden. Your midden is here, while mine is far away, therefore the contest in crowing is somewhat uneven. Nevertheless I indulge in a final flapping of my wings and an effort of the throat when I say that you will apologise, not by writing at your ease in Dunvegan Castle, but on your bended knees at Stirling."

"That's as may be," said the MacLeod indifferently, and it was quite obvious that he remained unmoved by the threat. "Gentlemen, I have the honour to wish you good morning."

"One moment. Are we then to consider ourselves prisoners?"

"You may consider yourselves whatever best pleases you. If you make another attempt like the one you indulged in this morning, I shall clap you both in the deepest dungeons I possess. Some would even go so far as to call that imprisonment, but if each gives me his word of honour that he will make no attempt at escape, and also that he will not communicate with Stirling, then you are as free of my house and my grounds as if you were the most welcome of guests. But I warn you that if, when you pass your words, you attempt to tamper with any of my men, I shall know of it very soon after, and then comes the dungeon."

The king hesitated and looked at his friend, but MacDonald, who had taken no part in this conversation, seemed in an absent dream, his eyes gazing on vacancy, or perhaps beholding a vision that entranced him.

"What do you say, MacDonald?" enquired the king sharply.

MacDonald recovered himself with a start.

"To what?" he asked.

"To the terms proposed by our gaoler."

"I did not hear them; what are they?"

"Will you give your word not to escape?"

"Oh, willingly."

"And not to communicate with Stirling?"

"I don't care if I never see Stirling again."

The king turned to the chief.

"There is little difficulty, you see," he said, "with your fellow Highlander. I however, am supposed to be a Lowlander, and therefore cautious. I give you my word not to communicate with Stirling. As for the other proviso, I amend it as follows. I shall not leave this island without your knowledge and your company. If that is satisfactory, I pledge my faith."

"Perfectly satisfactory," answered the MacLeod, and with that the two young men took their departure.

Once more in the king's room, from which, earlier in the day they had set out so confidently, MacDonald flung himself upon a bench, but the king paced up and down the apartment. The former thought the latter was ruminating on the conditions that had been wrung from him, but the first words of the king proved his mistake.

"Jamie, you hardly gave me fair play, you and your Gaelic, with that dainty offspring of so grim a sire."

"Master of Ballengeich," replied the Highlander, "a man plays for his own hand. You should have learned the Gaelic long ago."

The king stopped abruptly in his walk.

"Why do you call me by that name?"

"Merely to show that in this ploy the royal prerogative is not brought into play; it is already settled that when I meet the king, I am defeated. It remains to be seen what luck plain James MacDonald has in a contest with plain James Stuart."

"Oh, it's to be a contest then?"

"Not unless you wish it so. I am content to exchange all the fair damsels of Stirling for this one Highland lassie."

"You'll exchange!" cried the king. "I make bold to say she is not yours to exchange."

"I intend to make her mine."

"Ah, we'll see about that, Jamie."

"We will, Ballengeich," said MacDonald with confident precision. And so the contest began.

The girl, who saw few in her father's castle to be compared with those whom she supposed to be mere visitors at Dunvegan, was at first equally charming to each. A younger sister was her almost constant companion, which was very well at first but latterly became irksome to both the suitors. Occasionally, however, one James or the other saw her alone and made the most of the opportunity presented, but the king soon found himself tremendously handicapped in the matter of language. The young lady possessed a keen sense of humour, and this, with the ever present knowledge that her English was not that of the schools, made her loth to adventure in that tongue before one accustomed to its polished use. This same sense of humour was equally embarrassing when the king madly plunged into the intricacies and ambushes of the Gaelic. His majesty was brave enough for anything and did not hesitate, as a forlorn hope, to call his scant knowledge of the Gaelic to his aid, but even he could see that the result was invariably unhappy, for although the girl made every endeavour to retain her composure, there were times when some unfortunate phrase made her slight frame quiver with suppressed merriment, and no one knew better than the baffled king, that laughter banishes sentiment. The serious Highlander, not less manly and handsome than his competitor, was gifted with an immeasurable advantage in his familiarity with every phase and inflection of his native vernacular. In his despair the king struck up a close friendship with Donald, the second son of the MacLeod, the elder son being absent on some foray or expedition, and his majesty made a frantic effort to learn the only speech with which his new comrade was equipped. But this race against time gave MacDonald long and uninterrupted conferences with his inamorata, and the king saw, too late, the futility of his endeavour. It might have been wiser if he had taken his lessons from the girl herself instead of from her brother, but his majesty was more proficient in teaching than in learning from the fair sex. He had come to the conclusion that his uninteresting rambles with Donald were not likely to further his quest, and was sitting in his room cogitating upon some new method of attack when MacDonald burst into the apartment with radiant face. The king looked up at his visitor with no great good nature, and said sharply,—

"Well, what is it?"

"Your majesty," cried MacDonald jubilantly, "I think I have found a method of escape, and that without in any way impugning our pledges."

"Oh, is that all," said the king, with the air of snubbing too enthusiastic a courtier. "I thought the house was on fire."

"And I thought, your majesty," returned MacDonald, "that this subject was ever uppermost in your mind."

The king rested his closed fist on his hip, leaned his head a little to one side and examined his rival critically.

"Why have you returned so unexpectedly to the phrase, your majesty?"

"Because, your majesty," answered MacDonald laughing, "the phrase, Guidman of Ballengeich, no longer matters."

"I do not understand you."

"It is to make myself understood that I have come so hurriedly. I beg then to inform your majesty, that Miss MacLeod has consented to become my wife. I have spoken to her father, who has somewhat grudgingly and conditionally given his consent. It occurred to me that if I wedded the daughter of your gaoler, I may have enough influence with the family to secure your majesty's release."

"I have no doubt," said the king, "that this was your object from the beginning. And so you have exchanged a temporary gaoler for one that will last you all your life."

The Highlander knit his brow and compressed his lips, as if to hold back some retort which later he might regret. There was a moment's constrained silence, then the king flung off his ill-humour as if it were a cloak.

"Forgive me, Jamie," he cried, springing to his feet. "Forgive the wounded vanity of the vanquished."

He extended his hand impetuously, which the other grasped with eager cordiality.

"Jamie, my lad, you were right. The crown weighs heavy when it is thrown into the scale, but with this lassie I well believe it would have made not an ounce of difference. Let the best man win, say I, and you're the victor, so you have my warmest congratulation. Still, Jamie, you must admit that the Gaelic is the cursedest lingo ever a poor Lowland-bred man tried to get his tongue round. So now you see, Jamie, we are even again. You think the crown defeated you at Stirling, and I hold the language defeated me in Skye; thus we are both able to retain a good opinion of ourselves, which is the splendid privilege of every Scotchman to hold. Your bravery deserves success, for it requires some courage to face your future father-in-law. What did the old curmudgeon say?"

"He gave little indication of pleasure or the reverse. He offered me my liberty, now that I had pledged it in another direction, but he refused to release you, so I declined to accept his clemency."

"Then my proposed rescue must await the marriage ceremony?"

"Not so. I have a more immediate and practical remedy. You have not forgotten the twenty-six oared barge which the MacLeod was to keep for the king, and which Malcolm MacLeod built for him."

"It is not very likely, when I issued a proclamation commending Malcolm as the greatest shipbuilder in the world."

"Well, Malcolm has arrived at Dunvegan to receive into his own hands once more that same proclamation. I asked him, in MacLeod's presence, if the fleet still lingered in Torridon Bay, and he answered that it did. MacLeod pricked up his ears at this, and thinking he was to get some information, now that I proposed myself as a member of his family, inquired if I knew why it remained so long. I said I had a suspicion of the cause. If Malcolm had not replied to the king's proclamation it was natural that the fleet would wait until he did. Old Alexander and Malcolm seemed surprised that a response was expected, Malcolm being but a simple yeoman. However, we wrote out a courteous reply to the king, in Gaelic, and Malcolm is to send it to the fleet as soon as he returns to the northern coast."

"I don't see how that is to help us," demurred his majesty.

"Here is my proposal. If you will now write out an order to the admiral commanding the fleet to appear before Dunvegan Castle, I will ride part of the way home with Malcolm, and suggest to him at parting, that perhaps none of the officers of the fleet understand Gaelic, or at least that none can read it, so I will fasten your letter to the other document, and tell Malcolm it is a translation of his Gaelic effusion. Neither Malcolm nor any of his friends at the port can read English, and as he is a simple minded man it is not likely that he will return and allow the laird a perusal. So in that way we may get word to the fleet. Even if the letter is discovered, you will have kept your word, for you promised only not to communicate with Stirling."

The king pronounced the device a feasible one, and set himself at once to the writing of the letter.

MacDonald succeeded in getting the unsuspicious Malcolm to take charge of the supposed English version of his note, and the king was left to await the result with whatever patience was vouchsafed him. The island had suddenly lost all interest for him and he fervently wished himself safely in Stirling once more. He complimented the girl on the excellent choice she had made, and she returned his compliment laughingly in Gaelic, glancing timidly at MacDonald as she asked him to be her interpreter.

Two or three days later there was a commotion in the castle. The guards on the western headlands reported the approach of numerous ships, and by-and-by from the castle wall itself the fleet could be seen sailing slowly up Loch

Follart. For the first time since they had known him, lines of deep anxiety marked the frowning brow of MacLeod as he stood gazing at the approaching vessels. Here were visitors who, if they proved not to his liking, he could scarcely threaten with the dungeons of Dunvegan.

"What do you make of this, MacDonald?" said the chieftain, turning to his future son-in-law, as if already he looked to him for support and counsel.

But MacDonald shook his head, in spite of the fact that his wife who-was-to-be, stood very close to him.

"All negotiations have been carried on by my friend here, and so to him I must refer you. He is the leader of our expedition of two."

During his brief acquaintance MacLeod had but thinly veiled his dislike of the Lowlander, who had always ventured to speak with him in a free and easy manner to which he was unaccustomed. Instead then of addressing his question to the other, he returned to his occupation of watching the ships manœuvring in the loch before him. But his air of expectancy seemed to indicate that he thought the usual glibness exhibited by the man at his right would bring forth some sort of explanation, but the king stood as silent as himself, his eyes fixed on the fleet. One by one the ships came to anchor and even an amateur in the art of naval warfare could see by the protruding guns that they were prepared for action.

MacLeod could restrain his impatience no longer, so without glancing at his visitor, he said,—

"Perhaps you, sir, can tell me the purport of all this display."

"Assuredly," answered the king with a trace of sternness in his tone that had hitherto been absent in his converse with his gaoler. "The fleet comes at the command of the king to take away your prisoners, if they are unharmed, or to batter down your castle if they have been molested."

"I suppose then I should be thankful they are unharmed?"

"You have reason," said the king shortly.

"His majesty must set great value on your heads if he sends his whole fleet to succour you."

"He does."

"How did he know you were here if you did not break your parole and communicate with Stirling?"

"The king knows there is more going on in Skye than the making of strong drink. I did not break my parole, neither did MacDonald."

"In spite of what you said to me, you must have told the king before you left Stirling where you were going."

"I did not."

"Then word must have been brought to him from Skye?"

"It was not."

"In that case the only conclusion I can come to is that the king is unaware of your presence here."

"He is well aware of it."

"You speak in riddles, my friend. However, I had no real wish to detain you, and you might have gone where you pleased any time this fortnight or more."

"So you say now."

"It's true enough, and if you wish to visit the fleet one of my boats will be ready to carry you the moment you give the order. I told you the first day that if you were a friend of the king's, or an emissary of his, you could go on your way unchecked. Did I not, MacDonald?"

"You said something of that sort, sir."

"You denied being a friend of the king's," persisted MacLeod, "and said you were but a small farmer near Stirling."

"I deny yet that I am a friend of the king. On the contrary, I don't mind confessing to you that I am the greatest enemy he has in the world, and it's well he knows it."

"You amaze me. Then you do not wish to meet the fleet."

"On the contrary, I do, and I ask you to order a suitable boat for me."

"You shall have the best boat in my possession," said MacLeod leaving them for a moment to give his command.

In a short time a large boat with ten oarsmen was waiting at the landing.

"They are ready for you," said MacLeod with an effort at geniality, which gave a most sinister effect to his face. "I am sorry to bid you good-bye, but I hope you bear away with you no ill will against Dunvegan."

"Sir," said the king ignoring his compliments, "that boat will not do for me."

"It is the best I have," said MacLeod looking at his truculent guest with new anxiety.

"The boat you must bring to the landing is the twenty-six oared barge, which Malcolm MacLeod builded so well."

The MacLeod stepped back two paces.

"That boat is for the king," he said in a voice scarcely above a whisper.

"Yes, it is for the king, therefore the king demands it. Give the order instantly that it be brought to the landing, well manned with twenty-six rowers."

All colour left MacLeod's face. His next words were to MacDonald.

"Is this true?" he said.

"Yes," answered MacDonald, "it is true."

The girl, her wide eyes distended with fear, clutched the arm of her lover. Even she knew this was a case for the headsman, but MacLeod, with not a quiver in his voice, called down to his followers,—

"Bring round the king's barge, and see it is well manned. I myself will take the rudder."

The stern face of the king relaxed as he saw this chieftain stand straighter than ever before since he had known him, ready to take on his head whatever might befall.

The girl impetuously flung herself at the king's feet, and in her excitement forgetting the limitations of his learning, she poured forth a plea for her father in Gaelic. The king smiled as he stooped and raised the suppliant.

"My dear," he said, "I shall never hear that language without thinking of you, and of my own discomfiture. If it were not that MacDonald stands there with that dour Highland look on his face, it is I would kneel at your feet. Your father is to come with me to Stirling, for I have said he should, and I must keep my word with myself as well as I have kept it with him. Do not draw away your hand, in spite of MacDonald's scowls, for I have this to promise you. If you and he will accompany us to Stirling, I pledge to you the king's word that I shall grant you whatever you ask. So you see you need have no fear for your father's safety." Saying this, the king, with that courtly manner which so well became him, gave the hand of the girl into that of MacDonald.

Thus it came about that the MacLeod took a voyage he had not intended, and came so unscathed from it that he long outlived the man who was the cause of his journey.

The King Weds

Even a stranger in Stirling must have been impressed by the fact that something unusual was afoot, not to be explained by the mere preparation for ushering in the New Year. Inquiry soon solved the problem of the decorations and the rejoicings. James the Fifth, the most popular king Scotland had possessed since the days of Bruce, was about to be married, and most of his subjects thought it high time, for he had reached the mature age of twenty-six, and monarchs are expected to take a mate somewhat earlier than other folk. As the king, with a splendid retinue, was to depart shortly after the new year on a journey to France to claim his bride, the capital city flung its bunting to the breeze, and the inhabitants thereof pledged each other and the king in bumpers of exhilarating beverages; indeed all Scotland was following the example set to it by Stirling, for the marriage was extremely well liked throughout the land.

The king's father had linked himself to an English princess, and the Scottish people thought little of her. The precipitate marriage of this queen, only a few months after her husband's death, still further lowered her in public estimation. Scotland professed slight regard for Margaret of England, and was glad when her son refused the offer of his uncle, Henry the Eighth, to provide him with a wife. Indeed, James was at that moment the most sought-after young man in the world, so far as matrimony was concerned. The Pope, who now addressed him as Defender of the Faith, had a favourite candidate for his hand. Henry the Eighth was anxious that he should have all England to pick and choose from. The Emperor Charles the Fifth wished him to marry Princess Mary of Portugal; Francis the First of France was eager to supply him with a well-dowered bride. Never before had any youth such an embarrassment of choice, but James himself decided that he would go a-wooing to France, and his subjects universally applauded his preference. James's elderly relative, John, Duke of Albany, had married the heiress of De la Tour d'Auvergne, and the young king resolved to follow his example. Apart from this, James, in a manner, was pledged from the time he was three years of age, for Albany, when Regent of Scotland, had promised France that the young ruler should seek his consort in that country; so there had now been chosen for him Mary, daughter of the Duc de Vendôme, who was reported beautiful, and, what was more to the purpose in a thrifty nation, was known to be wealthy.

This courting by all Europe might have turned the head of a less sensible young man than James, but he well knew the reason that so many distinguished persons desired his alliance. Henry the Eighth was at loggerheads with France; the Emperor Charles and Francis the First were engaged in one of their customary aimless wars, the advantage as usual inclining rather to the emperor's side. Scotland was at peace with itself and with all the world. The Scots were excellent fighters in whatever part of the world they encountered an enemy, and the strong fleet which James the Fourth had builded was augmented by his son and might prove a powerful factor in European politics. France and Scotland had long been traditional friends, and so this new mating aroused enthusiasm in both countries.

Thus Stirling put on gay attire and her citizens went about with smiles on their faces, all except one, and that one was James himself, who became more and more gloomy as the time for his departure approached. He had no desire to take upon himself the trammels of the matrimonial estate, and although his uncle, the strenuous Henry, was ultimately to set an example before the world of the ease with which the restrictions of marriage were to be shuffled off, yet at this time Henry himself was merely an amateur at the business, engaged in getting rid of Catherine of Arragon, a task which he had not yet succeeded in accomplishing. James had postponed and re-postponed the fateful journey; but at last he saw it must be taken, or a friendly country, one of the proudest on earth, would be deliberately insulted in the face of the world. Not only this, but his own subjects were getting restive, and he knew as well as they that a disputed succession in the event of his early death might lead to civil war. So, making the best of the hard bargain which is imposed on princes, where what should be the most endearing ties of human affection are concerned, James set his face resolutely towards the south, and attended by a brilliant escort, sailed for France. After a stormy voyage, for the month was January, the royal party landed in France, and was met by a company of nobles, only less splendid than itself in that a king was one of the visitors; for Francis had remained at Loches, to welcome his brother sovereign at that great and sinister stronghold, where the Court of France for the moment held its seat. Both time and weather seemed unpropitious for joyous occasion. News arrived at Loches that the French army had suffered defeat in its invasion of the Duke of Savoy's territory, and these tidings exercised a depressing influence on the welcoming delegation.

As the united escorts of France and Scotland set out on their journey to Loches a flurry of damp snow filled the air, raw from off the Channel, and the road proved wellnigh impassable through depth of mud. The discontented countenance of the king, who was wont to be the life of any party of which he was a member, lowered the spirits of his Scottish followers to the level of those saddened by military defeat and the horsemen made their way through the quagmires of Northern France more like a slow funeral procession than wedding guests.

At the castle where they halted at the end of the first day's journey, the King speedily retired to the apartment assigned to him without a word of cheer even to the most intimate of his comrades.

The travellers had accomplished only about twelve leagues from the sea-coast on their first day's journey, and darkness had set in before the horsemen clattered through the narrow streets of a little town and came to the frowning gates of a great castle, whose huge tower in the glare of numerous torches loomed out white against the wintry sky. The chief room of the suite reserved for the king was the only cheerful object his majesty had seen that day. A roaring bonfire of bulky logs shed a flickering radiance on the tapestry that hung along the wall, almost giving animation to the knights pictured thereon, sternly battling against foes in anger, or merrily joisting with friends for pleasure at some forgotten tournament.

The king, probably actuated by the military instincts of his race urging him to get his bearings, even though he was in the care of a friendly country, strode to one of the windows and looked out. Dark as was the night and cloudy the sky, the landscape was nevertheless etched into tolerable distinctness by the snow that had fallen, and he saw far beneath him the depths of a profound valley, and what appeared to be a town much lower than the one through which he had just ridden. The stronghold appeared to stand on a platform of rock which was at least impregnable from this side. James turned from the wintry scene outside to the more alluring prospect within the apartment. A stout oaken table in the centre of the room was weighted with a sumptuous repast; and the king, with the stalwart appetite of youth and health augmented by a tiresome journey in keen air, forthwith fell to, and did ample justice to the providing of his unknown host. The choicest vintages of France did something to dispel that depression which had settled down upon him, and the outside glow of the great fire supplemented the inward ardour of good wine.

The king drew up his cushioned chair to the blaze, and while his attendants speedily cleared the board, a delicious drowsiness stole over him. He was partially aroused from this by the entrance of his poetical friend and confidant, Sir David Lyndsay.

"Your majesty," said the rhymster, "the constable of these towers craves permission to pay his respects to you, extending a welcome on behalf of his master, the King of France."

"Bring him in, Davie," cried James; "for in truth he has already extended the most cordial of welcomes, and I desire to thank him for my reception."

Shortly after Sir David Lyndsay ushered into the room a young man of about the same age as the king, dressed in that superb and picturesque costume which denoted a high noble of France, and which added the lustre of fine raiment to the distinguished court of Francis the First. The king greeted his visitor with that affability, which invariably drew even the most surly toward him, without relaxing the dignity which is supposed to be the heritage of a monarch.

"I am delighted to think," said the newcomer, "that the King of Scotland has honoured my house by making it his first halting-place in that realm which has ever been the friend of his country."

"Sir," replied James, "the obligation rests entirely upon me. After a stormy voyage and an inclement land journey, the hospitality of your board is one of the most grateful encounters I have ever met with. I plead an ignorance of geography which is deplorable; and cannot in the least guess where I am, beyond the fact that the boundaries of France encompass me."

"I shall not pretend," said the young man, "that my house is unworthy even of the distinguished guest which it now holds. Your majesty stands within historic walls, for in an adjoining apartment was born William, the founder of a great race of English kings. Scotchmen have defended this castle, and Scotchmen have assaulted it, so its very stones are linked with the fortunes of your country. Brave Henry the Fifth of England captured it, and France took it from his successor. My own family, like the Scotch, have both stood its guard and have been the foremost through a breach to sack it. I am but now employed in repairing the ravages of recent turmoil."

Here the King interrupted him, as if to mend the reputation of ignorance he had bestowed upon himself.

"I take it, then, that I speak to one of the renowned name of Talbot, and that this fortress is no other than the Castle of Falaise?" and the king impetuously extended his hand to him. "We both come of a stormy line, Talbot. Indeed we are even more intimately associated than you have hinted, for one of your name had the temerity to invade Scotland itself in the interests of Edward Baliol—yes, by the Rood, and successfully too."

"Ah, your majesty, it does not become the pride of our house to refer to Richard Talbot, for three years later the Scots took him prisoner, and he retired defeated from your country."

"Indeed," replied the king gaily, "if my memory serves me truly, we valued your valiant ancestor so highly that we made the King of England pay two thousand marks for him. We Scots are a frugal people; we weigh many of the blessings of life against good hard coin, and by Saint Andrew of Scotland, Talbot, I hold myself to-day no better than the rest, for, speaking as young man to young man, I think it unworthy of either king or peasant to take a woman to his bosom for aught save love of her."

"In that I cordially agree with your majesty," said Talbot, with a fervour that made the king glance at him with even more of sympathy than he had already exhibited. A wave of emotion seemed to overwhelm the sensitive James, and submerge for the moment all discretion; he appeared to forget that he spoke to a stranger and one foreign to him, yet James rarely mistook his man, and in this case his intuition was not at fault. To lay bare the secrets of his heart to one unknown to him shortly before, was an experiment of risk; but, as he had said, he spoke as young man to young man, and healthy youth is rarely cynical, no matter to what country it belongs. The heart knows nothing of nationality, and a true man is a true man wherever he hails from.

James sprang to his feet and paced the long room in an excess of excitement, a cloud on his brow; hands clenching and unclenching as he walked. Equally with the lowest in his realm he felt the need of a compassionate confidant. At last the words poured forth from him in an ecstasy of confession.

"Talbot," he cried, "I am on a journey that shames my very manhood. I have lived my life as others of my age, and whatever of contrition I may feel, that rests between my Maker and myself. I am as He formed me, and if I was made imperfect I may be to blame that I strove so little to overcome my deficiency, but, by God, I say it here, I never bought another nor sold myself. Now, on the contrary, I go to the loud marketplace; now I approach a woman I have never seen, and who has never seen me, to pledge our lives together, the consideration for this union set down on parchment, and a stipulated sum paid over in lands and gold."

The king stopped suddenly in his perambulation, raised his hands and said impressively,—

"I tell you, friend and host, I am no better than my fellows and worse than many of them, but when the priest mutters the words that bind, I say the man should have no thought in his mind, but of the woman who stands beside him; and she no thought in hers but of the man in whose hand she places her own."

"Then why go on with this quest?" cried young Talbot with an impetuosity equal to that of his guest.

"Why go on; how can I stop? The fate of kingdoms depends on my action. My honour is at stake. My pledged word is given. How can I withdraw?"

"Your majesty need not withdraw. My master, Francis, is the very prince of lovers, and every word you have uttered will awake an echo in his own heart, although he is our senior by twenty years. If I may venture to offer humbly such advice as occurs to me, you should tell him that you have come to France not to be chosen for, but to choose. France is the flower garden of the human race; here bloom the fairest lilies of womanhood, fit to grace the proudest throne in Christendom. Choice is the prerogative of kings."

"Indeed, Talbot, it is not," said the king dolefully.

"It should be so, and can be so, where a monarch boldly demands the right exercised unquestioned by the meanest hind. Whom shall you offend by stoutly claiming your right? Not France, for you will wed one of her daughters; not the king, for he is anxious to bestow upon you the lady you may prefer. Whom then? Merely the Duke of Vendôme, whose vaulting ambition it is to place a crown upon the head of his daughter, though its weight may crush her."

The king looked fixedly at the perturbed young man, and a faint smile chased away the sternness of his countenance.

"I have never known an instance," he said slowly, "where the burden of a crown was urged as an objection even by the most romantic of women."

"It would be so urged by Mary of Vendôme, were she allowed to give utterance to her wishes."

"You know her then?"

"I am proud to claim her as a friend, and to assert she is the very pearl of France."

"Ha, you interest me. You hint, then, that I come a bootless wooer? That is turning the tables indeed, and now you rouse an emulation which heretofore was absent in me. You think I cannot win and wear this jewel of the realm?"

"That you may wear it there is no doubt; that you may win it is another matter. Mary will place her listless hand in yours, knowing thus she pleases the king and her father, but it is rumoured her affections are fixed upon another."

"Sir, you stir me up to competition. Now we enter the lists. You bring the keen incentive of rivalry into play."

"Such, your majesty, was far from my intention. I spoke as a friend of the lady. She has no more choice in this bargain than you deplored the lack of a moment since."

The former gloom again overspread the king's face.

"There is the devil of it," he cried impatiently. "If I could meet her on even terms, plain man and woman, then if I loved her I would win her, were all the nobles of France in the scales against me. But I come to her chained; a jingling captive, and she approaches me alike in thrall. It is a cursed fate, and I chafe at the clanking links, though they hold me nevertheless. And all my life I can never be sure of her; the chiming metal ever between us. I come in pomp and display, as public as the street I walk on, and the union is as brazen as a slave market, despite cathedral bells and archbishop's blessing. Ah, well, there is nothing gained by ranting. Do you ride to Loches with me?"

"I follow your majesty a day behind, but hope to overtake you before you are well past Tours."

"I am glad of it. Good-night. I see you stand my friend, and before this comes to a climax we may have need to consult together. Good-night; good-night!"

Next morning early the itinerants were on horseback again, facing southward. The day was wild and stormy, and so was the next that followed it; but after leaving Tours they seemed to have entered an enchanted land, for the clouds were dispersed and the warm sun came forth, endowing the travellers with a genial climate like late springtime in Scotland. As they approached Loches even the king was amazed by the striking sight of the castle, a place formidable in its strength, and in extent resembling a small city.

The gay and gallant Francis received his fellow monarch with a cordiality that left no doubt of its genuine character. The French king had the geniality to meet James in the courtyard itself; he embraced him at the very gates as soon as James had dismounted from his horse. Notwithstanding his twenty years of seniority Francis seemed as young as the Scottish king.

"By Saint Denis, James," he cried, "you are a visitor of good omen, for you have brought fine weather with you and the breath of spring. All this winter we have endured the climate of Hades itself, without its warmth."

The two rulers stood together in the courtyard, entirely alone, for no man dare frequent their immediate neighbourhood; but in a circle some distance removed from their centre, the Scotch and the French fraternised together, a preeminent assemblage numbering a thousand or more; and from the balconies beautiful ladies looked down on the inspiring scene.

The gates were still open and the drawbridge down, when a horseman came clattering over the causeway, and, heedless of the distinguished audience, which he scattered to right and left, amid curses on his clumsiness, drew up his foaming horse in the very presence of royalty itself.

Francis cried out angrily at this interruption.

"Unmannerly varlet, how dare you come dashing through this throng like a drunken ploughman!"

The rider flung himself off the panting horse and knelt before his enraged master.

"Sire," he said, "my news may perhaps plead for me. The army of the Emperor Charles, in Provence, is broken and in flight. Spain has met a crushing defeat, and no foe insults the soil of France except by lying dead upon it."

"Now, my good fellow," cried the king with dancing eyes, "you are forgiven if you had ridden down half of my nobility."

The joyous news spread like wildfire, and cheer upon cheer rose to heaven like vocal flame to mark its advance.

"Brother," cried the great king to his newly arrived guest, placing an arm lovingly over his shoulder, his voice with suspicion of tremulousness about it, "you stalwart Scots have always brought luck to our fair land of France. This glad news is the more welcome to me that you are here when I receive it."

And so the two, like affectionate kinsmen, walked together into the castle which, although James did not then know it, was to be his home for many months.

There was a dinner of state that evening, so gay and on a scale so grand that James had little time or opportunity for reflection on his mission. Here indeed, as Talbot had truly said, was the flower garden of the human race; and the Scottish king saw many a proud lady to whom probably he would have been delighted to bend the knee. But his bride was not among the number. The Duchesse de Vendôme explained to the king that her daughter was suffering from a slight illness, and apart from this was anxious to greet her future husband in a conference more private than the present occasion afforded. This was certainly reasonable enough, and the important meeting took place the following afternoon.

Mary of Vendôme might truly be called the Pearl of France, if whiteness of visage gave claim to that title. The king found himself confronted by a drooping young woman whose stern mother gave her a support which was certainly needed. Her face was of the pallor of wax; and never once during that fateful interview did she raise the heavy lids from her eyes. That she had once been beautiful was undoubted, but now her face was almost gaunt in its excessive thinness. The death-like hue of her delicate skin, the fact that she seemed scarce to breathe, and that she never ventured to speak, gave her suitor the impression that she more resembled one preparing for the tomb than a young girl anticipating her bridal. She courtesied like one in a trance; but the keen eyes of the king saw the tightening of her mother's firm hand on her wrist while she made the obeisance which etiquette demanded. Short as was their formal greeting, it was too long for this anæmic creature, who would have sunk to the floor were it not for the clutch in which the determined mother held her. Even the king, self-contained as he usually was, found little to say beyond empty expressions of concern regarding her recent illness, ending with a brief remark to the effect that he hoped she would soon recover from her indisposition. But once the ordeal was over, James was filled with a frenzy to be alone, tortured as he was by an agony of mind which made any encounter with his fellows intolerable. He strode through the seemingly interminable corridors of the great castle, paying slight heed to his direction. All doors opened before him, and sentinels saluted as he passed. At last, not knowing where he was, or how to get outside, he said to one of the human statues who held a pike,—

"Tell me, good fellow, the quickest way to the outer air; some spot where I can be entirely alone?"

The guard, saluting, called a page, whispered a word to him, and the boy led the king to a door which gave access to a secluded garden, enclosed on every side by high battlements, yet nevertheless filled with great trees, under which ran paths both straight and winding. Beside one wall lay the longest walk of this little park, and up and down this gravelled way, his hands clasped behind him, the young king strode in more disturbance of mind than had ever before afflicted him.

"Oh, God save me; God save me!" he cried; "am I to be wedded to a ghost? That woman is not even alive, to say whether she is willing or no. Have I come to France to act the ghoul and rob the grave of its due? Saints in heaven, help me! What am I to do? I cannot insult France, yet I cannot chain my living body to that dead woman. Why is not Talbot here? He said he would overtake me at Tours, and yet is he not come. The Pearl of France, said he, the jewel of a toad's head, say I. My honour staked, and to that unbreathing image of tallow! Is this my punishment? Do the sins of our youth thus overtake us, and in such ghastly form? Bones of my ancestors, I will not wed the grave, though war and slaughter come of it. And yet—and yet, my faith is plighted; blindly, unknowingly plighted. Why does not Talbot come? He knew what my emotions would be on seeing that denizen of another world, and so warned me."

These muttered meditations were suddenly interrupted by a clear sweet voice from above.

"Écossais! Scottish knight! Please rescue for me my handkerchief, which I have, alas, let fall. Wrap a stone in it and throw it hither, I beg of you."

The startled king looked up and beheld, peering over at him from the battlements above, one of the most piquant and pretty, laughing faces he had ever seen. Innocent mischief sparkled in the luscious dark eyes, which regarded him from a seemingly inaccessible perch. A wealth of dark tousled hair made a midnight frame for a lovely countenance in the first flush of maidenly youth. Nothing could be more marked than the difference between the reality which thus came unexpectedly into view, and his sombre vision of another. There also sifted down to him from aloft, whisperings that were evidently protests, from persons unseen; but the minx who was the cause of them merrily bade her counsellors be quiet. She must get her handkerchief, she said, and the Scot was the only one to recover it. Fluttering white from one of the lower branches was a dainty bit of filmy lace, much too fragile a covering for the stone she had suggested. The despair which enveloped the king was dispelled as the mist vanishes before the beaming sun. He whipped out his thin rapier and deftly disentangled the light burden from the detaining branch. It fluttered to his hand and was raised gallantly to his lips, at which the girl laughed most joyfully, as if this action were intensely humorous. Other faces peeped momentarily over the balustrade to be as quickly withdrawn when they saw the stranger looking up at them; but the hussy herself, whoever she was, seemed troubled by no such timorousness, resting her arms upon the stone balustrade, with her chin above them, her inviting eyes gazing mockingly on the man below. The king placed the handkerchief in the bosom of his doublet, thrust home the rapier in its scabbard, grasped the lower branch of the tree and swung himself up on it with the agility of an acrobat. Now the insolence of those eyes was chased away by a look of alarm.

"No, no," she cried, "stay where you are. You are too bold, Scottish knight."

But she had to reckon with one who was a nimble wall climber, either up or down, whose expertness in descent had often saved him from the consequences of too ambitious climbing. The young man answered not a word, but made his way speedily up along the branches until he stood at a level with the parapet. Across the chasm which divided him from the wall he saw a broad platform, railed round with a stone balustrade, this elevated floor forming an ample promenade that was nevertheless secluded because of the higher castle walls on every side, walls that were unpierced by any window. A door at the farther end of the platform gave access to the interior of the palace. A short distance back from the balustrade stood a group of some half-dozen very frightened women. But the first cause of all this commotion remained in the forefront of the assemblage, angry and defiant.

"How dare you, sir?" she cried. "Go back, I command you." Then seeing he made no motion to obey her, but was measuring with his keen eye the distance between the bending limb on which he held his precarious position, and the parapet, something more of supplication came into her voice, and she continued,—

"My good fellow, place the handkerchief on the point of your sword and one of my women will reach for it. Be careful, I beg of you; that bough will break under your weight if you venture further. The outreached arm and the sword will span the space."

"Madam," said the king, "the sword's point is for my enemy. On bended knee must I present a lady that which belongs to her."

And with this, before further expostulation was possible, the young man made his perilous leap, clutched the parapet with his left arm, hung suspended for one breathless moment, then flung his right leg, a most shapely member, over the balustrade, and next instant was kneeling at her feet, offering the gosamer token. In the instant of crisis the young lady had given utterance to a little shriek which she instantly suppressed, glancing nervously over her shoulder. One of her women ran towards the door, but the girl peremptorily ordered her to return.

"The Scot will not eat you," she cried impatiently, "even if he is a savage."

"Madam, your handkerchief," explained the savage, still offering it.

"I shall not accept it," she exclaimed, her eyes blazing with resentment at his presumption.

The king sprang to his feet and swept off his plumed hat with the air of an Italian.

"Ten thousand thanks, madam, for your cherished gift." Saying which he thrust the slight web back into his doublet again.

"'Tis not a gift; render it to me at once, sir," she demanded with feminine inconsistency. She extended her hand, but the king, instead of returning the article in dispute, grasped her fingers unawares and raised them to his lips. She drew away her hand with an expression of the utmost contempt, but nevertheless stood her ground, in spite of the evident anxiety to be elsewhere of the bevy behind her.

"Sir, you are unmannerly. No one has ever ventured to treat me thus."

"Then I am delighted to be the first to introduce to you so amiable a custom. Unmannerly? Not so. We savages learn our manners from the charming land of France; and I have been told that in one or two instances, this country has known not only the fingers, but the lips to be kissed."

"I implore you, sir, to desist and take your departure the way you came; further, I warn you that danger threatens."

"I need no such warning, my lady. The danger has already encompassed me, and my heart shall never free itself from its presence, while remembrance of the lightning of those eyes abides with me."

The girl laughed with a trace of nervousness, and the rich colour mounted to her cheek.

"Sir, you are learning your lesson well in France."

"My lady, the lowest hind in my country could not do otherwise under such tutelage."

"You should turn your gifts to the service of your master. Go, woo for him poor Mary of Vendôme, and see if you can cure her who is dying of love for young Talbot of Falaise."

For a moment the king stood as if struck by the lightning he had just referred to, then staggering back a step, rested his hand on the parapet and steadied himself.

"Good God!" he muttered in low tones, "is that true?"

All coquetry disappeared from the girl as she saw the dramatic effect her words had produced. She moved lightly forward, then held back again, anxiety on her brow.

"Sir, what is wrong with you? Are you ill? Are you a friend of Talbot's?"

"Yes, I am a friend of his."

"And did you not know this? I thought every one knew it. Does not the King of Scotland know? What will he do when he learns, think you, or will it make a difference?"

"The King of Scotland is a blind fool; a conceited coxcomb, who thinks every woman that sees him must fall in love with him."

"Sir, you amaze me. Are you not a subject of his? You would not speak so in his hearing."

"Indeed and that I would, without hesitation, and he knows it."

"Is he so handsome as they say? Alas, I am thought too young to engage in court festivities, and in spite of my pleadings I was not allowed even to see his arrival."

The king had now recovered his composure, and there was a return of his gallant bearing.

"Madam, tell me your name, and I shall intercede that so rigid a rule for one so fair may be relaxed."

"Ah, now your impudence reasserts itself. My name is not for you. How can a humble Scottish knight hope to soften a rule promulgated by the King of France himself?"

"Madam, you forget that we are guests of France, and in this courteous country nothing is denied us. We meet with no refusals except from proud ladies like yourself. I shall ask my captain, he shall pass my request to the general, who will speak to the King of Scotland, and the king, when he knows how beautiful you are, will beg the favour from Francis himself."

The girl clasped her hands with exuberant delight.

"I wonder if it is possible," she said, leaning towards the gay cavalier, as if he were now her dearest friend—for indeed it was quite evident that she thought much of him in spite of his irregular approach. She was too young to feel the rules of etiquette otherwise than annoying bonds, and like an imprisoned wild bird, was willing to take any course that promised liberty.

"Your name, then, madam?"

"My name is Madeleine."

"I need not ask if you are noble."

"I am at least as noble as Mary of Vendôme, whom your king is to marry, if he is cruel enough."

At this point one of the women, who had stationed herself near the door, came running towards the group and warned them that somebody was approaching. The attendants, who had hitherto remained passive, probably with some womanly curiosity regarding the strange interview, now became wild with excitement, and joined their mistress in begging the stranger to depart.

"Not until I have whispered in your ear," he said stoutly.

"I cannot permit it; I cannot permit it. Go, go at once, I implore you."

"Then I escort you within the hall to meet whoever comes."

"Sir, you are importunate. Well, it doesn't matter; whisper."

He bent toward her and said:—

"Madeleine, you must meet me here alone at this time to-morrow."

"Never, never," she cried resolutely.

"Very well then; here I stay until you consent."

"You are cruel," she said, tears springing in her eyes. Then appealingly, as a knock sounded against the door, she added, "I promise. Go at once."

The young man precipitated himself over the parapet into the tree. The fortune which attends lovers and drunkards favoured him, and the last bending branch lowered him as gently to the gravel of the walk as if he were a son of the forest. He glanced upward, and saw that the luminous face, in its diaphanous environment of dark hair was again bent over the parapet, the lips apart and still, saying nothing, but the eloquent eyes questioning; indeed he fancied he saw in them some slight solicitude for his safety. He doffed his hat, kissed the tips of his fingers and wafted the salutation toward her, while a glow of satisfaction filled his breast as he actually saw a similar movement on the part of her own fair fingers, which was quickly translated into a gesture pointing to the garden door, and then she placed a finger-tip to her lips, a silent injunction for silence. He knew when to obey, as well as when to disobey, and vanished quickly through the door. He retreated in no such despairing phase of mind as he had advanced, but now paid some attention to the geography of the place that he might return unquestioning to his tryst. Arriving at the more public corridors of the palace, his first encounter was with the Constable of Falaise. Talbot's dress was travel-stained, and his youthful face wore almost the haggardness of age. He looked like a man who had ridden hard and slept little, finding now small comfort at the end of a toilsome journey. The king, with a cry of pleasure at the meeting, smote his two hands down on the shoulders of the other, who seemed unconsciously to shrink from the boisterous touch.

"Talbot," he cried, "you promised to overtake me at Tours, but you did not."

"It is not given to every man to overtake your majesty," said Talbot hoarsely.

"Constable of Falaise, you were not honest with me that night in your castle. I spoke to you freely from the bottom of my heart; you answered me from your lips outward."

188

"I do not understand your majesty," replied the young man grimly.

"Yes, you do. You love Mary of Vendôme. Why did you not tell me so?"

"To what purpose should I have made such a confession, even if it were the fact?"

"To the purpose of truth, if for nothing else. God's sake, man, is it thus you love in France! Cold Scotland can be in that your tutor. In your place, there had been a quick divorce between my sword and scabbard. Were my rival twenty times a king, I'd face him out and say, by Cupid's bow, return or fight."

"What! This in your castle to your guest?" exclaimed Talbot.

"No, perhaps not. You are in the right, constable, you are in the right. I had forgotten your situation for the moment. I should have been polite to him within my own walls, but I should have followed him across my marches and slit his gullet on the king's highway."

Notwithstanding his distraction of mind the newcomer smiled somewhat wanly at the impetuosity of the other.

"You must remember that while your foot presses French soil, you are still the guest of all true Frenchmen, nevertheless your majesty's words have put new life into my veins. Did you see Mary of Vendôme?"

"Yes, and there is not three months' life left to her unless she draws vitality from your presence. Man, man, why stand you here idling? Climb walls, force bolts, kidnap the girl and marry her in spite of all the world."

"Alas, there is not a priest in all France would dare to marry us, knowing her pledged to your majesty."

"Priests of France! I have priests in my own train who will, at a word from me, link you tighter than these stones are cemented together. God's will, Talbot, these obstacles but lend interest to the chase."

"Is it possible that you, having opportunity, care not to marry Mary of Vendôme?" cried the amazed young man, who could not comprehend that where his preference fell another might be indifferent; for she was, as he had said, the Pearl of France to him, and it seemed absurd to imagine that she might not be so to all the world.

"United Europe, with Francis and the Emperor Charles for once combined could not force me to marry where I did not love. I failed to understand this when I left Scotland, but I have grown in wisdom since then."

"Who is she?" asked the constable, with eager interest.

"Hark ye, Talbot," said the king, lowering his voice and placing an arm affectionately over the shoulder of the other. "You shall be my guide. Who is the Lady Madeleine of this court?"

"The Lady Madeleine? There are several."

"No, there is but one, the youngest, the most beautiful, the most witty, the most charming. Who is she?"

The constable wrinkled his brows in thought.

"That must be Madeleine de Montmorency. She is the youngest of her name, and is by many accounted beautiful. I never heard that she was esteemed witty until your majesty said so. Rather reserved and proud. Is that the lady?"

"Proud, yes. Reserved—um, yes, that is, perhaps not when she meets a man who knows enough to appreciate her. However, I shall speedily solve the riddle, and must remember that you do not see the lady through a lover's eyes. But I will not further keep you. A change of costume may prove to your advantage, and I doubt not an untroubled night's sleep will further it."

"Your majesty overwhelms me with kindness," murmured the young lover, warmly grasping the hand extended to him. "Have I your permission to tell Mary of Vendôme?"

"You have my permission to tell her anything, but you will bring her no news, for I am now on my way to see her."

The king gaily marched on, his head held high, a man not to be denied, and as he passed along all bowed at his coming, for everyone in the court admired him. There was something unexpectedly French in the dash of this young Scotchman. He strode across the court and up the steps which led into the Palais Vendôme. The duchess herself met him with a hard smile on her thin lips.

"Madam," he said bruskly, "I would see your daughter alone."

The grim duchesse hesitated.

"Mary is so shy," she said at last.

But the king interrupted her.

"I have a cure for that. Shyness flees in my presence. I would see your daughter alone, madam; send her to me."

There being no remedy when a king commands, the lady made the best of a dubious proceeding.

James was pacing up and down the splendid drawing-room when, from the further door the drooping girl appeared, still with downcast eyes, nun-like in her meek obedience. She came forward perhaps a third the length of the room, faltered, and stood.

"Mary," said the king, "they told me you were beautiful, but I come to announce to you that such is not my opinion. You are ambitious, it would seem, so I tell you frankly, you will never be Queen of Scotland."

For the first time in his presence the girl uncovered her eyes and looked up at him.

"Yes," said the king, "your eyes are fine. I am constrained to concede that much, and if I do not wed you myself it is but right I should nominate a candidate for your hand. There is a friend of mine for whom I shall use my influence with Francis and your father that they may persuade you to marry him. He is young Talbot, Constable of Falaise, a demented stripling who calls you the Pearl of France. Ah, now the colour comes to your cheeks. I would not have believed it. All this demureness then———" But the girl had sunk at

191

his feet, grasped his hand and pressed it to her lips.

"Tut, tut," he cried hastily, "that is a reversal of the order of nature. Rise, and when I send young Talbot to you, see that you welcome him; and now, good-day to you."

As he passed through the outer room the duchesse lay in wait for him and began murmuring apologies for her daughter's diffidence.

"We have arranged all about the wedding, madam," said the king reassuringly as he left the palace.

The next day at the hour when the king had met Madeleine for the first time, he threaded his way eagerly through the mazes of the old castle until he came to the door that led him out into the Elysian garden. The weather still befriended him, being of an almost summer mildness.

For several minutes he paced impatiently up and down the gravel walk, but no laughing face greeted him from the battlements above. At last, swearing a good round Scottish oath he said, "I'll solve the mystery of the balcony," and seizing the lower branch of the tree, he was about to climb as he had done before, when a tantalizing silvery laugh brought his arms down to his sides again. It seemed to come from an arbour at the further end of the grounds, but when he reached there the place proved empty. He pretended to search among the bushes, but nevertheless kept an eye on the arbour, when his sharp ear caught a rustling of silk from behind the summer-house. He made a dash towards it, then reversed his direction, speeding like the wind, and next instant this illusive specimen of Gallic womanhood ran plump into his arms, not seeing where she was going, her head averted to watch the danger that threatened from another quarter.

Before she could give utterance to more than one exclamatory "Oh," he had kissed her thrice full on the lips. She struggled in his arms like a frightened bird, nobly indignant with shame-crimsoned cheeks, smiting him with her powerless little snowflake of a hand. Her royal lover laughed.

"Ha, my Madeleine, this is the second stage of the game. The hand was paradise on earth; the lips are the seventh heaven itself."

192

"Release me, you Scottish clown!" cried Madeleine, her black eyes snapping fire. "I will have you whipped from the court for your insolence."

"My dear, you could not be so cruel. Remember that poor Cupid's back is naked, and he would quiver under every stroke."

"I'd never have condescended to meet you, did I dream of your acting so. 'Tis intolerable, the forwardness of you beggarly Scots!"

"Nay, never beggarly, my dear, except where a woman is concerned, and then we beg for favours."

"You little suspect who I am or you would not venture to misuse me thus, and be so free with your 'my dears.'"

"Indeed, lass, in that you are mistaken. I not only found you in the garden, but I found your name as well. You are Madeleine de Montmorency."

She ceased to struggle, and actually laughed a little.

"How clever you are to have discovered so much in such a short time. Now let me go, and I will thank you; nay more, I promise that if you ask the Duke of Montmorency for his permission, and he grants it, I will see you as often as you please."

"Now Madeleine, I hold you to that, and I will seek an introduction to the duke at once."

She stepped back from him panting, and sank into a deep courtesy that seemed to be characterised more by ridicule than politeness.

"Oh, thank you, sir," she said. "I should dearly love to be an eavesdropper at your conference."

Before he could reply, the door opened by which he had entered the park.

"In the fiend's name, the king!" muttered James, in no manner pleased by the unwelcome interruption.

All colour left the girl's face, and she hastily endeavoured to arrange

193

in brief measure the disordered masses of her hair, somewhat tangled in the struggle. As Francis advanced up the walk, the genial smile froze on his lips, and an expression of deep displeasure overshadowed his countenance, a look of stern resentment coming into his eyes that would have made any man in his realm quail before him. The girl was the first to break the embarrassing silence, saying breathlessly,—

"Your majesty must not blame this Scottish knight. It is all my fault, for I lured him hither."

"Peace, child," exclaimed Francis in a voice of cold anger. "You know not what you say. What do you here alone with the King of Scotland?"

"The King of Scotland!" echoed Madeleine, in surprise, her eyes opening wide with renewed interest as she gazed upon him. Then she laughed. "They told me the King of Scotland was a handsome man!"

James smiled at this imputation on his appearance, and even the rigour of the lord of France relaxed a trifle, and a gleam of affection for the wayward girl that was not to be concealed, rose in his eyes.

"Sire," said James slowly, "we are neither of us to blame. 'Tis the accident that brought us together must bear the brunt of consequence. I cannot marry Mary of Vendôme, and indeed I was about to beg your majesty to issue your command that she may wed your Constable of Falaise. If there is to be a union between France and Scotland other than now exists, this lady, and this lady alone, must say yes or no to it. Premising her free consent, I ask her hand in marriage."

"She is but a child," objected Francis, breathing a sigh, which had, however, something of relief in it.

"I am fully seventeen," expostulated Madeleine, with a promptness that made both men laugh.

"Sire, Youth is a fault, which alas, travels continually with Time, its antidote," said James. "If I have your good wishes in this project, on which, I confess, my heart is set, I shall at once approach the Duke of Montmorency and solicit his consent."

The face of Francis had cleared as if a ray of sunshine had fallen upon it.

"The Duke of Montmorency!" he cried in astonishment; "what has he to do with the marriage of my daughter?"

James murmured something that may have been a prayer, but sounded otherwise, as he turned to the girl, whose delight at thus mystifying the great of earth was only too evident.

"I told him he little suspected who I was," said Madeleine, with what might have been termed a giggle in one less highly placed; "but these confident Scots think they know everything. Indeed, it is all your own fault, father, in keeping me practically a prisoner, when the whole castle is throbbing with joy and festivity." Then the irrepressible princess buried her flushed face in her hands, and laughed and laughed, as if this were the most irresistible comedy in the world, instead of a grave affair of state, until at last the two monarchs were forced to laugh in sympathy.

"I could not wish her a braver husband," said Francis at last. "I see she has bewitched you as is her habit with all of us."

And thus it came about that James the Fifth of Scotland married the fair Madeleine of France.

THE END

LORD STRANLEIGH
ABROAD

I.—LORD STRANLEIGH ALL AT SEA.

A few minutes before noon on a hot summer day, Edmund Trevelyan walked up the gang-plank of the steamship, at that moment the largest Atlantic liner afloat. Exactly at the stroke of twelve she would leave Southampton for Cherbourg, then proceed across to Queenstown, and finally would make a bee-line west for New York. Trevelyan was costumed in rough tweed of subdued hue, set off by a cut so well-fitting and distinguished that it seemed likely the young man would be looked upon by connoisseurs of tailoring as the best-dressed passenger aboard. He was followed by Ponderby, his valet, whose usually expressionless face bore a look of dissatisfaction with his lot, as though he had been accustomed to wait upon the nobility, and was now doomed to service with a mere commoner. His lack of content, however, was caused by a dislike to ocean travel in the first place, and his general disapproval of America in the second. A country where all men are free and equal possessed no charms for Ponderby, who knew he had no equal, and was not going to demean himself by acknowledging the possibility of such.

Once on deck, his master turned to him and said—

"You will go, Ponderby, to my suite of rooms, and see that my luggage is placed where it should be, and also kindly satisfy yourself that none of it is missing."

Ponderby bowed in a dignified manner, and obeyed without a word, while Trevelyan mounted the grand staircase, moving with an easy nonchalance suited to a day so inordinately hot. The prospect of an ocean voyage in such weather was in itself refreshing, and so prone is mankind to live in the present, and take no thought of the morrow, that Trevelyan had quite forgotten the cablegrams he read in the papers on his way down from London, to the effect that New York was on the grill, its inhabitants sweltering—sleeping on the house-tops, in the parks, on the beach at Coney Island, or wherever a breath of air could be had. On the upper deck his slow steps were arrested by an exclamation—

"Isn't this Mr. Trevelyan?"

The man who made the enquiry wore the uniform of the ship's company.

"Ah, doctor, I was thinking of you at this moment. I read in the papers that you had been promoted, and I said to myself: 'After all, this is not an ungrateful world, when the most skilful and most popular medical officer on the Atlantic is thus appreciated.'"

"Ah, you put it delightfully, Trevelyan, but I confess I hesitated about adding, at my time of life, to the burden I carry."

"Your time of life, doctor! Why you always make me feel an old man by comparison with yourself; yet you'll find me skipping about the decks like a boy."

"If you'll take the right-hand seat at my table, I'll keep an eye on you, and prevent you from skipping overboard," laughed the doctor.

"Indeed, that was the boon I intended to crave."

"Then the seat is yours, Trevelyan. By the way, I read in the newspapers that Evelyn Trevelyan is none other than Lord Stranleigh; but then, of course, you can never believe what you see in the press, can you?"

"Personally, I make no effort to do so. I get my news of the day from Ponderby, who is an inveterate reader of the principal journals favoured by what he calls the 'upper classes.' But I assure you that Evelyn Trevelyan is a name that belongs to me, and I wear it occasionally like an old, comfortable-fitting coat."

"Ah, well, I'll not give you away. I'll see you at lunch between here and Cherbourg." And the doctor hurried away to his duties.

The young man continued his stroll, smiling as he remembered some of the doctor's excellent stories. He regarded his meeting with that friendly officer as a good omen, but hoped he would encounter no one else who knew him.

The next interruption of his walk proved to be not so pleasant. There came up the deck with nervous tread a shabbily-dressed man, who appeared from ten to fifteen years older than Stranleigh, although in reality there was no great disparity in their ages. His face was haggard and lined with anxiety, and his eyes had that furtive, penetrating glance which distinguishes the inveterate gambler. Stranleigh watched his oncoming with amazement.

The Hon. John Hazel had been a member of some of the most exclusive clubs in London; but whether or not Nature had endowed him with a useful talent, he had become notorious as a reckless cardsharper, quite unscrupulous when it came to obtaining money. No one knew this better than Lord Stranleigh, who had been so often his victim, yet had regarded his losses lightly, and forgiven the Hon. John time and again. But recently this younger son of an ancient and honourable house had committed the unpardonable sin—he had been found out, and had been permitted to resign from all his clubs but one, and from which he was expelled by a committee not so lenient. After that he disappeared. He was done for, so far as England was concerned, and he knew it.

"John, is this possible?" cried Lord Stranleigh, as the other approached.

Hazel stopped, his eyes veiling over, as though he held a hand at poker that was unbeatable.

"I haven't the pleasure of knowing you, sir," he said haughtily.

"I'm glad of that, because I'm Edmund Trevelyan at the moment, and was just hoping I should meet no one on board who would recognise me."

"I don't know Edmund Trevelyan, and have no wish to make his acquaintance," returned the other coldly.

"That's quite all right, and your wish does you credit. Trevelyan has no desire to force his friendship on any man. Nevertheless, Jack, time was when I helped you out of a hole, and, if occasion arose, I should be glad to do it again."

"You could have prevented my expulsion from the Camperdown Club, had you but cared to raise a finger," said the other hotly.

"Hazel, you are mistaken. I did all I could for you, as in other crises of the same nature. The committee proved to be adamant, and rather prided themselves on their independence, as if they were a group of blooming Radicals. The House of Lords isn't what it was, Jack, as, alas, you may learn, should you ever come into the title of your family, although many people stand between you and it at the present moment. Indeed, Jack, it has been on my conscience that my urgent advocacy prejudiced your case instead of helping it."

"Ah, well, that's all past; it doesn't matter now," said the other, with a sigh. "I have shaken the dust of England for ever from my feet."

"The mud, you mean."

"Oh, I admit I wallowed in the mud, but it was dust when I left London this morning. Ah, we're off! I must be going." And he moved away from the rail of the ship, where he had been gazing over the side.

"Going? Where?"

"Where I belong. I'm travelling third-class. The moment the steamer gets under way, I have no right on the cabin deck. Before she left, I took the liberty of a sightseer to wander over the steamship."

"My dear Jack," said his former friend, in a grave voice, "this will never do; you cannot cross the Atlantic in the steerage."

"I have visited my quarters, and find them very comfortable. I have been in much worse places recently. Steerage is like everything else maritime— like this bewilderingly immense steamer, for example—vastly improved since Robert Louis Stevenson took his trip third-class to New York."

"Well, it is a change for a luxury-loving person like my friend the Hon. John Hazel."

"It is very condescending of you to call me your friend. Nobody else would do it," replied the Hon. John bitterly.

"Condescension be hanged! I'm rather bewildered, that's all, and wish for further particulars. Are you turning over a new leaf, then?"

"A new leaf? A thousand of them! I have thrown away the old book, with its blotches and ink-stains. I'm starting a blank volume that I hope will bear inspection and not shock even the rectitude of the Camperdown Committee."

"What's the programme?"

"I don't quite know yet; it will depend on circumstances. I think it's the West for me—sort of back-to-the-land business. I yearn to become a kind of moral cowboy. It seems the only thing I'm at all equipped for. I can ride well and shoot reasonably straight."

"I thought," said Stranleigh, "that phase of life had disappeared with Bret Harte. Is there any money in your inside pocket?"

"How could there be?"

"Then why not let me grub-stake you, which I believe is the correct Western term."

"As how, for instance?"

"I'll secure for you a comfortable cabin, and you will pay the damage when you strike oil out West, so, you see, there's no humiliating condescension about the offer."

"I'm sure there isn't, and it's very good of you, Stranleigh, but I can't dress the part."

"That's easily arranged. Ponderby always over-dresses me. His idea of this world is that there is London, and the rest of the planet is a wilderness. You could no more persuade him that a decent suit might be made in New York than that I am the worst-dressed man in London. You and I are about the same height and build. Ponderby will have in my mountainous luggage anywhere from twenty-five to forty suits never yet worn by me. I don't know on what principle he goes, but as the last time we went to America he took twenty-five new suits, and we crossed in a twenty-five thousand ton boat, he is likely to have at least forty-five suits for this forty-five thousand ton steamship, and he will feel as much pleasure in rigging you out as he took in the crowning of the new King."

"Very good of you, Stranleigh, but I cannot accept."

"I am pleading for Ponderby's sake. Besides, there's one practical point you have overlooked. If you attempt to land from the steerage—travelling under an assumed name, I suppose——"

"Like yourself, Stranleigh."

"No, I own the name 'Trevelyan.' But, as I was saying, if you attempt to land rather shabbily dressed and almost penniless, you will find yourself turned back as an undesirable alien, whereas you can go ashore from the first cabin unquestioned, save for those amazing queries the U.S.A. Government puts to one, the answers to which Ponderby will be charmed to write out for you."

Hazel without reply walked back to the rail, leaned his arms on it, and fell into deep thought. Stranleigh followed him.

"Give me your ticket," he said.

Hazel took it from his pocket and handed it over.

"Have you any luggage?"

"Only a portmanteau, which I placed in my bunk. It contains a certain amount of necessary linen."

"Wait here until I find out what there is to be had in the first cabin."

Stranleigh went down to the purser, and that overworked official threw him a friendly glance, which nevertheless indicated that his time was valuable.

"My name is Trevelyan," said the young man.

"Oh, yes, Mr. Trevelyan. You have our premier suite. How do you like your accommodation?"

"I haven't seen it yet. I have just discovered a friend, a rather eccentric man, who had made up his mind to cross the Atlantic in the steerage. One of those silly bets, you know, which silly young men make in our silly London clubs, and I have persuaded him out of it."

"Our steerage is supposed to be rather comfortable, Mr. Trevelyan."

"So he says, but I want his company on deck, and not on the steerage deck at that. Have you got anything vacant along my avenue?"

The purser consulted his written list.

"Nobody with him?"

"He's quite alone."

"All the larger cabins are taken, but I can give him No. 4390."

"I suppose, like your steerage, it is comfortable?" said Stranleigh, with a smile.

"It is, yet it's not a private hotel like your quarters."

"Oh, he'll not grumble. Will you send a steward to carry his portmanteau from the number indicated on this steerage ticket to his new room? Meanwhile, I'll have transferred to him his luggage that I brought from London."

The purser rapidly wrote out a new ticket, and took the difference in five-pound notes.

"Are you going to your quarters now?" the purser asked.

"Yes, I must give some instructions to my man."

"Then it will give me great pleasure to show you the way there," said the purser, rising and locking the door; and in spite of Stranleigh's protest against his taking the trouble, he led him to a series of rooms that would have satisfied a much more exacting person than his young lordship. When the purser had returned to his duties, Stranleigh said to Ponderby—

"The Hon. John Hazel is aboard, and his cabin is No. 4390. He had to leave London in a great hurry and without the necessary luggage."

Ponderby's eyes lit up with an expression which said—"I knew that would happen sooner or later." But he uttered no word, and cast down his eyes when he saw his master had noticed the glance. Stranleigh spoke coldly and clearly.

"How many new suits have you provided for me?"

"Thirty-seven, my lord."

"Very well. Clear out one or two boxes, and pack a dress-suit and two or three ordinary suits; in fact, costume the Hon. John Hazel just as you would costume me. Call a steward, and order the box to be taken to his room. Lay out for him an everyday garb, and get all this done as quickly as possible."

His lordship proceeded leisurely to the upper deck once more, and found Hazel just as he had left him, except that he was now gazing at the fleeting shore, green and village-studded, of the Isle of Wight.

"Here you are," said Stranleigh breezily, handing the Hon. John the cabin ticket.

There was a weak strain in Hazel's character, otherwise he would never had come to the position in which he found himself, and he now exhibited the stubbornness which has in it the infallible signs of giving way.

"I really cannot accept it," he said, his lower lip trembling perceptibly.

"Tut, tut! It's all settled and done with. Your room is No. 4390. You will find your bag there, and also a box from my habitation. Come along—I'll be your valet. Luncheon will be on shortly, and I want your company."

Stranleigh turned away, and Hazel followed him.

Cabin 4390 could not be compared with the luxurious suite that Stranleigh was to occupy, yet, despite the purser's hesitation to overpraise it, the cabin was of a size and promise of comfort that would have been found in few liners a decade ago. Ponderby was on hand, and saved his master the fag of valeting, and when finally the Hon. John emerged, he was quite his old jaunty self again—a well-dressed man who would not have done discredit even to the Camperdown Club.

"I have secured a place for you," said Stranleigh, "next to myself at the doctor's table. I flatter myself on having made this transfer with more tact than I usually display, for I am somewhat stupid in the main, trusting others to carry out my ideas rather than endeavouring to shine as a diplomatist myself. The purser—the only official aware of the change—thinks you made a bet to go over steerage, and will probably forget all about the matter. The question is, under what name shall I introduce you to the doctor?"

"What would you advise?" asked Hazel. "The name on my steerage ticket is William Jones."

"Oh, that's no good as a nom de guerre—too palpably a name chosen by an unimaginative man. I should sail under your own colours if I were you."

"Good! Then John Hazel I am, and so will remain. As a guarantee of good faith, I promise you not to touch a card all the way across."

"A good resolution; see that you keep it." And thus they enjoyed an appetising lunch together, and were regaled with one of the doctor's best salads.

They got away from Cherbourg before the dinner hour, and after that meal Stranleigh and Hazel walked together on the main deck, until the latter, admitting he was rather fagged after the exciting events of the day, went off to his cabin, and Stranleigh was left alone to smoke a final cigar. He leaned on the rail and gazed meditatively at the smooth sea.

It was an ideal evening, and Stranleigh felt at peace with all the world. There exists a popular belief that the rich are overburdened with care. This may be true while they are in the money-making struggle, but it is not a usual fault when the cash is in the bank or safely invested. Stranleigh occasionally lost money, but an immense amount had been bequeathed him, and he made many millions more than he had parted with, although he claimed this was merely because of a series of flukes, maintaining that, whenever he set to work that part of him known as his brains, he invariably came a cropper.

"You are Mr. Trevelyan, are you not?" said a very musical feminine voice at his elbow. Stranleigh turned in surprise, and seeing there a most charming young woman, he flung his partially consumed cigar into the sea.

"Yes," he replied, "my name is Trevelyan. How did you know?"

That rare smile came to his lips—a smile, people said, which made you feel instinctively you could trust him; and many ladies who were quite willing to bestow their trust, called it fascinating.

"I am afraid," said the girl, whose beautiful face was very serious, and whose large dark eyes seemed troubled—"I am afraid that I enacted the part of unintentional eavesdropper. I had some business with the purser—business that I rather shrank from executing. You came to his window just before I did, for I was hesitating."

"I am sorry," said Stranleigh, "if I obtruded myself between you and that official. Being rather limited in intelligence, my mind can attend to only one thing at a time, and I must confess I did not see you."

"I know you did not," retorted the girl. "There was no obtrusion. You were first comer, and therefore should have been first served, as was the case."

"I would willingly have given up my place and whatever rights I possessed in the matter, had I known a lady was waiting."

"I am sure of it. However, your conversation with the purser gave me a welcome respite, and, thinking over the crisis, I determined to consult you before I spoke to him; thus I have taken the unusual step of bringing myself to your notice."

"In what way can I assist you, madam?" asked Stranleigh, a return of his usual caution showing itself in the instant stiffening of manner and coldness of words.

"I learned you were exchanging, on behalf of a friend, a third-class ticket for a place in the cabin. I judged from this that you are a good-hearted man, and my attention was attracted when you introduced yourself to the purser as Trevelyan, because Trevelyan is my own name."

"Really?" ejaculated his lordship. "Have you relatives near Wychwood?

You are English, are you not?"

"I am English, and a distant connection with the family of Trevelyan, near Wychwood, none of whom, however, I have yet met, unless you happen to belong to that branch."

"I do," said Stranleigh. "And now tell me, if you please, what is your difficulty?"

"I wish to ask you if the steerage ticket you gave the purser was taken in part payment for the cabin ticket, or did you forfeit it altogether?"

"That I can't tell you," said Stranleigh, with a laugh. "I am not accustomed to the transaction of business, and this little arrangement had to be made quickly."

Although his lordship spoke lightly and pleasantly the girl appeared to have some difficulty in proceeding with her story. The large eyes were quite evidently filling with tears, and of all things in the world Stranleigh loathed an emotional scene. The girl was obviously deeply depressed, whatever the cause.

"Well," he said jauntily and indeed encouragingly, "we were talking of first and third-class tickets. What have you to say about them?"

"I speak of the steerage ticket only. If you haven't forfeited it, you have the right to demand its return."

"I suppose so. Still, it is of no particular use to me."

"No, but it would be vital to me. Coming down in the train from London, my purse was stolen, or perhaps I lost it when giving up my railway ticket. So I am now without either money or transportation voucher."

"Was it for cabin passage?"

"Yes."

"In that case you will have no difficulty; your name will be on the purser's list. Do you know the number of your state-room?"

"No, I do not, and, so far as my name goes, I can expect no help from that quarter, because the name I travel under is not Miss Trevelyan."

"Good gracious," cried Stranleigh, "there are three of us! This ship should be called Incognita. Was your money also in that purse?"

"Yes, all my gold and bank-notes, and I am left with merely some silver and coppers."

"Then the third-class ticket would not be of the slightest use to you. As I had to point out to another person on a similar occasion, you would not be allowed to land, so we will let that third-class ticket drop into oblivion. If you are even distantly related to the Trevelyan family, I could not think of allowing you to travel steerage. Are you alone?"

"Yes," she murmured almost inaudibly.

"Well, then, it is better that you should make all arrangements with the purser yourself. As I told you, I am not particularly good at business affairs. You give to him the name under which you purchased your ticket. You bought it in London, I suppose?"

"Yes," she murmured again.

"Mention to him the name you used then. He will look up his list, and allot you the state-room you paid for. It is probable he may have the power to do this without exacting any excess fare; but if such is not the case, settle with him for your passage, and take his receipt. The money will doubtless be refunded at New York. Here is a fifty-pound note, and you can carry out the transaction much better than I. But stop a moment. Do you remember how much you paid for the room?"

"Twenty-five pounds."

"That will leave you only the remaining twenty-five for New York, which is an expensive place, so we must make the loan a hundred pounds. Leave me your address, and if you do not hear from your people before that loan is expended, you may have whatever more you need. You will, of course, repay me at your convenience. I will give you the name of my New York agents."

210

The eyes had by this time brimmed over, and the girl could not speak. Stranleigh took from his pocket-book several Bank of England notes. Selecting two for fifty pounds each, he handed them to her.

"Good-night!" he said hurriedly.

"Good-night!" she whispered.

After dinner on the day the liner left Queenstown, Lord Stranleigh sat in a comfortable chair in the daintily furnished drawing-room of his suite. A shaded electric light stood on the table at his elbow, and he was absorbed in a book he had bought before leaving London. Stranleigh was at peace with all the world, and his reading soothed a mind which he never allowed to become perturbed if he could help it. He now thanked his stars that he was sure of a week undisturbed by callers and free from written requests. Just at this moment he was amazed to see the door open, and a man enter without knock or other announcement. His first thought was to wonder what had become of Ponderby—how had the stranger eluded him? It was a ruddy-faced, burly individual who came in, and, as he turned round to shut the door softly, Stranleigh saw that his thick neck showed rolls of flesh beneath the hair. His lordship placed the open book face downwards on the table, but otherwise made no motion.

"Lord Stranleigh, I presume?" said the stranger.

Stranleigh made no reply, but continued gazing at the intruder.

"I wish to have a few words with you, and considered it better to come to your rooms than to accost you on deck. What I have to say is serious, and outside we might have got into an altercation, which you would regret."

"You need have no fear of any altercation with me," said Stranleigh.

"Well, at least you desire to avoid publicity, otherwise you would not be travelling under an assumed name."

"I am not travelling under an assumed name."

The stout man waved his hand in deprecation of unnecessary talk.

"I will come to the point at once," he said, seating himself without any invitation.

"I shall be obliged if you do so."

The new-comer's eyes narrowed, and a threatening expression overspread his rather vicious face.

"I want to know, Lord Stranleigh, and I have a right to ask, why you gave a hundred pounds to my wife."

"To your wife?" echoed Stranleigh in amazement.

"Yes. I have made a memorandum of the numbers, and here they are—two fifty-pound notes. Bank of England. Do you deny having given them to her?"

"I gave two fifty-pound notes to a young lady, whose name, I understood, was Trevelyan—a name which I also bear. She informed me, and somehow I believed her, that her purse containing steamship ticket and money, had been lost or stolen."

A wry smile twisted the lips of the alleged husband.

"Oh, that's the story is it? Would you be surprised if the young lady in question denied that in toto?"

"I should not be astonished at anything," replied his lordship, "if you are in possession of the actual bank-notes I gave to her."

"She describes your having taken these flimsies from a number of others you carry in your pocket. Would you mind reading me the number of others you carry in your pocket. Would you mind reading me the number of the next note in your collection?"

"Would you mind reading me the numbers on the notes you hold?" asked Stranleigh, in cool, even tones, making no sign of producing his own assets.

"Not at all," replied the other; whereupon he read them. The notes were evidently two of a series, and the numbers differed only by a single unit. Stranleigh nonchalantly took out his pocket-book, and the intruder's eyes glistened as he observed its bulk. Stranleigh glanced at the number on the top bank-note, and replaced his pocket-book, leaning back in his easy chair.

"You are quite right," he said. "Those are the notes I gave to Miss Trevelyan."

"I asked why."

"I told you why."

"That cock-and-bull story won't go down," said the other. "Even the richest men do not fling money about in such reckless fashion. They do it only for a favour given or a favour expected."

"I dare say you are right. But come to the point, as you said you would."

"Is that necessary?"

"I don't know that it is. You want money—as large an amount as can be squeezed from a man supposedly wealthy. You use your good-looking wife as a decoy——"

"You are casting aspersion on a lady quite unknown to you!" cried his visitor, with well-assumed indignation.

"Pardon me, you seem to be casting aspersion on her whom you say is your wife. I don't know how these notes got into your hands, but I'd be willing to stake double the amount that the lady is quite innocent in the matter. She certainly is so far as I am concerned. If the lady is your wife, what is her name? She told me she was travelling under a different title from that written on the lost ticket."

"I am not ashamed of my name, if you are of yours. My name is Branksome Poole."

"Ah, then she is Mrs. Branksome Poole?"

"Naturally."

213

Stranleigh reached out and drew towards him a passenger list. Running his eye down the column of cabin passengers, he saw there the names: "Mr. and Mrs. Branksome Poole."

"Well, Mr. Poole, we come to what is the final question—how much?"

"If you give me the roll of Bank of England notes which you exhibited a moment ago, I shall say nothing further about the matter, and, understand me, there is no coercion about my request. You may accept or decline, just as you like. I admit that my wife and I do not get along well together, and although I consider I have a grievance against you, I am not assuming the injured husband rôle at all. If you decline, I shall make no scandal aboard ship, but will wait and take action against you the moment we arrive in New York."

"Very considerate of you, Mr. Poole. I understand that in New York the fountains of justice are perfectly pure, and that the wronged are absolutely certain of obtaining redress. I congratulate you on your choice of a battle-ground. Of course, you haven't the slightest thought of levying blackmail, but I prefer to spend my money on the best legal talent in America rather than trust any of it to you. It's a mere case of obstinacy on my part. And now, if you will kindly take your departure, I will get on with my book; I am at a most interesting point."

"I shall not take my departure," said Poole doggedly, "until we have settled this matter."

"The matter is settled." Stranleigh touched an electric button. An inside door opened, and Ponderby entered, looking in amazement at his master's visitor.

"Ponderby," said Lord Stranleigh, "in future I desire you to keep this outer door locked, so that whoever wishes to see me may come through your room. Take a good look at this gentleman, and remember he is not to be allowed within my suite again on any pretext. Meanwhile, show him into the corridor. Take him through your room, and afterwards return and lock this other door."

Then occurred an extraordinary thing. Ponderby, for the first time in his life, disobeyed his master's instructions. Approaching the seated Poole, he said—

"Will you go quietly?"

"I'll not go, quietly or otherwise," answered the man stubbornly.

Ponderby opened the door by which Poole had entered, then, seizing him by the collar, lifted him, led him to the door, and pitched him out of the room across the corridor. Returning, he closed, locked, and bolted the door.

"I beg your pardon, my lord," said the panting Ponderby to his amazed master, "but I dare not take him through my room. His wife is there. She appears to have followed him. Anyhow, she recognised his voice, and told me hurriedly why she came. I locked the door to the passage, for, as I heard her story, I felt it might be serious, and at least you ought to hear what she has to say before you acted. I hope you will excuse the liberty I have taken, my lord."

"Ponderby, as I have often told you, you are a gem! I will go into your room, but you must remain there while I talk to this lady. No more tête-à-tête conversations with the unprotected for me."

"I think she is honest, my lord, but in deep trouble."

"I am glad to have my opinion corroborated by so good a judge of character as yourself, Ponderby."

They went together to the valet's sitting-room, and there sat the woman, with her dark head bowed upon arms outstretched along the table, her shoulders shaking. She was plainly on the verge of hysterics, if, indeed, she had not already crossed the boundary line.

"Here is Mr. Trevelyan, madam," said Ponderby. "You wanted to speak with him."

She raised her head, dabbed her wet eyes nervously with her handkerchief, and made an effort to pull herself together. When she spoke, it was with rapid utterance, reeling off what she had to say as if it were a task learned by rote.

"I have at last come to the end of my tether, and to-night, if there is no prospect of freedom, I shall destroy myself. Before this I have often thought of suicide, but I am a cowardly person, and cling to life. Five years ago my father went out to America bent on a motor tour; he took me with him. Among other servants he engaged Charles Branksome, who had proved himself an expert chauffeur. He was English, and came to us well recommended. He intimated that he was of good family, but had his living to earn. He was handsome then, and had a most ingratiating manner. The person who called on you to-night bears little resemblance to the Branksome of five years ago. I had often gone motoring with him while in America, and I was young, and rather flighty: a foolish person altogether. Perhaps you read about it in the papers. I cannot dwell on the appalling mistake I made.

"We became very well acquainted, and at last he professed to have fallen in love with me, and I believed him. We were secretly married before a justice of the peace in America, and I was not long left in doubt as to the disaster that had befallen me. His sole desire was money. My father being wealthy, he hoped to get all he cared to demand. My father, however, is a very stubborn man, and, after his first shock on finding the episode made much of by the American papers, he refused to pay Branksome a penny, and returned forthwith to England. I never saw him again, nor could I get into communication with him. Two years after my mad act he died, and never even mentioned me in his will.

"My husband is a liar, a thief, a forger, a gambler, and a brute. He has maltreated me so that I have been left once or twice for dead, but finally he broke me to his will. He is known as a cheat in every gambling resort in Europe, and on the Atlantic liners. Lately I have been used as a decoy in the way of which you have had experience. Somehow he learned—indeed, that is his business—who were the rich travellers on this boat. He thought, as this was the newest and largest steamship on the ocean, its staff would not at first be thoroughly organised, and that he might escape detection. He pointed you out to me as you came on board, and said you were Lord Stranleigh, travelling as Mr. Trevelyan. The rest you know. He forced me to hand to him the money you had given, and told me it might be necessary for me to go on the witness-stand when we reached New York, but, as you were very wealthy, it is not likely you would allow it to go so far as that. His plan was to demand a very moderate sum at first, which was to be a mere beginning, and each exaction would be but a prelude for the next. He is old at the game, and is wanted now by the authorities in New York for blackmailing a very well-known millionaire."

"Do you know the name of the millionaire?"

She gave him the information.

"Very well, madam. In the first place, you must do nothing reckless or foolish. I shall see that this man is detained at New York on some pretext or other—in fact, I shall arrange for this by wireless. You should journey to one of the states where divorces are easily obtained. If you will permit me, I shall be your banker. Even if Branksome got free in New York, it will cost him dear, and his supplies are precarious. You should experience no difficulty in evading him with money in your possession. Do you agree?"

"Oh, yes!"

"That's settled, then. Ponderby, look into the corridor, and see that the way of escape is clear."

"I am sorry, my lord," she said, rising, "to cause you such trouble and inconvenience."

"No inconvenience at all," said Stranleigh, with his usual nonchalance, "and I never allow myself to be troubled."

Ponderby reported the way open, and the lady disappeared silently along the passage. Stranleigh betook himself to Room 4390, and had a long talk with the Hon. John Hazel, who, for the first time during the voyage, seemed to be enjoying himself.

Next morning the Hon. John paced up and down one deck after another, as if in search of someone. On an almost deserted lower deck he met the person whom he sought.

"I beg your pardon," said Hazel in his suavest manner, "but I am trying to find three men as tired of this journey as I am. I have never been on a voyage before, and I confess I miss London and the convenience of its clubs. A quiet little game of poker in the smoking-room might help to while away the time."

The keen eyes of Mr. Branksome Poole narrowed, as was a custom of theirs, and he took in the points of the man who addressed him.

"I am not much of a hand at poker," he said hesitatingly and untruthfully.

The Hon. John laughed.

"Don't mind that in the least," he said. "The requirement for this game is cash. I have approached several men, and they object to playing for money; but I confess I don't give a rap for sitting at a card-table unless there's something substantial on."

"I'm with you there," agreed the stout man, his eyes glistening at the thought of handling a pack of cards once more. His momentary hesitation had been because he feared someone might recognise him, for he felt himself quite able to cope with anyone when it came to the shuffle and the deal. They were a strangely contrasted pair as they stood there, the pleb and the patrician—the pleb grim and serious, the patrician carrying off the situation with a light laugh—yet it was hard to say which was the more expert scoundrel when it came to cards.

A little later four men sat down to a table. Hazel ordered a new pack of cards from the smoke-room steward, broke the seal, and pulled off the wrapper.

It is not worth while to describe the series of games: only the one matters. At first Poole played very cautiously, watching out of the tail of his eye for any officer who might spot him as one who had been ordered off the green, and so expose him for what he was. The consequence of this divided attention was soon apparent. He lost heavily, and finally he drew a couple of fifty-pound notes from his pocket-book. He fingered them for a moment as if loath to part with paper so valuable.

"Where's that steward?" he asked.

"What do you want?" demanded Hazel, as though impatient for the game to go on.

"Change for a fifty."

"I'll change it for you." And the Hon. John drew from his pocket a handful of gold and five-pound bank-notes, counted out fifty pounds, and shoved them across the table to Poole, who, still hesitating, was forced reluctantly to give up the big bank-note. Now Poole began to play in earnest, but still luck was against him, and soon the second fifty-pound note was changed, for they were playing reasonably high. Hazel, after glancing at the number on the note, thrust it carelessly into his waistcoat pocket alongside its brother, as if it were of no more account than a cigarette paper. Little did the pleb dream that he was up against a man of brains. Hazel now possessed the two bank-notes that could have been used in evidence against Lord Stranleigh, and he drew a sigh of satisfaction. Poole only saw that here was a man, evidently careless of money, possessing plenty of it, and extremely good-natured. He had already recognised him as an aristocrat, and expected that, whatever happened, he would treat it with a laugh, and perhaps leave the table, so the pleb now began some fine work. Two games were played in silence, and in the third it was the deal of Branksome Poole. Hazel watched him like a beast of prey, conscious of every crooked move, yet he did not seem in the least to be looking. He gazed at the cards dealt him, rose to his feet, and spread the hand face upward on the table.

"Sir, you are cheating," he said crisply.

"You lie!" roared Branksome Poole, turning, nevertheless, a greenish yellow, and moistening his parched lips. At the sound of the loud voice, a steward came hurrying in.

"Show your hand, if you dare!" challenged Hazel. "You have dealt yourself——" And here he named the concealed cards one after another. Poole made an effort to fling his hand into the rest of the pack, but Hazel stopped him.

"Show your hand! Show your hand!" he demanded. "These two

gentlemen will witness whether I have named the cards correctly or not. Steward, ask the chief officer to come here, or, if he is not on duty, speak to the captain."

The steward disappeared, and shortly returned with the chief officer, to whom Hazel briefly and graphically related what had happened.

"Will you come with me to the captain's room?" requested the chief officer.

Branksome Poole had been through the mill before, and he offered no resistance.

When the wireless came in touch with the American shore, a dispatch reached police headquarters in New York, informing them that Charles Branksome, wanted for blackmailing Erasmus Blank, the millionaire, was detained by the ship's authority for cheating at cards.

When the great vessel arrived at her berth, Mrs. Branksome Poole was quite unmolested as she took her ticket for the West. She was amply supplied with money, and among her newly-acquired funds were two fifty-pound notes which had been previously in her possession.

II.—AN AUTOMOBILE RIDE.

When Lord Stranleigh of Wychwood came to New York under his family name of Trevelyan, he had intended to spend several weeks in that interesting metropolis, but newspaper men speedily scattered his incognito to the winds, and, what with interviewers, photographers, funny paragraphists and the like, the young lord's life was made a burden to him. Despite his innate desire to be polite to everyone, he soon found it impossible to receive even a tenth part of those who desired speech with him. This caused no diminution of interviews or special articles regarding his plans, and his object in revisiting America. The sensational papers alleged that he had untold millions to invest; that he had placed cash on all the available projects in Europe, and now proposed to exploit the United States in his insatiable desire to accumulate more wealth.

Stranleigh changed his quarters three times, and with each move adopted a new name. He endured it all with imperturbable good-nature, despite the intense heat, but Ponderby was disgusted with the state of affairs, and wished himself and his master back once more in that quiet village known as London.

"By Jove! Ponderby," said Stranleigh, "they say three moves are as bad as a fire, and the temperature to-day seems to corroborate this, for we are making our third move. Have you anything to suggest?"

"I should suggest, my lord," said Ponderby, with as much dignity as the sweltering day would allow, "that we return to London."

"A brilliant and original idea, Ponderby. Many thanks. Go down at once to the steamship office, and book the best accommodation you can get on the first big liner leaving New York."

Ponderby departed instantly, with a deep sigh of relief.

Stranleigh's life had been made more of a burden to him than was necessary through the indefatigable exertions of a fellow countryman, whose name was Wentworth Parkes. This individual brought with him a letter of introduction from the Duke of Rattleborough. Rattleborough was an acquaintance, but not a particular friend of Stranleigh's; nevertheless, a Duke overtops a mere Earl in social eminence, much as the Singer building overtops the structure next to it.

Wentworth Parkes told Stranleigh he had been in America for something more than a year. He had been very successful, making plenty of money, but expending it with equal celerity. Now he determined to get hold of something that contained princely possibilities for the future. This he had secured by means of an option on the Sterling Motor Company at Detroit, and the plant alone, he alleged, was worth more than the capital needed to bring the factory up to its full output. J. E. Sterling, he went on to explain, knew more about automobile designing than anyone else in the world, notwithstanding the fact that he was still a young man. He would undoubtedly prove to be the true successor of Edison, and everyone knew what fortunes had come to those who interested themselves in the products of the great Thomas Alva, who up to date had proved to be the most successful money-making inventor the world had ever seen, to which Lord Stranleigh calmly agreed. Well, J. E. Sterling was just such another, and all a man required to enter the combination, was the small sum of one hundred thousand dollars. This would purchase a share in the business which might be sold within a year or two for millions. Detroit was the centre of automobile manufacturing in America; a delightful city to live in; the finest river in the world running past its doors, with a greater tonnage of shipping than passed through the Suez Canal.

Mr. Parkes was a glib and efficient talker, who might have convinced anyone with money to spare, but he felt vaguely that his fluency was not producing the intended effect on Lord Stranleigh. His difficulty heretofore had been to obtain access to men of means, and now that he had got alongside the most important of them all, he was nonplussed to notice that his eloquence somehow missed its mark. Stranleigh remained scrupulously courteous, but was quite evidently not in the least interested. So shrewd a man as Parkes might have known that it is not easy to arouse enthusiasm in a London clubman under the most favourable auspices, and this difficulty is enormously increased when the person attacked is already so rich that any further access of wealth offers no temptation to him.

Parkes had come to believe that the accumulation of gold was the only thing the average man really cared about, so he failed, by moving against the dead wall of Stranleigh's indifference towards money, whereas he might have succeeded had he approached the sentimental side of the young man. Indeed, Mr. Wentworth Parkes seemed to catch a glimmering of this idea as his fairy visions of the future fell flat, so he reversed his automobile talk, and backed slowly out.

Conversation lagging, his lordship asked a few casual questions about the Duke of Rattleborough and other persons he knew in London, but if any of these queries were intended to embarrass his visitor, Stranleigh's failure was equal to that of Parkes himself. The latter answered all enquiries so promptly and correctly that Stranleigh inwardly chided himself for his latent distrust of the man who now, quick to see how the land lay, got his motor car in position once more, but took another direction. He mopped his forehead with his handkerchief, and drew a slight sigh.

"You see," he said, in a discouraged tone, "a person brought up as I have been, to do nothing in particular that is of any use to the world, finds himself at a great disadvantage in a hustling land like the United States, where the fellows are all so clever, and have been trained from their very boyhood to be alert business men. I have a good thing in this option, and if once I got upon my feet, I could soon build up a great and profitable business. My chief trouble is to convince any capitalist of this, and if he asks me whether or not the scheme will produce a fortune within six months or a year, I am forced to admit there is little chance of it. An American wishes to turn over his money quickly; a long look into futurity is not for him. He wishes to buy one railway on Monday, another on Tuesday, amalgamate them on Wednesday, and sell out the stock to the public at several millions profit on Thursday, then rake in the boodle on Friday, which proves an unlucky day for the investors. When I truthfully confess it will be a year before I get fairly under way, I am immediately at a discount. Capitalists won't listen any further."

Parkes saw that for the first time during the interview Lord Stranleigh began to show interest, reserved though it was.

"Do you know anything about cars?" asked his lordship.

"I can take apart any motor in the market, and put it together again, always leaving it a little better than when I found it."

"And this machine—invented by the Detroit man—does it fill the bill?"

"It's the best motor in the world to-day," asserted Parkes, with a return of his old confidence.

Stranleigh smiled slightly.

"I think," he said, "you have been very successful in catching the enthusiasm of America. You deal glibly with superlatives. Mr. Sterling is the most remarkable man on earth, Detroit the most beautiful city on the globe, and your motor-car beats the universe."

"Well, my lord, I don't disclaim the superlatives, but I insist on their truth. As I said, I deal in truth, and have suffered somewhat in pocket by doing so."

A slight shade of perplexity came into the young earl's face. There was something deferential in the tone used by Parkes when he enunciated the phrase "my lord," which Stranleigh did not like. Neither phrase nor tone would have been used by any person in his own circle of acquaintance addressing another in the same set. His former distrust was again aroused. As he remained silent, Parkes went on—

"You need not take my word for the automobile, which after all is the crux of the situation. I have one of them here in New York. I tested it very fully on the way from Detroit to this city, travelling in it the whole distance. Let me take you for a drive. You doubtless know all about a motor-car, for I was told in London that you owned at least a dozen of them."

"I daresay it's true. I'm not sure. Nevertheless, I am so unfortunate as to have only a slight knowledge of their mechanics. I have driven a good deal, but not being so energetic as Prince Henry of Prussia, I leave details to my chauffeurs."

"Very good. You are doubtless well acquainted with the merits of a car from the owner's point of view. Come out with me in this Detroit motor, and I will be your chauffeur, or you may drive the machine yourself, if you remember that in this country you keep to the right side of the road."

Thus the appointment was made, and was kept by Lord Stranleigh. At the end of his run, he said to Parkes—

"The car seems to be a satisfactory piece of construction, but I own two or three American cars in London, any one of which, I think, is equally good; in fact, as Mark Twain said about his Jumping Frog—'I see no points about this frog different from any other frog.' However, I will consider your proposal, and will let you know the result. Meanwhile, many thanks for a most interesting ride."

Stranleigh sauntered down town, and entered a cable office.

"Can I send a message to London, and leave a deposit here for the reply, that it may not cost my London friend anything?"

"Certainly, sir."

Stranleigh wrote—

"Duke of Rattleborough, Camperdown Club, London.

"A man calling himself Wentworth Parkes presented a letter of introduction from you to me. Please cable whether or not he is reliable."

Two days later, Stranleigh received a reply—

"Letter a forgery. Parkes was my valet for three years, then bolted, leaving a lot of little things behind him, but not if they were portable and valuable. Believe he is now abroad, though the London police are yearning for him.   Rattleborough."

Now began the persistent pursuit of Stranleigh, which culminated in his sending Ponderby down to the steamship office to buy tickets for England. The young man said nothing to anyone of the cablegram he had received, nor did he inform the police of London the whereabouts of their quarry. He rather pitied the poor wretch, as he called him, but he had no use for a thief and a liar, so he refused to hold further communication with him, or to make any explanation. Parkes, finding he could not gain admission to Stranleigh, took to sending letters by special messenger, first adopting an aggrieved tone, a reproachful suggestion of injured innocence running through his correspondence like a minor note in a piece of music; then he became the victim of an unscrupulous millionaire, asserting that Stranleigh had promised to finance the proposed company, and breathing threats of legal proceedings. Indeed, as the recipient read these later communications, he realised they were evidently written with a view to publicity in law courts, for there emanated from them sentiments of great patriotism. The United States, Stranleigh learned, would not put up with his villainy, as would have been the case with legal proceedings in decadent England, where judges were under the thumb of a debased aristocracy.

Stranleigh had no ambition to appear in the courts of either country, so he removed from one hotel to another, but apparently he was watched, for Parkes ran him down wherever he betook himself. Thus we come to the moment when the sedate but overjoyed Ponderby returned with the steamship tickets, which Stranleigh thrust into his pocket.

"Shall I pack up now, my lord?"

"I wish you would. The valet of the hotel will assist you. Prepare three boxes; one for yourself and two for me, filling mine with such clothing as I should take were I going to visit a friend in the country for a week or two. Place the other luggage in charge of the manager of the hotel, and say I will telegraph when I make up my mind where it is to be sent."

And then, to Ponderby's amazement, the young man left for Boston, and took passage in the steamer for St. John, New Brunswick.

"You see, Ponderby," said his lordship, when they got out into the ocean, "the estimable Parkes, if he is watching us, is already aware that you have booked for Southampton. He may possibly set the law in motion, and appear with some emissaries thereof aboard the liner before she sails, so we might be compelled to remain in this country which he so ardently loves."

"But the steamship tickets, my lord? They cost a lot of money."

"Quite so, my economical Ponderby, but remember for your consolation that when you step ashore from this boat, you will be under the British flag. You may telegraph to the company and tell them to sell the tickets, meanwhile sending them by post to New York. Here they are. Whatever money the company returns, is to be retained by you further to mitigate your disappointment. I have no doubt that in thus bolting for Canada you feel like a culprit escaping from justice, but we are only escaping from Parkes. Having pestered me as much about Detroit as he has done, that city will be the last place in which he is likely to look for me. We are making for Detroit, Ponderby, by the most roundabout route I could choose, seeing that the Panama Canal is not yet open, and thus I am unable to reach the autometropolis by way of San Francisco."

After passing through Canada, Lord Stranleigh settled himself very comfortably in a luxurious suite of rooms situated near the top storey of a luxurious hotel in the city of the Straits, under the assumed commonplace name of Henry Johnson. The windows of his apartment afforded wide and interesting views of skyscrapers and noble public edifices, with a wilderness of roofs extending towards the misty horizon to the west, north, and east, while to the south flowed the majestic river, its blue surface enlivened by stately steamers and picturesque sailing craft.

The gloomy valet did not share his master's admiration of the scene. Ponderby was heart and soul a Londoner, and although forced to admit that the Thames was grey and muddy, and its shipping for the most part sombre and uncouth, that tidal water remained for him the model of all other streams. He was only partially consoled by the fact that five cents brought him across to the Canadian shore, where he might inhale deep breaths of air that fluttered the Union Jack.

Stranleigh, confident that he had shaken off pursuit, enjoyed himself in a thoroughly democratic manner, sailing up stream and down, on one of the pearl white passenger boats, that carried bands which played the immortal airs of Sousa.

He began his second week in Detroit by engaging a motor to make

227

a tour of the motor manufacturing district. He was amazed at the size and extent of the buildings, and recognised, among the names painted thereon, the designation of cars that were familiar to him. He had come to believe Parkes such an untruthful person, that he had taken a big discount from everything he said, and so was unprepared to find the reality far in advance of the description. However, he saw no sign bearing the name of the Sterling Motor Company, so asked his chauffeur to convey him thither. The chauffeur, pondering a moment, was forced to admit that he had never heard of the firm.

"Then be so good," requested Stranleigh, "as to drop into one of these offices and enquire. It is likely that someone will know the names of all other companies in the same line of manufacture."

"I don't doubt," said the chauffeur, "that they know all about it, but it wouldn't be business to direct a possible customer to a rival firm."

Stranleigh smiled.

"I have not been in this country so long as you have," he said, "but I think you will find an American business man ignores rivalry when he has an opportunity of doing an act of courtesy."

The chauffeur drew up at a huge factory and went inside. Returning very promptly, he informed his fare that they knew of no Sterling Motor Company, but there was in Woodbridge Street a young engineer named J. E. Sterling, who, they believed, made motor-cars.

"J. E. Sterling! That's the man I want. Where is Woodbridge Street?"

"Right away down town; next door, as you might say, to the river front."

"Very good; we'll go there. Just drive past Mr. Sterling's place, for if I do not like the look of it I shall not go in."

By and by they turned into Woodward Avenue, and raced down town at a speed which Stranleigh thought must surely exceed the legal limit, if there was one. Woodbridge Street proved to be crowded with great lumbering trucks, loaded with vegetables for the most part, and among these vehicles the chauffeur threaded his way cautiously. They passed a small, rather insignificant shop, above whose window was painted—

"J. E. Sterling. Motor Engineer. Repairs

promptly executed. Satisfaction guaranteed."

When the chauffeur came to a halt a little further on, Stranleigh said—

"The place doesn't look very inviting, but as Mr. Sterling guarantees satisfaction, I think it but right to call upon him. I sha'n't need you any more to-day."

The door being open, Stranleigh walked in unannounced. A two-seated runabout, evidently brand new, stood by the window, where it could be viewed by passers-by. Further down the room rested a chassis, over which two men, one middle-aged and the other probably twenty-five, were bending, with tools in their hands. They were dressed in grease-stained blue overalls, and they looked up as Stranleigh entered.

"I wish to see Mr. J. E. Sterling," he said.

"My name is Sterling," replied the younger man, putting down his tools, and coming forward.

"I understood," went on Stranleigh, "that there was a Sterling Motor Car Company."

"There will be," answered the young man confidently, "but that's in the sweet by and by. It hasn't materialised so far. What can I do for you?"

"Well, you can give me some information regarding J. E. Sterling. I want to learn if it tallies with what I have heard."

The young man laughed.

"It depends on who has been talking about me. I daresay you have been told things that might require explanation."

"I heard nothing but praise," his lordship assured him. "It was said you were the true successor of Thomas Alva Edison."

Sterling laughed even more heartily than before.

"I'm afraid they were getting at you. A man may be a creditable inventor, and a good, all-round engineer without being able to hold a candle to Edison. Are you looking for an automobile?"

"No; as I told you at first, I am looking for J. E. Sterling."

"I was going to say that I am not yet prepared to supply cars. I do repairing and that sort of thing, merely to keep the wolf from the door, and leave me a little surplus to expend in my business. My real work, however, is experimenting, and when I am able to turn out a machine that satisfies me, my next business will be to form a company, for one can't do anything in this trade without capital."

"The competition must be intense."

"It is, but there's always room for a first-rate article, and the production of a first-rate article is my ambition."

"Is that your work in the window?"

"Yes."

"Does it come up to your expectations?"

The young man's face grew serious; his brow wrinkled almost into a frown, and he remained silent for a few moments.

"Well, I can't exactly say that it does," he answered at last, "still, I think the faults I have found can be remedied with a little patience. On the other hand, I fear the improvement I have put in this car may not be as great as I thought when I was working at it."

Lord Stranleigh looked at the young man with evident approval; his frankness and honesty commended themselves to him.

"Do you mind showing me your improvement and explaining its function?"

"Not at all. You will remember, however, that this exhibition is confidential, for I have not yet patented the mechanism."

"I shall not mention to anyone what you show me. You asked me a moment ago if I wished to buy an automobile, and I said I did not. I have made a little money in my time, but mostly, it seems to me, by flukes. I do not pretend to be a business man, yet such is the conceit of humanity that I wish to invest some of my money to back my own judgment. If I lose the cash, it won't cripple me to any appreciable extent. On the other hand, should the investment prove satisfactory, I shall have more faith in my judgment than has hitherto been the case. In any event, I promise to assist you in the formation of your company."

"That's all right!" cried the young engineer, with enthusiasm. "My own judgment of men is frequently at fault, but somehow I'd stake my bottom dollar on you. Come over to the window, and I'll show you how the wheels go round."

The two men approached the car in the window, and as they did so a third person on the pavement outside stopped suddenly, and regarded them with evident astonishment. Neither of those inside saw him, but if one or the other had looked through the glass, he would have recognised the sinister face of Wentworth Parkes who, having satisfied himself as to the visitor's identity, turned away and retraced his steps.

Sterling lifted up a leather curtain which hung down in front from the passenger's seat and disclosed a line of three upright pegs, rising two or three inches from the floor of the car. They were concealed when the curtain was lowered.

"If you give the matter any thought," said Sterling, "you will discover that the passenger in an automobile is in rather a helpless position. His chauffeur may faint, or even die at his wheel from heart failure, as has been the case in several instances I know of, or he may be drunk, and therefore unreasonable or obstinate, driving the car with danger to all concerned, yet if his master attempt to displace him while the car is going at high speed, disaster is certain. Now, the centre peg here will stop the engine and put on the brakes. A pressure by the foot on the right-hand peg turns the car to the right; and on the left-hand to the left. In the ordinary car the passenger can

231

do nothing to save himself, but here he may stop the car dead, or, if he prefers it, may disconnect the steering wheel, and guide the car at his will."

"Why, I think that's an excellent device!" cried Stranleigh.

"I thought so, too, but there are disadvantages. The crises in which it could be brought to play are rare. As a general rule, a chauffeur is much more to be trusted than the owner, and if the owner happens to be a nervous man, he might interfere, with deplorable results."

"Yes," said Stranleigh, "it's like the pistol in Texas. You may not need it, but when you do you want it very badly. Has anyone else seen this contrivance?"

"No one except my assistant."

"Could you lend me this car to-morrow?"

"Certainly."

"Then place the car in charge of a competent chauffeur, who knows nothing of your safety device, and send it up to my hotel at eleven o'clock. Tell him to ask for Henry Johnson. I'll take a little trip into the country, where I can test the car on some unfrequented road."

"Better cross the river to Canada," said Sterling, with a smile. "Things are quiet over there."

"Very well," agreed Stranleigh. "You are a busy man, and I have taken up a considerable amount of your time. You must allow me to pay you for it."

The young man's face grew red underneath its spots of grease, and he drew back a step.

"You have spent your own time to an equal amount, so we'll allow one expenditure to balance the other."

"My time is of no account. I'm a loafer."

"I could not accept any money, sir."

The two looked at one another for a moment, and gentlemen understand

232

each other even though one wears the greasy clothes of a mechanic.

"I beg your pardon," said Stranleigh, softly. "Now, let me ask you one question. Have you given an option on this business to anyone?"

Sterling glanced up in surprise.

"Why, yes, I did give an option to an Englishman. By the way, you're English, are you not?"

"I was born over there."

"This Englishman wasn't your sort. He was a most plausible talker, and as I told you, my judgment of men is sometimes at fault. I gave him an option for two months, but I think all he wanted was to get an automobile for nothing. He said he represented a syndicate of English capitalists, some of whom were in New York, and he borrowed the only car I had completed at that time. That was four months ago. Like the preacher after the futile collection, I wanted to get back my hat at least, but although I wrote letter after letter, I never received any answer. It wasn't worth my while to set the police on his track, so I tried to forget him, and succeeded until you spoke of an option just now."

"That agreement lapsed two months ago?"

"Yes."

"Then write out an option for me, good for a week. I'll pay you five hundred dollars down, to be forfeited if I fail to do what I promise."

"I'll give you the document with pleasure, but it is unnecessary to make a deposit."

"This is business, you know, Mr. Sterling. You are pretending you are as bad a business man as I am. I don't know much about the law of America, but I think you will find that unless a deposit is made, your instrument would be invalid in a court of law. There must be value received, I believe, when a bargain is made."

"All right," said Sterling, "but I'll give you back your money if you regret the deal."

He went to a desk in the corner, and wrote out the agreement, in which he acknowledged the receipt of five hundred dollars. Stranleigh selected from his wallet five bills for a hundred dollars each, and handed them over, then bidding farewell to the engineer, walked to his hotel, followed at a discreet distance by Mr. Wentworth Parkes.

Having located his quarry, Parkes retraced his steps to Woodbridge Street, deep in thought. His first resolution was to try bluster, but he abandoned that idea for two reasons, each conclusive in its way. His slight acquaintance with the engineer had convinced him that while much could be done with Sterling by persuasion, he would not yield to force, and secondly, the motor builder had no money. Whatever gold he was to acquire in his deal must come from Lord Stranleigh. It was, therefore, a mild and innocent lamb of a man who entered the machine shop of Woodbridge Street.

"Hello!" cried Sterling, who seemed taken aback by the encounter. "What have you done with my automobile, and why did you not answer my letters?"

"Your automobile is here in Detroit; a little the worse for wear, perhaps, but there is nothing wrong with it that you cannot put right in short order. As for letters, I never received any. I thought I had notified you of my changed address."

"As a matter of fact, you didn't."

"In that case, I apologise most humbly. The truth is, Mr. Sterling, I have been working practically night and day, often under very discouraging circumstances. Until quite recently there was nothing hopeful to tell, and the moment I struck a bit of good luck, I came on here in the car to let you know. You see, it was very difficult to interest capital in a proposition that apparently has no substantiality behind it. If you had possessed a big factory in going order, that I could have shown a man over, the company would have been formed long ago. It therefore surprised me exceedingly, when I passed your shop less than a hour ago, to see standing in this window, while you were explaining the car to him, the man on whom I chiefly depended. You must put it down to my credit that instead of coming in as I had intended, thus embarrassing him, and perhaps spoiling a deal by my interference, I passed on, waited until he came out, and followed him to his hotel."

Sterling was plainly nonplussed.

"I wish you had come in an hour earlier," he said. "You couldn't have interfered with a deal, because your option ran out two months ago."

"I know that," said Parkes regretfully, "but I thought the good work on my part would have made up for a legal lapse. Indeed, Mr. Sterling, if you will allow me to say so, I had such supreme faith in your own honesty, that I believed you would not hesitate to renew our arrangement."

"That's just the point," said Sterling. "Had you come in an hour sooner, you would have been in time. As it is, I have granted a new option to the man you saw here with me."

"What name did he give you? Trevelyan?"

"No; the name he mentioned was Henry Johnson."

Parkes laughed a little, then checked himself.

"He went under the name of Trevelyan in New York, but I know neither that nor Johnson is his true title. Well, is he going in with you, then?"

"He has asked for a week to decide."

Now Parkes laughed more heartily.

"I took him out in your motor in New York, and there also he asked for a week in which to decide. He seems to have taken the opportunity to come West, and try to forestall me."

"Oh, I don't believe he's that sort of man," cried Sterling, impatiently.

"Perhaps I do him an injustice. I sincerely hope so. Of course you're not compelled to show your hand, but I think, in the circumstances, you might let me know just how far you've got."

"Yes, I think you are entitled to that. I remember I was rather astonished when I learned he knew I had given a former option, but I shall be very much disappointed if he doesn't run straight. Still, I have been mistaken in men before. He took an option for a week, and paid me five hundred dollars down in cash, to be forfeited if he does not exercise it."

"Well, if the money is not counterfeit, that certainly looks like running straight. And meanwhile, what are you to do?"

"I am to do nothing, except send this car up to his hotel with a suitable chauffeur, at eleven o'clock to-morrow. He is going to test it along the Canadian roads."

"Was anything said about the amount of capital he was to put up?"

"Not a word; we didn't get that far."

Parkes took a few turns up and down the room then he said suddenly:

"Have you any particular chauffeur in mind?"

"No; I was just going out to make arrangements."

"You don't need to make any arrangements. I'll be your chauffeur, and can show off this car better than a stranger, who perhaps might be interested in some other automobile, and try to get your customer away. It's to my interest, having spent so much time on it, to see the deal put through. Besides, I know your man, and now that I have encountered him here in Detroit, he cannot deny that I sent him to your shop. I think he owes me at least a commission for bringing you together. I realise, of course, that I have no legal claim on either of you, yet I am sure, if the facts were proved, any court would allow me an agent's commission."

"I'll pay your commission," said Sterling.

"You haven't got the money, and he has."

"Very well; I will let you go as chauffeur, but I must inform him who you are."

Parkes shook his head.

"My dear Sterling, you are the most honest and impractical man I ever met. If you give him warning, he'll merely leave you in the lurch as he did me."

"Do you intend to disguise yourself?"

"Certainly not."

"Then he will recognise you at once."

"I understand that class of Englishman much better than you do. He will never see me, and I don't know that I shall call myself to his attention at all. My own idea is to let the deal go through, claiming only the privilege of being your adviser, and keeping altogether in the background. I can give you valuable hints about dealing with this sort of man. He will regard me as a servant, and unless I said to him: 'Lord Stranleigh of Wychwood, why did you bolt so suddenly from New York?' he would never have the least idea who was sitting beside him, and even then he would exhibit no surprise."

"Lord Stranleigh?" echoed Sterling in amazement.

"Yes; that's the man you're dealing with, and he's worth untold millions. I'll go up to this hotel now, and see him, if you prefer that I should do so."

"No; you may take him out to-morrow, but I advise you to say nothing to him about me or my business. Whatever arrangement we come to finally, you shall be recompensed for your share in the negotiations."

Parkes' prediction regarding Stranleigh's non-recognition of him proved accurate. The young man simply said—

"We will cross the ferry, and run up along the Canadian shore as far as Lake St. Clair."

The road continued along the river bank, with no fences on the left side. Although residences were fairly numerous, there was little traffic on the highway. The car was running at a moderate pace when the chauffeur suddenly diverted it towards the river, and with an exceedingly narrow margin escaped tumbling down the bank.

"I say," murmured Stranleigh, "I don't like that you know."

"There's worse to come," said the chauffeur menacingly. "You will promise to pay me a hundred thousand dollars, or I will dash you and the car over the edge into the river. If you consider your life worth that sum, speak quickly."

"Ah, it is you, Parkes? I hope you realise that you will dash yourself over at the same time?"

"I know that, but I'm a desperate man. Just get that through your head."

"You are aware that a promise given under duress is not binding?"

"Stow talk!" roared Parkes. "Say 'yes' or 'no.'"

"I say 'No!'" replied Stranleigh, so quietly that the other was unprepared for the prompt action which followed. Stranleigh flung his arms around the man, and jerked him backward from his wheel. His lordship was in good athletic condition; the ex-valet had looked too much on the wine when it was red, and on the highball when it sparkled in the glass. He felt helpless as a child.

"Now," said Stranleigh, "we will see who is the coward. I'll lay a wager with you that this car tumbles off the bank before five minutes are past."

Stranleigh with his heels was working the two outside pegs, and the car acted as if it were drunker than a lord, and almost as drunk as the valet.

"In God's name," cried the latter, "let me go. We shall be wrecked in a moment."

"No, we won't."

"I implore you, Lord Stranleigh!"

"I'll save your life, but will give you a lesson against attempted blackmail."

He steered to the edge of the bank, then pressed the middle peg, and stopped the car. Rising and carrying Parkes with him, he hurled him headlong over the slight earthy precipice into the water, which was shallow at that point. Parkes arose spluttering, and found Stranleigh had turned the car round, and with a smile on his face, was looking down at his dripping victim.

"You'll suffer for this!" cried Parkes, shaking his fist at him. "We're in a country, thank God, where we think very little of lords."

"Oh, I don't think much of lords myself, in any country," replied Stranleigh suavely, "and even less of their valets, notwithstanding I've a very good one myself. Now listen to my advice. I shall be in the United States before you can reach a telephone, and I don't see how you can get me back unless I wish to return. I advise you not to stir up the police. The Duke of Rattleborough cabled to me that a certain section of that useful body is anxious to hear of you. Call on Mr. Sterling, and whatever he thinks is just compensation for your introduction I will pay, but before you get the money, you must ensure both of us against further molestation in any way."

Stranleigh drove up to the shop on Woodbridge Street, and listened to the account Sterling gave of Parkes' visit and conversation, and his explanation of how he had come to allow him to drive the car.

"That's quite all right and satisfactory," said his lordship. "I never for a moment distrusted you. Still, I did get your name from Parkes, and I owe him something for that. What do you think would be a fair payment to make? I threw him into the river, but though it's clean, clear water, I expect no reward."

"If you'll allow me to pay him the five hundred dollars you gave me yesterday, I think the rogue will get much more than he deserves."

"Very good; I'll add another five hundred, but see that he signs some legal promise not to molest us further. I'll capitalise your company to the extent of any amount between a hundred thousand dollars and half a million."

III.—THE GOD IN THE CAR.

Young Lord Stranleigh always proved a disappointment to a thorough-going Radical, for he differed much from the conventional idea of what a hereditary proud peer should be. He was not overbearing on the one hand, nor condescending on the other, being essentially a shy, unassuming person, easily silenced by any controversialist who uttered statements of sufficient emphasis. He never seemed very sure about anything, although undoubtedly he was a judge of well-fitting clothes, and the tailoring of even the remoter parts of America rather pleased him.

One thing that met his somewhat mild disapproval was undue publicity. He shrank from general notice, and tried to efface himself when reporters

got on his track. In order, then, to live the quiet and simple life, his lordship modified a stratagem he had used on a previous occasion with complete success. He arranged that the obedient but unwilling Ponderby should enact the country gentleman of England, bent on enlarging his mind, and rounding out his experiences by residence in the United States. Ponderby wished to get back to the old country, but was too well-trained to say so. Lord Stranleigh, under the humble designation of Henry Johnson, set for himself the part of Ponderby's chauffeur, a rôle he was well fitted to fill, because of his love for motoring, and his expertness in the art. He dressed the character to perfection, being always particular in the matter of clothes, and was quite admirable in raising his forefinger deferentially to the edge of his cap, a salute whose effect Ponderby endangered by his unfortunate habit of blushing.

Accustomed to self-suppression though he was, Ponderby could not altogether conceal from Lord Stranleigh his dislike of the metamorphosis that was proposed. He had been born a servant and brought up a servant, with the result that he was a capable one, and posing as a gentleman was little to his taste. Of course, he would do anything Lord Stranleigh commanded, and that without consciously hinting disapproval, but the earl shrank from giving a command as much as he would have disliked receiving one. He was suave enough with the general public, but just a little more so in dealing with those who depended on him.

"Did you ever visit the ancient village of Burford, Ponderby?" he asked on this occasion.

"Burford in England, my lord?"

"Ponderby," pleaded Stranleigh, "kindly oblige me by omitting the appellation."

"Burford in England, sir?"

"That's better," said the earl with a smile, "but we will omit the 'sir' in future, also. I am a chauffeur, you know. Yes, I do mean Burford in Oxfordshire, nestling cosily beside the brown river Windrush, a village of very ancient houses."

"I have never been there." Ponderby swallowed the phrase "my lord" just in time.

"Then you have not seen the priory of that place; the ruins of a beautiful old English manor-house? It forms the background of a well-known modern picture by Waller—'The Empty Saddle.' The estate was purchased by Lenthall, Speaker of the House of Commons during the Long Parliament. Kings have put up at the Priory, the last being William the Third. Think of that, Ponderby! Royalty! I know how you will respect the house on that account. One of Lenthall's descendants was served by an ideal butler, who was happy, contented, well-paid; therefore, to all outward appearances, satisfied. One day he fell heir to three thousand pounds, which at present would be not quite fifteen thousand dollars, but at that time was a good deal more. Against his master's protests, he resigned his butlership.

"'I have always wished to live,' he confessed, 'at the rate of three thousand a year; to live as a gentleman for that period. I will return to you a year from to-day, and if you wish to engage me, I shall be happy to re-enter your service.'

"He spent his long-coveted year and the three thousand pounds, returning and taking up his old service again on the date he had set. Now,

Ponderby, there's a precedent for you, and I know how you love precedents. Remembering this historical fact, I have placed in the bank of Altonville fifteen thousand dollars to your credit. You cannot return to old England just yet, but you may enjoy New England. Already constituting myself your servant, I have taken a furnished house for you, and all I ask in return is that I may officiate as your chauffeur. I hope to make some interesting experiments with the modern American automobile."

And so it was arranged. Lord Stranleigh at the wheel saw much of a charming country; sometimes with Ponderby in the back seat, but more often without him, for the inestimable valet was quite evidently ill-at-ease through this change of their relative positions.

One balmy, beautiful day during the exceptionally mild Indian summer of that year, Stranleigh left Altonville alone in his motor, and turned into a road that led northward, ultimately reaching the mountains to be seen dimly in the autumn haze far to the north. It was a favourite drive of his, for it led along the uplands within sight of a group of crystal lakes with well-wooded banks on the opposite shore. The district was practically untouched by commerce, save that here and there along the valley stood substantial mills, originally built to take advantage of the water power from the brawling river connecting the lakes. Some of these factories had been abandoned, and were slowly becoming as picturesque as an old European castle. Others were still in going order, and doubtless the valley had once been prosperous, but lagging behind an age of tremendous progress, had lost step, as it were, with the procession. Lack of adequate railway connection with the outside world was the alleged cause, but the conservatism of the mill-owners, who, in an age of combination, had struggled on individually to uphold the gospel of letting well alone, a campaign that resulted in their being left alone, had probably more to do with bringing about adversity than the absence of railways. Some of the mills had been purchased by the Trusts, and closed up. One or two still struggled on, hopelessly battling for individualism and independence, everyone but themselves recognising that the result was a foregone conclusion.

Yet for a man who wished to rest, and desired, like the old-fashioned millers, to be left alone, this countryside was indeed charming. The summer visitors had all departed, missing the sublimest time of the year. Stranleigh had the road to himself, and there was no annoying speed limit to hamper the energy of his machine. Without any thought of his disconsolate valet moping about an unnecessarily large and well-furnished house, the selfish young man breathed the exhilarating air, and revelled in his freedom.

He passed a young couple, evidently lovers, standing on a grassy knoll, gazing across a blue lake at the wooded banks on the other side, seemingly at a fine old colonial mansion which stood in an opening of the woods, with well-kept grounds sloping down to the water's edge.

A man driving a car enjoys small opportunity for admiring scenery and architecture, so Stranleigh paid little regard to the view, but caught a fleeting glimpse of a beautiful girl, in whose expression there appeared a tinge of sadness which enhanced her loveliness; then he was past, with the empty road before him. He fell into a reverie, a most dangerous state of mind for a chauffeur, since a fall into a reverie on the part of a driver may mean a fall into a ravine on the part of the machine. The reverie, however, was interrupted by a shout, and then by another. He slowed down, and looking back over his shoulder saw that the young man was sprinting towards him at a record-breaking speed. Stranleigh declutched his automobile, and applying the brakes came to a standstill. The young man ran up breathlessly.

"You are the chauffeur of that Englishman in Altonville, are you not?" he panted, breathing hard.

"Yes."

"Are you going to meet him, or anything of that sort?"

"No; I'm out for my own pleasure."

"I'll give you a dollar if you take my wife and me back to Altonville."

Stranleigh smiled.

"I'll go, my chief; I'm ready," he murmured. "It is not for your silver bright, but for your winsome lady."

"My wife has sprained her ankle, and cannot walk," explained the young man.

"I am sorry to hear that," replied Lord Stranleigh. "Get in, and we will go back to her in a jiffy."

The young man sprang into the car, which the amateur chauffeur turned very deftly, and in a few moments they drew up close to the grassy bank where the girl was sitting. The young husband very tenderly lifted her to the back seat, and the polite chauffeur, after again expressing his regret at the accident, drove the car swiftly to Altonville, stopping at the office of the only doctor.

The young man rang the bell, and before the door was opened, he had carried the girl up the steps. Presently he returned, and found Stranleigh still sitting in the chauffeur's seat, meditatively contemplating the trafficless street. His late passenger thrust hand in pocket, and drew forth a silver dollar.

"I am ever so much obliged," he said, "and am sorry to have detained you so long."

"The detention was nothing. To be of assistance, however slight, is a pleasure, marred only by the fact of the lady's misadventure. I hope to hear that her injury is not serious, and then I shall be well repaid."

"You will not be repaid," returned the young man, with a slight frown on his brow, "until you have accepted this dollar."

Stranleigh laughed gently.

"I told you at the beginning that I was not working for coin."

The young man came closer to the automobile.

"To tell the truth," he said earnestly, "I fear that now we are in Altonville that pompous gentleman, your boss, may come along, and you will get into trouble. Masters do not like their motors used for other people's convenience."

"Don't worry about Mr. Ponderby. He is a very good-hearted person, and his pomposity merely a mannerism. I am waiting to take madame and yourself to your residence."

"It isn't much of a residence," laughed the young man rather grimly, "only a couple of rooms and a small kitchen, and is less than a hundred yards from this spot."

"Then I'll take you that hundred yards."

"I work in Fulmer's grist mill," explained the husband, "and business is not very good, so I had the day off. This is a time of year when we ought to be busy, but the trade is merely local. The huge concerns down east, and further west, do practically all the grinding nowadays."

The door opened, and the doctor appeared at the top of the steps.

"It's all right, Mr. Challis," he said encouragingly. "Mrs. Challis must stay indoors for a few days, and be careful to rest her foot. The cure may be tedious, but not painful, thanks to prompt treatment."

Challis brought out his wife, and Stranleigh took them to the two-storied frame house, of which they occupied part. When the young man came out to thank the chauffeur, he found the street empty.

A week later, Stranleigh's passengers heard the purr of an automobile outside the cottage. Challis opened the door in response to the chauffeur's knock.

"Good morning," said Stranleigh, shaking hands cheerfully. "What a lovely day! I am delighted to know that Mrs. Challis has completely recovered. I did not care to trouble you with repeated calls, but the doctor has been very kind, and has kept me informed of her progress. It is with his permission that I come to offer you a spin in the car. I'll take you anywhere you wish to go, and this invitation is extended with the concurrence of Mr. Ponderby, so you may enjoy the run to the full. My name's Johnson; not Jack, the celebrated, but Henry, the unknown."

Challis laughed.

"I'm delighted to meet you again," he said.

"Come in and see my wife. Her worry has been that she has never had the opportunity to thank you for your former kindness. Yes; I shall be glad of a ride. I have been too much in the house lately."

"Another day off, eh?"

"All days are off days now," growled Challis. "The grist mill has shut down."

Mrs. Challis received the alleged Johnson with a graciousness that was quite charming. She thanked him in a manner so winning that Stranleigh sat there overcome with an attack of the shyness he had never been able to shake off. He could not help noticing the subtle melancholy of her beautiful face, a hint of which he had received in that brief first glance as he passed in the automobile. He attributed it then to her mishap, but now realised its cause was something deeper and more permanent. He was astonished later to find her so resolute in refusing his invitation. She wished her husband to go for a drive, but would not avail herself of that pleasure. In vain Stranleigh urged the doctor's dictum that it would be good for her especially as the day was so fine, and she had endured a week of enforced idleness indoors.

"Some other day perhaps," she said, "but not now," and he speedily recognised that her firmness was not to be shaken.

All her own powers of persuasiveness, however were turned upon her husband.

"You must go, Jim," she insisted. "I have kept you a prisoner for a week, and you need the fresh air much more than I do."

James Challis, protesting more and more faintly at last gave way, and the two men drove off together while Mrs. Challis fluttered a handkerchief from her window in adieu.

Challis had refused to sit in the back seat, and took his place beside the chauffeur.

"Where shall we go?" asked the latter.

"Drive to the place where you found us," said his passenger, and there they went. On the way thither, neither spoke, but at a sign from Challis,

Stranleigh stopped the car.

"You must not think," began the former, "that my wife did not wish to come. I know from the expression of her eyes that she did. Her reason for declining was one that I imagine any woman would consider adequate, and any man the reverse."

"I am an exception so far as the men are concerned," said Stranleigh, coming much nearer the truth than he suspected, "for I am sure that whatever motive actuated Mrs. Challis, it was commendable and right."

"Thank you," responded the other. "I am with you there. It is all a matter of clothes. My wife possesses no costume suitable for a motor excursion."

"In that case," cried Stranleigh impulsively, "the defect is easily remedied. I have saved a bit from the ample salary Mr. Ponderby allows me, and if I may offer you——"

"I could not accept anything," interrupted Challis.

"Merely a temporary loan, until the grist mill begins operations."

Challis shook his head.

"That mill will never grind again with the water that is past, nor the water that is to come. Fulmer has gone smash, and I could not accept a loan that I do not see my way to repay. Nevertheless, I appreciate fully the kindness of your offer, and if you don't mind, I will tell you how I got myself entangled, for there is no use in concealing from you what you must already have seen—that I am desperately poor, so much so that I sometimes lose courage, and consider myself a failure, which is not a pleasant state of mind to get into."

"Oh, I've often felt that way myself," said Stranleigh, "but nobody's a failure unless he thinks he is. You strike me as a capable man. You have youth and energy, and added to that, great good luck. I'm a believer in luck myself."

This commendation did not chase the gloom from the face of Challis.

"You have knocked from under me," he said, "the one frail prop on which I leaned. I have been excusing myself by blaming the run of horrid bad luck I have encountered."

Stranleigh shook his head.

"You can't truthfully say that," he rejoined quietly, "while you have had the supreme good fortune to enlist the affection of so clever and charming a wife."

The gloom disappeared from Challis's countenance as the shadow of a cloud at that moment flitted from the surface of the lake. He thrust forth his hand, and there being no onlookers, Stranleigh grasped it.

"Shake!" cried Challis. "I'll never say 'ill-luck' again! I wish she had come with us."

"So do I," agreed Stranleigh.

"I'd like her to have heard you talk."

"Oh, not for that reason. I'd like her to enjoy this scenery."

"Yes, and the deuce of it is, she practically owns the scene. Look at that house across the lake."

"A mansion, I should call it."

"A mansion it is. That's where my wife came from. Think of my selfishness in taking her from such a home to wretched rooms in a cottage, and abject poverty."

"I prefer not to think of your selfishness, but rather of her nobility in going. It revives in a cynical man like myself his former belief in the genuine goodness of the world."

"It all came about in this way," continued Challis. "I graduated at a technical college—engineering. I began work at the bottom of the ladder, and started in to do my best, being ambitious. This was appreciated, and I got on."

"In what line?" asked Stranleigh.

"In a line which at that time was somewhat experimental. The firm for

248

which I worked might be called a mechanical-medical association, or perhaps 'surgical' would be a better term. We had no plant, no factory; nothing but offices. We were advisers. I was sent here and there all over the country, to mills that were not in a good state of health; dividends falling off, business declining, competition too severe, and what-not. I looked over the works, talked with managers and men, formed conclusions, then sent a report to my firm containing details, and such suggestions as I had to offer. My firm communicated with the proprietor of the works accordingly, and collected its bill."

"That should be an interesting occupation," said Stranleigh, whose attention was enlisted.

"It was. One day, I was sent up here to inspect the factory of Stanmore Anson, a large stone structure which you could see from here were it not concealed by that hill to the right. It has been in the Anson family for three generations, and had earned a lot of money in its time, but is now as old-fashioned as Noah's Ark. It was cruelly wasteful of human energy and mechanical power. It should have had a set of turbines, instead of the ancient, moss-grown, overshot waterwheels. The machinery was out of date, and ill-placed. The material in course of manufacture had to go upstairs and downstairs, all over the building, handled and re-handled, backward and forward, instead of passing straight through the factory, entering as raw material, and coming out the finished product. I reported to my firm that the establishment needed a complete overhauling; that it ought to have new machinery, but that if it was compulsory to keep the old machines at work, they should be entirely rearranged in accordance with the sketch I submitted, so that unnecessary handling of the product might be avoided. I set down the minimum expense that must be incurred, and also submitted an estimate covering the cost of turbines and new machinery, which I admit was large in the bulk, but really the most economical thing to do."

"I see. And the old man objected to the expense, or perhaps had not the necessary capital to carry out your suggestion? What sort of a person is he? Unreasonable, I suppose you consider him?"

"Strangely enough, I never met him in my life."

"And you married his daughter?"

"Had to. I was determined to take the girl away, whether I reformed the factory or not, and here you see where good luck and the reverse mingled. When I arrived at Mr. Anson's factory, the old man was in New York, for the purpose, as I learned, of raising a loan, or of selling the property, neither of which projects was he able to carry out."

"That was his misfortune, rather than his fault, wasn't it?"

"In a way, yes; still, the Trust had offered him a reasonable figure for his factory. He not only refused, but he fought the Trust tooth and nail, thinking that with low taxation, and country wages, he could meet the competition, which, of course, with the factory in its present state, he could not do. The fact that he was up against the Trust became well known, so that he could neither borrow nor sell. While in New York, he called several times on Langdon, Bliss, and Co., the firm that employed me. When my report came in and was read to him, I understand he fell into a tremendous rage, and characterised our company as a body of swindlers. Mr. Langdon ordered him out of the office.

"That was the first spoke in my wheel. Mr. Langdon was a capable man, always courteous and very calm when dealing with his fellows, so I am sure that my father-in-law must have been exceedingly violent when he provoked Langdon to vocal wrath. I judge that Langdon, when he recovered from his outbreak, regretted it extremely, and was inclined to blame me for rather muddling the affair of Anson's mill. I may say that I had been placed in rather a difficult position. The proprietor was absent, and had not taken his foreman into his confidence, therefore this foreman put difficulties in the way of investigation. The employees were suspicious, not knowing what this research by a stranger meant, so I went to Anson's house, hoping to find there someone with sufficient authority to enable me to get the information I must have.

"I met Mrs. Anson, a kindly woman, but realised in a moment that no authority had been delegated to her. She appeared afraid to suggest anything, but called in her only daughter to assist at our conference. The girl at once said she would accompany me to the mill, and did so. I shall never forget with what infinite tact and persuasiveness she won over the foreman, and it was quite evident that the workmen all knew and liked her, for her very presence appeared to dissipate distrust. I saw Miss Anson home, and it seemed, as my investigations progressed, many conferences became more and more necessary. You're a young man, and doubtless you know how it is yourself."

"As a matter of fact, I don't," interjected Stranleigh, "but I can guess."

"Well—your guess is right. We had no difficulty with Mrs. Anson, but both mother and daughter were uneasy about how the father would take it. I wrote him what I hoped was a straightforward letter, putting the case to him as man to man. He answered with a very brief and terse letter that left me no doubt regarding his opinion, but my own communication had arrived at an unfortunate time; the day after he had been ordered out of our office. He at once enclosed my letter to Mr. Langdon, saying in effect:—

"'This is the sort of man you sent like a wolf in sheep's clothing to my home.'"

"Langdon telegraphed, asking if this was true. I, of course, had to admit it was, with the result of instant dismissal. I never would have let either mother or daughter know about this, but my reticence was vain, for Mr. Anson wrote a stinging letter to his daughter saying she could do what she pleased about marrying me, but that he had secured my dismissal. It is strange," Challis murmured reflectively, speaking more to himself than to his companion, "it is strange that a father rarely recognises that when he comes to a difference with one of his children, he is meeting, in part at least, some of his own characteristics. I wonder if I shall ever be so unreasonable as——"

Stranleigh's eye twinkled as he remembered how firm the girl had been in refusing the automobile invitation, yet giving no explanation of that refusal.

"What Gertrude said to me was, holding her head very proudly: 'I have received my father's permission to marry you, and if you are ready for an immediate ceremony, I am willing.'

"We were married before the old man returned from New York."

251

"Has there been no further communication between Mr. Anson and yourself?"

"On my part, yes; ignored by him. It was Gertrude who wished to stay in Altonville. She knew a financial crisis was threatening her father, and she hoped that in some way I should be able to advise him. That was not to be. She requested permission to take away her belongings. This was refused. Everything she possessed, Mr. Anson said, had been purchased with his money. They remained at his home, and she was welcome to use them at his house, any time she chose to return, but having exchanged his care for that of another man, it was the other man's duty to provide what she needed. This ended our communication, and brings us to the present moment."

"Can you drive a car?" asked Stranleigh.

"Yes."

"The immediate question strikes me as being that of wearing apparel. I propose to return with at least a box full. I don't like to be baffled, and I wish Mrs. Challis to come out with us for a run. Will you exchange seats, and drive me down to the mill?"

"You're up against a tough proposition," demurred Challis.

"A proposition usually gives way if you approach it tactfully, as Miss Anson approached the manager. If you have never seen her father, he will not recognise you, so let us call at the mill."

"He would not recognise me, but the foreman would, also many of the men."

"We must chance that."

The two young men exchanged seats, and Challis at the wheel, with more caution than ever Stranleigh used, sent the car spinning down the slightly descending road by the margin of the lake, until they came to the water level. No word was spoken between them, but his lordship studied with keen scrutiny from the corner of his eye, the profile of the intent driver. He was immensely taken with the young man, and meditated on the story to which he had listened. The effect left on his mind by that recital surprised him. It was a feeling of sympathy with the old man who had acted so obstreperously, and gradually he placed this feeling to the credit of Challis, who had shown no rancour against his father-in-law, either in word or tone. Yes; he liked Challis, and was sorry for the elderly Anson, one evidently advanced in years, battling against forces that were too much for him, stubbornly using antiquated methods in a world that had out-grown them; the muzzle-loader against the repeating rifle. These two men should be pulling together.

"There's the factory," said Challis, at last, and Stranleigh, looking up, beheld further down the valley a three-storied structure, unexpectedly huge, built apparently for all the ages. There was no sign of activity about it; but the roar of waters came to their ears; idle waters, nevertheless, that were turning no wheels, the muffled sound of an unimpeded minor cataract.

"By Jove!" cried Stranleigh, jumping out as the car stopped.

Challis said nothing, but an expression of deep anxiety darkened his countenance. There were plastered here and there on the stone walls great white posters, bearing printing like the headings of a sensational newspaper, magnified several hundred times.

AUCTION SALE.

BY ORDER OF THE BANKRUPTCY COURT,

that desirable property known as Anson's Mill, fully equipped with machinery, in condition for immediate use, with never-failing water power, which at slight expense may be enormously increased; together with ten acres of freehold land; without reserve to the highest bidder; on the Seventeenth of November!

"A desirable property," said Challis, sadly, "which nobody desires except the Trust, and probably it cares nothing about it now."

"You forget that it is desired by Stanmore Anson."

"I am afraid that even he is tired of it by this time. I am sorry, but I feared it was inevitable."

Stranleigh looked up at him.

"Could you make this factory pay, if it were given into your charge?"

"Not in its present condition."

"I mean, of course, with your recommendations carried out. If the mill, free from all encumbrances, filled with modern machinery, rightly placed, were put under your management, could you make it pay?"

Challis did not answer for some moments. His brow was wrinkled in thought, and he seemed making some mental calculations.

"There would need to be a suitable amount of working capital——"

"Yes, yes; all that is understood. Could you make it pay?"

"I am almost sure I could, but there is that incalculable factor, the opposition of the Trust."

"Damn the Trust!" cried Stranleigh. "I beg your pardon; I should have said, blow the Trust! I thought I had lost the power of becoming excited, not to say profane. It must be the exhilarating air of America. The sale is a good way off yet, and I think it will be further off before I get through with it. If you will accept the management, and your father-in-law proves at all reasonable, I guarantee to find the necessary money."

"You mean that, Mr. Ponderby——"

"Exactly. I am his chief business adviser, as well as his only chauffeur. But we are forgetting the matter in hand. We must rescue the wardrobe of Mrs. Challis. Drive on to the mansion. You know the way, and I don't."

"I'm a warned-off trespasser, but here goes."

"You won't be called on to trespass very much. You're my chauffeur, pro tem. Perhaps you won't need to enter the house at all. I shall see Mrs. Anson before I meet her husband, if possible, and will try to persuade her to give me the wardrobe."

"She would not have the courage to do that without her husband's permission, and he will never give it."

"We'll see about that. Ah, the mill is not the only piece of property to be sold!"

They had turned into a well-shaded avenue, to the massive stone gate-pillars of which were attached posters similar to those at the mill, only in this case it was "This valuable, desirable and palatial residence," with the hundreds of acres of land attached, that were to be knocked down by the auctioneer's hammer.

"I might have known," commented Stranleigh, "that if Mr. Anson was bankrupt at his mill, he was also bankrupt at his house."

They drew up at the entrance. Stranleigh stepped down, and rang the bell, Challis remaining in the car. Shown into the drawing-room, the visitor was greeted by a sad-looking, elderly woman.

"Mrs. Anson," said the young man, very deferentially, "I expect your forgiveness for this intrusion on my part when I say that I am here in some sense as an ambassador from your daughter."

"From my daughter!" gasped the old lady in astonishment. "Is she well, and where is she?"

"She is very well, I am glad to say, and is living with her husband over in the village."

"In her last letter she said her husband was taking her to New York. There had been a—misunderstanding." The old lady hesitated for a moment before using that mild term. "On the day her letter was received, I went to the hotel at which they were stopping, and was told by the landlord they had gone, he did not know where. Do you tell me they have been living in Altonville all the time?"

"I think so, but cannot be sure. I met Mr. and Mrs. Challis for the first time only a week ago."

"I hope she is happy."

"She is," said Stranleigh confidently, "and before the day is done her mother will be happy also."

Mrs. Anson shook her head. She was on the verge of tears, which Stranleigh saw and dreaded. So he said hurriedly:

"You will select me what you think she should have at once, and I will take the box or parcel to Altonville in my car."

"When at last her father saw that everything we possessed must be sold," rejoined Mrs. Anson, "he packed up in trunks what belonged to Gertrude,

and as we could not learn where to send them, Mr. Asa Perkins, a friend of ours, who lives in Boston, lent us a room in which to store the things, and they are there now."

"How odd!" exclaimed Stranleigh. "I met Mr. Perkins just before he left his summer residence, and took the place furnished, acting for the present tenant. It is much too large for him, and some of the rooms are locked. Do you happen to have the key?"

"No; it is in the possession of the housekeeper. She is there still, is she not?"

"Yes; I took the house as it stood, servants and all."

"I'll write a note to the housekeeper, then. What name shall I say?"

"Please write it in the name of Mr. Challis. He's outside now, in my car."

"May I bring him in?" she asked, eagerly.

"Certainly," said Stranleigh, with a smile. "It's your house, you know."

"Not for long," she sighed.

"Ah,——" drawled Stranleigh, "Mr. Challis and I propose that this sale shall not take place. If I may have a short conversation with your husband, I think we shall come to terms."

An expression of anxiety overspread her face.

"Perhaps I had better not ask Jim to come in," she hesitated.

"Your husband does not know him, and I would rather you did not tell him who is with me. Just say that Henry Johnson and a friend wish to negotiate about the factory."

Stanmore Anson proved to be a person of the hale old English yeoman type, as portrayed by illustrators, although his ancestors originally came from Sweden. His face was determined, his lips firm, and despite his defeats, the lurking sparkle of combat still animated his eyes.

"Before we begin any conversation regarding a sale," he said, "you must answer this question, Mr. Johnson. Are you connected in any way, directly or indirectly, with the G.K.R. Trust?"

"I am not connected with it, directly or indirectly."

"You state that on your honour as a man?"

"No; I simply state it."

"You wouldn't swear it?"

"Not unless compelled by force of law."

"Then I have nothing further to say to you, sir."

The old man seemed about to withdraw, then hesitated, remembering he was in his own house. Stranleigh sat there unperturbed.

"You have nothing further to say, Mr. Anson, because two thoughts are sure to occur to you. First, a man whose word you would not accept cannot be believed, either on his honour or his oath. Second, the Trust doesn't need to send an emissary to you; it has only to wait until November, and acquire your factory at its own figure. No one except myself would bid against the Trust."

"That's quite true," agreed Anson. "I beg your pardon. What have you to propose?"

"I wish to know the sum that will see you clear and enable you to tear down those white posters at the gates, and those on the mill."

Stanmore Anson drew a sheet of paper from his pocket, glanced over it, then named the amount.

"Very good," said Stranleigh, decisively. "I'll pay that for the mill and the ten acres."

"They are not worth it," said Anson. "Wait till November, and even though you outbid the Trust, you'll get it at a lower figure."

"We'll make the mill worth it. You may retain the residence and the rest of the property."

"There is but one proviso," said the old man. "I wish to name the manager."

"I regret I cannot agree to that, Mr. Anson, I have already chosen the manager, and guarantee that he will prove efficient."

"I'll forego your generous offer of the house and property if you will allow me to appoint the manager."

"I am sorry, Mr. Anson, but you touch the only point on which I cannot give way."

"Very well," cried Anson, angrily, his eyes ablaze. "The arrangement is off."

Both young men saw that Stanmore Anson was indeed difficult to deal with, as his ancestors had been in many a hard-fought battle.

"Wait a moment! Wait a moment!" exclaimed Challis. "This will never do. It is absurd to wreck everything on a point so trivial. I am the man whom Mr. Johnson wishes to make manager. I now refuse to accept the position, but if the bargain is completed, I'll give Mr. Anson and his manager all the assistance and advice they care to receive from me, and that without salary."

"Be quiet, Challis!" cried Stranleigh.

"Challis! Challis!" interrupted the old man, gazing fiercely at his junior.

258

"Is your name Challis?"

"Yes, sir."

"You're not my son-in-law?"

"I am, sir."

"I did you a great injustice," admitted Anson. "No man has a right to deprive another of his livelihood. I have bitterly regretted it. It is you I wish appointed manager."

"Challis," said Stranleigh, "take the car, and bring your wife. Say her father wishes to see her."

Challis disappeared, and in an incredibly short space of time, during which Anson and Stranleigh chatted together, the door opened, and Gertrude Challis came in.

"Father," she cried, "Jim says he's going to scrap all the machinery in the factory. Shall we throw our differences on that scrap-heap?"

The old man gathered her to his breast, and kissed her again and again. He could not trust his voice.

IV.—THE MAD MISS MATURIN.

"Would you like to meet the most beautiful woman in America?" asked Edward Trenton of his guest.

Lord Stranleigh drew a whiff or two from the favourite pipe he was smoking, and the faint suggestion of a smile played about his lips.

"The question seems to hint that I have not already met her," he said at last.

"Have you?"

"Of course."

"Where?"

"In every town of any size I ever visited."

"Oh, I daresay you have met many pretty girls, but only one of them is the most beautiful in America."

Again Stranleigh smiled, but this time removed his pipe, which had gone out, and gently tapped it on the ash tray.

"My dear Ned," he said at last, "on almost any other subject I should hesitate to venture an opinion that ran counter to your own experience, yet in this instance I think you wrong the great Republic. I am not very good at statistics, but if you will tell me how many of your fellow-countrymen are this moment in love, I'll make a very accurate estimate regarding the number of most beautiful women there are in the United States."

"Like yourself, Stranleigh, I always defer to the man of experience, and am glad to have hit on one subject in which you are qualified to be my teacher."

"I like that! Ned Trenton depreciating his own conquests is a popular actor in a new rôle. But you are evading the point. I was merely trying in my awkward way to show that every woman is the most beautiful in the world to the man in love with her."

"Very well; I'll frame my question differently.

Would you like to meet one of the most cultured of her sex?"

"Bless you, my boy, of course not! Why, I'm afraid of her already. It is embarrassing enough to meet a bright, alert man, but in the presence of a clever woman, I become so painfully stupid that she thinks I'm putting it on."

"Then let me place the case before you in still another form. Would your highness like to meet the richest woman in Pennsylvania?"

"Certainly I should," cried Stranleigh, eagerly.

Trenton looked at him with a shade of disapproval on his brow.

"I thought wealth was the very last qualification a man in your position would care for in a woman, yet hardly have I finished the sentence, than you jump at the chance I offer."

"And why not? A lady beautiful and talented would likely strike me dumb, but if she is hideously rich, I may be certain of one thing, that I shall not be asked to invest money in some hare-brained scheme or other."

"You are quite safe from that danger, or indeed from any other danger, so far as Miss Maturin is concerned. Nevertheless, it is but just that you should understand the situation, so that if you scent danger of any kind, you may escape while there is yet time."

"Unobservant though I am," remarked Stranleigh, "certain signs have not escaped my notice. This commodious and delightful mansion is being prepared for a house-party. I know the symptoms, for I have several country places of my own. If, as I begin to suspect, I am in the way here, just whisper the word and I'll take myself off in all good humour, hoping to receive an invitation for some future time."

"If that's your notion of American hospitality, Stranleigh, you've got another guess coming. You're a very patient man; will you listen to a little family history? Taking your consent for granted, I plunge. My father possessed a good deal of landed property in Pennsylvania. This house is the old homestead, as they would call it in a heart-throb drama. My father died a very wealthy man, and left his property conjointly to my sister and myself. He knew we wouldn't quarrel over the division, and we haven't. My activity has been mainly concentrated in coal mines and in the railways which they feed, and financially I have been very fortunate. I had intended to devote a good deal of attention to this estate along certain lines which my father had suggested, but I have never been able to do so, living, as I did, mostly in Philadelphia, absorbed in my own business. My sister, however, has in a measure carried out my father's plans, aided and abetted by her friend, Miss Constance Maturin. My sister married a man quite as wealthy as herself, a dreamy, impractical, scholarly person who once represented his country as Minister to Italy, in Rome. She enjoyed her Italian life very much, and studied with great interest the progress North Italy was making in utilising the water-power coming from the Alps. In this she was ably seconded by Miss Maturin, who is owner of forests and farms and factories further down the river which flows past our house. Her property, indeed, adjoins our own, but she does not possess that unlimited power over it which Sis and I have over this estate, for her father, having no faith in the business capacity of woman, formed his undertakings into a limited liability company where, although he owned the majority of stock during his life, he did not leave his daughter with untrammelled control. Had the old man known what trouble he was bequeathing to his sole heir, I imagine he would have arranged things a little differently. Miss Maturin has had to endure several expensive law-suits, which still further restricted her power and lessened her income. So she has ceased to take much interest in her own belongings, and has constituted herself adviser-in-chief to my dear sister, who has blown in a good deal of money on this estate in undertakings that, however profitable they may be in the future, are unproductive up to date. I am not criticising Sis at all, and have never objected to what she has done, although I found myself involved in a very serious action for damages, which I had the chagrin of losing, and which ran me into a lot of expense, covering me with injunctions and things of that sort. No rogue e'er felt the halter draw, with a good opinion of the law, and perhaps my own detestation of the law arises from my having frequently broken it. If this long diatribe bores you, just say so, and I'll cut it short."

"On the contrary," said Stranleigh, with evident honesty, "I'm very much interested. These two ladies, as I understand the case, have been unsuccessful in law——"

"Completely so."

"And unsuccessful in the projects they have undertaken?"

"From my point of view, yes. That is to say, they are sinking pots of money, and I don't see where any of it is coming back."

"Of what do these enterprises consist?"

"Do you know anything about the conservation controversy now going on in this country?"

"I fear I do not. I am a woefully ignorant person."

"My father had ideas about conservation long before the United States took it up. It is on these ideas that Sis has been working. You preserve water in times of flood and freshet to be used for power or for irrigation throughout the year. Her first idea was to make a huge lake, extending several miles up the valley of this river. That's where I got into my law-suit. The commercial interests down below held that we had no right to put a huge concrete dam across this river."

"Couldn't you put a dam on your own property?"

"It seems not. If the river ran entirely through my own property, I could. Had I paid more attention to what was being done, I might perhaps have succeeded, by getting a bill through the Legislature. When I tried that, I was too late. The interests below had already applied to the courts for an injunction, which, quite rightly, they received. Attempting to legalise the action, not only did I find the Legislature hostile, but my clever opponents got up a muck-raking crusade against me, and I was held up by the Press of this State as a soulless monopolist, anxious to increase my already great wealth by grabbing what should belong to the whole people. The campaign of personal calumny was splendidly engineered, and, by Jupiter! they convinced me that I was unfit for human intercourse. Tables of statistics were published to prove how through railway and coal-mine manipulation I had robbed everybody, and they made me out about a hundred times richer than I am, although I have never been able to get any of the excess cash. Sermons were preached against me, the Pulpit joining the Press in denunciation. I had no friends, and not being handy with my pen, I made no attempt at defence. I got together a lot of dynamite, blew up the partially-constructed dam, and the river still flows serenely on."

"But surely," said Stranleigh, "I saw an immense dam on this very river, when you met me at Powerville railway station the other day?"

Trenton laughed.

"Yes; that was Miss Maturin's dam."

"Miss Maturin's!" cried Stranleigh in astonishment.

"It was built years ago by her father, who went the right way about it, having obtained in a quiet, effective way, the sanction of legislature. Of course, when I say it belongs to Miss Maturin, I mean that it is part of the estate left by her father, and the odd combination of circumstances brought it about that she was one of my opponents in the action-at-law, whereas in strict justice, she should have been a defendant instead of a plaintiff. The poor girl was horrified to learn her position in the matter, and my sister was dumbfounded to find in what a dilemma she had placed me. Of course, the two girls should have secured the advice of some capable, practical lawyer in the first place, but they were very self-confident in those days, and Sis knew it was no use consulting her husband, while her brother was too deeply immersed in his own affairs to be much aid as a counsellor.

"Well, they kept on with their conservation scheme after a time, and both on this property and on Miss Maturin's, dams have been erected on all the streams that empty into the river; streams on either side that take their rise from outlying parts of the estate. They have built roads through the forest, and have caused to be formed innumerable lakes, all connected by a serviceable highway that constitutes one of the most interesting automobile drives there is in all the United States; a drive smooth as a floor, running for miles through private property, and therefore overshadowed by no speed limit."

"By Jove, Ned," exclaimed Stranleigh, "you must take me over that course."

"I'll do better than that, my boy. Constance Maturin is one of the best automobilists I know, and she will be your guide, for these dams are of the most modern construction, each with some little kink of its own that no one understands better than she does. There is a caretaker living in a picturesque little cottage at the outlet of every lake, and in each cottage hangs a telephone, so that no matter how far you penetrate into the wilderness, you are in touch with civilisation. From this house I could call up any one of these water-wardens, or send out a general alarm, bringing every man of the corps to the 'phone, and the instructions given from here would be heard simultaneously by the whole force. I think the organisation is admirable, but it runs into a lot of money."

"'But what good came of it at last,

Quoth little Peterkin,'"

asked Stranleigh. "Do these artificial lakes run any dynamos, or turn any spindles? Now tell me all about the war, and what they dammed each streamlet for."

"Ah, you have me there! The ladies have not taken me into their counsel: I've got troubles enough of my own. One phase of the subject especially gratifies me: their activities have in no instance despoiled the landscape; rather the contrary. These lakes, wooded to their brims, are altogether delightful, and well stocked with fish. A great many of them overflow, causing admirable little cascades, which, although not quite so impressive as Niagara, are most refreshing on a hot day, while the cadence of falling waters serves as an acoustic background to the songs of the birds; a musical accompaniment, as one might call it."

"Bravo, Ned; I call that quite poetical, coming as it does from a successful man of business. I find myself eager for that automobile ride through this forest lakeland. When do you say Miss Maturin will arrive?"

"I don't know. I expect my sister will call me up by telephone. Sis regards this house as her own. She is fond of leaving the giddy whirl of society, and settling down here in the solitude of the woods. I clear out or I stay in obedience to her commands. You spoke of a house-party a while ago. There is to be no house-party, but merely my sister and her husband, with Miss Maturin as their guest. If you would rather not meet any strangers, I suggest that we plunge further into the wilderness. At the most remote lake on this property, about seven miles away, quite a commodious keeper's lodge has been built, with room for, say, half a dozen men who are not too slavishly addicted to the resources of civilisation. Yet life there is not altogether pioneering. We could take an automobile with us, and the

telephone would keep us in touch with the outside world. Fond of fishing?"

"Very."

"Then that's all right. I can offer you plenty of trout, either in pond or stream, while in a large natural lake, only a short distance away, is excellent black bass. I think you'll enjoy yourself up there."

Stranleigh laughed.

"You quite overlook the fact that I am not going. Unless ejected by force, I stay here to meet your sister and Miss Maturin."

For a moment Trenton seemed taken aback. He had lost the drift of things in his enthusiasm over the lakes.

"Oh, yes; I remember," he said at last. "You objected to meet anyone who might wish you to invest good money in wild-cat schemes. Well, you're quite safe as far as those two ladies are concerned, as I think I assured you."

Ned was interrupted, and seemed somewhat startled by a sound of murmured conversation ending in a subdued peal of musical laughter.

"Why, there's Sis now," he said, "I can tell her laugh anywhere."

As he rose from his chair, the door opened, and there entered a most comely young woman in automobile garb, noticeably younger than Trenton, but bearing an unmistakable likeness to him.

"Hello, Ned!" she cried. "I thought I'd find you here," then seeing his visitor, who had risen, she paused.

"Lord Stranleigh," said Trenton. "My sister, Mrs. Vanderveldt."

"I am very glad to meet you, Lord Stranleigh," she said, advancing from the door and shaking hands with him.

"Why didn't you telephone?" asked her brother.

His sister laughed merrily.

"I came down like a wolf on the fold, didn't I? Why didn't I telephone? Strategy, my dear boy, strategy. This is a surprise attack, and I'd no wish that the garrison, forewarned, should escape. I am sure, Lord Stranleigh, that he has been descanting on the distraction of the woods and the camp, or perhaps the metropolitan dissipation of Philadelphia, depending on whether the yearning for sport, or his business in town was uppermost in his mind."

"My dear Sis," cried Ned with indignation, "that is a libellous statement. I never so much as mentioned Philadelphia, did I, Stranleigh? You can corroborate what I say."

"I'm not so sure about that," said Stranleigh, lightly. "Your attempt to drag me into your family differences at this point of the game is futile. I'm going to lie low, and say nothing, as Brer Rabbit did, until I learn which of you two is the real ruler of this house. I shall then boldly announce myself on the side of the leader. My position here is much too comfortable to be jeopardised by an injudicious partisanship."

"As for who's boss," growled Ned, "I cravenly admit at once that Sis here is monarch of all she surveys."

"In that case," rejoined Stranleigh, heaving a deep sigh of apparent relief,

"I'm on the side of the angels. Mrs. Vanderveldt, he did mention Philadelphia and his office there, speaking much about business interests, coal-mines, and what not, during which recital I nearly went to sleep, for I'm no business man. He also descanted on the lakes and the waterfalls and the fishing, and on trout and black bass, and would doubtless have gone on to whales and sea-serpents had you not come in at the opportune moment. Please accept me as your devoted champion, Mrs. Vanderveldt."

"I do, I do, with appreciation and gratitude," cried the lady merrily. "I've long wished to meet you, Lord Stranleigh, for I heard such glowing accounts of you from my brother here, with most fascinating descriptions of your estates in England, and the happy hours he spent upon them while he was your guest in the old country. I hope we may be able to make some slight return for your kindness to this frowning man. He is always on nettles when I am talking; so different from my husband in that respect."

"Poor man, he never has a chance to get a word in edgewise," growled Ned. "My soul is my own, I'm happy to say."

"Ah, yes," laughed the lady, "pro tem. But although I am saying so much for myself, I speak with equal authority for my friend Constance Maturin."

"Did you bring her with you, or is she coming later?" asked Trenton with some anxiety.

"She is here, dear brother, but I could not induce her to enter this room with me. Doubtless she wishes to meet you alone. She is a dear girl, Lord Stranleigh, and it will be my greatest joy to welcome her as a sister-in-law."

A warm flush was added to the frown on her brother's brow, but he made no remark.

"Gracious me!" cried the lady, laughing again "have I once more put my foot in it? Why Ned, what a fine confidential friend you are. If I were a young man, and so sweet a girl had promised to marry me, I should proclaim the fact from the house-tops."

"You wouldn't need to," groaned Ned, "if you had a sister."

"Never mind him," said Stranleigh, "you have betrayed no secret, Mrs. Vanderveldt. His own confused utterances when referring to the young lady, rendered any verbal confession unnecessary. I suspected how the land lay at a very early stage of our conversation."

"Well, I think he may congratulate himself that you do not enter the lists against him. You possess some tact, which poor Ned has never acquired, and now I'll make him sit up by informing him that Connie Maturin took a special trip over to England recently, in order to meet you."

"To meet me?" cried Stranleigh in astonishment.

"Yes, indeed, and an amazed girl she was to learn that you had sailed for America. She came right back by the next boat. She has a great plan in her mind which requires heavy financing. My brother here isn't rich enough, and I, of course, am much poorer than he is, so she thought if she could interest you, as the leading capitalist of England——"

"Good heavens, girl," interrupted Ned, the perspiration standing out on his brow, "do show some consideration for what you are saying! Why, you rattle on without a thought to your words. Lord Stranleigh just made it a proviso that——. Oh, hang it all, Sis; you've put your foot in it this time, sure enough."

The lady turned on him now with no laughter on her lips, or merriment in her tone.

"Why, Ned, you're actually scolding me. I promised Connie Maturin to help her, and my way of accomplishing anything is to go directly for it."

"Oh, heaven help me," murmured Ned, "the law courts have already taught me that."

"Mrs. Vanderveldt," said the Earl of Stranleigh, very quietly, "please turn to your champion, and ignore this wretched man, whose unnecessary reticence is finding him out."

The only person to be embarrassed by this tangle of concealments and revelations was Constance Maturin, who had indulged in neither the one nor

269

the other. The Earl of Stranleigh found it difficult to become acquainted with her. She seemed always on her guard, and never even approached the subject which he had been given to understand chiefly occupied her thoughts.

On the day set for their automobile ride, Miss Maturin appeared at the wheel of the very latest thing in runabouts; a six-cylindered machine of extraordinary power, that ran as silently and smoothly as an American watch, and all merely for the purpose of carrying two persons. Stranleigh ran his eye over the graceful proportions of the new car with an expert's keen appreciation, walking round it slowly and critically, quite forgetting the girl who regarded him with an expression of amusement. Looking up at last, he saw a smile playing about her pretty lips.

"I beg your pardon," he said.

"I'm not sure that I shall grant it," she replied, laughing. "To be ignored in this callous fashion for even the latest project of engineering, is not in the least flattering."

"Not ignored, Miss Maturin," said Stranleigh, "for I was thinking of you, although I may have appeared absorbed in the machine."

"Thinking of me!" she cried. "You surely can't expect me to believe that! The gaze of a man fascinated by a piece of machinery is quite different from that of a man fascinated by a woman. I know, because I have seen both."

"I am sure you have seen the latter, Miss Maturin. But what I have just been regarding is an omen."

"Really? How mysterious! I thought you saw only an automobile."

"No, I was looking through the automobile, and beyond, if I may put it that way. I am quite familiar with the plan of this car, although this is the first specimen that I have examined. The car is yours by purchase, I suppose, but it is mine by manufacture. Your money bought it, but mine made it, in conjunction with the genius of a young engineer in whom I became interested. Perhaps you begin to see the omen. Some time ago I was fortunate enough to be of assistance to a young man, and the result has been an unqualified

270

success. To-day perhaps I may be permitted to aid a young woman with a success that will be equally gratifying."

Stranleigh gazed steadily into the clear, honest eyes of the girl, who returned his look with a half-amused smile. Now she seemed suddenly covered with confusion, and flushing slightly, turned her attention to the forest that surrounded them. Presently she said—

"Do you men worship only the god of success? You have used the word three or four times."

"Most men wish to be successful, I suppose, but we all worship a goddess, too."

"I'm sorry," said Miss Maturin, "that Mrs. Vanderveldt mentioned my search for a capitalist. I have abandoned the quest. I am now merely your guide to the lakes. Please take a seat in this automobile of yours, Lord Stranleigh, and I will be your conductor."

The young man stepped in beside her, and a few moments later they were gliding, rather than running over a perfect road, under the trees, in a machine as noiseless as the forest. The Earl of Stranleigh had seen many beautiful regions of this world, but never any landscape just like this. Its artificiality and its lack of artificiality interested him. Nothing could be more businesslike than the construction of the stout dams, and nothing more gently rural than the limpid lakes, with the grand old forest trees marshalled round their margins like a veteran army that had marched down to drink, only to be stricken motionless at the water's edge.

It seemed that the silence of the motor-car had enchanted into silence its occupants. The girl devoted her whole attention to the machine and its management. Stranleigh sat dumb, and gave himself up to the full enjoyment of the Vallombrosic tour.

For more than half an hour no word had been spoken; finally the competent chauffeur brought the auto to a standstill at a view-point near the head of the valley, which offered a prospect of the brawling main stream.

"We have now reached the last of the lakes in this direction," she said quietly. "I think your automobile is admirable, Lord Stranleigh."

The young man indulged in a deep sigh of satisfaction.

"As a landscape gardener on a marvellous scale, you are without a competitor, Miss Maturin."

The girl laughed very sweetly.

"That is a compliment to nature rather than to me. I have merely let the wilderness alone, so far as road-making and dam-building would allow me."

"In that very moderation lies genius—the leaving alone. Will you forgive the inquisitiveness of a mere man whom you suspected at our outset of success-worship, if he asks what practical object you have in view?"

"Oh, I should have thought that was self-evident to an observant person like yourself," she said airily. "These lakes conserve the water, storing it in time of flood for use in time of scarcity. By means of sluices we obtain partial control of the main stream."

"You flatter me by saying I am observant. I fear that I am rather the reverse, except where my interest is aroused, as is the case this morning. Is conservation your sole object, then?"

"Is not that enough?"

"I suppose it is. I know little of civil engineering, absorbing craft though it is. I have seen its marvels along your own lines in America, Egypt, India, and elsewhere. As we progressed I could not help noticing that the dams built to restrain these lakes seemed unnecessarily strong."

A slight shadow of annoyance flitted across the expressive countenance of Constance Maturin, but was gone before he saw it.

"You are shrewder than you admit, Lord Stranleigh, but you forget what I said about freshets. The lakes are placid enough now, but you should see them after a cloud-burst back in the mountains."

"Nevertheless, the dams look bulky enough to hold back the Nile."

"Appearances are often deceitful. They are simply strong enough for the work they have to do. American engineering practice does not go in for useless encumbrance. Each dam serves two purposes. It holds back the water and it contains a power-house. In some of these power-houses

turbines and dynamoes are already placed."

"Ah, now I understand. You must perceive that I am a very stupid individual."

"You are a very persistent person," said the young woman decisively.

Stranleigh laughed.

"Allow me to take advantage of that reputation by asking you what you intend to do with the electricity when you have produced it?"

"We have no plans."

"Oh, I say!"

"What do you say?"

"That was merely an Anglicised expression of astonishment."

"Don't you believe me?"

"No."

They were sitting together on the automobile seat, deep in the shade of the foliage above them, but when he caught sight of the indignant face which she turned towards him, it almost appeared as if the sun shone upon it. She seemed about to speak, thought better of it, and reached forward

to the little lever that controlled the self-starting apparatus. She found his hand there before she could carry out her intention.

"I am returning, Lord Stranleigh," she said icily.

"Not yet."

She leaned back in the seat.

"Mr. Trenton told me that you were the most polite man he had ever met. I have seldom found him so mistaken in an impression."

"Was it a polite man you set out to find in your recent trip to Europe?"

As the girl made no reply, Stranleigh went on—

"My politeness is something like the dams we have been considering. It contains more than appears on the surface. There is concealed power within it. You may meet myriads of men well qualified to teach me courtesy, but when this veneer of social observance is broken, you come to pretty much the same material underneath. I seldom permit myself the luxury of an escape from the conventions, but on rare occasions I break through. For that I ask your pardon. Impressed by your sincerity, I forgot for the moment everything but your own need in the present crisis."

"What crisis?" she asked indignantly.

"The financial crisis caused by your spending every available resource on this so-called conservation policy. To all intents and purposes you are now a bankrupt. Mrs. Vanderveldt has contributed all she can, and both you and she are afraid to tell her brother the true state of the case. You fear you will get little sympathy from him, for he is absorbed in coal-mines and railways, and both of you have already felt his annoyance at the law-suit in which you have involved him. Hence your desperate need of a capitalist. A really polite man would be a more pleasant companion than I, but he is not worth that, Miss Maturin!"

Stranleigh removed his hand from the lever long enough to snap fingers and thumb, but he instantly replaced it when he saw her determination to start the machine.

"The man of the moment, Miss Maturin, is a large and reckless capitalist. I am that capitalist."

He released his hold of the lever, and sat upright. The sternness of his face relaxed.

"Now, Miss Maturin, turn on the power; take me where you like; dump me into any of those lakes you choose; the water is crystal clear, and I'm a good swimmer," and with this Stranleigh indulged in a hearty laugh, his own genial self once more.

"You are laughing at me," she said resentfully.

"Indeed I am not. Another contradiction, you see! I am laughing at myself. There's nothing I loathe so much as strenuousness, and here I have fallen into the vice. It is the influence of that brawling river below us, I think. But the river becomes still enough, and useful enough, when it reaches the great lake at Powerville, which is big enough to swallow all these little ponds."

The girl made no motion towards the lever, but sat very still, lost in thought. When she spoke, her voice was exceedingly quiet.

"You complimented Nature a while ago, intending, as I suppose, to compliment me, but I think after all the greater compliment is your straight talk, which I admire, although I received it so petulantly. I shall make no apology, beyond saying that my mind is very much perturbed. Your surmise is absolutely correct. It isn't that I've spent the whole of my fortune and my friend's fortune in this conservation scheme. It is because I have built a model city on the heights above Powerville. I was promised assistance from the banks, which is now withheld, largely, I suspect, through the opposition of John L. Boscombe, a reputed millionaire. To all intents and purposes Boscombe and I are the owners of Powerville and the mills there, but although this place was founded and built up by my father, I am a minority stock-holder, and powerless. Boscombe exercises control. Any suggestions or protests of mine are ignored, for Boscombe, like my father, has little faith—no faith at all, in fact—in the business capacity of a woman.

"I have tried, as I hinted, to enlist the co-operation of other capitalists, but experience has taught me that any appeal is futile that does not impinge

directly upon cupidity. If there is the least hint of philanthropy in the project, every man of money fights shy of it."

"I am an exception," said Stranleigh, eagerly. "Philanthropy used to be a strong point with me, though I confess I was never very successful in its exercise. What humanitarian scheme is in your mind, Miss Maturin?"

Again she sat silent for some moments, indecision and doubt on her fair brow. Presently she said, as if pulling herself together—

"I will not tell you, Lord Stranleigh. You yourself have just admitted disbelief, and my plan is so fantastic that I dare not submit it to criticism."

"I suppose your new city is in opposition to the old town down in the valley? You alone are going to compete with Boscombe and yourself."

"That is one way of putting it."

"Very well, I am with you. Blow Boscombe! say I. I've no head for business, so I sha'n't need to take any advice. I shall do exactly what you tell me. What is the first move?"

"The first move is to set your brokers in New York at work, and buy a block of Powerville stock."

"I see; so that you and I together have control, instead of Boscombe?"

"Yes."

"That shall be done as quick as telegraph can give instructions. What next?"

"There will be required a large sum of money to liquidate the claims upon me incurred through the building of the city."

"Very good. That money shall be at your disposal within two or three days."

"As for security, I regret——"

"Don't mention it. My security is my great faith in Ned Trenton, also in yourself. Say no more about it."

"You are very kind, Lord Stranleigh, but there is one thing I must say. This may involve you in a law-suit so serious that the litigation of which Ned complains will appear a mere amicable arrangement by comparison."

"That's all right and doesn't disturb me in the least. I love a legal contest, because I have nothing to do but place it in the hands of competent lawyers. No personal activity is required of me, and I am an indolent man."

The second part of the programme was accomplished even sooner than Stranleigh had promised, but the first part hung fire. The brokers in New York could not acquire any Powerville stock, as was shown by their application to Miss Maturin herself, neither had their efforts been executed with that secrecy which Stranleigh had enjoined. He realised this when John L. Boscombe called upon him. He went directly to the point.

"I am happy to meet you, Lord Stranleigh, and if you'll excuse me, I'd like to say that you are more greatly in need of advice at this moment than any man in America."

"You are perfectly right, Mr. Boscombe. I am always in need of good advice, and I appreciate it."

"An application was made to me from New York for a block of stock. That stock is not for sale, but I dallied with the brokers, made investigations, and traced the inquiry to you."

"Very clever of you, Mr. Boscombe."

"I learn that you propose to finance Miss Constance Maturin, who is a junior partner in my business."

"I should not think of contradicting so shrewd a man as yourself, Mr. Boscombe. What do you advise in the premises?"

"I advise you to get out, and quick, too."

"If I don't, what are you going to do to me?"

"Oh, I shall do nothing. She will do all that is necessary. That woman is stark mad, Lord Stranleigh. Her own father recognised it when he bereft her of all power in the great business he founded. If she had her way, she'd ruin the company inside a year with her hare-brained schemes; love of the dear people, and that sort of guff."

"I am sorry to hear that. I noticed no dementia on the part of Miss

Maturin, who seemed to me a most cultivated and very charming young lady. You will permit me, I hope, to thank you for your warning, and will not be surprised that I can give you no decision on the spur of the moment. I am a slow-minded person, and need time to think over things."

"Certainly, certainly; personally I come to sudden conclusions, and once I make up my mind, I never change it."

"A most admirable gift. I wish I possessed it."

Lord Stranleigh said nothing of this interview to Constance Maturin, beyond telling her that the acquisition of stock appeared to be hopeless, as indeed proved to be the case.

"Boscombe must be a stubborn person," he said.

"Oh, he's all that," the girl replied, with a sigh. "He cares for one thing only, the making of money, and in that I must admit he has been very successful."

"Well, we've got a little cash of our own," said Stranleigh, with a laugh.

Miss Maturin and Mrs. Vanderveldt celebrated a national holiday by the greatest entertainment ever given in that district. The mills had been shut down for a week, and every man, woman and child in the valley city had been invited up to the new town on the heights. There was a brass band, and a sumptuous spread of refreshments, all free to the immense crowd. The ladies, for days before, visited everyone in the valley, and got a promise of attendance, but to make assurance doubly sure, an amazing corps of men was organised, equipped with motor cars, which scoured the valley from Powerville downwards, gathering in such remnants of humanity as for any reason had neglected to attend the show. Miss Maturin said she was resolved this entertainment should be a feature unique in the history of the State.

The shutting down of the mills had caused the water in the immense dam to rise, so that now the sluices at the top added to the picturesqueness of the scene by supplying waterfalls more than sixty feet high, a splendid view of which was obtainable from the new city on the heights. Suddenly it was noticed that these waterfalls increased in power, until their roar filled the valley. At last the whole lip of the immense dam began to trickle, and an ever augmenting Niagara of waters poured over.

"Great heavens!" cried Boscombe, who was present to sneer at these activities, "there must have been a cloud-burst in the mountains!"

He shouted for the foreman.

"Where are the tenders of the dam?" he cried. "Send them to lower those sluices, and let more water out."

"Wait a moment," said Constance Maturin, who had just come out of the main telephone building. "There can be no danger, Mr. Boscombe. You always said that dam was strong enough, when I protested it wasn't."

"So it is strong enough, but not——"

"Look!" she cried, pointing over the surface of the lake. "See that wave!"

"Suffering Noah and the Flood!" exclaimed Boscombe.

As he spoke, the wave burst against the dam, and now they had Niagara in reality. There was a crash, and what seemed to be a series of explosions, then the whole structure dissolved away, and before the appalled eyes of the sight-seers, the valley town crumpled up like a pack of cards, and even the tall mills themselves, that staggered at the impact of the flood, slowly settled down, and were engulfed in the seething turmoil of maddened waters.

For a time no voice could be heard in the deafening

uproar. It was Boscombe who spoke when the waters began to subside.

"This," he cried, "is murder!"

He glared at Constance Maturin, who stood pale, silent and trembling.

"I told you she was mad," he roared at Stranleigh. "It is your money that in some devilish way has caused this catastrophe. If any lives are lost, it is rank murder!"

"It is murder," agreed Stranleigh, quietly. "Whoever is responsible for the weakness of that dam should be hanged!"

V.—IN SEARCH OF GAME.

The warm morning gave promise of a blistering hot day, as Lord Stranleigh strolled, in his usual leisurely fashion, up Fifth Avenue. High as the thermometer already stood, the young man gave no evidence that he was in the least incommoded by the temperature. In a welter of heated, hurrying people, he produced the effect of an iceberg that had somehow drifted down into the tropics. The New York tailor entrusted with the duty of clothing him quite outdistanced his London rival, who had given Lord Stranleigh the reputation of being the best-dressed man in England. Now his lordship was dangerously near the point where he might be called the best-dressed man in New York, an achievement worthy of a Prince's ambition.

His lordship, with nothing to do, and no companionship to hope for, since everyone was at work, strolled into the splendour of the University Club and sought the comparative coolness of the smoking room, where, seating himself in that seductive invitation to laziness, a leather-covered arm chair, he began to glance over the illustrated English weeklies. He had the huge room to himself. These were business hours, and a feeling of loneliness crept over him, perhaps germinated by his sight of the illustrated papers, and accentuated by an attempted perusal of them. They were a little too stolid for a hot day, so Stranleigh turned to the lighter entertainment of the American humorous press.

Presently there entered this hall of silence the stout figure of Mr. John L. Banks, senior attorney for the Ice Trust, a man well known to Stranleigh, who had often sought his advice, with profit to both of them. The lawyer approached the lounger.

"Hello, Banks, I was just thinking of you, reflecting how delightful it must be in this weather to be connected, even remotely, with the ice supply of New York."

Mr. Banks's panama hat was in one hand, while the other drew a

"I say nothing of the kind," replied his lordship calmly. "I am merely lost in admiration of a hard-working man, enduring the rigours of toil in the most

luxurious club of which I have ever been an honorary member. Let me soften the asperities of labour by ordering something with ice in it."

The good-natured attorney accepted the invitation, and then went on—

"We have a saying regarding any futile proposition to the effect that it cuts no ice. This is the position of the Trust in which I am interested. In this hot weather we cut no ice, but we sell it. Winter is a peaceable season with us, and the harder the winter, the better we are pleased, but summer is a time of trouble. It is a period of complaints and law-suits, and our newspaper reading is mostly articles on the greed and general villainy of the Trust. So my position is literally that of what-you-may-call-him on the burning deck, whence almost all but he have fled to the lakes, to the mountains, to the sea shore. Now, I don't intend to do this always. I have set a limit of accumulated cash, and when I reach it I quit. It would be high falutin' if I said duty held me here, so I will not say it."

"A lawyer can always out-talk a layman," said Stranleigh, wearily, "and I suppose all this impinges on my ignorance."

"Certainly," said Banks. "It's a large subject, you know. But I'll leave theory, and come down to practice. As I said before, you've had too much of New York. You are known to have a little money laid by against a rainy day, so everybody wants you to invest in something, and you've got tired of it. Have you ever had a taste of ranch life out West?"

"I've never been further West than Chicago."

"Good. When you were speaking of setting a limit to financial ambition, I remembered my old friend, Stanley Armstrong, the best companion on a shooting or fishing expedition I ever encountered. It is not to be wondered at that he is an expert in sport, for often he has had to depend on rod and gun for sustenance. He was a mining engineer, and very few know the mining west as well as he does. He might have been a millionaire or a pauper, but he chose a middle course, and set his limit at a hundred thousand pounds. When land was cheap he bought a large ranch, partly plain and partly foothills, with the eternal snow mountains beyond. Now, if you take with you an assortment of guns and fishing rods, and spend a month with Stanley Armstrong, your pessimism will evaporate."

"A good idea," said Stranleigh. "If you give me a letter of introduction to Mr. Armstrong, I'll telegraph at once to be sure of accommodation."

"Telegraph?" cried the lawyer. "He'd never get your message. I don't suppose there's a telegraph office within fifty miles. You don't need a letter of introduction, but I'll write you one, and give your name merely as Stranleigh. You won't have any use for a title out there; in fact, it is a necessary part of my prescription that you should get away from yours, with the consequences it entails. Not that you're likely to come across would-be investors, or any one with designs on your wealth. As for accommodation, take a tent with you, and be independent. When I return to my office, I'll dictate full instructions for reaching the ranch."

"Is it so difficult of access as all that?"

"You might find it so. When you reach the nearest railway station, which is a couple of days' journey from the ranch, you can acquire a horse for yourself, and two or three men with pack mules for your belongings. They'll guide you to Armstrong's place."

Stranleigh found no difficulty in getting a cavalcade together at Bleachers' station, an amazingly long distance west of New York. A man finds little trouble in obtaining what he wants, if he never cavils at the price asked, and is willing to pay in advance. The party passed through a wild country, though for a time the road was reasonably good. It degenerated presently into a cart-track, however, and finally became a mere trail through the wilderness. As night fell, the tent was put up by the side of a brawling stream, through which they had forded.

Next morning the procession started early, but it was noon before it came to the clearing which Stranleigh rightly surmised was the outskirts of the ranch. The guide, who had been riding in front, reined in, and allowed

Stranleigh to come alongside.

"That," he said, pointing down the valley, "is Armstrong's ranch."

Before Stranleigh could reply, if he had intended doing so, a shot rang out from the forest, and he felt the sharp sting of a bullet in his left shoulder. The guide flung himself from the saddle with the speed of lightning, and stood with both hands upraised, his horse between himself and the unseen assailant.

"Throw up your hands!" he shouted to Stranleigh.

"Impossible!" was the quiet answer, "my left is helpless."

"Then hold up your right."

Stranleigh did so.

"Slide off them packs," roared the guide to his followers, whereupon ropes were untied on the instant, and the packs slid to the ground, while the mules shook themselves, overjoyed at this sudden freedom.

"Turn back!" cried the guide. "Keep your hand up, and they won't shoot. They want the goods."

"Then you mean to desert me?" asked Stranleigh.

"Desert nothing!" rejoined the guide, gruffly.

"We can't stand up against these fellows, whoever they are. We're no posse. To fight them is the sheriff's business. I engaged to bring you and your dunnage to Armstrong's ranch. I've delivered the goods, and now it's me for the railroad."

"I'm going to that house," said Stranleigh.

"The more fool you," replied the guide, "but I guess you'll get there safe enough, if you don't try to save the plunder."

The unladen mules, now bearing the men on their backs, had disappeared. The guide washed his hands of the whole affair, despite the fact that his hands were upraised. He whistled to his horse, and marched up the trail for a hundred yards or so, still without lowering his arms, then sprang into the saddle, fading out of sight in the direction his men had taken. Stranleigh sat on his horse, apparently the sole inhabitant of a lonely world.

"That comes of paying in advance," he muttered, looking round at his abandoned luggage. Then it struck him as ridiculous that he was enacting the part of an equestrian statue, with his arm raised aloft. Still, he remembered enough of the pernicious literature that had lent enchantment to his early days, to know that in certain circumstances the holding up of hands was a safeguard not to be neglected, so he lowered his right hand, and took in it the forefinger of his left, and thus raised both arms over his head, turning round in the saddle to face the direction from whence the shots had come. Then he released the forefinger, and allowed the left arm to drop as if it had been a semaphore. He winced under the pain that this pantomime cost him, then in a loud voice he called out:

"If there is anyone within hearing, I beg to inform him that I am wounded slightly; that I carry no firearms; that my escort has vanished, and that I'm

going to the house down yonder to have my injury looked after. Now's the opportunity for a parley, if he wants it."

He waited for some moments, but there was no response, then he gathered up the reins, and quite unmolested proceeded down the declivity until he came to the homestead.

The place appeared to be deserted, and for the first time it crossed Stranleigh's mind that perhaps the New York lawyer had sent him on this expedition as a sort of practical joke. He couldn't discover where the humour of it came in, but perhaps that might be the density with which his countrymen were universally credited. Nevertheless, he determined to follow the adventure to an end, and slipped from his horse, making an ineffectual attempt to fasten the bridle rein to a rail of the fence that surrounded the habitation. The horse began placidly to crop the grass, so he let it go at that, and advancing to the front door, knocked.

Miss Armstrong applied the warm water.

"I must sacrifice your linen," she said calmly. "Please sit down again."

In a few moments his shoulder was bare; not the shoulder of an athlete, but nevertheless of a young man in perfect health. The girl's soft fingers pressed it gently.

"I shall have to hurt you a little," she said.

Stranleigh smiled.

"It is all for my good, as they say to little boys before whipping them."

The girl smiled back at him.

"Yes; but I cannot add the complementary fiction that it hurts me more than it does you. There! Did you feel that?"

"Not more than usual."

"There are no bones broken, which is a good thing. After all, it is a simple case, Mr. Stranleigh. You must remain quiet for a few days, and allow me to put this arm in a sling. I ought to send you off to bed, but if you promise not to exert yourself, you may sit out on the verandah where it is cool, and where the view may interest you."

"You are very kind, Miss Armstrong, but I cannot stay. I must return to Bleachers."

"I shall not allow you to go back," she said with decision.

Stranleigh laughed.

"In a long and comparatively useless life I have never contradicted a lady, but on this occasion I must insist on having my own way."

"I quite understand your reason, Mr. Stranleigh, though it is very uncomplimentary to me. It is simply an instance of man's distrust of a woman when it comes to serious work. Like most men, you would be content to accept me as a nurse, but not as a physician. There are two doctors in

Bleachers, and you are anxious to get under the care of one of them. No—please don't trouble to deny it. You are not to blame. You are merely a victim of the universal conceit of man."

"Ah, it is you who are not complimentary now! You must think me a very commonplace individual."

She had thrown the coat over his shoulders, after having washed and dressed the wound. The bullet had been considerate enough to pass right through, making all probing unnecessary. With a safety-pin she attached his shirt sleeve to his shirt front.

"That will do," she said, "until I prepare a regular sling. And now come out to the verandah. No; don't carry the chair. There are several on the platform. Don't try to be polite, and remember I have already ordered you to avoid exertion."

He followed her to the broad piazza, and sat down, drawing a deep breath of admiration. Immediately in front ran a broad, clear stream of water; swift, deep, transparent.

"An ideal trout stream," he said to himself.

A wide vista of rolling green fields stretched away to a range of foothills, overtopped in the far distance by snow mountains.

"By Jove!" he cried. "This is splendid. I have seen nothing like it out of Switzerland."

"Talking of Switzerland," said Miss Armstrong, seating herself opposite him, "have you ever been at Thun?"

"Oh, yes."

"You stopped at the Thunerhof, I suppose?"

"I don't remember what it was called, but it was the largest hotel in the place, I believe."

"That would be the Thunerhof," she said. "I went to a much more

290

modest inn, the Falken, and the stream that runs in front of it reminded me of this, and made me quite lonesome for the ranch. Of course, you had the river opposite you at the Thunerhof, but there the river is half a dozen times as wide as the branch that runs past the Falken. I used to sit out on the terrace watching that stream, murmuring to its accompaniment 'Home, sweet Home.'"

"You are by way of being a traveller, then?"

"Not a traveller, Mr. Stranleigh," said the girl, laughing a little, "but a dabbler. I took dabs of travel, like my little visit to Thun. For more than a year I lived in Lausanne, studying my profession, and during that time I made brief excursions here and there."

"Your profession," asked Stranleigh, with evident astonishment.

"Yes; can't you guess what it is, and why I am relating this bit of personal history on such very short acquaintance?"

The girl's smile was beautiful.

"Don't you know Europe?" she added.

"I ought to; I'm a native."

"Then you are aware that Lausanne is a centre of medical teaching and medical practice. I am a doctor, Mr. Stranleigh. Had your wound been really serious, which it is not, and you had come under the care of either physician in Bleachers, he would have sent for me, if he knew I were at home."

"What you have said interests me very much, Miss Armstrong, or should I say Doctor Armstrong?"

"I will answer to either designation, Mr. Stranleigh, but I should qualify the latter by adding that I am not a practising physician. 'Professor,' perhaps, would be the more accurate title. I am a member of the faculty in an eastern college of medicine, but by and by I hope to give up teaching, and devote myself entirely to research work. It is my ambition to become the American Madame Curie."

"A laudable ambition, Professor, and I hope you will succeed. Do you mind if I tell you how completely wrong you are in your diagnosis of the subject now before you?"

"In my surgical diagnosis I am not wrong. Your wound will be cured in a very few days."

"Oh, I am not impugning your medical skill. I knew the moment you spoke about your work that you were an expert. It is your diagnosis of me that is all astray. I have no such disbelief in the capacity of woman as you credit me with. I have no desire to place myself under the ministrations of either of those doctors in Bleachers. My desire for the metropolitan delights of that scattered town is of the most commonplace nature. I must buy for myself an outfit of clothes. I possess nothing in the way of raiment except what I am wearing, and part of that you've cut up with your scissors."

"Surely you never came all this distance without being well provided in that respect?"

"No; I had ample supplies, and I brought them with me safely to a point within sight of this house. In fact, I came hither like a sheik of the desert, at the head of a caravan, only the animals were mules instead of camels. All went well until we came to the edge of the forest, but the moment I emerged a shot rang out, and it seemed to me I was stung by a gigantic bee, as invisible as the shooter. The guide said there was a band of robbers intent on plunder, and he and the escort acted as escorts usually do in such circumstances. They unloaded the mules with most admirable celerity, and then made off much faster than they came. I never knew a body of men so unanimous in action. They would make a splendid board of directors in a commercial company that wished to get its work accomplished without undue discussion."

The girl had risen to her feet.

"And your baggage?" she asked.

"I suppose it is in the hands of the brigands by this time. I left it scattered along the trail."

"But, Mr. Stranleigh, what you say is incredible. There are no brigands, thieves or road agents in this district."

"The wound that you dressed so skilfully is my witness, and a witness whose testimony cannot be impugned on cross-examination."

"There is a mistake somewhere. Why, just think of it; the most energetic bandit would starve in this locality! There is no traffic. If your belongings were scattered along the trail, they are there yet."

"Then why shoot the belonger of those belongings?"

"That's just what I must discover. Excuse me for a moment."

She passed through the house, and the young man heard a shrill whistle blown, which was answered by a call some distance away. The girl returned, and sat down again, her brow perplexed, and presently there came on to the platform a stalwart, good-natured looking man, dressed in what Stranleigh took to be a cowboy costume; at least, it was the kind of apparel he had read about in books of the Wild West. His head was covered with a broad-brimmed slouch hat, which he swept off in deference to the lady.

"Jim," she said, "did you hear any shooting out by the Bleachers trail about an hour ago?"

"No, Ma'am; I can't say that I did, except a rifle I shot off."

"That you shot off! What were you shooting at?"

"Well," said Jim, with a humorous chuckle, "I guess perhaps it was this gentleman."

"Why did you wish to murder me?" asked Stranleigh, with pardonable concern.

"Murder you, sir? Why, I didn't try to murder you. I could have winged you a dozen times while you were riding down to the house, if I'd wanted to. Where were you hit?"

"In the left shoulder."

"Then that's all right. That's what I aimed to do. I just set out to nip you, and scare you back where you came from."

"But why?" insisted the perplexed Stranleigh.

"You came along with a posse behind you, and I thought you were the sheriff, but I wouldn't kill even a sheriff unless I had to. I'm the peaceablest man on earth, as Miss Armstrong there will tell you."

"If that's your idea of peace," said Stranleigh, puzzled, "I hope next time I'll fall among warlike people."

Jim grinned. It was Miss Armstrong who spoke, and, it seemed to Stranleigh, with unexpected mildness, considering she knew so much of the Eastern States and Europe.

"I understand," she said, "but next time, Jim, it will be as well merely to fire the gun, without hitting anybody."

"Oh," explained Jim, in an off-hand manner, "our folk don't pay any attention to the like of that. You've got to show them you mean business. If this gentleman had come on, the next shot would have hit him where it would hurt, but seeing he was peaceable minded, he was safe as in a church."

"Is the baggage where he left it?"

"Certainly, Ma'am; do you wish it brought here?"

"Yes; I do."

"All right, Ma'am; I'll see to that. It's all a little mistake, sir," he said amiably, as he turned to Stranleigh. "Accidents will happen in the best regulated family, as the saying goes," and with a flourish of the hat he departed.

Miss Armstrong rose as if to leave the verandah. As she did so Stranleigh said in a tone of mild reproach:

"I confess I am puzzled."

"So am I," replied the girl, brightly. "I'm puzzled to know what I can offer you in the way of books. Our stock is rather limited."

"I don't want to read, Miss Armstrong, but I do want to know why there is such a prejudice here against a sheriff. In the land I came from a sheriff is not only regarded with great respect, but even with veneration. He rides about in a gilded coach, and wears magnificent robes, decorated with gold lace. I believe that he develops ultimately into a Lord Mayor, just as a grub, if one may call so glorious a personage as a sheriff a grub, ultimately becomes a butterfly. We'd never think of shooting a sheriff. Why, then, do you pot at sheriffs, and hit innocent people, out here?"

The girl laughed.

"I saw the Lord Mayor of London once in his carriage, and behind it were two most magnificent persons. Were they sheriffs?"

"Oh, dear no; they were merely flunkeys."

"Our sheriffs are elected persons, drawn from the politician class, and if you know America, you will understand what that means. Among the various duties of a sheriff is that of seizing property and selling it, if the owner of that property hasn't paid his debts."

"They act as bailiffs, then?"

"Very likely; I am not acquainted with legal procedure. But I must go, Mr. Stranleigh, for whatever the position of a sheriff may be, mine is that of

assistant to my mother, who is just now preparing the dinner, a meal that, further East, is called lunch. And now, what would you prefer to read? The latest magazine or a pharmaceutical journal?"

"Thank you, Miss Armstrong; I prefer gazing at the scenery to either of them."

"Then good-bye until dinner time," whereupon she disappeared into the house.

The meal proved unexpectedly good. There was about it an enticing freshness, and a variety that was surprising when the distance from the house to the nearest market was considered. Stranleigh could not remember any repast he had enjoyed so much, although he suspected that horseback exercise in the keen air had helped his appreciation of it. When he mentioned his gratification at so satisfactory a menu, the girl smiled.

"Plain living and lofty thought is our motto on the ranch," she said.

"This is anything but plain living," he replied, "and I consider myself no mean judge in such matters. How far away is your market town?"

"Oh, a market is merely one of those effete contrivances of civilisation. What you buy in a market has been handled and re-handled, and artificially made to look what it is not. The basis of our provender is the farm. All round us here is what economists call, in a double sense of the term, raw material. Farm house fare is often what it should not be because art belongs to the city while nature belongs to the farm. To produce a good result, the two must be united. We were speaking just now of Thun. If, leaving that town, you proceed along the left hand road by the lake, you will arrive at a large institution which is devoted entirely to the art of cookery. The more I progressed with my studies at Lausanne, the more I realised that the basis of health is good food, properly prepared. So I interrupted my medical studies for a time, entered that establishment, and learned to cook."

"Miss Armstrong, you are the most efficient individual I ever met."

"You are very complimentary, Mr. Stranleigh, because, like the various meals you have enjoyed in different parts of the world, you must have met a great many people. To enhance myself further in your eyes, I may add that I have brought another much-needed accomplishment to the farm. I am an expert accountant, and can manage business affairs in a way that would startle you, and regarding this statement of mine, I should like to ask you, hoping you won't think I am impertinent, are you a rich man?"

Stranleigh was indeed startled—she had succeeded in that—and he hesitated before he answered—

"I am considered reasonably well off."

"I am very glad to hear it, for it has been the custom of my father, who is not a good business man, to charge boarders two or three dollars a week when they come with their guns and fishing tackle. Now, we are in a unique position. We have the advantage of being free from competition. The hotels of New York are as thick as blackberries. They meet competition in its fiercest form, yet the prices they charge are much more per day than we charge for a month. I am determined that our prices shall be equal to New York prices, but I think it is only fair to let any customer know the fact before he is called upon to pay his bill."

"A very excellent arrangement," said Stranleigh, heartily, "and in my case there will be an additional account for medical services. Will that be on the basis of professional charges in London, New York, Vienna, Berlin, or Lausanne?"

"Not on the basis of Lausanne, certainly, for there an excellent doctor is contented with a fee of five francs, so if you don't object, I'll convert francs into dollars."

"My admiration for your business capacity is waning, Miss Armstrong. If this is to be an international matter, why choose your own country instead of mine? Transpose your francs into pounds, Professor. There are five francs in a dollar, but five dollars in a pound sterling. Let me recommend to you my own currency."

"A very good idea, Mr. Stranleigh," rejoined Miss Armstrong, promptly. "I shall at once take it into consideration, but I hope you won't be shocked when the final round-up arrives."

"I shall have no excuse for astonishment, being so honestly forewarned, and now that we are conversing so internationally, I'd like to carry it a little further. In Italy they call an accident a 'disgrazia,' and when you read in an Italian paper that a man is 'disgraced,' you realise that he has met with an accident. Then the account ends by saying that the patient is guaranteed curable in two days, or a week, or a month, as the case may be. How long, then, doctor, must I rest under this 'disgrace'?"

"I should say a week, but that's merely an off-hand guess, as I suppose is the case with the estimate of an Italian physician."

"I hope your orders won't be too strict. By the way, has my luggage arrived?"

"It is all in the large room upstairs, but if you have any designs upon it, you are disobeying orders."

"I must get at a portmanteau that is in one of the bundles."

"I will fetch what you want, so don't worry about that, but come and sit on the verandah once more."

Stranleigh protested, and finally a compromise was arrived at. Miss Armstrong would whistle for Jim, and he would do the unpacking. She saw a shade of distrust pass over Stranleigh's face, and she reassured him that Jim was the most honest and harmless man in the world, except, perhaps, where sheriffs were concerned.

"Now," she continued, when he had seated himself, "you have talked enough for one day, so you must keep quiet for the rest of the afternoon. I will do the talking, giving you an explanation of our brigandish conduct."

"I shall be an interested listener," said Stranleigh, resignedly. "But permit me, before silence falls, to ask what you may regard an impertinent question. Do you smoke?"

"Goodness, no!" she replied, with widely opened eyes.

"Many ladies do, you know, and I thought you might have acquired the habit during your travels abroad. In that case, I should have been delighted to offer you some excellent cigarettes from my portmanteau."

Jumping up, the girl laughed brightly.

"Poor man! I understand at last. You shall have the cigarettes in less than five minutes. Give me your keys, please."

"That particular piece of luggage is not locked. I am so sorry to trouble you, but after such a memorable dinner——"

"Yes, yes; I know, I know!" she cried, as she vanished.

"Interesting girl, that," murmured Stranleigh to himself, "and unusually accomplished."

He listened for a whistle, but the first break in the silence was the coming of Miss Armstrong, holding a box of cigars in one hand and a packet of cigarettes in the other.

"Then you didn't call for help, after all," said Stranleigh, a shade of reproach in his tone.

"Oh, it was quite easy. By punching the bundles I guessed what they contained, and soon found where the portmanteau was concealed. Now, light up," she continued, "lean back, and smoke. I'll do the talking. My father, as I've told you, is a very poor business man, and that is why I endeavoured to acquire some knowledge of affairs. He is generous and sympathetic, believing no evil of anyone, consequently he is often imposed upon to his financial disadvantage. Our position as father and daughter is the reverse of what is usual in such relationships. I attempt to guide him in the way he should go, and as a general thing he accepts my advice and acts upon it, but on the occasion of which I speak, I was at work in New York, and knew nothing of the disastrous contract into which he had entered, until it was too late.

"I always come West and spend the vacation on the ranch, and this time brought with me all the money I had saved, but it proved insufficient to cope with the situation. In his early days my father was a mining engineer. He was successful, and might have been a very rich man to-day if—— But that 'if' always intervened. Nevertheless, he accumulated money, and bought this ranch, determined to retire.

"The lower part of the ranch is good grazing ground, but the upper or western part is rocky, rising to the foothills. My father was not a success as a rancher, partly because we are too far from the markets, and partly because he chose as cowboys men who did not understand their business. I told you that my father is a sympathetic man. No one ever appealed to him in vain. He has always been very popular, but it seems to me that his friends are always poorer than himself. Thus it came about that miners who knew him, and were out of work, applied for something to do, and he engaged them as cowboys, until he had half a dozen on his pay roll, and thus began the gradual loss of his money. These men were excellent as miners, but useless as cowboys, and there was no one here to teach them their duties, my father being himself a miner. It seemed, then, a dispensation of Providence that as he rambled over the western part of his property he struck signs of silver. He was not mistaken in his prospecting. He and the cowboys took hilariously to their old trade, and worked away at the rocks until all his money was gone."

"Did they find any real silver?" asked Stranleigh, interested.

"Oh yes, plenty of it," answered the girl. "It is evident they have opened a very rich mine."

"Then where is the difficulty?"

"The difficulty is the want of machinery, which there is no capital to purchase. My father tried to get that capital in this district, but there is very little ready money to be obtained out here. He enlisted the interest of Mr. Ricketts, a lawyer in Bleachers, and reputed the only rich man in the town. Ricketts came to the ranch with a mining engineer, and they examined the opening. Seemingly they were not impressed with the contents, and Ricketts advised my father to go East and form a company.

"My father explained his financial situation, and Ricketts, with apparent generosity, offered to lend him five thousand dollars on his note, to be paid on demand, with the ranch as security. Thus my father put himself entirely in the other's power.

Ricketts gave him the address of a lawyer in Chicago, who, he said, would be of assistance to him. The latest word we received from my father is that this lawyer, in one way or another, has got hold of all his money. Father telegraphed to Ricketts for help, which was refused. So he left Chicago on foot, determined to walk home, since he had not even money enough left to pay his fare home. Where he is at present, we have no idea, except that he is making for this ranch.

"Ricketts at once took action to sell the ranch. Apparently he is quite within his legal rights, but there are formalities to be gone through, and one of these is the arrival of the sheriff to seize the property. That arrival the men, headed by Jim, are determined to prevent, and now, perhaps, you understand why you rode into danger when you came from Bleachers this morning.

"When I learnt of my father's predicament, I went out to Bleachers to see Mr. Ricketts, offering him what money I had brought from New York if he would hold his hand for a year. He refused, and from his conversation I realised he was determined to secure the ranch for himself, and I believe the whole transaction is a plot toward that end."

"Then the mine must be a valuable one?"

"I am sure it is; indeed, my father could make no mistake in that matter."

"Well, the position seems very simple after all. What you need, Miss Armstrong, is a change of creditors. You want a creditor who is not in a hurry for his money. In other words, if you could transfer that debt, you would be out of immediate danger. Would you allow me to go into Bleachers to-morrow, and see Mr. Ricketts?"

"Most decidedly not!"

"How much money did you bring with you from New York?"

"Two thousand dollars."

"I brought just twice that amount, so I think the affair may be arranged, and you can go to Ricketts to-morrow, and take up the note. I think perhaps you had better have five thousand five hundred dollars with you, as there will certainly be some interest and expenses to pay, for if the case is as you state it, Ricketts will be reluctant to part with the document. Is there another lawyer in Bleachers?"

"Yes."

"Well, get him to accompany you, and make formal tender of the money."

The girl had reddened while he was speaking, and now she said, in tones of distress—

"I fear you completely misunderstood my object in telling you of my difficulties. My object was not to borrow money, but to explain why Jim Dean shot at you."

"Oh, I understand perfectly why you spoke as frankly as you did, and I am very much obliged to you for doing so, but you must have no diffidence in accepting the money. It is purely a business transaction, and, as you say, you are a business woman. Therefore, as a matter of business, it would be folly to reject an offer that is to our mutual advantage. The security is ample."

"That is true, Mr. Stranleigh, but, you see, I have no power, no authority, to give this ranch as security; it belongs to my father."

"True; but you are not nearly so competent a business woman as you would have me believe. You will receive from Ricketts your father's promissory note. That you will hand to me, then I shall be your debtor for two thousand dollars. Those two thousand dollars I shall pay as soon as I get some money from New York, and your father will become my debtor for five thousand dollars. All perfectly simple, you see. In the first instance I trust you for three thousand dollars, and in the second instance you trust me for two thousand dollars. After I have paid you the two thousand dollars, I hold the note, and can sell you up whenever I please. I give you my word I won't do that, though even if I did you would be no worse off than you are now."

"Very well, Mr. Stranleigh; I will take the money."

It was several days later when Miss Armstrong returned from Bleachers. Her first interest was to satisfy herself of the patient's progress. He had been getting on well.

"You are an admirable physician, Miss Armstrong," he said. "Now let me know whether you are equally capable as a financier."

"I have failed completely," she answered, dejectedly. "Mr. Ricketts has refused the money."

"Did you take the other lawyer with you?"

"Yes."

"What did he say?"

"He said Ricketts had no right to refuse, but a different question has arisen. The guide who accompanied you to the ranch brought back news of the shooting. Ricketts guessed at once why you were shot at, and the sheriff has signed an affidavit, or some such instrument, to show that his life, and his men's lives, are in danger if they go to seize the property, so this complication has been overcome by some order from the legislature, and the personal seizure is waived. The sale is announced to take place in Bleachers two weeks from to-day. Mr. Timmins—that is the other lawyer—fears that Ricketts is within his rights in refusing the money at this stage."

"This is all very interesting, Miss Armstrong, but we have a fortnight to turn round in."

"Yes; that is so."

"I am delighted, for now I shall have the pleasure of trying a fall with the estimable Mr. Ricketts."

VI.—THE BUNK HOUSE PRISONER.

As the wound in his shoulder healed, Stranleigh began to enjoy himself on the ranch. He was experiencing a life entirely new to him, and being always a lover of waving woods and rushing waters, even in the tamed state which England presents, he keenly appreciated these natural beauties in the wilderness, where so-called human improvements had not interfered with them. Without attempting to indulge in the sport for which he had come, he wandered about the ranch a good deal, studying its features, and at the same time developing an appetite that did justice to the excellent meals prepared for him. He visited Jim Dean, who had shot him, and tried to scrape acquaintance with his five aiders and abettors in that drastic act, but they met his advances with suspicion, naturally regarding him as a tenderfoot, nor were they satisfied that his long residence among them was as friendly as he evidently wished it to appear.

The men resided in a huge bunk house, which consisted of one room only, with a shack outside where the cooking was done. In the large room were a dozen bunks; half of them in a very dishevelled state, giving sleeping accommodation for the company, while the other half were ready in case of an accession of help, should the mine prosper.

The cabin was as securely built as a fortress, of the rugged stone which had been blasted from the rocks in opening the mine. The mine itself was situated about five hundred yards to the south of this edifice, but instead of being dug downwards, as Stranleigh expected, it extended westward on the level toward the heart of the mountain, so that a rudely built truck could carry out the débris, and dump it down the steep hill. To his æsthetic fancy this seemed a pity, because a short distance south from the opening of the mine, the river formed a cascade descending a hundred feet or more; a cascade of entrancing beauty, whose loveliness would be more or less destroyed as the mining operations progressed.

The rising sun illumined the tunnel to its final wall, and Stranleigh found no difficulty in exploring it to the remotest corner. He passed the abandoned truck partly turned over beside an assortment of picks, shovels, hand-drills and the like. To his unpractised eye there was no sign of silver on walls, floor or ceiling. At the extreme end was piled up a quantity of what appeared to be huge cartridges.

Before entering the cavern he had noticed three or four of the miners standing in front of the bunk house, evidently watching him, but he paid no attention to them, and while he was inside, the roar of the cataract prevented him from hearing approaching footsteps. As he came out to the lip of the mine, he found Jim and three others waiting for him. Each had a rifle on his shoulder.

"Inspecting the property?" said Jim, casually.

"Yes," replied Stranleigh.

"What do you think of it?"

"My opinion would be of very little value. I know nothing of mining."

"The deuce you don't!" said Jim. "What are you doing with that lump of rock in your hand?"

"Oh, that," said Stranleigh, "I happened to pick up. I wanted to examine it in clear daylight. Is there silver in it?"

"How should I know?" replied Jim, gruffly. "I'm not a mining engineer. I only take a hand at the drill or the pick, as the case may be. But when you throw that back where you got it, throw it carefully, and not too far."

"I don't intend to throw it," said Stranleigh. "I'm going to take it down to the house."

"Oh, you think you're not going to throw it, but you are. We've just come up to explain that to you."

"I see. If it is compulsory, why shouldn't I throw it as far as I can?"

"Because," explained Jim, politely, "there's a lot of dynamite stored in the end of that hole, and dynamite isn't a thing to fool with, you know."

Stranleigh laughed.

"I rather fancy you're right, though I know as little about dynamite as I do about mines. But to be sure of being on the right side, I will leave the tossing of the stone to you. Here it is," whereupon he handed the lump of rock to Jim, who flung it carelessly into the mine again, but did not join in his visitor's hilarity.

"You seem to regard me as a dangerous person?"

"Oh, not at all, but we do love a man that attends to his own business. We understood that you came here for shooting and fishing."

"So I did, but other people were out shooting before I got a chance. A man who's had a bullet through his shoulder neither hunts nor fishes."

"That's so," admitted Jim, with the suavity of one who recognises a reasonable statement, "but now that you are better, what do you come nosing round the mine for? Why don't you go on with your shooting and your fishing?"

"Because Mr. Armstrong was to be my guide, and he, I regret to say, has not yet returned home. As he is tramping from Chicago to the ranch, no one knows when he will put in an appearance."

"Well, Mr. Stranleigh, we are plain, ordinary backwoods folks, that have no reason for loving or trusting people who come from the city, as you do. You say that shooting is your game. Now, we can do a bit of shooting ourselves, and I tell you plainly that if any stranger was found prowling around here, he'd have got a bullet in a more vital spot than you did. Do you understand me?"

"Your meaning, sir, is perfectly plain. What do you want me to do? Go away from here before Mr. Armstrong returns?"

"No; we don't say that, but we draw an imaginary line, such as they tell me the equator is, past this end of the farm house, and we ask you not to cross it westward. There's all the fishing you want down stream, but there's none up here by the waterfall, neither is there any game to shoot, so you see we're proposing no hardship if your intentions are what you say they are."

"Sir, you speak so beautifully that I must address you less familiarly than I am doing. My own name is Ned, but few take the liberty of calling me by that title. I don't know that I should like it if they did. You are already aware, perhaps, that I answer to the name of Stranleigh. May I enquire what your name is?"

"I'm James Dean."

"Ah, the Dean of the Faculty? You are leader of this band of brothers?"

"In a manner of speaking, yes."

"Are they unanimous in restricting my liberty on this ranch?"

"You bet!"

"You've no right to do such a thing, and besides, it is inhospitable. I came to this ranch properly accredited, with a letter of introduction to Mr. Armstrong. He happens to be away; if he had been here, and I had seen that my visit was unwelcome to him, I should instantly have taken my leave, but I refuse to have my liberty restricted by Mr. Armstrong's hired men."

"That's exactly where you're wrong, Mr. Stranleigh. In the first place, we're not hired men; we're Mr. Armstrong's partners, and we don't restrict your liberty on the ranch."

"A partner contributes his share to the expenses of the combination. I understand Mr. Armstrong bears the burden alone."

"We contribute our labour, which is cash in another form, therefore whether Mr. Armstrong is here, or whether he is away, we mean to defend our property. So when you cross the imaginary line I spoke of, you are trespassing, and no jury will convict a man who shoots a trespasser after he has been fully warned, as we warn you."

"Well, Mr. Dean, I admit that you have right on your side, even if there is not much wisdom at the back of it. There is just one more thing I should like to know. Why do you treat me as an enemy?"

"As a possible enemy," corrected Dean.

"As a possible enemy, then?"

"Because we don't like your actions, and we don't think much of you. You're a city man, and we don't trust any such."

"But Mr. Banks, who gave me the letter to your chief, is not only a city man, but a lawyer. He has been here, and spoke highly of his reception."

"That was before the mine was opened, and as for being a lawyer, we hate 'em, of course, but they're like rattlesnakes. In some seasons of the year they are harmless. The opening of the silver mine opened the rattlesnake season, and that's why this lawyer snake in Bleachers is trying to cheat Armstrong out of his ranch. He came over here with a mining engineer and learnt the whole value of the ground. How do we know you're not a mining engineer?"

"I regret to say I'm nothing so useful."

"And didn't you send Miss Armstrong into Bleachers to see that villain Ricketts? What connection have you with him?"

"None at all, Mr. Dean. I never saw Ricketts in my life, and never heard of him before the day you mistook me for the sheriff."

Dean glanced at his companions, who had taken no part in the colloquy, but who listened with an interest at once critical and suspicious. It was evident that their distrust could not be dissipated, or even mitigated, by strenuous talk, and for a moment Stranleigh was tempted to tell them that he had lent three thousand dollars to Miss Armstrong, in the hope that this money, added to her own, would gain some sort of concession from the obdurate lawyer. But he remembered that the girl was in constant communication with these men, and if she had not already informed them of his futile assistance, it was because she did not want them to know.

Dean pondered for a few moments before he spoke. He seemed to have gathered in the purport of his men's thoughts without the necessity for words. At last he said:

"May I take it you agree hereafter to attend to your own business?"

Stranleigh laughed.

"There would be no use in my making that promise, for I have never in my life attended to my own business. My business affairs are all looked after by men who are experts. They live in New York and in London, and although I make a decision now and then, I do that as seldom as possible. It fatigues me."

"So you are a loafer?"

"That's it exactly, Mr. Dean, and I freely give you my promise not to loaf about your silver mine."

"Are you so rich as all that?"

"You are not consistent, Mr. Dean. How can you ask me to attend to my business if you do not attend to yours? Whether I am rich or poor is none of your affair?"

"Quite true," agreed Jim, nonchalantly, "we will let it go at that."

Stranleigh, with a smile, bowed courteously to the group.

"I wish you a very good day," he said, and turning, strolled down to the house at a leisurely gait, quite in keeping with his self-declared character of loafer. His back offered an excellent target, but no man raised his rifle, and Stranleigh never looked over his shoulder, never hurried a step, but walked as one very sure of himself, and in no fear of attack.

"Stuck up cuss," said Jim to his comrades. "I'd like to take that chap down a peg. Let's get back to the bunk house and talk it over," so they, too, left the pit mouth, and returned to their cabin.

When the Earl of Stranleigh entered the house, he was accosted by Miss Armstrong, on whose fair face were traces of deep anxiety, which his lordship thought were easily accounted for by the fact that the homestead was to be sold in less than a fortnight.

"I have been anxious to see you, Mr. Stranleigh," she said. "Won't you come out on the verandah where we can talk?"

"With great pleasure, Miss Armstrong."

When they were seated, she continued—

"You have been talking with the men?"

"Yes; we had a little chat together."

"Did they tell you anything of their intentions?"

"No; except in so far as they were determined not to let me examine the mine."

"Ah; they have distrusted you from the first. Did you insist on visiting it?"

"I have visited it."

"Without asking one of them to accompany you?"

"I regarded them as hired men. They say they are your father's partners."

"So they are."

"Ah, well, if that is really the case, I must apologise to them. I thought when you ordered Dean to bring in my luggage, and he obeyed with such docility, that he was your servant. I intended to offer him some money for that service, but I suppose I must not."

"Certainly not. Those men will do anything for a friend, but nothing for one of whom they are suspicious. Their distrust, once aroused, is not easily removed. I am sure, however, you were tactful with them."

Stranleigh smiled ruefully.

"I am not so certain of that myself. I fear I failed in diplomacy."

310

"I do wish my father were here," she said, ignoring his last remark. "I am very much worried about the men."

"What do they know of your trouble with that man Ricketts?"

"They know all about it, and they now threaten to march into Bleachers in a body and, as we say, shoot up the town, including Ricketts, of course."

"When do they intend to do this?"

"On the day of the auction sale."

"Don't they understand that that would be futile?"

"It would cause an infinite amount of harm, and ultimately might result in their being wiped out themselves. Not that Bleachers could do such a thing, but because they would be pitting themselves against the United States Government, which is a mere name to those men, carrying no authority. All their lives have been spent in camps, where the only law is that of the mob. I have tried my best to influence them, but they regard me merely as a woman, and a woman from the East at that, who has no knowledge of practical affairs, so I have every reason for wishing my father were here."

"I should not trouble about that if I were you, Miss Armstrong. If they intended to carry out their resolution to-morrow, or next day, there might be reason for anxiety, but we have luckily plenty of time in which to act. The one immediate thing is to find your father. I'll undertake that task. He's travelling somewhere between here and Chicago, on foot. May I see the latest letter he wrote you?"

The girl brought it to him.

"Might I take this with me?"

"Yes. What do you intend to do?"

Stranleigh smiled.

"Oh, I never do anything. As I was telling your men, who wished me to mind my own business, I always have people to do that for me. I am a great believer in the expert. Now, America seems to be the land of experts, and the man to deal with this case is Detective Burns, of New York. I shall get into touch with him by telegraph, and if he cannot attend to the matter himself, he will select the best substitute that is to be had, and as Burns and his men invariably track down anyone they want, even though he be seeking to elude them, it will be an easy task to find your father, who is tramping the straightest possible line between Chicago and this ranch. I shall give instructions for two or three hundred dollars to be handed to Mr. Armstrong, with directions to take the next train to Bleachers, as we need his presence here. I shall do nothing but send a telegram, and Mr. Burns will do the rest. Now, if you will assist me by ordering out my horse, I shall be ready to start within ten minutes. I'd order the horse myself, but I don't think your men would obey me."

In less than the time mentioned, Jim brought the horse to the door. All his men were standing in front of their cabin, looking on. They quite naturally

believed that their guest had taken alarm, and was making off to some district where he would be in less danger. When his lordship came downstairs and out to the front, Jim was overcome with astonishment. His lordship was accoutred amazingly, after the fashion of the English horseman. He had dressed himself in a riding costume such as an English gentleman would wear at home. Jim and his comrades had never seen such an outfit before, and they greeted his appearance with a roar of laughter.

Stranleigh sprang into his saddle with the agility of a cowboy, and smiling good-humouredly at his audience, raised his hat to them, and rode off.

As Stranleigh's horse entered the forest the young man began to ponder over the problem that confronted him. When the unfortunate Armstrong borrowed money from Ricketts, he had, of course, fully explained the situation. The lender had examined the property in company with a mining engineer, and this expert doubtless took away with him some ore to analyse at his leisure. Ricketts, being in possession of the engineer's estimate of the pit's value, had probably formed a syndicate, or perhaps made arrangements with other capitalists, to see him through with the speculation. Undoubtedly Ricketts expected no competition when the estate was put up at auction, but if he was a shrewd man, as was almost certain to be the case, events had occurred which might stimulate thought regarding his position.

Miss Armstrong had ridden out to Bleachers, having in her possession five thousand dollars, the face value of the notes. Ricketts would wonder how she had obtained the money. She possessed only two thousand dollars on her first visit, as he knew from the fact that she had offered it to him for refraining from action until her father returned. Who could have given her the extra three thousand? Whoever had done so must have known the girl could offer no security for its repayment. He was therefore a rich man, or he could not afford to throw away a sum so considerable.

It was likely that such reflections as these had put Ricketts on the alert, and the sudden advent in Bleachers of a smartly costumed stranger, a stranger coming from the direction of the ranch, would almost certainly convince Ricketts that here was his opponent. In Bleachers, too, each inhabitant very probably knew every one else's business. That he could elude the astute Ricketts was therefore exceedingly doubtful, and Stranleigh already knew enough about the lawlessness of the district to believe that he might ride into considerable danger. In that sparsely-settled country, people were not too scrupulous in their methods of getting rid of an enemy.

He wondered how far down the line the next town was, for he was certain that any telegraphing he did from Bleachers would speedily be known to Ricketts. Would it be possible to deflect his course, and make for the next station eastwards? He possessed no map of the State, however, and there was little chance of meeting anyone, so there seemed nothing for it but to push on to Bleachers.

At this point his meditations were interrupted by the dimly heard sound of horses' hoofs on the trail behind him. He pulled up and listened. Pausing for a few minutes, he heard nothing more, and so went on again, with an uneasy feeling of being followed. He determined not to camp out when night overtook him, but to hurry on until he reached Bleachers. He had made a two days' journey to reach the ranch, but that was because the laden mules were slow. Before dark he would be on the high road, and after that he could not lose his way. After all, perhaps it was better to reach Bleachers at night, and trust to rousing up the people in the one tavern of the place.

It was after midnight when his task was accomplished, and having seen to the accommodation of a very tired and hungry horse, Stranleigh threw himself down, dressed as he was, upon the bed to which he was shown by a sleepy ostler. He had had quite enough equestrian exercise for one day.

Ten o'clock had struck next morning before he woke, and went down to breakfast. His mind had become clarified, and he knew now exactly what he meant to do. To avoid the cognizance of Ricketts was impossible; of that he was certain. His first object, then, was to draw a red herring across the trail, so he enquired from the hotel-keeper the whereabouts of Ricketts' office, and was directed to it.

He crossed the street and ascended a stair. Ricketts kept neither clerk nor office boy, so Stranleigh knocked at the door, was gruffly commanded to enter, and obeyed.

Silas A. Ricketts was seated at a large table strewn with books and legal-looking documents, and he stared in astonishment at the figure which presented itself. He, like the men on the ranch, had never seen such a costume before.

"Are you Mr. Ricketts?" asked his lordship.

"Yes, sir."

"My name is Stranleigh. I took the liberty of calling upon you to learn, if possible, the whereabouts of Mr. Stanley Armstrong."

"Why should I know anything of his whereabouts?" demanded Ricketts.

"Permit me to explain——"

"Now, before we go any further," interrupted the lawyer, "I want you

314

to know that this is a business office, and I'm a business man. My time is valuable. I thought when you came in that you were a client. If you have come here for aimless gossip, I'm not your man. I have my own affairs to look after."

"You state the case very lucidly, Mr. Ricketts, and I congratulate your clients. My own time is far from precious, for I'm here after sport. How valuable is your time? How much does an hour's conference with you cost?"

"It all depends on the business transacted."

"I can't agree with you, Mr. Ricketts. An hour is an hour. I want to buy sixty minutes of your time and attention. What do you ask for it?"

"Five dollars!" snapped Ricketts.

Stranleigh drew forth a five-dollar bill, and placed it on the table.

"May I sit down?" he enquired. "No healthy man should be tired in the morning, but I endured a long horseback ride yesterday, and had an indifferent night's rest."

"Where did you come from?"

"I have been living for the past few days at Armstrong's ranch."

"Are you the man who was shot last week?"

"Yes; by mistake for your estimable sheriff I understand. You see, I came here from New York with a letter of introduction to Mr. Armstrong, being told that I might enjoy some good fishing and a little shooting, while Armstrong was described as a most admirable guide to these sports. I waited at the ranch day after day, hoping that Armstrong would return, but nobody seems to know yet where he is, or when he will return, so I came out here, hoping to get into telegraphic communication with him. I'm well enough now to take part in the chase, and I am loth to return to New York without having had any sport."

"I still don't understand why you come to me about the matter."

"I was told by his daughter that Armstrong had written to you. She does not know in the least where he is, and so on the chance of your having received a recent letter, I have called to enquire."

"I see. Armstrong's letter to me was written from Chicago. It was a request for money. I had already loaned him a considerable sum and was unable to accede to his further demand. I answered to this effect, but have heard no more from him. It is likely that his own people have received word since the letter to me was written. Of course, you don't know the date of their last letter from him?"

"Yes, I do," said Stranleigh, "I have the letter with me. It contains all the data of which Miss Armstrong is possessed, and she gave me the letter to assist me in my search."

He drew the letter from his pocket, and showed the date to the lawyer, who consulted his file, and then said—

"It is just as I expected. That letter was written ten days later than the one I received. Sorry I am unable to give you any definite assistance, Mr. Stranleigh."

Stranleigh rose.

"I am sorry also. I suppose there wouldn't be much use in telegraphing to the address he gives in Chicago?"

"I see no object in that. The place is probably a boarding-house, and he's not there."

"Thank you, Mr. Ricketts. Good morning."

Stranleigh went slowly down the steep stairs, and reaching the sidewalk, almost fell into the arms of Jim Dean. Here, then, was the man who had been following him.

"Good morning, Mr. Dean."

"Morning," snarled Jim, briefly.

"I've just been up to see Mr. Ricketts, whom I think you mentioned the other day."

"So I supposed," agreed Dean.

"I expected to get some information from him about Mr. Armstrong, but he doesn't appear to know very much."

"Well, you're the first man I ever heard say that S. A. Ricketts doesn't know very much, but I think by and by you will find that others know a great deal."

"Perhaps they know a great deal that is not so; there's a lot of knowledge of that kind lying around loose."

"Very likely," remarked Jim, laconically, then turned on his heel and walked down the street, while Stranleigh went towards the depôt to enlist the services of a telegraph operator, and learn when the next train left for the east.

Stranleigh found the telegraph operator dozing in a wooden chair tilted back against the wall, his soft hat drawn over his eyes, his feet resting on a rung of the chair. It was a hot day, and the commercial inactivity of Bleachers called for very little exertion on the part of the telegraphist. The young man slowly roused himself as the door opened and shut. His unexpected customer nodded good morning to him.

"Could you oblige me with some forms?" asked the newcomer.

"Forms? Forms of what?" The operator's feet came down with a crash on the board floor as he rose from his chair.

"Well, telegraph blanks, perhaps I should have said."

"Oh, certainly."

The young man fished one out from a drawer, and flung it on the counter.

"This will do excellently for a beginning," said Stranleigh, "but you'd better let me have a dozen to go on with."

The young man was waking up. He supplied the demand, and with ever-increasing amazement, watched his client write.

Stranleigh gave the New York detective particulars in great detail so far as he possessed them, asked him to spare no expense, and requested that Armstrong, when found, should be presented with two hundred dollars or more, as he required, with admonition to take the first train home, where his presence was urgently needed.

"Great Scott!" cried the operator, "is that all one message?"

"Yes," said Stranleigh.

"Where is it going?"

"I've written the address as plainly as I can. It's going to New York."

"I say, stranger," protested the telegraphist, "have you any idea what it costs to send a message across the Continent to New York?"

"No, I haven't, but I expect to be in possession of that information as soon as you have mastered my handwriting, and counted the words."

The operator was practically speechless when he reached the end of his enumeration, but after making a note on the pad, he was sufficiently recovered to remark—

"Say, stranger, you'll have to dig up a pretty big wad to pay for this. We don't give credit in a Western Union office."

"I shouldn't think of asking credit from a downtrodden monopoly," said Stranleigh, pulling out his pocket book, and liquidating his debt. "You ought to be happy if you get a percentage."

"Worse luck, I don't."

"Well, I think you're entitled to one. I've given a fee this morning and received no particular equivalent for it. Do you, being a useful man, object to accepting a five-dollar bill?"

"Not on your life!" assented the operator with great earnestness.

Stranleigh passed it over.

"I'm expecting a reply. At what time shall I call for it?"

"You don't need to call, Mr. Stranleigh. When it comes, I'll lock up the office, and find you if you're anywhere in town."

"I'm stopping over at the tavern."

"All right; you'll get it."

"Thanks. Good morning."

"See you later," said the now thoroughly-awakened operator, and Stranleigh proceeded to the railway station. He took the next train to the nearest town east, and there did some more telegraphing, but this time the message was in cypher, and it was addressed to his agent in New York. Translated, it read—

"Send me at once by express, registered and insured, twenty thousand dollars in currency, made up of five dollar, ten dollar, and hundred dollar bills."

The address was fully written out in plain English. He found there was time for a satisfactory lunch before the west-bound train arrived, and he partook of it in the chief hotel, whose accommodation was much superior to that of the Bleachers tavern.

On his return to headquarters, he called in at the telegraph office. The young man in charge, at once recognising him, announced—

"Nothing doing. The moment anything comes I'll take it over to the tavern. Say, is there anything secret about that telegram you sent?"

"No; why do you ask?"

"Well, Mr. Ricketts, a lawyer here, came in about ten minutes ago, and described you, and wanted to know if you had sent a telegram."

"What did you say to him?"

"I said nobody had sent a telegram, and that I knew nothing of you. He seemed powerful anxious, and offered me a dollar to let him know if you

319

telegraphed anything. I went over to the tavern to tell you about it, but they said you hadn't been in since breakfast."

"I suppose you haven't many chances of picking up an extra dollar in Bleachers?"

"No; I haven't. Ricketts is always mighty curious about anyone who arrives here, but I never knew him offer a cent for information before."

"I'm very much obliged to you. You go right over to Ricketts' office and pick up his dollar, but don't say I gave you the advice. By the way, wouldn't you be breaking the rules of the Western Telegraph Company if you divulged the purport of any message that passed through your hands?"

A look of trouble, almost of fear, came over the young man's face.

"If a telegram is secret," he said, "the sender usually writes it in cypher."

"Quite so, but even in that case wouldn't you be punished if it became known that you had shown Mr. Ricketts a private despatch entrusted to your care?"

"Certainly," admitted the telegraphist, exhibiting more and more uneasiness, "but I have not shown your telegram to anybody, and what I told you was entirely in confidence."

"Oh, you need have no fear of my rounding on you. I am merely endeavouring to put you in possession of that dollar without getting your neck in a noose. Don't you see that you are placing yourself entirely at Mr. Ricketts' mercy?"

"But you," protested the frightened young man, "advised me to do so."

"Undoubtedly. I want you to get that dollar, but not to place yourself in jeopardy. From what I saw of Ricketts this morning, I should not like to be in his power, yet his dollar is just as good as any other man's dollar, and I want you to detach it from him with safety, and profit to yourself. Let me have another telegraph blank."

Stranleigh wrote rapidly—

"Pinkerton Detective Agency, Chicago.

"I want to be put into communication with Stanley Armstrong, who left Chicago on foot ten days ago, for the West, and I am willing to pay one hundred dollars for the job.

"Edmund Stranleigh.

"White's Hotel, Bleachers."

"There," said Stranleigh, passing over the sheet to the operator, "you show that to our inquisitive friend Ricketts, but don't send it over the line."

Stranleigh slept that night at White's Hotel, and shortly after breakfast next morning the telegraph clerk came across with a very satisfactory telegram from New York. The sender could not positively predict the finding of Armstrong, but anticipated no difficulty in the task.

Stranleigh paid his bill at the hotel, ordered out his horse, and trotted off towards the ranch. He saw no more of Ricketts, who, if on any trail, was following the wrong one.

Dusk had fallen as he was about to emerge into the clearing which in daylight would have afforded him a sight of Armstrong's house. Suddenly and stealthily he was surrounded by six armed men, and the voice of Jim Dean broke the stillness.

"Good evening, Mr. Stranleigh. I must ask you to get down from your horse."

"Willingly," replied the rider. "I confess I have had enough equestrian exercise for one day."

"We have supper ready for you at the bunk house."

"Why at the bunk house? I am perfectly satisfied with the fare that Mr. Armstrong's family provides."

"We'd like a little conversation with you, and the conversation must take place in private."

"In that case, Mr. Dean, you could hardly find a better spot than this."

"We're a kindly set of chaps, and couldn't think of keeping a hungry man out here."

"But I'm not very hungry. I took a pocketful of sandwiches with me from the tavern."

"Nevertheless, you are coming with us, either peaceably, or by force, whichever you choose."

"Oh, quite willingly, of course. I should be ungrateful if I gave you any unnecessary trouble, while accepting your hospitality. I may add that I am unarmed, so if you keep your guns in readiness you need fear no reprisal on my part."

"That's all right," responded Jim. "We're not easily scared, but are prepared to protect ourselves should you try any funny business."

"Is Peter going to take my horse to the farm?"

"Sure; your horse will be put in its old quarters, and will be well taken care of."

"Then I should be glad if Peter would oblige me by telling Miss Armstrong that I have arrived safely, and will give her an account of my journey when next I have the pleasure of meeting her."

"I'm afraid Peter can't carry any messages; indeed, it's not at all necessary. I've told Miss Armstrong that your horse will be brought back, and that I saw you off on the east-bound train, which is quite true. You've brought back the horse, and you did go east on the train. Miss Armstrong thinks you have become tired of waiting for her father, and that you've gone either to Chicago or New York."

"Am I to regard myself as your prisoner, then?"

"Prisoner is an ugly word, and we are not entitled to call ourselves gaolers, but if you wouldn't mind looking on it in that way, it's all the same to us."

"Well, truthful Jim, I'm your man in every sense of the word. Let us begin our amicable journey. I yearn for the bunk house."

"You will keep silent? No shouting or calling for help? There's no help to be had anyhow, and a noise would merely alarm the women."

"I recognise the necessity for silence, and I shall make no outcry. Indeed, my whole future conduct while with you will be governed by the strictest secrecy. When I get tired of the bunk house I shall merely cut all your throats while you are asleep, and will do it in the quietest and gentlest manner."

Jim laughed.

"I guess we can take care of our throats, but I'm much obliged for the suggestion, which may come in handy if you get funny, as I said before."

They reached the bunk house by a circuitous route. A fine fire of logs was blazing on the ample hearth, for even in summer a fire was good to look at when night came on, at that elevation.

When Stranleigh sat down to supper, he regretted more than ever the civilised fare of the farm house. The menu was rough, but plentiful, and they all sat together at the long table. A meal was a serious event, and they partook of it in silence. It was evident that the men were going to adopt full precautions, for while they supped one of them sat by the door, a rifle over his knees. He came in for the second course, and another took his place. After the table was cleared, they all sat round the big fire, and smoked.

Remembering that the best tobacco in the world came from the southeast of their country, the aroma of the weed they had chosen was not as grateful to Stranleigh's nostrils as might have been expected, so partly for good fellowship, and partly for his own protection, he presented each with a fine Havana cigar, such as would be welcomed in a London club, where pipes are not permitted. The men amiably accepted this contribution, but each put the cigar in his pocket against a future occasion, and went on with his pipe. Cheap as was the tobacco they were using, it was naturally scarce among men who had received no money for some months.

"I don't wish to appear unduly inquisitive," began their guest, "but now that we have all night before us, would you mind telling me why I am thus taken charge of by strangers on whom I have no claim?"

"There are several reasons," replied Jim, who was always the spokesman for the company, "and we are quite willing to mention them. You appear to be a person of some intelligence——"

"Thanks," interjected Stranleigh.

Jim went on, unheeding the interruption—"and so perhaps you know that we suspect you of being in cohoots with Ricketts."

"Does 'cohoots' mean co-partnership?"

"Something of that sort. You partly persuaded us that wasn't so, but I followed you to make sure. Perhaps you remember that I caught you coming out from Ricketts' office. You made for that office the moment you reached Bleachers."

"Pardon me, but I went first to the hotel."

"Yes; and you enquired there where Ricketts hung out."

"Certainly; but that's in my favour. It showed that so far from being in the employ of the lawyer, I didn't even know where he lived."

"It was a good bluff."

"It's very circumstantial evidence of my innocence. But for the sake of argument, I will admit that I am in 'cohoots,' as you call it, with the estimable Ricketts. What next?"

"The next thing is that you learnt from Miss Armstrong of our intention to go into Bleachers and shoot up the town, including Ricketts."

"That is true."

"You didn't like the plan and said so."

"That also is correct."

"You said it should be stopped, not knowing the ways of this country."

"Certainly. Desirable as may be the shooting up of Bleachers, the odds 'e too strongly against you."

"Oh, we'll chance that. But the next thing you do is to put your funny clothes on, get out your horse, and ride directly to Mr. Ricketts. You are an informer."

"An informer is always a despicable character, Mr. Dean. What's the next item in the indictment?"

"Don't you think that's enough? Men have been hanged for less. An informer is the most poisonous wretch in the world except a horse thief."

"Then I am in danger of being hanged?"

"You sure are."

"Isn't there any way in which I can compound my felony?"

"Well, I don't quite know what confounding a felony is, but you're the sleekest fellow I ever met, and if you think you can palaver us to let you go, you've made the mistake of your life."

"I shouldn't think of attempting such a thing. I am merely endeavouring to discover your state of mind. You're strong on muscle, Jim, and I admire your build, but I'm beginning to doubt whether your brain equals your frame. There was a time when your equipment would have been victorious, but those days are long since past. Nowadays it's brain that wins every time, and in every country. Physical force has had to give way before it. Jimmy, my boy, you're out of date."

"Brain isn't going to help you any," said Dean, evidently annoyed by these strictures on his mentality.

"Perhaps it won't, but if there was a corresponding brain in your head, I'd appeal to it, and probably win. Are all your men here as stupid as you, Jim?"

Jim rose up from his chair, a forbidding frown on his brow.

"Look here, stranger," he called out, "I've had enough of that line of talk."

"Oh no, you haven't. Please sit down. This line of talk is only beginning, and I say, Jim, lay aside that pipe, and smoke the Havana cigar. It will put reason into your head if anything will."

Some of the company laughed, and Jim sat down, seeing that his opponent failed to show any fear at his captors' threatening attitude. He tried to change the course of the conversation into a less personal channel.

"You see, Mr. Stranleigh, we're short on tobacco, and I want to keep this cigar until to-morrow. I can tell by the smell it's a good one."

"That's all right," said Stranleigh, "I have plenty more of them down at the house, and when they are finished, I'll telegraph east for a fresh supply. If you will let me know your favourite brand of tobacco, I'll order a ton of it at the same time."

For a moment Jim's eyes twinkled, then they narrowed into their usual caution.

"Was that what you meant by confusing a penalty? Well, stranger, it doesn't go here. We ain't to be bought, even by a ton of tobacco."

"I hadn't thought of either buying or bribing you," said Stranleigh, "therefore we will get back to our original subject, the difference between brain and muscle. I see here on the table a pack of cards in a deplorably greasy condition. If you were playing a game with an opponent who was beating you, would you shoot him?"

"Yes," promptly replied Jim, "if I found he was cheating."

"Whereupon his friends would lynch you."

"A cheater hasn't any friends."

"Jim, I shouldn't like to sit down to a game with you. You would shoot first, and think afterwards, while I, being unarmed, should be at a disadvantage. That, indeed, is just what you are doing now. If you succeed in holding me here you will spoil my game. What I propose to do is not to attack Ricketts with a gun, but to learn his style of play, and beat him at it. Any confounded fool can shoot off a gun; there's no credit in that. It's a coward's trick."

"You say we'll spoil your game. You may bet your life we will. You daren't tell us what it is."

"Oh yes, I dare, because I have a trick that will quite delude you."

"I know you'll try to do that."

"Exactly. Well, my trick is to tell the truth. The situation is very simple. That morning when from the pit mouth you warned me off the premises, I found Miss Armstrong very much worried because she had learned of your intention to shoot up the town, and could not persuade you to abandon so foolish a project. It then became my duty to prevent you doing what you proposed."

"Do you think you can?"

"Of course; I knew it was no use attempting to reason with you, so the instant necessity was to get one man of common sense to counteract the stupidity of the bunk house. That I set out to do. I rode to Bleachers, called on Lawyer Ricketts, paid him five dollars down for whatever knowledge he could give me concerning the whereabouts of Mr. Armstrong. He could give me none that I did not already possess. He kept the five dollars, though. You saw me go off in the train. I merely went to the next town, to do some telegraphing that might be more or less secret from Ricketts. A detective agency will find Mr. Armstrong, and hand him two hundred dollars, asking him at the same time to make for home by the earliest train. Then, unless I'm much mistaken, Mr. Armstrong will see the idiocy of what you propose, and will prevent you from carrying out your scheme."

Jim pondered over this announcement for some minutes. At last he broke the silence.

"What you say may be true, but I don't believe a word of it. It's more likely Ricketts is your boss, and you went in to report to him and tell him what we intended to do. Then he'll see that Bleachers is prepared to meet us."

"Yes; that would be a simple way of turning the trick. There are good points about it, but it happens not to be my way, as you will learn in a few days when Mr. Armstrong returns."

Again Jim meditated for a while, and finally rose, walked to the further end of the room, and engaged for some minutes in earnest cogitation with his fellows, carried on in tones so low that Stranleigh could not hear. Resuming his seat, he spoke with deliberation—

"You want us to believe that you are a friend of Mr. Armstrong?"

"I don't care whether you believe it or not. I can hardly be a friend of Stanley Armstrong, because I've never seen him."

"Well, we'll put your good intentions to the test. When Mr. Armstrong gets here, he will have no money. Stony broke, that's what he is. Now, unless we shoot 'em up in Bleachers when they try to sell his place, Armstrong will lose it. We take it you are a rich man. Will you promise to lend him enough money to hold this ranch, and run the mine?"

"No; I won't," said Stranleigh, with decision.

"All right. Then you stay here until you cough up that cash. Even if Armstrong comes, he will never know you're here, because we shall tell him that you've gone East. Nobody else knows where you are, so there isn't any chance of a search being made."

"This is rank brigandage," remarked Stranleigh.

"I guess that's the right title, but a man who brags so much of his brains as you do, ought to see that if we're ready to shoot up a town, we won't stop at such a trifle as brigandage."

"That's so. And now, gentlemen, I'm tired after my long journey, and I think we've talked a great deal to very little purpose, so if you'll show me what bunk I am to occupy, I'll turn in."

"There are six unused bunks, Mr. Stranleigh, and you can take your choice. There's nothing mean about us."

Stranleigh made his selection, and rough as the accommodation was, he slept as soundly as ever he had done in his London palace, or his luxurious yacht.

Although the Earl of Stranleigh was naturally an indolent man, the enforced rest of the next few days grew very irksome. He had expected the guard set over him to relax as time went on, but this was not the case. The genial Jim saw to that, and it was soon evident to Stranleigh that Dean ruled his company with an iron hand. Such casual examination of the premises as he was able to make impressed him more and more with the difficulty of escape. Had the structure been built of logs, there might have been some hope, but the imperviousness of the thick stone walls was evident to the most stupid examiner. The place was lit in daytime by two slits, one at each gable, which were without panes, and narrow, so that they might as much as possible keep out the rain. No man could creep through, even if he could reach the height at which they were placed. During the day the stout door, fit to encounter a battering ram, was open, but a guard sat constantly at the sill, with a rifle across his knees. At night it was strongly locked. Stranleigh was handicapped by the fact that heretofore he had never been required to think out any difficult problem for himself. He had merely to give the order, and other people did his thinking for him, and when a plan was formed, there were others to carry it out, being well paid for doing so. Thus it happened that the means of escape were so obvious that a ten year old boy might have discovered them.

Each evening passed very pleasantly, for Stranleigh was a good story-teller, and had many interesting tales to relate. In spite of the fact that his gaolers were unanimous in their opinion that Stranleigh was a useless encumbrance upon earth, they began rather to like him. One night Stranleigh asked Jim if anything had yet been heard of Mr. Armstrong, and Dean, after hesitating a moment, replied that there was so far no news of him or from him.

"I'm sorry for Armstrong," said Stranleigh, more as if talking to himself than to anyone else. "Poor fellow, away from home all this time, and yet compelled to support six stalwart loafers without commonsense enough to do the obvious thing."

"What is the obvious thing?" asked Dean.

"Why, to work, of course. There's your mine; you've got plenty of dynamite to go on with, and yet you lounge about here not earning enough to keep yourselves in tobacco. If there is silver in that hole, you could by this time have had enough out to buy the ranch and furnish your own working capital. You say you are partners in the scheme, but you seem to be merely a blunderheaded lot of hired men, determined not to do any work."

Jim answered with acerbity—

"If you weren't a fool you'd know we'd gone already as far as hand work can go. We need a steam engine and a crusher."

"A steam engine?" echoed Stranleigh. "What on earth would you have to pay for coal, with railway haulage, and the cost of getting it out here from the line? Why, right there, rushing past you, is all the power you need. You've only to make a water-wheel, with a straight log, thrown across the falls as axle, and there you are. Pioneers have done that sort of thing since civilisation began, and here you don't need even to build a dam."

Jim was about to make an angry retort when the company were scattered by a roar and a heavy fall of soot on the log fire. The chimney was ablaze, but that didn't matter in the least, as the house was fireproof. In a short time the flames had died out, and the party gathered round the fire once more.

"Well," said Jim, "go on with your pretty advice."

Stranleigh replied dreamily, gazing into the fire.

"Oh, well, I think my advice doesn't amount to much, as you hinted. It is none of my affair. You are a most capable body of men, I have no doubt, only the fact has been concealed from me up to date. I find I am developing the vice of talking too much, so I'm going to turn in. Good-night!"

But the fall of soot had suggested to Stranleigh a method of escape.

VII.—THE END OF THE CONTEST.

A wood fire is an evanescent thing, having none of the calm determination of coal combustion. A wood fire requires constant replenishing, and that in the bunk house did not receive this attention. When the men, tired with doing nothing, overcome by the lassitude enduring an empty day had caused, turned into sleep, the wood fire, left to itself, crumbled into a heap of ashes. The guarding of Stranleigh became more perfunctory as time passed. He proved to be a model prisoner, and usually the sentinel at the door fell into peaceful slumber as night wore on. On the particular evening Stranleigh chose for his attempt, Jim Dean sat on the chair against the door. Jim's jaw worked so much during the day, he talked so incessantly, emptying his mind of all it contained, that he was naturally exhausted when his turn for watching came. Each of the men slumbered more or less soundly at his post, but the confident Jim outdid them all, so Stranleigh selected him as the man destined to hold the empty bag.

It was two hours after midnight when his lordship slipped down from his bunk. The fire had long since gone out, and the stone chimney was reasonably cool. The climbing of that ample flue presented no difficulty to an athletic young man who in his time had ascended the Matterhorn. The inside of the chimney offered to the amateur sweep walls of rough stone, which projected here and there, forming an effective, if unequal ladder. He attained the top with such ease that he wondered he had remained so long a prisoner. Descending the roof silently, he let himself down to the top of the lean-to which acted as kitchen and supply store, and dropped from that elevation lightly to the ground. It was a night of clear moonlight, and Stranleigh smiled to think how nearly he must represent the popular idea of the devil, covered as he was with soot from head to foot.

He made directly down the hill to the farm house by the stream, and risked a few minutes of time in washing his face in the rapid current. He now took off his boots, the better to enact the part of burglar. The doors of the house, he knew, were never locked. First he secured his favourite magazine rifle and a large quantity of cartridges, then as, after all, he was entitled to the board he paid for, he penetrated softly to the kitchen. Here he secured a couple of loaves of bread and a cooked ham, together with some other things he wanted, including a supply of tobacco, and thus overloaded as he had rarely been in his life before, he stole softly outside, slipped his feet into his boots, and slowly climbed the hill to the silver cavern. Depositing within his goods and chattels, he examined his store carefully to learn whether there was anything more he needed to stand a siege.

Bright as was the moonlight outside, the cavern was pitch dark, so Stranleigh determined on another expedition to the house, and he brought back a bunch of candles and an armful of bedclothes.

"Now for the night's work," he said to himself, and having lit a candle, which he placed at the remote end of the cave, he began picking up stones, and with them building a wall across the mouth of the pit. No Roman wall was ever built with such care, and no Roman wall ever contained within itself such possibilities of wholesale obliteration, because the structure was intersticed with sticks of dynamite, which Stranleigh carried with the most cautious tenderness from the rear to the front of the cavern. When his task was completed the moon had gone down, and the misty, luminous grey of the eastern sky betokened the approach of dawn. The young man was thoroughly tired, and with a sigh of relief he stretched himself out on the bedclothes he had brought from the house.

The early sun shining on his face awakened him. He knew from experience that the bunk house men were not afflicted with the vice of early rising. There was no aperture in their habitation, unless the door was open, through which the sun might shine upon them. He was therefore not surprised that no one was visible anywhere near the sleeping quarters. So he breakfasted in peace, alternating slices of bread with slices of ham, thus constructing some admirable sandwiches.

A providential jug, which doubtless in its time had contained whisky, was one of the utensils left when the mine was abandoned. Stranleigh took this, and stepping over the dangerous wall, filled it three or four times at the rushing cataract, rinsing out all indication of its former use. He brought it back, filled with very clear and cold water. He could not help thinking as he returned what an excellent place the waterfall would be for the washing of dishes, if a person ran the risk of standing upon spray-drenched, slippery rock ledges.

Stranleigh sat down where he could see the enemy's quarters, and carefully examined his rifle, assured himself that the magazine was full, then with the weapon over his knees in the fashion adopted by his recent gaolers, watched the bunk house patiently, wishing he had a morning paper to while away the time.

The laggard sentinel was the first to rouse himself. The broad door opened, and Jim Dean, palpably bewildered, stepped out. With hand shading his eyes he minutely examined the landscape, slowly turning his head from left to right as he scrutinised the distant horizon and the ground intervening. Stranleigh, kneeling, rested his rifle on the top of the wall, and as Jim's left ear, a rather prominent feature, became fully visible, the young man fired.

Jim's action instantaneously verified the Indian romances of Stranleigh's youth. He sprang clear up into the air and clapped a hand upon his wounded ear. He was at that moment the most astonished man on the western hemisphere. His first instinct being to bolt for cover, he did so without pausing to close the door, which opened outwards, and this broad piece of woodwork now offered a much more prominent target than Jim's ear had done a moment before.

Stranleigh, exercising a care that seemed unnecessary with so big a target, fired out the cartridges of his magazine, then immediately restocked it, and shot away the second charge. Putting in a third load, he sat there with his customary nonchalance, awaiting the turn of events. In that clear atmosphere, and with his sharp vision, he saw that he had accomplished his intention, and had punctured the letter "S" on the panel of the open door.

Meanwhile, there was commotion in the bunk house. The first sharp report, accompanied by Jim's yell, woke every man within. The subsequent fusilade engendered a belief that the enemy was in possession of a Maxim gun, and brought every man to the floor, thankful that he was under better cover than if he stood behind the door, through the panel of which all the bullets had penetrated.

"How did he escape?" demanded one, addressing Jim, who was holding his left hand to his ear.

"I don't know," said the wounded man ruefully. "You can search me."

"Seems from that shooting that we'd better search outside. What in the fiend's name made him batter the door?"

"Sorry he left us, I suppose," muttered Dean, grimly. "Knocking because he wanted to come in again."

"How did he get his gun?"

"Hanged if I know," said the questioned man, impatiently.

"But you were on guard. You ought to know something about it."

"Look here," said Jim. "There's no use in talking. He got out some way, and he's got his gun some way. He's holding us up, and we must make terms with him."

"But where is he?"

"I tell you I don't know! The bullet came from the direction of the mine. Now, one of you boys throw up your hands, and go outside and hail him."

At this command, Jim met the first rebellion against his authority.

"Go outside yourself. It is you who have brought all this upon us. You shot him through the shoulder; you proposed capturing him, and it was you who fell asleep last night and let him escape."

Jim did not combat their charges.

"All right," he said. "I'll go out, and you sit here and shiver while I enjoy a little conversation with him."

Raising his hands above his head, Dean stepped across the threshold into the open, and stood like an oriental about to begin his prayers. He saw at once the wall that had been built during the night, and then caught sight of Stranleigh standing behind it. Pulling out a white handkerchief, and waving it, Dean proceeded towards the mine.

"Have you got a revolver?" shouted Stranleigh.

"No," answered Dean.

"Then put down your hands, and approach as a Christian should."

Jim obeyed.

"Now stand where you are," said Stranleigh, when the other was within four or five yards of the wall. "I see your ear is bleeding. That was rather a neat shot of mine, don't you think?"

"It was," admitted Dean, without enthusiasm.

"When you shot at my shoulder, you had a bigger mark."

"Oh, not so very much," growled Dean. "My ears are celebrated for their size."

"You'd better wrap it up in this handkerchief," commented Stranleigh, rolling it up in a ball, and flinging it towards Jim. The wounded man tied it round his voluminous ear.

"And now," said Stranleigh, "get through with your parley as soon as possible, then go to Miss Armstrong, who will very expertly attend to your hurt. But in order to win the privilege of surgical treatment, you must recognise that you are a prisoner."

"A prisoner?" echoed Dean.

"Certainly. You must give me your word you will say nothing to Miss Armstrong to show that I have had a hand in the game. Make whatever excuse you like for the disaster, and then get back to the bunk house, tell your fellows the condition of the game as far as we have gone. I will allow you five minutes after your return to show those chaps the letter 'S' I have perforated in the door. They are a very unbelieving lot, and I wish to gain their affection and respect. Without hurting anybody I mean to prove that I am a dead shot. I'm well provisioned here, and prepared to stand a siege. Until Mr. Armstrong returns, not one of you will be allowed outside the châlet. Don't be misled by the fact that you outnumber me six to one. I hold a magazine rifle, possess an ample supply of ammunition, and have just given evidence of the rapidity with which reloading can be performed."

"Yes," said Dean, meditatively, "your position would be bull strong and hog tight, if you had a chum with you who could shoot as well as you do. But as it is, you've nobody to relieve you, and a man must sleep. It will only take one of us to defeat you. We've no magazine rifles and don't need none. I'll undertake the job myself."

"How do you propose to do it?"

"That would be telling," said Jim, craftily.

"Why not?" answered Stranleigh. "I'm placing my cards on the table. Why don't you do the same? I'm not yearning for war and bloodshed, but have inaugurated a sort of Hague tribunal. There were two things I determined to accomplish when I broke jail. I hope that wounded ear hasn't impaired your hearing, so that you may listen with attention. It's always as well to know what your enemy desires."

"I'm listening," said Jim.

"The first thing was to shoot you through the leg or the arm or the ear, choosing some spot that was not vital. This in return for your shooting me. One good turn deserves another, you know. That part of my programme I have accomplished."

"What's the other part?"

"The second is to keep you gentlemen in prison just as long as you kept me in prison. One good imprisonment deserves another. Now will you tell me what you intend to do?"

"No; I won't."

"That's mean of you, Jim; secretive, over-cautious and that sort of thing. I'm not so chary and so will give you the information. There are only two portions of the night during which you can come out unnoticed; before the moon rises and after it sets. You will steal out and take up a position where you can see the barricade when day begins to dawn. You'll need to chose a spot a long way off, because the explosion, when it comes, will wreck everything in the neighbourhood."

"What explosion?"

"The dynamite explosion. This wall is built of rock intersticed with those dynamite cartridges of yours. It is very likely you will obliterate the farm-house."

"I'll obliterate you, anyway."

"Quite so, but at a tremendous cost, because whatever the fate of Mr. Armstrong's residence, the doom of the bunk house is certain. You may be outside that danger, but you won't be free of another. You suppose, doubtless, that I shall be asleep in the cavern. As a matter of fact I shall be sleeping placidly under the stars, quite out of reach of the main disaster. Your first shot will awaken me. Now, it is by no means certain that your first shot will send off the dynamite. You may have to fire half a dozen times, and your best rifle is an old breech-loader. I use smokeless powder, and you don't. I could pepper away at you for half an hour and you'd never know where the bullets were coming from. The smoke from your rifle would give you away at once. When I fire at you next time, Jim, I shall aim at a more vital point, because, my dear boy, the person who sets off that dynamite is a murderer. So before you put your plan into operation, just consult your comrades and explain to them its disadvantages."

Dean stood there meditating for a few moments before he spoke.

"I'm very much obliged to you," he said at last, "for telling me what you mean to do. We'll change that plan a little, and come out of the bunk house together. We'll search the country for you, and so won't need to blow up the

337

mine."

"That's a much more humane expedient, and will prevent unnecessary loss of life. I shall be lying quiet under whatever cover I can find. Your crowd will perambulate the locality, and I may remind you that you are no lightfooted Cinderellas. A herd of elephants would make less noise. I shall see you long before you see me, and I leave the result to your own imagination. And now, Jimmy, take the advice of a true friend. Your time to act was when you were snoring at that door and I was climbing the chimney. Once you allowed me to get my rifle, you had permitted opportunity to pass you, because I am a good shot, and I came West in order to shoot. When a person accustomed to downy beds of ease slumbers peacefully, as I did this morning, on hard and jagged rocks thinly disguised by a blanket, with my right ear against a dynamite cartridge, there's nothing the matter with his nerves, is there?"

"No; there isn't," said Dean, with conviction.

"Now, what you chaps want is not a battle, but an armistice. Leave well enough alone, I say, and accept the status quo. If you remain in the bunk house, you are as safe as in a Presbyterian church."

Jim did not reply, but deliberated, his open palm against his bandaged ear.

"Hurt?" asked Stranleigh.

"Yes, it does," admitted Jim, ruefully.

"Well, my shoulder hurt a good deal after you fired at me. Now, I'll tell you what I'll do, Jim. Next time I shoot at you, I'll take the other ear. You're determined to prove yourself a brigand, or a pirate, or something of that sort, and as pirates always wear earrings, that will put you in a position to adopt them. What do you say to my proposal for an armistice?"

"I can't answer for the rest of the boys without consulting them. If we need an armistice or a status quo, why, I suppose we ought to have them."

"All right. If your ear hurts, the sooner you get it attended to, the better. You go directly down to the house and see Miss Armstrong, and you can reflect upon the situation while she is dressing the wound. Deep thinking will take your mind from the pain. Then go up and consult the company. Come and let me know what they decide. Meanwhile, I'll guarantee that no one comes out of that bunk house without being shot at."

"Mr. Stranleigh, I'll do what you say, but I'll change the order. I'll go first to our shack, and warn the boys. That's only fair, for they're watching from that door, and if they see me going to the house they may think it's all right, and come outside. After talking with them, I'll visit Miss Armstrong, and then come back here to tell you what the boys say."

"Yes, Jim; that's a better plan than mine. But first give me your word that you will take no advantage of this respite until war. An armistice, you know, is a cessation of hostilities."

"You mean that there will be no shenanigan? I give you my word."

The wounded man made his way to the bunk house. Shortly afterwards Stranleigh saw him emerge, and go towards the homestead. After a longer interval he came slowly up towards the fortress, his ear neatly bandaged in white linen, which showed up, as one might say, like a small flag of truce.

"Well, what did Miss Armstrong say about the wounded ear?"

"She says it's about as serious as the sting of a bee, and won't hurt much longer than that would, and will be cured nearly as soon."

"That's first-rate, and relieves my conscience, which has been troubling me, because I'd much rather smite a man on the ear with my fist than with a bullet. For the same reason I hope you found your messmates undergoing a spasm of common sense."

"They agreed with me that it wasn't very healthy to take outdoor exercise for a while. If we decide to begin fighting again, we'll give you twelve hours' notice. Will that suit you?"

"I don't know that it does, quite. I want you to promise that you will not break loose either until Mr. Armstrong returns, or the auction is over."

"The boys wouldn't agree to that, Mr. Stranleigh. We're bound to attend that auction."

Stranleigh sighed.

"Very good," he conceded. "I must content myself with what you offer. I accept your proposal, for I feel certain that Mr. Armstrong will return before the ranch is sold. So good-bye. Give my love to the boys."

Stranleigh watched the retreating figure until it disappeared into the bunk house. A moment later the perforated door was drawn shut, and then he rolled up the bedclothes into a bundle, and deposited it at the further end of the cavern. This done, he took his rifle under his arm, crossed the barricade, and strolled down to the farm-house. Miss Armstrong greeted him with surprise.

"I thought you had gone to New York," she said.

"I took the train east, but only to the next station from Bleachers."

"You've not been stopping at that wretched hotel in Bleachers ever since?"

"Oh no; I received a pressing invitation from some friends of mine to be their guest, with a prospect of a little shooting, so I've been staying with them ever since."

"Did you have a pleasant time?"

"Oh, excellent, and I heard more entertaining stories than ever I listened to in a similar period."

"Good shooting?"

"First rate. Limited in quantity, but of finest quality. Indeed, I may boast of a record; I hit everything I aimed at. Camp fare, however, left a good deal to be desired, so you may imagine how glad I am to return."

"I'm very pleased to have an opportunity of giving you something better. How would you like some nice broiled trout, freshly caught this morning?"

"Oh, heavenly!" cried Stranleigh, enthusiastically. "I haven't had anything but bread and salt pork since I saw you. Who caught the trout?"

"I did. I went down the river early this morning. I must have had a premonition that you would return, famished for trout, and I had quite an adventure, or rather, plunged into a mystery which I have not yet solved. I heard the sound of firing; first a single shot, then a fusilade. I could not tell from whence the sound came. I hurried home with my basket, but there was no one in sight. After a while Jim came in, very much crestfallen, it seemed to me, with his ear tied up clumsily in a handkerchief. He had been shot through the ear, and of course I came to his aid at once. With a woman's curiosity, I asked him how the accident happened. Now, one of Jim's infirmities is that he can only tell the truth when it suits his convenience."

"Many of us are like that," said Stranleigh.

"Well, this time it didn't suit his convenience."

"What did he say?"

"That the boys were having a sort of shooting match. I told him I had heard the firing, and feared that there had been a battle of some sort. He said it was the first shot that did for him. They had some bet on as to who could fire the quickest at a flying mark. In his hurry to get ready he had mishandled his gun, and sent a bullet through his ear. The other men had then fired almost simultaneously."

"Miss Armstrong, I fear you are too sceptical. Why shouldn't that be a true story?"

"Mr. Stranleigh, you quite underrate my intelligence.

The wound in Jim's ear was not caused by the gun he held. In the first place, his ear would have been blackened with gunpowder, and likely would have been partly torn off. Secondly, a mishandled gun would have fired upwards. The bullet that wounded him was fired from a distance by someone higher up than the spot where Jim stood. The wound was clean cut, slightly inclining downwards. Besides all that, Jim's bullet, coming from an old-fashioned rifle, would make a bigger hole. I know that, for you remember

341

I tended your shoulder, through which his bullet had gone."

"By Jove, Miss Armstrong, if Sherlock Holmes had a daughter, she would be just about your age. Was there anything else?"

"Yes; I looked at the handkerchief in which he had bound his ear. It was of a finer cambric than we have ever seen in this district, or indeed, than I have seen anywhere else. The corner was embroidered with a very delicately-worked crest."

"A crest?" said Stranleigh, rather breathlessly.

"I asked Jim where he had got this handkerchief. He seemed confused, but said he had always had it. Bought it once at a five-cent store in Denver."

Stranleigh could not refrain from laughing.

"You think it cost more than five cents?"

"Yes; I am sure it cost more than twenty-five."

"Perhaps he stole it?"

"Jim might shoot a man, but he'd never steal."

"I think that when you discover the owner of that handkerchief, you will have solved the mystery," remarked Stranleigh calmly.

"I think so, too," said the girl quietly. "Now I am going to cook your trout."

The three days following were among the most enjoyable Stranleigh had ever spent. He asked Miss Armstrong to show him the portion of the river in which she had caught those delicious trout. Heretofore, she had used a baited hook when fishing, landing her spoil with a trout pole, but now she was to be initiated in the delicate mysteries of fly fishing. Stranleigh remembered the story told of an English official sent to view the debateable land adjoining the far western boundary of Canada who reported the territory useless, because the fish wouldn't rise to the fly. He wondered what lure the official used, for here they rose readily enough, and fought like demons until Miss Armstrong deftly lifted them from the water in the new-fangled landing net, the like of which she had never seen before.

But in spite of the excellent sport he was enjoying, Stranleigh became more and more anxious as time went on. Nothing had been heard from Stanley Armstrong. The fisher began to fear that the detective had failed in his search. On the morning of the fourth day he dressed in his ordinary tweed suit. The riding costume attracted more attention than was altogether convenient. He put in his pocket an automatic revolver of the latest construction; light, accurate and deadly. The day of the auction was drawing uncomfortably near, and he was determined that his journey should not be interrupted, as his former ride had been. Aside from this, he expected to carry with him a large amount of money, and if any word of that got abroad, he knew a holdup was quite within the range of possibility. The coterie confined in the bunk house would doubtless learn that they were their own gaolers, and with that gang once free upon the landscape, he anticipated interruption which, if successful, would completely nullify his plans.

"Are you going fishing to-day?" asked Miss Armstrong, when he came downstairs. He had appeared unexpectedly soon that morning. The young woman was always an early riser.

"Fishing!" echoed Stranleigh. "Yes, in a manner of speaking. Isn't there a text which refers to fishers of men? I'm going fishing for your father. We should have had him here before this, but now the need of him becomes imperative. I imagine that a telegram awaits me in Bleachers. If not, I must communicate with New York, and wait for a reply."

Stranleigh walked up the hill to the bunk house, and rapped at the panel with the butt of his riding whip. Dean himself threw open the door, and he could not conceal his astonishment at seeing the young man standing there, apparently unarmed.

"Good morning, Jim," said Stranleigh cordially.

"I wish to enjoy a few minutes' conversation with the company before leaving for Bleachers."

"None of the company are out of their bunks yet, except myself, but I guess they're wide enough awake to hear what you say. Won't you come inside?"

"Thank you," said Stranleigh, stepping across the threshold; then, to the sleeping beauties—"The top of the morning to you! Early to bed and late to rise, makes a man healthy, wealthy, and wise. Has wisdom come to you since I left? Do you still intend to shoot up Bleachers on auction day?"

"You bet we do," said Dean.

Stranleigh seated himself upon the chair he had formerly occupied.

"How did you propose to get out?"

"By the same way you escaped," responded Dean with determination.

"What an inconvenient exit! I speak from sooty experience. Why not have gone by the doorway?"

"We didn't want to get shot," said Jim.

"There was no danger of that. I have been spending my days in fishing, and my nights in sound sleep."

"Do you mean to say," cried Jim, "that there's been nobody on guard?"

"No; you've been as free as air to go where you pleased."

Dean laughed heartily, and the others joined him. The joke was on them, but they seemed to enjoy rather than resent it.

"You were right about brain and muscle," observed Jim at last.

Stranleigh ignored the compliment.

"I've got a proposal to make to you men," he went on. "I'm off to Bleachers to do some telegraphing, trying to learn the whereabouts of Mr. Armstrong, who has not yet put in an appearance. The sale takes place day after to-morrow."

Stranleigh paused in his recital. He noticed a stealthy movement among the bunkers. He had observed that the first to sit up cast a longing glance at the rifles stacked in the corner, and it seemed to him that a simultaneous rush towards them was going to take place.

"As you know, gentlemen," he went on, "I have an objection to shooting as a settlement of any legal question, but if shooting has to be done, I am quite prepared for it, and the inhabitants of Bleachers will regret provoking me to a fusilade."

He took from his pocket the neat little automatic pistol.

"I don't suppose," he went on, "that you ever saw anything exactly like this. It will simply rain bullets, and I can re-load before any of those Bleachers men can get his hand to his hip pocket. Next to the Maxim gun, it's the most deadly object in existence." Casually he cast his eye along the bunks. Each man had withdrawn the leg that had been quietly reaching for the floor. Stranleigh still fondled his weapon.

"Just before you captured me, I had sent to New York for a considerable sum of money, which was to reach me by express. I thought it better to have no dealings with the bank, as I didn't wish Ricketts to learn what I was doing. I expect that sum of money is at this moment resting in the express office, and on the day of the sale I shall have more currency on my person than is perhaps quite safe to carry. I therefore wish to engage you as a bodyguard, if you agree to certain conditions. I shall expect you all in Bleachers day after to-morrow, and shall pay each of you fifty dollars for the day, and so that there may be no mistake, I tender you the money now. Do you agree?"

"What are the conditions?" asked Jim, cautiously.

"First, you will keep clear of the tavern, and not drink."

"That's easy. What next?"

"You will not shoot until I give the word of command, and until I have emptied my pistol."

Jim consulted with his fellows, then turned to Stranleigh.

"We agree," he said.

"Right you are." Stranleigh rose, took from his pocket-book six fifty-dollar bills, and laid them on the table.

"Look here," cried Dean, "we don't want any money for this job."

"I'm quite sure of that, but six honest men are as much entitled to their pay as is a dishonest lawyer like Ricketts. So good-bye, until I see you at Bleachers day after to-morrow."

Stranleigh went down to the house, mounted his horse, and rode away.

He had accomplished little more than half the distance when he perceived a horseman coming towards him. They approached one another with some caution. Stranleigh would have passed in silence had not the other accosted him.

"Hello, stranger!" he said. "You from the ranch?"

"Yes."

"Been stopping there?"

"Yes."

"How's everything? Folks all well?"

"Yes; they were when I left. Is there any chance that you are Mr. Armstrong?"

"That's my name."

"I'm very glad to meet you, sir. I'm Stranleigh, who telegraphed the detective to find you and hand you two hundred dollars, begging you to get home in a hurry."

"Well, Mr. Stranleigh, all that was done, and here I am, but as for paying back that two hundred dollars and expenses, I don't see how I am to do it. I'm broke."

"So I understand. Do you know your place is to be disposed of by forced sale day after to-morrow?"

"Yes; they've got me with my hands up."

"I don't think so. I'm going to attend that sale, and probably our friend Ricketts will regret the fact. Now, you turn your horse round and accompany me to the settlement. I've got some money coming by express, and being rather a stupid sort of person, it never occurred to me until half an hour ago that I'd need to be identified before I got my hands on that express package. So if you'll take my word that I am Stranleigh, we'll collar the currency and attend the sale. I have a letter of introduction to you from Mr. Banks, of New York, but I left it at your house."

"That's all right. I'll go surety that you're the man. I'd like mighty well to see a little money, even if it belongs to another fellow."

Armstrong turned his horse, who was not loth to set his face in the other direction, because he belonged to White's Tavern. As the two men jogged along together, Stranleigh explained the situation. Armstrong was silent for some time, evidently in a state of dejection.

"Well, Mr. Stranleigh," he said at last, "as you know, I am quite helpless. I haven't a cent to bless myself nor curse an enemy with. I'm no good as a business man, and the slick way in which those rascals in Chicago separated me from what cash I had would make you laugh at me if you knew how it was done."

"I shouldn't be inclined to laugh. We read in Scripture of the man who fell among thieves, and I imagine Chicago is a good place to find such cattle, although I believe there are a few of them further west. I think that Ricketts, in refusing the money when it was offered to him, exceeded his legal rights."

"Our sharpers out here," said Armstrong, "are always exceeding their legal rights, but they get rich all the same. I confess I haven't so much dependence on legality as a law-abiding citizen should have."

"Your men on the ranch seem to hold the same opinion. In spite of all I could say, they were determined to make a raid on Bleachers."

"Did you manage to stop them?" enquired Armstrong eagerly.

"I think I did," was the reply.

There had been a flash of hope in Armstrong's eyes, but it now died down to dejection again.

"I am sorry for that," he said.

Stranleigh gazed at him in astonishment.

"You don't mean to say that you approve of such violence?"

"Oh, well," said Armstrong nonchalantly, "when a man's in a corner, he'll do most anything, and at such times a little gun play is not out of place. I'll bet the boys would have stopped that sale."

"Doubtless, but what good would that do?"

"We should gain breathing space, and perhaps Ricketts wouldn't go on with his villainy."

"But it would land all your men in gaol."

"Don't you believe it. The sheriff would have to catch the boys first, and they know every ravine and stream and gully in the mountains, and every trail in the woods, and if Ricketts was sacrificed in the scrimmage, I, for one, wouldn't be chief mourner. These boys might not be much good in Chicago, but they are very useful out here. A scoundrel like Ricketts, who tries legally to steal a man's property, takes big chances and runs a lot of risks, and no one knows that better than himself. He has taken advantage of my being away from home."

"It's not too late yet to carry out your plan. Although your men hold to their resolve to visit Bleachers on the day of the sale, they have promised not to shoot until I give the word of command."

"They will be there, then, after all?" cried Armstrong, eagerly.

"Certainly; I have engaged them as bodyguard, because, as I told you, I shall have a considerable sum of money in my possession, and I don't wish to be detached from that cash, either by Chicago methods, or those of Bleachers.

I want the sale to go on without any disturbance."

"What's your plan?"

"I intend to buy the ranch."

"Do you imagine for a moment that you'll be allowed to?"

"How can they prevent me if I've got the cash in my pocket?"

"Why, first thing they'll do is to postpone the sale."

"Has Ricketts power to do that?"

"No; but the sheriff has, and the sheriff is Ricketts' man."

"Official bribery, eh? Are you personally acquainted with the sheriff?"

"Yes; I voted for him."

"Is he a man who would rather do right than wrong?"

"It depends how much money there is in either course."

"Then I think our path is reasonably clear. If Ricketts can bribe him to do wrong, we can bribe him to do right."

Armstrong shook his head doubtfully.

"It's not so easy as you think. He would take our money all right, but he might not deliver the goods. He wouldn't stay bought."

"That is a useful thing to know. We'll pay him half the money cash down, and the other half when he has delivered the goods. Would a hundred dollars be sufficient?"

"Oh, lord, yes! It gives Ricketts a pain when he parts with a ten-dollar bill, so it won't take very much money to compete with him."

"As you know the man, and as it's your ranch that is in jeopardy, you can carry out the negotiations better than a stranger like myself."

"That's so; if I have the cash. A hundred dollars would turn the trick."

"Better take five hundred dollars and be sure of it."

They stopped their horses and made the transfer of money where they stood, as being safer than in the tavern.

Arriving at Bleachers, they found the express office closed for the night, but next day his lordship, with Armstrong as his identifier, secured the package.

The land sale took place in the Agricultural Hall, the largest building in town. Stanley Armstrong's six armed followers arrived in good time, and quite unobtrusively seated themselves in a row on a bench at the rear of the hall. When Stranleigh, accompanied by Armstrong, came in, the half dozen shook hands with their chief, and expressed no more surprise at meeting him than if he had left them the week before. Large as the hall was, it speedily filled up, but Lawyer Ricketts, on entering, as he cast his eye over the assemblage, knew there were few moneyed men among the crowd gathered there, and so anticipated no serious opposition when the bidding began.

The lawyer was accompanied by two friends; strangers in Bleachers, who took their places beside him on the chairs provided near the auctioneer's desk. Ricketts was an important man, and quite entitled to reserved seats for himself and his friends. Last of all the sheriff entered, and mounted the platform, bowing graciously to the meeting, which was composed of constituents whose votes he would need next year. It was quite evident that the sheriff was a popular man, for there was a round of applause the moment he appeared.

He got down to business without any unnecessary loss of time, reading the documents giving the conditions of the sale, the item on which Stranleigh was relying being that no cheques would be accepted, or credit allowed. Payment must be cash down on the fall of the auctioneer's gavel. This the clever lawyer had insisted upon, to prevent all possibility of his being outbid by someone who desired time for payment. Thus he dug a pit for his own undoing.

Having finished this reading, the sheriff took a sip from the glass supposed to hold water, and promptly began—

"You all know the property, gentlemen, so I need not detain you by any lengthy description of it. How much am I offered for Armstrong's ranch?"

"Three thousand dollars," said Ricketts.

"Five thousand," promptly outbid the Earl of Stranleigh.

There was a buzz of interest in the crowd, as if some one had stirred up a nest of bees. They had not expected competition. Ricketts stood up and scrutinised the numerous faces turned towards him, endeavouring to discover from whom the bid came.

Then he sat down, and whispered to each of the men beside him. They nodded, and one of them stole quietly out through the door by which the sheriff had entered.

"He's gone for more money," said Stranleigh quietly to Armstrong.

"Five thousand dollars I am bid," went on the sheriff. "Is there any advance on five thousand dollars?"

His gavel hovered over the table.

"Six thousand," said Ricketts.

"Ten thousand," offered Stranleigh, realising that his opponent was playing for time.

"Ten thousand dollars!" echoed the sheriff, then, glancing at the lawyer; "It's against you, Mr. Ricketts."

The lawyer hesitated.

"Eleven thousand!" he said at last.

"Fifteen thousand," bid Stranleigh, promptly.

There were two anxious men in that hall. Stranleigh was wishing he had sent for a hundred thousand dollars. It was evident that Ricketts possessed good backing, but he had no means of knowing whether or

not these men had the necessary money actually in hand. Ricketts was the second anxious man, and he was now gazing with apprehension at the door through which his companion had disappeared. He was called to attention by the strident voice of the sheriff.

"Fifteen thousand dollars is the last bid. Going at fifteen thousand once; going at fifteen thousand twice——"

"Wait a moment, Mr. Sheriff: there's no hurry."

"The sale must go on, Mr. Ricketts."

"Certainly," replied the lawyer, "but it's your duty to get as much as you can for the property. We all sympathise very much with our neighbour, Mr. Armstrong, and whatever is paid over and above his debt to me, goes to him."

"I am aware of that, Mr. Ricketts, and your compassion for Mr. Armstrong does you credit. Still, as I have said before, the sale must go on, and unless there is another bid, I am compelled to knock the property down to the last offer. Fifteen thousand dollars I am bid, and for the third time———"

"Sixteen thousand," cried Ricketts, taking out a handkerchief, and mopping his brow.

The missing man now re-appeared, and took his place beside the lawyer. The three heads came closer together, and Stranleigh watched them with half-closed eyes, apparently indifferent.

"The bid is against you, sir," said the Sheriff. "By the way, what name, please?"

"Stranleigh."

"Well, Mr. Stranleigh, I'm waiting for your bid."

"Don't wait any longer, Mr. Sheriff. I'm anxious to know how much money Mr. Ricketts possesses at the present moment. The ranch belongs to him if he can hand over to you sixteen thousand dollars."

Down came the gavel on the table.

"Mr. Ricketts, the ranch is yours."

Mr. Ricketts rose to his feet.

"I ask for a postponement of this sale for a week from to-day."

"I have no objection," said the Sheriff, "as of course I shall earn another fee."

There was a laugh at this, then the Sheriff continued—

"But I cannot postpone the sale without the consent of Mr. Stranleigh. What do you say, Mr. Stranleigh?"

"A postponement would be very inconvenient to me, much as I should like to oblige Mr. Ricketts. I therefore refuse my consent."

"If the Sheriff is willing," roared Ricketts, "we will postpone without your consent, even if we have to turn you out by force."

"I shouldn't try that if I were you, Mr. Ricketts. There are six friends of mine sitting beside me, who are dead shots, and I don't think this crowd would stand in the way if the first gun were levelled at you. I ask that the sale go peacefully on, Mr. Sheriff."

"There must be a postponement! The Sheriff has control over this meeting!"

"I am counting on that," said Stranleigh, "and I am sure that the Sheriff will adhere strictly to the law. How much money have you collected, Mr. Ricketts?"

"That's none of your business."

"Perhaps not; and so to make everything easy and agreeable to all concerned, I bid seventeen thousand dollars for the property."

"Show your money," demanded Ricketts.

"You wouldn't show yours, so why should I show mine?"

"Knock it down to him, Sheriff. I don't believe he has the cash."

"Seventeen thousand I am offered. Going at seventeen thousand once; going at seventeen thousand twice; going at seventeen thousand third and last time. Going! Gone!"

Down came the mallet.

"I shall be obliged if you will hand over to me seventeen thousand dollars, Mr. Stranleigh."

"Certainly. With your permission, gentlemen!" and the crowd parted good-naturedly. Stranleigh counted out the money on the Sheriff's table.

Armstrong and his men went home directly the sale was over, but Stranleigh remained until all the legal business was finished, and the documents were in his possession. As he rode back to the ranch, he meditated upon the situation in which he found himself. The object of his trip to the West had been achieved. He had left New York tired of its noise, its heated pavements and other uncomfortable disadvantages. He had thought he would never care to see the metropolis again, but now he was yearning for the atmosphere of a large city; London for choice. He determined to bid farewell at once to the Armstrongs and the bunk house men, then turn his face eastwards.

Miss Armstrong was amazed to learn his decision.

"But you haven't had even one day's shooting!" she protested.

"Oh, I'll come for that another time," he assured her.

"Before you go away, my father would like to make some arrangement with you about this ranch."

"I shall be very glad to come to an agreement with him."

The girl sped up to the silver mine, where her father was superintending the removal of the dynamite to its proper place, a job requiring some little care. Armstrong accompanied his daughter down to the house, and greeted Stranleigh with eagerness.

"I am anxious to lease this place from you, Mr. Stranleigh, with the option of buying it later on. I am sure I can make money from the silver

354

mine."

"You must apply to the owner of the ranch, Mr. Armstrong."

"The owner!" echoed Armstrong, in some alarm.

"You haven't sold the ranch since I saw you, I hope?"

"No; but like most other men, I am in debt, and I intend to use this property in payment of my obligation."

Armstrong was taken aback by this declaration. Turning to Miss Armstrong, Stranleigh took from his pocket a long, well-filled envelope.

"These, Professor, are all the legal documents necessary to make you the owner of the ranch, including deed and what-not. I am quite incapable of understanding the red tape wound round the transaction, but I am assured it is all right. I tender this in payment of my medical bill."

"Oh," cried the girl, softly. Then she smiled. "As the sensational plays have it, this is too much!"

"Not a bit of it," returned Stranleigh. "You have no idea of the appalling charges made by specialists in New York and London. Besides, this includes payment of Jim's bill. You cured Jim's ear as well as my shoulder, and I am responsible for Jim. His ear is the only shooting I have had since I came to the ranch."

The girl again began to protest, but Stranleigh interrupted.

"As you are so loth to receive the property, I shall burden it with some conditions. Your father will ask you to mortgage this land to raise money for him. You must refuse that. Keep the ranch in your own name. You have just seen how much trouble has been caused by Ricketts getting his claws on the place. Your father has got, or will get, something between ten and twelve thousand dollars from the proceeds of the sale. Will you put that money into your daughter's hands, Mr. Armstrong?"

"I suppose I'll have to if you say so," rather grudgingly conceded the rancher.

355

"Yes; I say so, because she is a good business woman. Now, Miss Armstrong, you own the ranch, and with this money at your disposal, you should be able to prove conclusively whether there is profitable ore in that mine. When you are ready to demonstrate that fact, write to me, and I'll get together the capital you need for the energetic development of the mine. And now I must be off. Will you bid good-bye for me to my friends, the bunk house men?"

"Certainly; where shall I write to you when there is news of the mine to send?"

"Mr. Banks of New York always has my address."

The girl held forward her hand.

"Good-bye to you, Lord Stranleigh of Wychwood," she said.

For the first time in his life, his lordship neglected to take the proffered hand of a lady.

"Are you making a guess, or stating a certainty, Miss Armstrong?"

"I guess it's a certainty. I saw in a New York paper that Earl Stranleigh of Wychwood was coming into this district to shoot. Then from Jim's ear I unbound a handkerchief with a crest and a monogram on it."

Stranleigh laughed, and took the hand still outstretched to him.

THE END.

About Author

Robert Barr (16 September 1849 – 21 October 1912) was a Scottish-Canadian short story writer and novelist.

Early years in Canada

Robert Barr was born in Barony, Lanark, Scotland to Robert Barr and Jane Watson. In 1854, he emigrated with his parents to Upper Canada at the age of four years old. His family settled on a farm near the village of Muirkirk. Barr assisted his father with his job as a carpenter, and developed a sound work ethic. Robert Barr then worked as a steel smelter for a number of years before he was educated at Toronto Normal School in 1873 to train as a teacher.

After graduating Toronto Normal School, Barr became a teacher, and eventually headmaster/principal of the Central School of Windsor, Ontario in 1874. While Barr worked as head master of the Central School of Windsor, Ontario, he began to contribute short stories—often based on personal experiences, and recorded his work. On August 1876, when he was 27, Robert Barr married Ontario-born Eva Bennett, who was 21. According to the 1891 England Census, the couple appears to have had three children, Laura, William, and Andrew.

In 1876, Barr quit his teaching position to become a staff member of publication, and later on became the news editor for the Detroit Free Press. Barr wrote for this newspaper under the pseudonym, "Luke Sharp." The idea for this pseudonym was inspired during his morning commute to work when Barr saw a sign that read "Luke Sharp, Undertaker." In 1881, Barr left Canada to return to England in order to start a new weekly version of "The Detroit Free Press Magazine."

London years

In 1881 Barr decided to "vamoose the ranch", as he called the process of immigration in search of literary fame outside of Canada, and relocated to London to continue to write/establish the weekly English edition of the Detroit Free Press. During the 1890s, he broadened his literary works, and started writing novels from the popular crime genre. In 1892 he founded the magazine The Idler, choosing Jerome K. Jerome as his collaborator (wanting, as Jerome said, "a popular name"). He retired from its co-editorship in 1895.

In London of the 1890s Barr became a more prolific author—publishing a book a year—and was familiar with many of the best-selling authors of his day, including :Arnold Bennett, Horatio Gilbert Parker, Joseph Conrad, Bret Harte, Rudyard Kipling, H. Rider Haggard, H. G. Wells, and George Robert Gissing. Barr was well-spoken, well-cultured due to travel, and considered a "socializer."

Because most of Barr's literary output was of the crime genre, his works were highly in vogue. As Sherlock Holmes stories were becoming well-known, Barr wrote and published in the Idler the first Holmes parody, "The Adventures of "Sherlaw Kombs" (1892), a spoof that was continued a decade later in another Barr story, "The Adventure of the Second Swag" (1904). Despite those jibes at the growing Holmes phenomenon, Barr remained on very good terms with its creator Arthur Conan Doyle. In Memories and Adventures, a serial memoir published 1923–24, Doyle described him as "a volcanic Anglo—or rather Scot-American, with a violent manner, a wealth of strong adjectives, and one of the kindest natures underneath it all".

In 1904, Robert Barr completed an unfinished novel for Methuen & Co. by the recently deceased American author Stephen Crane entitled The O'Ruddy, a romance.Despite his reservations at taking on the project, Barr reluctantly finished the last eight chapters due to his longstanding friendship with Crane and his common-law wife, Cora, the war correspondent and bordello owner.

Death

The 1911 census places Robert Barr, "a writer of fiction," at Hillhead, Woldingham, Surrey, a small village southeast of London, living with his wife, Eva, their son William, and two female servants. At this home, the author died from heart disease on 21 October 1912.

Writing Style

Barr's volumes of short stories were often written with an ironic twist in the story with a witty, appealing narrator telling the story. Barr's other works also include numerous fiction and non-fiction contributions to periodicals. A few of his mystery stories and stories of the supernatural were put in anthologies, and a few novels have been republished. His writings have also attracted scholarly attention. His narrative personae also featured moral and editorial interpolations within their tales. Barr's achievements were recognized by an honorary degree from the University of Michigan in 1900.

His protagonists were journalists, princes, detectives, deserving commercial and social climbers, financiers, the new woman of bright wit and aggressive accomplishment, and lords. Often, his characters were stereotypical and romanticized.

Barr wrote fiction in an episode-like format. He developed this style when working as an editor for the newspaper Detroit Press. Barr developed his skill with the anecdote and vignette; often only the central character serves to link the nearly self-contained chapters of the novels. (Source: Wikipedia)

NOTABLE WORKS

In a Steamer Chair and Other Stories (Thirteen short stories by one of the most famous writers in his day -1892)

"The Face And The Mask" (1894) consists of twenty-four delightful short stories.

In the Midst of Alarms (1894, 1900, 1912), a story of the attempted Fenian invasion of Canada in 1866.

From Whose Bourne (1896) Novel in which the main character, William Brenton, searches for truth to set his wife free.

One Day's Courtship (1896)

Revenge! (Collection of 20 short stories, Alfred Hitchcock-like style, thriller with a surprise ending)

The Strong Arm

A Woman Intervenes (1896), a story of love, finance, and American journalism.

Tekla: A Romance of Love and War (1898)

Jennie Baxter, Journalist (1899)

The Unchanging East (1900)

The Victors (1901)

A Prince of Good Fellows (1902)

Over The Border: A Romance (1903)

The O'Ruddy, A Romance, with Stephen Crane (1903)

A Chicago Princess (1904)

The Speculations of John Steele (1905)

The Tempestuous Petticoat (1905–12)

A Rock in the Baltic (1906)

The Triumphs of Eugène Valmont (1906)

The Measure of the Rule (1907)

Stranleigh's Millions (1909)

The Sword Maker (Medieval action/adventure novel, genre: Historical Fiction-1910)

The Palace of Logs (1912)

"The Ambassadors Pigeons" (1899)

"And the Rigor of the Game" (1892)

"Converted" (1896)

"Count Conrad's Courtship" (1896)

"The Count's Apology" (1896)

"A Deal on Change " (1896)

"The Exposure of Lord Stanford" (1896)

"Gentlemen: The King!"

"The Hour-Glass" (1899)

"An invitation" (1892)

" A Ladies Man"

"The Long Ladder" (1899)

"Mrs. Tremain" (1892)

" Transformation" (1896)

"The Understudy" (1896)

" The Vengeance of the Dead" (1896)

"The Bromley Gibbert's Story" (1896)

" Out of Thun" (1896)

"The Shadow of Greenback" (1896)

"Flight of the Red Dog" (fiction)

"Lord Stranleigh Abroad" (1913)

"One Day's Courtship and the Herald's of Fame" (1896)

"Cardillac"

"Dr. Barr's Tales"

"The Triumphs of Eugene Valmont"